"The game is up, girl,"
Valcour bit out.
"Whatever game you are playing. . . ."

"I'm not *playing* anything, damn you! I—I—" protested Lucy.

"What are you? Some sort of spy, poking around in gaming halls, bewitching vulnerable boys? Or have you set your sights on marrying an English title?" Valcour glowered down at her. "Tell me, damn you, or I'll—"

"You'll what? Drag me off, kicking and screaming, to lock me in a tower?"

Valcour's eyes narrowed, ~~~~~~~~~~~~~~~~~~~ sual mouth curling in an expressi~~~~~~~~~~~~~~~~~~~~~~~ lickered to life in Lucy's ch~~~~~~~~~~~~~~~~~~~~~~~~ heartbeat, tried to skitt~~~

The Earl of ~~~~~~~~~~~~~~~~~~~~~~~~~ s mouth claiming hers ~~~~~~~~~~~~~~~~~~~~~ her bones melt, her heart ~~~~~~~~~~~~~~~~~~~ ut of her chest . . . and into Valcour~~~~

She had been k~~~~~y boys before—tentative gropings that had been uncomfortable and vaguely embarrassing.

Valcour was a man.

She could feel it in every sinew of his body, pressed so intimately against her. She could taste it on his lips—a drugging passion that whispered of dark pleasures she had never explored. His hands seemed alive with power, as if he could dominate her at will. . . .

Turn the page to find praise for
Kimberly Cates's previous novels . . .

Books by Kimberly Cates

Crown of Dreams
Only Forever
The Raider's Bride
The Raider's Daughter
To Catch a Flame

Published by POCKET BOOKS

The RAIDER'S DAUGHTER

KIMBERLY CATES

POCKET BOOKS

New York   London   Toronto   Sydney   Tokyo   Singapore

An *Original* Publication of POCKET BOOKS

 POCKET BOOKS, a division of Simon & Schuster Inc.
1230 Avenue of the Americas, New York, NY 10020

Copyright © 1994 by Kim Ostrom Bush

ISBN: 0-671-75509-9

First Pocket Books printing October 1994

10 9 8 7 6 5 4 3 2 1

POCKET and colophon are registered trademarks of Simon & Schuster Inc.

Cover art by Jacqui Morgan

Printed in the U.S.A.

The RAIDER'S DAUGHTER

1

*L*ucinda d'Autrecourt Blackheath scaled the branches of the oak tree that rambled up the side of Blackheath Hall, oblivious to the limbs that tossed in the waning storm. The golden glow of her bedchamber window beckoned at a height the most hardened adventurer would have found dizzying on the best of days, and simply terrifying tonight, with the lightning dancing against the sky.

Lucy was soaked bone-deep, from the rags she had stitched to the sleeves of the scarlet regimental coat she wore, to the lead paint she had used to transform her winsome features into a ghastly mask. But no trace of fear or discomfort shone in her cornflower-blue eyes, only unabashed merriment and fierce satisfaction.

Tonight had been perfect. She laughed aloud, savoring the memory of three burly men cowering beneath their beds, terrified of the phantom who had risen up before them.

It had been almost too easy to convince the thick-skulled Baumgartens that she was a denizen of the Underworld. She'd appeared as one of the undead, come to stalk them as mercilessly as they had tormented Cotton Wells, a broken old man who had lost everything in the war—his beloved king, his fortune, and all three of his sons.

Throughout the War for Independence and during its aftermath, the Tories who remained in America were considered fair game, bears in a pit to be tortured at will. But Lucy couldn't tolerate the tyranny of Americans against the defeated loyalists any better than she had been able to tolerate the tyranny of the English king.

In spite of the love that had been lavished on her for the past twelve years by her adoring mother and adoptive father, Lucy remembered all too vividly the dark time in her own life, when she had been afraid and alone.

She brushed away thoughts of the child she had been and gripped the stone window ledge, pulling herself up to the level of her room. Beyond the glass she could see the fire on the grate, and she couldn't wait to toast her chilled fingers above the blaze and clean off the paint that was dribbling in rivulets down her neck.

Bracing herself in the fork of a branch, Lucy tugged the length of rawhide she'd used to open the window countless times before. This time the pane wouldn't budge.

Damn the thing. She'd left it ajar when she'd slipped out hours before. Had one of the maids locked it?

The very thought was enough to fill Lucy with her first twinge of misgiving. *Thunderation!* It would be just like Tansy, the upstairs maid, to discover that the lumps beneath Lucy's coverlets were nothing but artistically arranged bolsters and announce it to the world.

Lucy's jaw set hard at the image of the girl tripping delightedly down to the drawing room, where Lucy's parents were entertaining a few remaining guests, then spilling out her discovery, a properly horrified expression on her sly face. If Tansy had frightened Lucy's mother, Lucy swore she'd wring the chit's neck.

The possibility of gentle Emily Blackheath's distress was enough to dampen Lucy's spirits as the rain had not. Muttering an oath she'd learned around the campfires of her father's soldiers, she jammed her boot against the wall and gave a mighty yank.

The window came open with such force she all but tumbled from the tree, her honey-gold curls straggling across her eyes. Gripping the window frame, she started to climb into the room.

Hands shot out and jerked her into the room as abruptly as a sinner being dragged down to hell.

She struggled for an instant before her boots landed square on the floor, then she froze, peering up at her captor through the sodden lengths of her hair.

Lucy's gaze locked on the man who had struck terror into the hearts of English troops throughout the War for Independence. Pendragon, the Patriot raider who had darted like quicksilver through the English ranks, stood before her. His arms were crossed in the timeless attitude of parental displeasure, and he regarded his adopted daughter with eyes that were unaccustomedly stern, his mouth grim enough to sour new milk.

Considering the expression on Ian Blackheath's face, Lucy figured she should have spent the rest of the night in the tree.

"Why, Papa," she said, excruciatingly aware that her guileless expression was being undermined by the garish makeup covering her face, "what a surprise."

Ian snorted. "I would imagine so. All this time I thought you had excused yourself because you were bored with our chatter about John Wilkes's diplomatic mission to London. But no. You just slipped off to run wild through the night. Most fathers of twenty-year-old girls would question their daughters about lovers and trysts and elopements in such a case. But I suppose I can hardly hope you've been out trying to captivate some young buck."

"No, Papa. I've been out haunting."

Ian sighed. "Terrorizing the neighborhood again?"

"It was a very selective haunting this time, I promise. Those fish-headed Baumgarten bastards have been tormenting Cotton Wells for weeks, so I dressed up as one of his dead sons and told them I didn't appreciate their treatment of my father."

She could see the corner of Ian's mouth twitch, but he lowered his brows even more ominously to compensate.

"Lucy, you must stop flinging out the word 'bastard' as if it is no more potent than 'by your leave.' A young lady—"

Lucy sashayed to the washstand and wrapped her hair in a towel. "A young lady is supposed to mince about, hiding behind her fan and fainting at the first sign of danger. But every time I faint I bruise my tender places, and 'bastard' is a deliciously chewy sort of word. Quite perfect, in fact, when I'm in a temper."

She dampened the corner of another cloth and went to work scrubbing away her makeup. "I'm very sorry, Papa. I know what a horrible disappointment I am to you."

It was a long-cherished joke between father and daughter, one that brought a bark of laughter from Ian. He crossed the room with a limp caused by a British musketball still lodged in his right hip—his personal barometer for foretelling tempests of two kinds, he always claimed: vagaries in the weather and those in his eldest daughter's formidable temper.

"Impertinent baggage," he said, taking the towel from her fingers and tipping her face up to the firelight the way he had when she was small. He began dabbing at her cheek. "I thought we had come to an agreement regarding these late-night adventures you are so fond of. Your mama worries dreadfully—"

"You didn't tell her?" Lucy demanded, alarmed. The fierce protectiveness both Lucy and Ian felt toward the

4

woman who had made them a family was yet another trait they shared.

"No, I didn't tell her. Though if I had an ounce of sense, I'd drag you down to the drawing room by the scruff of your neck right now and show her what mischief you've been up to tonight. Unfortunately, that would be a trifle awkward at the moment, with John and Claree Wilkes still lingering about, singing the praises of my so charming, so talented daughter. I wonder what they would say if I told them about the more unconventional talents you possess, in addition to your magnificence on the pianoforte."

Ian grimaced and paced to the window, closing it against the rain. He peered toward the dark tangle of branches beyond the pane. "Your mother has begged me for years to saw off that damnable branch in an effort to keep you tucked up safe inside your room. The only reason I don't is because I know it wouldn't put a hitch in your escapades. You would just make some sort of ladder out of sheets and break your neck trying to climb down another way."

"What can you expect from the Raider's daughter?" Lucy asked with a toss of her head. "You know what Vicar Dobbins always sermonizes: The sins of the fathers will be visited on the sons. What's bred in the bones will come out in the blood."

"I had nothing to do with your breeding, Madame Impudence. You were dumped on my doorstep half grown. But all of Virginia holds me responsible for your disgraceful antics." The teasing was softened by the deep bond that shone in Ian's eyes. For just an instant, Lucy felt a rare twinge of sentimentality.

Even though the Blackheath cradle had been filled three times since Ian had married Lucy's mother twelve years before, Lucy had always known she had a special portion of her adoptive father's generous heart.

Lucy had always been astonished that she was so little like her beloved mother, yet had so many of the traits that belonged to the men who'd played the role of her father. From Alexander d'Autrecourt, the young English nobleman she barely remembered, Lucy had inherited the love of music that flowed like a fiery spell from her fingertips. While Ian Blackheath had bequeathed her a thirst for adventure, a restlessness of spirit, and a keen sense of loyalty and justice that got her into trouble more often than her mother's nerves could stand.

Lucy shrugged out of the soaked regimental coat and slipped a pistol from the waistband of her breeches, laying it on the chair. The instant Ian's eyes locked on the weapon and darkened, she regretted her action.

"Lucy, there are times I fear that you're going to put yourself in real danger. What if the Baumgartens hadn't been taken in by your masquerade? What if they had fired shots at you or given chase?"

"It would only have made it more amusing." Lucy sighed. "Oh, Papa. I can't explain it. When the war was going on, there was always an adventure. I could dash out to visit you when your troops were near and listen to the stories your men told around the campfire. But now, with everything peaceful, I get so jittery inside that I have to play abominable pranks just to stir things up. I can't help it. There's this fire in my blood that keeps pulsing and pulsing."

There was a twinge of sadness in Ian Blackheath's smile. "Maybe if you paid more attention to the beaux that hover around you like a honey pot, you would find the source of that fire."

"I'd find nothing but trouble," Lucy scoffed. "The love you and Mama share is wonderful. And maybe when I am old and gray and doddering about, I'd like it too. But the moment a woman slips a wedding ring on her finger, her life becomes so boring. I can hardly imagine some ox-brained husband letting me play ghost or ride in a storm. And besides, every stupid boy I know runs around puffing up with pride as if they are so much stronger and smarter than me when they're really absolute block-heads. Just the other day, Wesley Mabley criticized the way I was carrying the reins when all Virginia knows he's so cow-handed he's ruined the mouth of every horse in his father's stable. Of course, he was probably still mad because I pointed out the cards he had tucked beneath his lace at the Grays' house party three weeks ago."

Ian chuckled. "It's hard for a man to admit that a slip of a girl like you can beat him at every pastime there is—riding, shooting, gaming."

"*You* aren't like that, Papa. I've not met a man who can hold a candle to you. Perhaps if I do, I'll consider hearts and flowers. Until then I shall stick to playing ghost, thank you very much. Now, if you're finished lecturing, you can kiss me on the cheek and carry yourself off to Mama. I know you can't bear to spend ten minutes away from her when she's in a family way."

"Actually, I came to your chamber for a purpose other than helping you climb through the window, my dear. Tony Gray stopped by. He'd been to Williamsburg on some goose chase for his own brood of daughters, and he discovered this package waiting to be delivered to you. A mysterious package, I might add. I tried to peek inside it myself, but your mother rapped my knuckles with her fan and sent me to carry it upstairs."

For the first time Lucy noticed the parcel setting on the pie-crust table. Pleasure set her a-tingle. "It's from England, Papa! Mama ordered the music I wanted, and it's finally come!"

Lucy raced over and tore open the wrappings as enthusiastically as a child. But she hesitated, confused, when she discovered no music. But, rather, a sealed letter tucked atop a jumble of strange objects, the message penned in an unfamiliar hand.

A sliver of unease pierced Lucy's excitement. Prodded

by some instinct she didn't understand, she turned away from the perceptive gaze of her father and held the missive to the light.

The package had been addressed to "Miss Lucinda Blackheath," but the name inscribed on the outside of this letter was "Jenny."

Lucy stared at the name as if it were a ghost from another world. Maybe it was.

Jenny d'Autrecourt—the name Lucy had been christened with in far-off England, by the father she remembered only through the hauntingly lovely music he had left behind.

The name she had forgotten during the five years she had been cruelly separated from her mother.

A rebellious waif known as Lucy Dubbonet had been left in Jenny d'Autrecourt's place. A child lost in anger and darkness that the love of Ian and Emily had healed.

Lucy's hand trembled.

"Lucy? Is there something amiss?"

Her father's voice jerked Lucy back to the present with a force that made her heart stumble. For a moment, she was tempted to hand the letter to her father, but the worried expression on his features stopped her.

In spite of twelve years of happiness, Lucy knew her parents still mourned what had happened to her as a child and that both, in their own way, blamed themselves for some portion of her pain.

Lucy stuffed the note back in the box and forced her face into an expression of displeasure. "No wonder we trounced the English in the war. They can't even get a simple order for music right."

"There was a mistake?" Ian moved to peer into the box, but Lucy swept it out of the way.

"This music will do well enough, I suppose. It's just that there was a particular piece I was looking forward to and it's not here. You won't tell Mama, will you? I don't want her to think the surprise was spoiled."

"Of course I won't tell her." Ian moved to cup Lucy's chin in his hand. "But I am sorry you're disappointed, angel. Why don't you mop yourself up and come downstairs again? John has spent half the night chuckling over your opinion of the king. And Claree is so delighted with your company that I think she would tuck you in her pocket and carry you away with her if she could. As much as they adore children, it's a pity that the Wilkeses cannot have their own brood—" Ian stopped and cleared his throat. Lucy knew it was a gruff attempt to change the subject from something so indelicate as the wound that had cost John Wilkes his ability to have a family.

"They'll be gone for several years, you know," Ian said. "You'll probably be terrorizing your own husband and have a nursery full of babes by the time they return." There was a certain sadness in her father's eyes, along with resignation.

"Not me, Papa. You're going to be saddled with me forever. I'm going to be the Mad Spinster of Blackheath Hall and set the whole parish on its ear with the scandals I stir up." Lucy attempted to tease, but her heart wasn't in it. It was as if the box in the corner were a living thing, lying in wait for her.

Ian kissed her on the cheek. "You're far too much like me to escape that easily, my child. I predict that you'll careen into love the way that I did: like a runaway carriage hurtling over the edge of a cliff. Before you know what's happening, it'll be too late to stop it."

Lucy chuckled in spite of herself. "I'm sure Mama will love to hear *that* description. I was there when the two of you met, if you remember, sir. And I was old enough to see that you were on the path straight to hell *before* you fell in love with her. She was the one who turned you back from the edge just in time."

"She did at that, bless my poor beleaguered angel. Now I'd best get back to her. I wouldn't want her lifting anything heavy."

"Like her teacup?"

Ian looked a little sheepish. Lucy went to him and laid a hand on her father's arm. "Mama will be fine, Papa. She'll go through hours of agony, then look like an angel when she lays a beautiful babe in your arms. She'll be beaming and bonnie, and you'll spend three weeks recovering, as if you were the one who had gone through childbirth."

"I just wish that I could help her through it. It's not easy, this being a woman." Those eyes that could be so bright and teasing and tender were more than a little sad. He kissed her on the forehead. "I love you, moppet."

"I love you too, Papa. So much."

He chucked her under the chin, then turned and walked out the door. Lucy hesitated until she heard the uneven tread of his boot soles on the stairs, then she hurried to the box. Collapsing before the fire, she picked up the sealed letter.

The skin on her arms crawled as she stared once again at the inscription. Lucy shuddered, hastily shoving the vellum aside. Her young sisters feared monsters hiding beneath the staircase or underneath their beds. Lucy's childhood monsters had been terrifyingly real.

It had always chilled her blood—the knowledge that in England there was a grave with her christened name inscribed on the headstone, a tomb with a tiny empty coffin buried beneath the earth. Jenny d'Autrecourt's false death had been orchestrated with sinister perfection.

For five years Emily d'Autrecourt had grieved for her three-year-old daughter, believing the fever that had taken her young husband had also stolen her child. For five years Lucy had been neglected and frightened and alone.

From the first moment Lucy heard the story of her abduction, she had cast her grandparents, the duke and duchess of Avonstea, in the role of scurrilous monsters.

They were aristocratic beasts who had developed a sadistic plan to rid themselves forever of the wife and child that were a reminder of their son's shameful alliance with a simple vicar's daughter.

Only a handful of people had ever known the truth about what the duke and duchess had done, and most of those were dead now. Lucy had been content to let Jenny rest in peace, while Ian Blackheath had let it be known that any further attempts to harm mother or child would result in his publishing the d'Autrecourts' entire villainous scheme in the London *Gazette*.

Thirteen years had passed since the confrontation between Pendragon and Avonstea. Years of silence when that other life had seemed like nothing but a dream. But now someone was turning up a spadeful of that grave, releasing a thousand buried questions and nameless fears.

Lucy's eyes fixed on the box as if it were waiting to poison her. Maybe it already had, filling her with sick trepidation and dizzying doubts. Hazy memories and terrors that still whispered to her in nightmares.

Slowly she peeked over the edge of the box. A jumble of objects had been packed in straw to preserve them on their journey: a rag-stuffed doll that must have belonged to Jenny long before, a gold watch engraved with Alexander d'Autrecourt's name. An odd shiver worked through Lucy as she cupped the latter in her hand. It was the first time she ever touched anything that had belonged to the young musician who'd sired her.

Emily d'Autrecourt hadn't been able to save a single keepsake from the life she'd known in England. Even her wedding ring had been pawned to keep the family from debtors' prison.

As Lucy fingered her father's watch, it was as if the ghostly man she'd idealized as a young god of music were taking on substance, an aura of reality both intriguing and unnerving.

She reached into the box again, her fingers closing on another sheet of vellum, its edges crumbling with age. Musical staffs were ruled across it with precision, inked notes rambling across them. Her eyes skimmed the notes, the music playing in her mind, as if it were her father's voice beckoning her from the realm of the dead. She glanced at the blotted inscription at the bottom of the page: "For Master St. Cyr on the occasion of his twelfth birthday, Harlestone Castle. Lord Alexander d'Autrecourt."

A birthday gift? Written for another child? An odd sense of hurt streaked through Lucy. She had always cherished the fact that her father had composed the "Night Song" for her alone. It was a part of him that only she could possess. Some shared secret, a special bond. Never once had she considered that he might have written melodies for his students as well, rewarding them for their work the way many music masters did.

It shouldn't have bothered her so much, but as Lucy set the pages aside, she realized that it did.

The knot in her throat tightened as she reached into the box for the last object, a jeweled miniature suspended from a faded black ribbon.

Lucy took the case gingerly in her hand. A folded scrap of vellum had been slipped between the gold frame and the porcelain.

Lucy tugged the bit of paper free and let it fall to her lap. Then she held the miniature to the fire, eyeing the image of her birth father with an inner hunger that astonished her.

Light danced across the features of a youth who looked seventeen. He was dressed in stiff aristocratic splendor, but his face was that of a poet, framed in an aura of soft gold hair. His lips curved in an uncertain smile that was far too sensitive for the harsh reality of the world, but his eyes brimmed with dreams, dreams that had been woven in the music he had written. Dreams he had passed to his daughter, along with the blue of his eyes and the gold of his hair.

Lucy stared into those features, trying desperately to conjure up her own memories of the man, but there was only the music, a silken web of mystery, magic, that spoke to her heart in a language far more eloquent than words.

The St. Cyr boy for whom her father had written the birthday song would have memories of Alexander d'Autrecourt, Lucy thought bitterly. The boy would remember Alexander's face, eyes, the way his voice had sounded. She felt a swift stab of animosity toward this boy she had never met.

"I don't remember you, Papa," Lucy whispered to the painted image. "It isn't fair—"

She felt a quick jolt of anger at herself, a sense that she was being disloyal to Ian Blackheath, the man who had loved her and taken care of her for the past twelve years. The father she adored more than anyone on earth.

She should just stuff the things back into the box and shove them into the fire, obliterating them along with the gnawing feeling that she had been waiting a lifetime for this box to arrive.

Instead, she looked at the letter, which had fallen to the floor beside her, the red sealing wax clinging to it like a gobbet of blood. For an instant she hesitated. Then she picked it up and cracked the wafer of wax with her thumbnail. She unfolded the page, time seeming to freeze as she looked down at what appeared to be a verse, fresh and newly inked in an elegant hand.

> *Roses watered by a grieving mother's tears*
> *Bloom where an angel-child is said to sleep*
> *Beside her long-dead father,*
> *Stolen by fever, rapacious, wild.*
> *But I know it was not cruel fates that swept them*
>   *both away.*

*Rather, the powerful hand of a Lion who would play
   God.*
*A Lion who roasts now upon hell's grate for his dark
   deeds.*
By all that is holy, I beg this of you.
Do not let the Lion triumph in the end.
Come home, Jenny.
*Undo his demon madness with the secret I tell to
   you.*
The roses weep, not over one empty grave, but two.

Lucy scrambled to her feet, her heart thundering. What kind of brutal joke was this? Who would have sent this to her? Tempt her to believe . . . *what?* That Alexander d'Autrecourt was alive?

It was ludicrous to think that possible for even a heartbeat. This was some monster's attempt to torment her, terrify her. Someone else playing at ghosts to amuse themselves.

But nothing about the objects scattered across the floor was amusing. Something about this rang of a subtle cruelty, of something sinister. She held the note to the light again and scanned the final lines.

Jenny,
   *I will await our reunion at Perdition's Gate, Fleet
Street. I regret bringing you to such a place, but
circumstances are such that it is unavoidable. I shall
be in the third room on the second floor every
Thursday evening for the next three months only. Be
swift, my beloved daughter. Yr. Obedient*

Daughter . . . My God, this person expected her to believe that he was her father? Expected her to race across the ocean, to meet him in a place called Perdition's Gate? She would have to be insane. It was far more likely that the person who'd sent her the box was some miscreant who wanted to extort money from the wealthy Ian Blackheath. A cutthroat who intended to kidnap her or worse.

She might even be willing to believe that the box was from the d'Autrecourts, that they were plotting to finish the dastardly deed they had begun when she was a child so they could wipe away the scandal of her existence in the most permanent manner possible.

But a letter from Alexander d'Autrecourt?

No. She could not believe that it was so.

Lucy grabbed up a petticoat, dragging it on with trembling fingers. Her chin bumped up a notch. If some maniac thought they could terrorize the Blackheaths, they were dead wrong. She'd tell her father, and that would be the end of this scheme. Pendragon and his daughter would make whoever was responsible for this sorry they had ever been born!

Half an hour later, dressed and determined, she marched into the drawing room. She fully intended to demand a private interview with her father. But as the door opened, Lucy's heart wrenched, her fingers folding tight over the disturbing letter.

Emily Rose d'Autrecourt Blackheath was sitting in a wing-backed chair, her mahogany tresses glistening in the candle shine, her face radiant as she smiled up at her husband. Five-year-old Norah had obviously escaped Nurse again and was curled up asleep on what little remained of Emily's lap, while the legendary Raider Pendragon stroked his tiny daughter's cheek as if she were an angel fallen straight down from heaven.

Emily caught sight of Lucy hovering at the doorway and gave her daughter a beatific smile. "So there is the guilty party," she said. "You are in very deep trouble, Lucy-love."

Lucy stuffed the hand that held the note behind her back, alarmed. "G-Guilty? I—"

"Norah told us that you'd taught her how to sneak out

of the nursery. She was to hide like a wee little mouse in the shadows, until Mrs. Gamp slipped out to gossip with Tansy, then all Norah had to do was scurry down the back stairs."

Lucy flushed, relief surging through her. "Norry's bright as a new button. She would have figured it out for herself soon enough."

Ian chuckled. "Especially since you told her there were 'sweet cakies' down here on a tray."

Lucy stared down at her tiny sister, who was blissfully unaware that there were more frightening monsters than the imaginary ones that lurked beneath the bed, and truths that were far more bitter than Nurse's tonics.

The letter seemed to cut Lucy's fingers, burn them with the secrets that it held. She trembled, suddenly stricken by what it would mean to her sister and to her parents if there were any truth at all in the message from England.

If Alexander d'Autrecourt were alive it would shatter twelve years of laughter and love, invalidate the marriage of Emily and Ian. It would brand the little ones in the Blackheath nursery with the label of bastard.

Lucy reeled at the implications. Hadn't her mother endured enough pain? Hadn't Ian Blackheath sacrificed enough?

How could she tell them? Her mother was blossoming with yet another child, while her father was half crazed with worry over her. What could the dread Raider Pendragon do? Sail to England, find whoever was behind this twisted jest, and make certain they could never hurt those he loved?

What if what the letter claimed were true? The thought of Ian Blackheath and Alexander d'Autrecourt confronting each other was so ghastly it made Lucy's stomach churn. She couldn't risk that happening, no matter how unlikely it was that her birth father was alive. Pendragon could never be told, could never confront whoever was responsible for this.

But the Raider's daughter could.

The idea struck her with the force of a lightning bolt.

She could go to England and take care of this matter, and no one else would ever have to know. No one else would have to be savaged by these terrible doubts.

This was insane! It would be a mad goose chase, with nothing to guide her but a musical score dedicated to some total stranger and a clandestine meeting at an establishment whose name already whispered of hell.

But what other choice did she have?

Lucy's fingers tightened, crumpling the note. She surreptitiously stuffed it beneath the lace at her wrist. When she turned to face the others in the room, Lucy's eyes had that determined gleam her parents had learned to regard with a healthy dose of dread.

"I've been feeling a need to escape myself lately, just like Norah has," Lucy said airily. "So I've come up with the most marvelous idea." She turned to Claree Wilkes with a smile that could wheedle the key to heaven right out of St. Peter's hands. "Claree, how would you like some company on your journey to England?"

Emily gasped, her teacup clattering against its saucer.

Ian's eyes filled with astonishment, then the dangerous glint that had been the signature of Pendragon. "What the blazes, girl? Did you hit your head when you were out riding?"

Emily eased herself out from beneath the drowsing Norah. The swell of pregnancy made her look all the more fragile and ethereal. "Lucy, this is so—so sudden."

"Not really, Mama. I've been thinking about it for a long time, but I never knew how to broach the subject with you and Papa."

"You've been lambasting us with your opinions from the first moment you set foot on Blackheath land," Ian challenged. "Why should this be any different?"

Lucy groped for a reason her parents would believe, praying that for once Ian wouldn't be able to see through her dissembling. "I didn't know how to tell you that . . . that . . ." She turned back to her mother and caught up her hands. "Mama, please try to understand. There's this empty place inside me that needs to be filled. Filled with music that I can't experience here in Virginia. London would be a feast of concerts and operas, theater. I could stay for six months or so, maybe a year, until Claree is settled in. You know how nervous she is around strangers. She'll be miserable in England without anyone she knows."

Lucy turned to Claree Wilkes. "I know it's abominably rude of me to invite myself along. But you're leaving so soon, there's hardly time for delicate hints and proper languishing looks."

"I'd a-adore having you, dear. You can't imagine how much," Claree said with the endearing lisp that had made her painfully shy. She darted a questioning glance at Ian and Emily. "I've been p-pure dreading being a diplomat's wife. All the entertaining, and—and . . . It would be so comforting to have someone from home to keep me company, child. And as for you, it would be the opportunity of a lifetime."

Claree turned pleading eyes to her husband, and Lucy could see the shadowy grief in her eyes for the daughters they would never have. "J-just think, John. We could give Lucy a London season."

"You could spend a season in hell, you mean!" Ian blustered. "You're going on a diplomatic mission. Knowing Lucy, she'll stir up another war!" He shot his daughter a glare so blistering she half expected her skin to peel. "What about your mother, Lucy? The baby coming?"

Lucy felt a quick jab of guilt.

"Ian, hush," Emily chided. "If Lucy lingers about, waiting for all the babes we intend to put in that cradle, she'll never leave Blackheath Hall. She's a woman grown. She has her own life to lead."

"I've no objection as long as she leads it on this side of the ocean!"

"But there are things we can never give Lucy here, no matter how much we might wish to. She would be with Claree and John. She would be loved, safe."

"That girl wouldn't be safe if she were shackled in the Williamsburg gaol!" Ian bellowed. "We're talking about Lucy here. A loose cannon, unleashed in England. For God's sake, an hour ago the little hellion was dangling out windows and dressing up like a ghost!"

His hands closed over Emily's arms, his voice tight. "Don't you understand, Emily Rose? *They* would be in England. The d'Autrecourts. God knows what they might do!"

"They can't hurt us now," Emily insisted. Lucy winced, her mother's soft words cutting like a lash.

"The old duke died eight years ago," Emily said. "And Granville, the eldest, died before that. Alexander's brother Edward holds the dukedom now. Edward would never hurt her. He adored Alexander. As for the rest of the d'Autrecourts, they won't even acknowledge she's alive."

"How could they?" Ian demanded. "They have their tidy little grave tucked up in the family crypt and their tragic little story about how she died. It might prove a trifle awkward if their long-dead granddaughter popped up in the middle of a London soiree."

"The d'Autrecourts have more reason to hide the truth than anyone. Besides, Lucy would be the guest of one of the first diplomats England has dealt with since the war. I hardly think they'd care to alienate her guardians."

"She doesn't belong in the midst of a pack of aristocratic dogs with their noses stuck so high in the air they don't give a damn who they trample over. That was why we fought the blasted war, to make certain our children were free of their power. Lucy belongs here with us."

"Do you really believe that?" Emily cupped her palm

tenderly along the stubborn jut of her husband's jaw. "Or are you afraid that some dashing English rogue will carry her off to his castle and we'll never see her again?"

Lucy saw her father flinch, his cheekbones flooding with color. "Of course not! No Englishman in his right mind would take on a headstrong, wild-blooded, impossible little termagant like Lucy."

His words trailed off, and Lucy could see the very real dread in her father's eyes. "There's not an Englishman alive who could tame her," he said softly. "Or one who could be worthy of such a treasure."

"I'm not trundling off with 'prospective bride' painted on my forehead, Papa. All I want to do is take a holiday with John and Claree. For a year at most."

"Barely an hour ago you were claiming you would stay here forever, the next moment you're packing your trunk for England. I don't understand. Lucy, help me to understand."

The words hurt Lucy more than any others could have. From the first moment she had squared off against Ian Blackheath they had discovered they were kindred spirits, so much alike that they understood each other without words.

She had told him everything: from the fact that his amber waistcoat made him look like an overripe squash, to the sad, secret fear she'd had when she'd first arrived at Blackheath Hall so many years before—the fear that she was so wicked inside no one could ever love her.

For the first time in her life, Lucy turned away from the question in Ian Blackheath's crystal-blue eyes.

Papa, I can't tell you this, she wanted to cry.

Someone might be trying to hurt you and Mama, and I have to stop them. Alexander d'Autrecourt might be alive. And if he is . . . oh, God. If he is it could destroy you.

The guilt twisted deep, a voice inside her whispering: *If he is, I could meet him, Papa. The father who wrote my*

"Night Song," the only memory I have of my life in England.

The prospect was a terror and a sweet temptation.

Lucy crossed to where Norah lay dreaming her sweet dreams—confident that when she awakened Mama would be there, with indulgent smiles and kisses, and Papa would be there to toss her up in his arms until she squealed with laughter.

Lucy knelt beside her small sister, brushing a dark curl from the child's dewy brow.

Was she doing the right thing in going to England? Lucy wondered desperately. It was as if she were being torn in two by the strange mixture of uncertainty and fear and anticipation she couldn't quite crush.

For the first time since she'd come to Blackheath Hall so many years before, Lucy was reaching into a past shrouded in mystery and haunting sorrow.

Perdition's Gate . . . The name of the rendezvous point echoed in her mind.

What was it that she was about to embrace?

A dream so impossible she'd never dared to dream it at all?

Or a nightmare that could destroy everyone she had ever loved?

2

*L*ondon stirred like a nocturnal beast hungry for prey. Its eyes glowed orange, in the form of newly lit street-lamps. Its claws were unsheathed as footpads and high-waymen, cutthroats and harlots crept from the doors of the buildings that huddled along streets littered with garbage and human filth.

By day cherry vendors and orange girls and bevies of ragged children filled the area. But night exposed the repulsive underbelly of the city, revealing the lost souls who scraped out an existence there.

Never had Lucy seen such poverty, so much hopeless-ness. For the first time she fully understood why men and women sold seven years of their lives for indentured servitude to escape this festering sore of humanity. For the first time in her life Lucy understood the horrors her mother must have faced wandering this city alone.

Lucy urged her mare to a brisker pace. Taking comfort from the weight of her pistol against her thigh, hidden behind her male disguise, she rode deeper into the labyrinth where the most notorious gaming hells and brothels held court.

Twelve days she had been searching for information that would lead to her destination. Twelve days of struggling against rules of society that were so ridiculous they'd made her want to box someone's ears. But tonight her battle for information and her struggle to escape Claree Wilkes's watchful eyes would finally come to an end. Lucy was going to Perdition's Gate.

An ironic smile tugged at her lips. From the time she was three years old, she had heard the predictions that she was a devil-spawned brat destined to roast in hell. But even she had never expected that she would enter its gate in the middle of an English slum, while she was searching for a ghost.

It might even have been amusing if she hadn't felt this sensation of danger—like a slender blade pressed against her spine, waiting, just waiting to be driven home.

Was it possible that Alexander d'Autrecourt, the dreamy youth in the miniature, had descended into this hell? Was it possible that a gentle musician could find himself lost in this miasma of human suffering?

There had to be some sort of mixup, Lucy reasoned grimly. Either that, or she was walking straight into some sort of bizarre trap.

She tugged at the neckcloth that fell in ruffles beneath the gentleman's waistcoat that was part of her disguise. What if she had been a fool not to tell Pendragon? What if she were making the biggest mistake of her life?

And what if you're turning coward? Lucy berated herself inwardly. *You've come too far to turn back now.*

But the temptation to do just that grew stronger. She was sucking in a steadying breath when she caught a glimpse of yet another shadowy street.

An innocuous-looking building stood halfway down the lane. Its windows were heavily curtained, and a man stood guard outside the door in case constables happened by. Lit by a single flambeau, a badly executed statue of Hades dragging Persephone down to hell stood at the entryway to alert patrons that the pleasures of the flesh and the lure of gambling were within.

The sight of that statue should have filled Lucy with triumph. Instead, her stomach pitched with an ambivalence that infuriated her. For a heartbeat she was uncertain whether to rein the horse toward the establishment or turn and flee back to the Wilkes's townhouse as if her coattails were afire.

But before she could reach a decision a commotion erupted. A bundle of rags and carroty hair scaled the statue like a bear cub treed by a pack of hounds. Or, rather, one very large hound. A giant of a man with a patch over one eye was attempting to drag the boy down by the seat of his ragged breeches.

"I be tryin' to get work, Pappy Blood! I do!"

Lucy heard the high-pitched shriek as the man cracked his paw hard against the boy's backside.

"Oww! My arse!"

Outrage flooded through Lucy when the guard looked away, as if the boy were no more than a roach to be stepped upon. In a heartbeat, Lucy spurred her horse toward the statue, pistol in hand. The man with the eyepatch wheeled at the sound of the horse thundering toward him, his face ashen as he saw the pistol pointed square at his chest.

"It seems you are accosting the boy's arse," Lucy said smoothly. "Unhand it at once."

The man the child had called Pappy Blood slunk back a few steps, his pock-marked features shifting from cruelty and anger to an obsequiousness that made Lucy want to pull her pistol's trigger.

"A thousand pardons, me fine sir. But the boy is rotten to the very heart of him."

"The most insufferable child ever born?" Lucy inquired silkily.

Blood nodded eagerly, until her gaze chilled even further.

"People once said the same of me. I had a marked aversion to the sentiment. I think I *will* shoot you."

Blood cowered back as the brash little boy scrambled down from his perch and straightened his stained jerkin.

"Ye don't have to shoot him on my account." The boy beamed. "Make a nasty mess to step over when you gentlemen are done flinging away a fortune at cards." He turned to Blood. "Go home, old man. I be tired o' looking at yer ugly mug." Supreme satisfaction darted across the boy's face as Blood skulked away.

Something about the cocky waif made Lucy warm to him. His pug nose thrust up at an engaging angle. There was a scrape on his chin and a gap in his grin where a tooth should be. He looked barely six years old, but there was an aura about him far older and much wiser.

"What is your name?" she asked the boy as she swung down from her mare.

"Natty. Natty Scratch. I hold horses for the gentlemen." Natty hitched up the breeches that were sagging low on his skinny buttocks. "Pissin' grand night for losin' a fortune, eh?"

"I suppose so."

"This ain't no gentlemen's club like Brook's or White's. Hazard table has weighted dice, an' the dealer at the second Faro table has cards up his sleeve. I'm only tellin' ye this for yer own edif-edification. It ain't a service I usually provide to me customers."

Lucy fingered the leather of her reins, glancing again at the guard, who was digging amongst rotted teeth with a metal toothpick.

"I'm grateful for the warning." She fished a coin from her pocket, wishing she could stay longer and talk to this charming little rogue. Wishing she never had to enter those doors that seemed even more ominous.

"I don't take charity," said Natty, thrusting his skinny chest out. "I'm a workin' man. Got my pride."

With the utmost dignity, she gave him the reins of her

horse. She started to walk toward the entrance, but Natty's grubby fingers caught at the sleeve of her frockcoat. She all but jumped out of her skin.

"Most o' all, beware o' Lord Jasper, devil take him. Got a streak in 'im that makes Pappy Blood look sweet as a sugar cone." Natty wriggled his brows. "Jasper's a bit withered in the cucumber, if ye catch my meaning. Can't service the ladies. Takes it out on everybody, he does. I heard tell he's got a 'pointment to blow some poor bastard's head off tomorrow morning in a duel." He heaved a pensive sigh. "Wish't I could see it. Never seen a duel before. Anyhow, about yer visit t' the Gate. Long as you stay clear o' everyone I warned ye about, I be certain you'll win a king's ransom. If ye have the luck, that is."

Shrewd green eyes peered up at Lucy above a sprinkling of freckles all but lost in the grime. "Course, I could help ye along a little. I'm Irish, ye know."

"I'm not interested in gaming."

"Very wise, me lord. Very wise." The boy nodded sagely.

She hesitated for a moment. "Natty, can you tell me what . . . entertainment is on the second floor?"

"Whores, sir. Bess be the prettiest, but what Josyphine lacks in the face she makes up for in her netherparts, they say."

Lucy went scarlet. The boy's eyes twinkled knowingly.

"First time, eh? Don't worry. Got a girl up there that's real good wi' virgins. I'll tell 'er to be gentle with ye."

"Th-That's not necessary," Lucy stammered. "I . . . there must be a mistake. Another room. The third one down the hall."

"That one's got whores in it too. I should know. I sneak in sometimes an' watch through the knothole." He whistled through the gap in his teeth. "If ye didn't come to gamble, an' ye didn't come for dipping in Josy's tup, what did ye come for?"

Lucy cringed at the clatter of an approaching coach. She swallowed hard, looking at the door. "I came here to meet someone." Of their own volition, her fingers reached out to brush over Natty's hair, an imitation of her affectionate greetings to her own sisters for so long.

The boy drew back, his eyes widening, wary. "Say, ye don't fancy boys, do ye? 'Cause I ain't interested, no matter how fat yer purse is."

With these words, Lucy understood the full impact of the life Natty had lived. One beyond most people's comprehension. "Of course you're not interested. You're a man of business."

She turned and walked to the door. Her fingers trembled as she opened it and stepped inside. She froze just inside the entryway, her vision blurring at the blaze of light inside the gaming hell. Slowly it pulled into focus, and she couldn't stop her jaw from dropping in astonishment.

If Lucifer provided the accoutrements of this establishment, she was certain most men would trip merrily down to the devil.

Garish red velvet-draped portraits of ladies seductively displaying their charms. Wreaths of smoke circled tables crowded with players, while women, the rouged tips of their breasts displayed above edgings of lace, draped themselves over patrons who were obviously the most debauched rakehells of the aristocracy.

Lucy fumbled with the fastening of her cloak and tried to stop the blush that spilled onto her cheeks as across the room a youth who looked barely out of the schoolroom popped one of some trollop's nipples into his mouth as if it were a sweetmeat.

Dear God, Lucy thought wildly, as a footman took her cloak from numb fingers. This was insane. What would a gentle musician be doing in such a place? In spite of her masculine disguise, Lucy felt as if her own breasts were visible to the lascivious men here. For the first time

Lucy feared she would not be able to carry off her deception.

A shiver scuttled down her spine as a sudden hush fell over the room, as if a hundred throats had been slit. Hands holding cards stilled, dice rattled against the table and lay there, unretrieved by the players. Women licked their lips, their eyes afire, while their men . . . they stared as if they were confronting Mephistopheles himself.

Sweet Jesus, what were they gaping at? Her? The entire room seemed charged with a menace that made Lucy's blood run cold, and her gaze clashed with that of a man at the table nearest her. A girl who looked incredibly young and frightened was perched on his knee, one of her breasts streaked with reddening fingermarks where she had been squeezed too tightly. Tears clung to her lashes, but her lips were curved into a most desperate smile. Lucy could tell that the man who held her enjoyed subjecting the girl to his abuse.

She remembered Natty's warning about the cruel Lord Jasper, and in that instant she was certain she was staring into that man's face.

Once Lucy had watched her father put down a rabid dog at the edge of Blackheath land. She'd seen the wild glimmer in those eyes, the savage curl of foam-flecked lips over its fangs. She had known that it wasn't the animal's fault that it was ill. But as she looked into Lord Jasper's face, she sensed that he had embraced his sickness and would have loved nothing better than to infest others with his poison.

"I should have known that you would come," the man purred, gazing straight at her.

A band of alarm tightened around Lucy's chest. Thunder in heaven, was this who had sent the parcel? What kind of twisted trap had she walked into? This man could murder her where she stood, and no one would ever know what had become of her. She'd taken so much care to conceal her destination that the only one who'd ever know she'd come here would be Natty Scratch. And despite the fact that she'd saved his "arse," she wasn't deluded that he'd trouble himself very long over her disappearance.

She heard Pendragon's voice whispering inside her. *Courage is not only knowing when to fight, girl, but when to retreat. Some say there is honor in dying nobly, but I'd rather live long enough to make my enemies miserable another day.*

She groped for her pistol beneath the shield of her coat, bracing herself with the feel of its smooth warm grip against her palm. With the weight of those staring eyes pushing her as if they were a tangible force, Lucy backed one step toward the door.

And slammed hard against a surface as unyielding as a castle wall.

She stifled a scream and wheeled, almost losing her balance, but powerful hands caught her arms, the man who had doubtless been the real target of those awed stares reaching out to steady her. Lucy struggled to breathe as she gaped at a froth of white lace neckcloth bare inches from her face, a diamond glinting in its snowy folds.

She brought her head back until her neck ached, tracing past the glittering stickpin, to where a flowing roquelaure was flung back over impressive shoulders, the cloak revealing a severe black frockcoat with touches of silver trimming.

In the frozen instant that she raised her eyes to the man's face, his features branded themselves in her mind.

He had the face of a Celtic warrior. Intense. Unrelenting. His hair, unpowdered in defiance of fashion, flowed like liquid midnight to skim his shoulders, as if torn from the customary neat queue by the fingers of the wind.

The silken strands tangled about the angular planes of a narrow face that seemed burnished not by the sun and wind, but rather by the harsh edges of life itself. A thin white scar, slashing from one high cheekbone to the bottom of his jaw, only added to the erotic potency of those features.

But it was the man's eyes Lucy knew she would never forget. Flaming ebony, with a ruthless power that terrified and seduced, mesmerized and repelled. Piercing as a dagger's blade, they were the sort of eyes to make the most courageous of men turn coward and the most chaste of women fantasize about stirring them to passion.

That hawklike gaze seared Lucy's face, and for a moment those dark eyes filled with another emotion Lucy couldn't name. "Don't tell me this is a children's gaming hell," he drawled, unfastening the roquelaure with one careless hand and throwing it, without a glance, to where a servant scrambled to catch it.

"What are you here for, boy?" he demanded of Lucy. "Are you all impatience to gamble away your inheritance, or are you looking for a pretty harlot to give you the French pox?"

The tension that had been building inside Lucy for the past hours burst free. "Actually, I came here looking for someone to gun down in a duel. You look as if you might do."

"Is that so?" The corner of that hard mouth tightened, his eyes glittering ebony slits. "I'm afraid you shall have to wait your turn." There was something about the face that made Lucy wonder for the first time in her life if her acid tongue had gotten her into something her wits would not be able to get her out of.

She was painfully aware of every eye in the room trained on them. At that moment the man's hard gaze swept the tables with such menace that even the most curious returned to their card playing and dice casting with such intensity that a bullet could have whizzed past their noses and they'd not have dared look up.

Evidently satisfied, the black-garbed man turned those unsettling eyes back to Lucy's face. "What is your name, boy?" he inquired. "It's a peculiar trait of mine. I like to know the name of someone before I kill him."

"Lucien Dubbonet," she answered.

"And where are you from, Mr. Dubbonet? By your accent, I'd say the colonies."

"The United States of America."

"Mr. Dubbonet, I give you a word of advice your father should have given long ago: Never make a threat you don't intend to carry out. And never ride alone at night in London. Tell me, have you ever wondered what it would feel like to have your throat slit?"

"Excuse me?" Lucy choked out.

"An unpleasant sensation, I would imagine. There are plenty of brigands just outside this door who would be more than happy to demonstrate it to you. And you would be far safer at their mercy than in the hands of most of the patrons inside these walls."

Lucy thrust out her chest with indignation, until for a moment she was afraid the binding about her breasts would snap free. "What I choose to do with my own neck isn't your affair."

"You're right. You came looking for trouble. Perhaps I should help you find it."

She wanted to pull away, find some way to retreat, but before she could answer a sinister laughter rose from behind her. A laughter that made her skin crawl. She knew it belonged to the man she had identified as Lord Jasper.

"Minding the nursery again, my lord Valcour? It must get excessively tiring."

Lucy's sparring partner's face darkened with a controlled fury more terrifying than any raging temper she'd ever encountered.

Lucy knew she should skitter up the stairs at the back

of the establishment. But before she could move, Valcour had grasped her arm so tightly she was certain the marks would remain on the morrow.

"Of course," Lord Jasper continued, "after tomorrow morning you'll have one less rebellious cub to trouble yourself with. I wonder what your hotheaded brother will choose as his weapons. Pistols or swords? No matter. The boy is hopelessly clumsy with either weapon."

"D'Autrecourt. You have no objection to my young friend and I joining your table, I presume?"

The name struck Lucy like a mace to the chest. "I thought—I mean, I heard him called Lord Jasper. . . ."

"Jasper d'Autrecourt." The man gave a curt bow. "Your obedient servant."

Lucy felt sick to her stomach. Was this the man who had brought her here? This beast with madness lurking in his eyes? Her knees were so weak she was almost glad of Valcour's hand shoring her up, until she realized he was dragging her with him to the table.

She made a half-frantic attempt to free herself, but Valcour slammed her buttocks down onto the seat of a vacant chair with a force that all but drove her spine through the top of her head. Lucy could hardly breathe as she realized Valcour had positioned her directly between Lord Jasper and himself.

Any other time Lucy might have been amused, watching the rest of the players at the table scatter like a flock of terrified children. Yet at this moment she would have been glad to join them, except for two facts.

First, this d'Autrecourt might well be the person she was here to meet. Second, she had the distinct impression that if she tried to bolt, Lord Valcour would haul her back into the chair in the same ignominious manner Pappy Blood had used with Natty.

Valcour signaled for wine for both of them and a fresh packet of cards. "D'Autrecourt, this is Mr. Dubbonet."

"Delighted. Delighted." Lord Jasper fingered the cards

as if they were razor blades and he was selecting one with which to draw blood.

"It is a pity your brother has turned out to be such a disappointment, Valcour," Lord Jasper said. "That a family with such a delightfully long and scandalous history as yours could spawn a thin-blooded whelp like him is hard to imagine. I do hope you are fitting up a space for him amongst the rest of the wastrels in the family plot."

"A tedious business, but I suppose I'll have no choice but to deal with it when the time comes." Valcour gave a careless brush of his hand. "It must be a relief that you don't have to make any such preparations, Lord Jasper."

Lucy stiffened against her chair back, disliking this discussion of grave sites. She already had one headstone with her name carved on it. She wasn't eager to make it a pair.

"Mr. Dubbonet, you might be interested to know that Lord Jasper is to fight a duel with my brother at Chalk Fields tomorrow."

"No. I—I'm not particularly interested at all."

"Nonsense, boy. Did you not come here specifically searching for a bit of excitement? Lord Jasper is just the sort to entertain a young rakehell like you with stories of his prowess. Lord Jasper, do tell my young friend how many duels you have fought. A dozen?"

"Fifteen. And not once have I tasted another man's steel."

Lucy swallowed hard, as both men stared at her expectantly. "You must be an estimable swordsman."

"It's a respectable sum," Valcour allowed, "though it doesn't near my record. Of course, it must be difficult for you to enjoy your notorious reputation, Lord Jasper, considering the humiliating things people say about your battles."

Jasper's hand knotted around his glass. "Humiliating?"

"Just so. In fact, Mr. Dubbonet, just last night while I was dining at White's, we came to the consensus that it's not because Lord Jasper has any skill with sword or pistol that he's accomplished this feat. It's because of the poor fools he challenges."

"What the devil are you implying?" Jasper growled.

Valcour emitted such a cold laugh that Lucy's fingers burned with the chill. "My ninety-year-old grandmama could look like an accomplished duelist if she only fought children or doddering old men."

Lord Jasper's face stilled, the wild look deepening in his eyes. "I think that when I meet your brother in the morning I shall insist on fighting with swords, Valcour. That way I can slash away his life by painful inches instead of blasting him into eternity with one quick pistolball."

"As you wish." Valcour shrugged, his long tapered fingers curled negligently about his wineglass. "I doubt you could make much of an impression on the boy no matter what weapon you used. I would avoid aiming for his head, in particular, if I were you. It's so bloody hard it would probably damage your sword."

Lucy couldn't help gaping at the man next to her so coolly discussing the impending death of his brother. No wonder her mother had fled England. These people were insane!

All of a sudden Jasper's eyes grew canny. "I know what you're doing, Valcour. You are trying to goad me into a temper to protect your brother. It won't work."

"I? Goad you into a temper? I am far too busy to waste my time in such an impossible pursuit. After all, I'm a grown man with a reputation for being a complete swordsman, not some youth barely out from beneath his schoolmaster's willow switch. I could fling this glass of wine in your face and you would not cross swords with me. Now Dubbonet here had best be careful not to give some grave offense to you, like stepping on your cloak, or he will find himself facing pistols for two, breakfast for one in the morning."

"I—I didn't really mean it," Lucy stammered. "About wanting to duel."

She could have told the two men that their hair was on fire and it would have had no effect. Tension sizzled between them as if no one else were in the room.

"Are you insinuating that I am a coward, sir?" Jasper hissed.

"Insinuating? No." Valcour sipped from the crystal goblet of wine, then stared contemplatively into its rosy depths. "I am saying it quite plainly." He raised his eyes to Lord Jasper's fury-reddened face. "You are a coward, d'Autrecourt."

Veins bulged in Lord Jasper's temples, his lips twisting. "You'd like nothing more than for me to fight you in an effort to save your brother from his death. But honor demands I not schedule another altercation until I've met him on the dueling field."

Lucy was stunned as Valcour flung back his head and laughed. "A fine speech, d'Autrecourt, but I know exactly how cowards like you behave. You'll cut down Aubrey, a seventeen-year-old boy. And while there you'll get some trifling injury that will make you unable to meet me. Then you'll take an unavoidable trip to the continent, quite out of my reach. Business, of course. And that will be the end to it."

Valcour sighed. "Ah, well. I suppose we are both to be disappointed. But you are a great deal more used to disappointment than I am. You've had plenty of practice at it in women's bedchambers."

Valcour stood as if oblivious to the murderous rage exploding in those evil eyes. Then with bored indifference he tossed the contents of his glass into Jasper d'Autrecourt's face.

3

$\mathcal{V}$alcour might as well have slung boiling oil into d'Autrecourt's face. Lord Jasper exploded from his chair as if he intended to kill the earl with his bare hands.

Lucy bounded to her feet, and the rest of the room erupted in shouts of excitement and shrieks of dismay. Only Valcour looked unperturbed. His eyes flicked to the playing cards, red wine pooling about them like blood.

"I believe Lord Jasper shall have need of another deck," Valcour told a gaping servant, then started to stride from the room.

"Valcour!" d'Autrecourt bellowed. "You cursed bastard, turn and fight!"

Slowly the nobleman turned, and Lucy was terrified to see that for the first time Lord Valcour's mouth was curved in a smile. Saturnine, chilling. "As you wish."

At that instant Lucy knew it would be a fight to the death. And death to Lord Jasper, no matter how loathsome he was, might mean that she would never find out why the parcel had been sent to her, might mean that Alexander d'Autrecourt—if he were indeed alive—would be lost to her forever.

While death to Valcour . . . Lucy couldn't imagine why the thought should distress her so.

She flung herself between the two men, unnerved as Valcour began stripping off his frockcoat in preparation for the duel. "My lord, you mustn't do this!"

Valcour's fingers made quick work of the buttons of his silver waistcoat. "Why Dubbonet, I'm touched. I didn't realize you had developed such a deep affection for me in so short a time."

"Don't be ridiculous!" Lucy snapped, the sound of the other clients scattering grating on her nerves. "It's just that—that it's a mistake to allow yourself to be carried away on a wave of anger." Lucy couldn't help remembering her reaction to such warnings.

"I am not angry in the least," Valcour said with arctic civility. Lucy was stunned to sense that he spoke the truth.

The realization that bets were being laid on the outcome of the duel made her stomach churn. She glanced over at Lord Jasper. His cohorts were clustered eagerly around him, while Jasper himself was practically frothing at the mouth in his eagerness to warm his steel in Valcour's blood. He was already stripped to his shirtsleeves, his face twisted with a violence that portended ill.

Lucy turned back to Valcour and tried another approach. "There are certain rules in dueling," Lucy objected, positioning herself between the earl and his enemy. "Someone has to serve as your second."

Valcour tossed his coat into her arms. "I suppose you'll do well enough."

Lucy clutched the garment, still warm from his body, smelling of sandalwood and leather and very real danger, a danger building heartbeat by heartbeat in this suddenly stifling room.

"If you kill d'Autrecourt you will have to flee to the continent. There must be someone who would grieve for your loss. A wife?" Lucy offered hopefully. "A mistress? What about your mama? You would break her heart."

Valcour's long fingers froze on the hilt of his sword. Lucy retreated a step from the black fire in his eyes—a conflagration of something raw and dark burning through that icy facade.

Steel hissed as Valcour drew his sword, light shimmering in a deadly river of blue down its length.

A space had been cleared, and the patrons of the gaming hell pressed up against tables, their eyes expectant, as Lord Valcour strode to the center of the room where Jasper was waiting.

Black breeches clung to the earl's powerful thighs and impossibly narrow hips, his ice-white shirt a startling contrast to his hair. His neckcloth had been loosened just enough to expose the tanned hollow of his throat.

His right cuff had been turned back to reveal a wrist that was sinewy and supple, the sword a mere extension of his arm.

"En garde." Valcour began to make the traditional salute with his sword, but without so much as that courtesy Jasper d'Autrecourt charged him, lashing out with his blade.

Valcour leapt back light as a cat, his steel flashing out to intercept the lethal blow. Jasper grunted in frustration and fury and slashed out again.

He outweighed Valcour by forty pounds of pure animal rage, but while d'Autrecourt battled as if consumed by a hundred demons, Valcour parried and thrust with the grace of a dancer, the lethal expertise of an cold-blooded assassin. Lucy had seen masterful swordplay before, had even amused herself by fencing with her father. But even Ian Blackheath could not have withstood the calculated onslaught of Lord Valcour's sword.

The tip danced, a will-o'-the-wisp, tormenting d'Autrecourt with his own death, like a cat toying with its prey. Valcour's blade flashed past his opponent's guard, biting with sinister delicacy into the flesh of Lord Jasper's shoulder. Red stained his shirt, and he gave a guttural cry of pain, but Valcour seemed not to notice at all.

Sweat dripped down Lord Jasper's face and darkened his dull gold hair until it was the hue of tarnished brass. Lucy could see his sword hand quiver just a little, heard his breath rasp. Valcour gave him no quarter, driving him harder, faster. Another wound bloomed on Lord Jasper's thigh, then Valcour's sword point ripped the front of his opponent's shirt, leaving a shallow gash.

Ruthless. Almost inhumanly cold, Valcour battled, his lips curled in a feral smile. Time after time Lucy saw openings where he could have driven his blade home. He chose not to, and Lucy was certain he was just extending the pleasure of this battle before he finished Jasper. After all, the only other reason Valcour could be leashing himself would be to keep from killing Lord Jasper, and that was the most preposterous possibility of all.

Valcour had come looking for this duel, and he had gotten it. Everyone in the room, including the winded d'Autrecourt, had to know that. Four times Valcour had dampened his sword with Sir Jasper's blood. It was only a matter of time before he would strike the final blow.

"Please, milord!" the proprietor of the gaming hell begged. "'Twill be the ruin of me if you murder him here!"

At that instant Jasper channeled all his waning strength and flung himself one last time at Valcour.

As if suddenly tiring of the game, Valcour flicked his supple wrist, driving the blade through Sir Jasper's shoulder.

The nobleman bellowed in pain and crumpled to his knees as Valcour pulled his weapon free.

Desperate to stop the death blow, Lucy flung herself

between them, clutching at Valcour's sword arm, "You've got what you wanted! He can't fight your brother tomorrow! There's no need to kill him!"

Valcour's eyes darkened for a heartbeat, his other hand coming up to shove her aside. His hard palm flattened against the front of Lucy's frockcoat.

Lucy cried out as Valcour's powerful hand closed upon the unmistakable swell of her bound breasts.

Stunned disbelief flashed like quicksilver across that arrogant countenance, but in a heartbeat the emotion vanished.

He turned away from the groaning d'Autrecourt and withdrew a black silk handkerchief to wipe the blood from his sword.

"I suppose it would be the height of vulgarity to kill a man in front of a group of ladies, however questionable their virtue." Valcour sheathed his sword. "But remember this, d'Autrecourt. My death blow is just one indiscretion away from your cowardly throat. My brother may be a fool. But at the moment I prefer him to be a living fool instead of a dead one. And I am well used to getting what I want. Now if you'll excuse us." He dug a wad of currency from his pocket and dropped it onto the floor. "This should cover damages."

Lucy shrank back, grateful that Valcour would be leaving. Grateful that d'Autrecourt was alive. If only she could question him a little before he was carted away to the surgeon's, perhaps this night's excursion would not have been in vain.

She started toward Sir Jasper when a hard hand knotted at the scruff of her neck.

"Did you not hear me, Dubbonet?" Valcour said through gritted teeth. "I said it is time for us to leave."

"You leave!" Lucy struggled against his grasp. He dragged her along as if she were no more trouble than a recalcitrant kitten. "I have business to conduct—"

"You have business to conduct, all right," Valcour

muttered, retrieving their cloaks. His voice dropped to a level that could reach her ears alone. "You can begin this *business* by explaining exactly what you are hiding beneath your frockcoat."

"They're called breasts," Lucy snapped, yanking against his grasp. The only thing it earned her was a bruise on her wrist. "I assume you know what they are."

"I know what breasts are, madam," Valcour said. "I just don't expect to find them beneath a frockcoat on a hotheaded boy in a gaming hell."

"You make a habit of checking beneath boys' frockcoats, do you?" she countered. She was about to further insult her tormentor, but at that moment her gaze snagged on the lone figure of a man standing at the top of the stairs on the far side of the room.

He was slender, with an ethereal grace. His hair was the soft hue of candlelight. Lucy's heart leapt to her throat. His features were obscured by shadow, only the sickly pallor of his skin visible across the smoke-filled room. As if the scene had pained him, he turned away, disappearing down the hall.

In pure desperation, Lucy did the only thing she could think of to get Valcour to release her. She turned and sank her teeth into his hand.

Valcour let fly a hoarse oath of surprise, his fingers loosening just a whisper. It was enough. Lucy ripped free of him and ran across the crowded room, dashing up the stairs two at a time with Valcour in hot pursuit. She plunged into the relative dimness of the upstairs corridor, her heart pounding.

Nothing. No one. Frustration, desperation balled in her chest. "Wait! Wait, please!" The man had to be here somewhere.

She was aware of the sound of Valcour's boot soles behind her, gaining on her, was aware of the gasps of harlots opening their boudoir doors.

At the third door, Lucy shoved the panel wide with such force it crashed against the inner wall.

She froze on the threshold, staring into the room.

A meager fire flickered on the grate. A single candle on a desk drove back the darkness. A quill was soaking in an open inkwell, while the pounce full of sand sat ready beside it. Almost as if in a trance, Lucy slipped inside the room. Blank sheaves of parchment were spread across the desk, while scattered on the floor were three pages, crumpled up as if in frustration. Lucy knelt and picked one up, her fingers unsteady as she smoothed it open. Her fingers came away stained with the ink still wet upon the page.

"It's music," she whispered. "Sweet Jesus. Music." She swayed, her head reeling, her knees weak. "It wasn't Sir Jasper. It was someone else."

"What the blazes?" She barely felt Valcour's hand curve beneath her arm. That harsh face swam before her eyes, his brows a slash of confusion over hawklike eyes.

"Damme girl, you look like you've seen a ghost."

I have. She wanted to shriek, her heart racing.

A gust of wind made the candle flame flicker, filling the room with writhing shadows. Lucy wheeled to see the shutters of a narrow window open to the night.

She tore away from Valcour and dashed to the opening, peering out. Fury, helplessness surged inside her as she caught a glimpse of pale hair disappearing into the maze of streets.

She braced one foot on the sill, ready to vault out after him, but before she could do it, Valcour's arm shot around her waist, all but crushing her ribs as he hauled her back against the granite-hard wall of his chest. She fought like a tigress, slamming her elbow into him, kicking back at him with the heels of her boots. Valcour gave a grunt of pain, his arm tightening until she couldn't draw breath.

"Stop this, you little hellcat! Don't make me hurt you!"

"You're the one who's going to be hurt, you interfering sonofabitch!" Lucy fought as if her life depended on it. And maybe it did. The life she had known since she was eight years old—the world Emily and Ian's love had created for her.

He dragged her to the desk chair and slammed her down on it so hard her buttocks stung.

"You have some questions to answer, girl. Now," he snarled, ripping off her ornate wig. A wealth of guinea-gold curls tumbled about Lucy's defiant face.

"This is all your fault!" Lucy raged, slapping the hair back over her shoulders. "Damn you and your accursed duel! You could've just waylaid Sir Jasper in the streets. Wounded him in his own bed. But no! You *goddamn* English have to be so civilized! You have to follow five pages of instructions before you can skewer an enemy with your sword! And as if that wasn't bad enough, you have to drag me into the affair!"

"I have no interest in your opinion of English custom," Valcour said. "What I will know, at once, is what your real name is and who the devil you belong to!"

"Belong to? I'm no man's lapdog!"

Valcour gave an ugly laugh. "I'd pity the man who got himself saddled with you. Your temper is so vicious you'd probably unman him the first chance you got!"

The words were flame to tinder. Before she'd even fully comprehended the idea, Lucy's boot flashed out, the hard leather toe connecting solidly with Valcour's groin.

"I appreciate the suggestion, my lord," Lucy taunted as the earl doubled over with a bellow of pain and fury. She bolted out of the chair, pausing just a heartbeat in her flight to snatch up her wig and one of the crumpled sheets of parchment that had been left behind. She plopped the wig on her head, stuffed the music down her shirtfront, and ran even faster as she heard Valcour struggling to come after her.

She took the one route she knew he could not follow. She vaulted onto the window ledge and jumped.

Her booted feet slammed upon the ground with bone-jarring force, Valcour's curses ringing in her ears.

Within moments she was astride her mare. Natty—obviously knowing a quick escape when he saw one—flung the reins into her hands. She glanced over her shoulder for just an instant to see Valcour silhouetted in the narrow window, his imposing frame still bent in pain, his dark hair tangled about a face like that of some pagan god of vengeance.

Heaven only knew what he would do if he ever caught her.

Lucy spurred her mare down into the maze of dark London streets, thanking God that she would never have to see the earl of Valcour again.

At nearly three o'clock in the morning, Dominic St. Cyr, the sixth earl of Valcour, strode down the corridor of Valcour House. The servants bolted for cover the moment the earl strode through the door, goaded by some instinct for self-preservation.

Hellfire, Valcour thought grimly, he'd gotten no more than he'd deserved when that Satan-spawned female had exacted her revenge. At thirty-five, a man should have more sense than to go thrusting his nose into other people's business—even if the person in question was barely more than a child, with huge blue eyes and a face that had seemed far too sweet even before Dominic had realized she was a girl.

A girl! Sashaying into one of the worst gaming hells in London, totally unprotected. A girl who had made fools of them all, from Jasper d'Autrecourt to the gaming hell's servants to the earl himself.

Valcour should have known better than to interfere. After these past two years with his seventeen-year-old brother, Aubrey, he'd begun to think he could sit without raising so much as an eyebrow and watch someone set their own hair afire. Unfortunately, Valcour's conscience balked at standing back and letting the boy fight a duel he could never win.

And of course, there were even more pleasures to come, Valcour thought with an ironic twist to his lips. Aubrey would be spitting fury when he discovered that the earl had saved his neck. However, another person would be more than grateful. Their mother.

Valcour approached the library, knowing he would find her there. She lay, a fragile figure, curled up in his favorite chair. Silver threads wove through hair that had once been soft, glossy gold. Dominic could remember her face when it was fresh with youth, a rosy bloom in her cheeks. Now it was pallid with sorrow and exhaustion.

Any other man would have crossed to the woman immediately and stooped to gently waken her and wipe away the tears that clung to her cheeks.

Dominic crossed to a mahogany table and poured himself a generous draught of brandy in hopes that the liquor would be able to loosen the knot that tightened in his gut whenever he looked into the face of his mother.

His voice was emotionless as he said, "Madam. It is done."

Catherine St. Cyr started awake, her blue-green eyes lost in bruised circles of hope and haunted despair.

"Dominic," she breathed, her simple white gown falling about a body slender to the point of frailty as she struggled to her feet. "Dominic, please tell me that you made Sir Jasper see reason."

"Actually, what Sir Jasper saw was the point of my sword. And a quantity of his own blood."

"You . . . fought?" She gasped, stricken.

"It was carried out with the height of discretion. You've no need to fear a scandal."

"You think I care about that? Just tell me you were not injured!" Lady Catherine rushed over to him, her fingers on his shirtfront as if searching for any sign of a wound.

Dominic disentangled himself from her. "Do not distress yourself, madam. I sustained . . ." Dominic's mouth quirked at the corners as he remembered Lucien Dubbonet, a termagant with glorious blue eyes and the most stubborn chin he'd ever seen. "I sustained one minor injury, and not at the hands of d'Autrecourt."

Lady Catherine stuffed her hands behind her back like a child caught touching some forbidden treasure. "Dominic, when I told you of Aubrey's predicament, I did not want you to charge out and place yourself in danger in his stead! I only—"

Dominic hated the stirring of pain beneath scars long buried. "What did you expect me to do? Slap Sir Jasper on the hand and lock Aubrey in his room? Or did you think I would just ignore the whole incident and order the young fool a shroud? There was nothing else to be done."

"No. I suppose I should have known that you would take care of him. The way you care for your estates. The way you care for me." Why did her voice sound so infernally sad? "You will not have to flee to the continent, will you, Dominic? You did not—not—"

"Kill him? No."

"I just feared that—"

"That even after all these years, I would be so hungry for d'Autrecourt blood I'd not be overly particular which d'Autrecourt was beneath my sword?" The words were cruel, a weapon to drive Lady Catherine away. But they were his only chance to fend off the throb of pain he felt at the unguarded emotion in her eyes. When she flinched, Dominic felt the pain in his own body.

"You had best go to bed, madam. I believe I hear Aubrey's carriage, and I can assure you, the boy's reaction to what I have to tell him will be quite spectacular. You will need your rest to play Lady Comforter to his wounded pride in the morning."

"Dominic, let me stay, try to explain. Perhaps if we both speak to Aubrey, he will not . . . not . . ."

"Goodnight, madam."

Those eyes that had once been bright with innocence seemed raw and stricken. But Lady Catherine crossed to where Dominic stood, awkwardly brushing back a tendril of midnight hair from his brow. She looked incredibly small and fragile, as if a single harsh word would make her dissolve into nothingness.

Dominic wanted nothing more than to reach out to her, pat her shoulder, to soothe her. But all he could do was gentle the timbre of his voice. "It will be all right, madam."

"Will it?" Tears welled against Lady Catherine's lashes. "I wonder, Dominique."

It was the pet name she had given him when he was small. A tender endearment that had once made him drag his gruff boyish dignity about him, though secretly he'd been pleased whenever she used it. Now Lady Valcour stared into his face, wanting something he knew he could not give her. A man's forgiveness for what a boy could never understand.

He saw the familiar disappointment shadow her gentle mouth. Then she slipped from the room.

Dominic downed the rest of his brandy. He crossed to the table and poured another, aware of the muffled commotion of Aubrey's arrival in the entry hall.

The boy was laughing with one of the under footmen, telling some preposterously bawdy story as he shed his cloak. Aubrey's tread was unsteady as he started down the corridor. Dominic went to his desk and sat down, watching through the doorway until he glimpsed a dashing scarlet frockcoat and a flash of disheveled gold hair.

"Aubrey." The mere name was a command. The youth blinked, peering into the library with eyes bleary from too much liquor.

"Dom!" the boy exclaimed, shoring himself up by leaning on the door jamb. "Waiting up for another one of our charming brotherly chats? Too bad. I haven't time to listen to your lecture right now. You see, I have an appointment at an ungodly early hour this morning."

"I regret to inform you that there has been a change of plans. Sir Jasper d'Autrecourt met with an accident."

"What?" The flush of drink drained from Aubrey's face, the scorn in his eyes shifting to almost wild fury. "It was you, wasn't it? Blast you, Dominic, if you interfered in this I'll never forgive you!"

"I shall try not to be heartbroken at the prospect. Feel free to add saving your fool hide from d'Autrecourt's sword to my numerous other transgressions."

"Damn you, this was *my* affair! Mine!" Aubrey staggered toward Valcour. "How the devil did you even find out we were to fight?"

Dominic looked down at a sheaf of papers on his desk and tried to blot out the image of Lady Catherine wringing her hands. Her eyes had been so huge and terrified, he'd wanted to murder Aubrey himself rather than rescue the boy from this latest disaster.

"You won't tell me who carried the tale to you, will you? Oh, no! You prefer to be the great, omniscient earl of Valcour, all-seeing, all-knowing! Well, damn your black soul to hell, I deserve at least to know exactly how you shamed me."

"I merely visited some gaming hell and pointed out to the assembled company what everyone already whispers about in private: the fact that Sir Jasper only challenges babes fresh from the cradle. That he hasn't the courage to fight a grown man." Aubrey reeled back as if Dominic had slapped him. "D'Autrecourt felt compelled to prove differently."

"You didn't. Dom, tell me you didn't!" The boy looked ashen. Doubtless he would have preferred dying nobly to facing a few moments of disgrace. Dominic remembered a time when he had felt the same. He stood up and paced to the window.

"You've made me the laughingstock of the season," Aubrey flung out. "How dare you! I won't endure it. Tomorrow I'll leave for Brighton."

"A magnificent idea. Order your valet to prepare at once."

Aubrey gaped, obviously thunderstruck at Dominic's quick acquiescence. "What did you say?"

"A retreat to Brighton is a brilliant idea. I shall be delighted to be rid of you. Of course, there will be those who say you are proving the gossips right if you go."

"Proving them right?"

"They will say that you had me interfere in the duel because you are a coward. That you fled London because you were ashamed to show your face. Of course, their opinion is worth no more than this." Valcour gave a dismissing snap of his long fingers.

"I've nothing to be ashamed of! I did nothing wrong!"

"Quite a pretty case of righteous indignation. It is possible that you would be able to play the wounded hero to a more sympathetic audience if you attended some social function and aired your opinion of my interference to the world. There are those who claim that if you show the gossips no fear they'll forget the scandal soon enough. But if you quake before them . . ." Valcour met his brother's eyes. "You will live with the disgrace of it forever."

"Do you think me a fool?" Aubrey challenged. "You know it will be the topic of conversation for months!"

"I didn't say this was my opinion, Aubrey. Only that there are some who believe it so. The one thing I know for certain is that you will not die of the scandal. However, you would have died at the point of d'Autrecourt's sword."

"Maybe that would have been better for everyone concerned!"

"Quite dramatic. You might have had a career on the stage, though I must say, actors are rather a more stable lot. You might care to remember that your mother adores you, in spite of all you do to make her feel otherwise. Any harm befalling you would break her heart."

The mention of Lady Catherine sobered Aubrey as little else could have.

"Of course, when you flee to Brighton, you will be abandoning *her* to the sharp tongues of the gossips. It is a pity, but she will feel compelled to defend you. Of course, considering what a cold-hearted villain I am, I will not lift a finger to help her."

Dominic crossed to his desk, where a dozen invitations to various social functions were scattered. He grimaced, knowing it was in Aubrey's best interests to brazen out this new scandal in the social whirl as soon as possible.

"I was intending to send my regrets to most of these," Valcour observed with feigned carelessness. "But now I suppose I will have to discuss them with Lady Catherine. I wonder which she will choose to attend to mount your defense, Aubrey. Addison's soiree? Newton's musicale? No. Most likely the ball the new American ambassador is giving a week from tonight. There will be such a large assembly, she can make a single sweep to defend your honor."

Aubrey was trembling, his cheeks flushed, his eyes filled with loathing. "You think I would leave my mother to suffer for me? I love her! Unlike you! I'll go to the accursed ball, damn your eyes to hell."

Dominic raised one brow. "I beg you to reconsider. It would be a hideously humiliating experience. I can even spare my traveling coach for your escape. And a generous amount of money. It goes without saying that you have none of your own. Perhaps you could even sail to the continent. France is lovely this time of year."

"Keep your coach and your accursed money! I'm attending that ball, and there is nothing you can do to stop me!"

"I see. Perhaps I will attend as well. It should prove quite entertaining to see such a brave young knight take the town dragons by storm."

The boy's face flooded with something akin to hurt. So much so that Dominic had to turn away from him.

"Damn you, Dominic, why can't you leave Mama and me alone? Why must you torment us?"

"It is my duty as head of the family to . . . torment you, as you so ungraciously put it."

"What else would you call it when you interfere in an affair of honor? Unman me before all England?" Aubrey challenged.

"I beg to correct you," Dominic said, smiling a little at the memory of flashing blue eyes and tumbled gold curls. "I saved you at considerable risk to my own . . . er . . . manhood."

"We both know you didn't charge into the breach because of your great love for me! You barely tolerate me as it is. For once, I thought I was living up to your expectations. D'Autrecourt insulted me, and I met that insult with a gentleman's challenge. But no. Even that was wrong! I don't understand, Dom! For Christ's sake, you're the one who is always so all-fired determined to defend the St. Cyr honor!"

Dominic wheeled on his brother. "Don't talk to me of honor, boy! It's only been three days since I hauled you out of a sponging house for gaming debts. You swore to me . . ." Dominic's mouth twisted at the bitter futility.

"I didn't ask for your help then, either!" Aubrey retorted. "One of your precious friends ran tattling to you that I was in trouble, just like they did tonight. Why didn't you let me rot there? Because I'm a St. Cyr? Because I was dishonoring your precious name?"

"You're the legal heir to the earldom." Dominic struggled to keep his temper leashed. "And you're my brother. I'm responsible for your actions."

Aubrey gave a choked laugh. "You mean I'm the millstone slung about your neck, the cross the great martyred earl has to drag through society because he's too honorable to throw me into the gutter as I deserve? You might as well let me revel in my destruction and be done with the whole affair, Dom. I'm sure I'll find plenty of our illustrious ancestors wallowing in hell to keep me company. Our father, the fifth earl, to begin with."

Pain and fury tore jagged edges through Dominic's chest. His arm flashed up, but he slammed it to a halt just before backhanding his brother across the jaw.

Aubrey leapt back, his eyes wide. Even his drunkenness couldn't mask his shock.

The sick sensation in the earl's stomach mingled with despair as he stared into Aubrey's face. Suddenly Dominic felt unutterably old.

It seemed an eternity before Aubrey spoke, low, fierce. "I can only hope you suffer the same hell you have put me through, *Brother.*"

Dominic looked away, for once no mocking sneer touching those sensual lips. "Mine is a very different corner of hell. Be grateful you will never feel its fires along with me."

4

*I*t was the perfect night to return to Perdition's Gate.

Satin shimmered, jewels flashed, the light from three hundred candles fragmenting in crystal prisms rained down on the guests who crammed the Wilkes's ballroom. The most powerful men in England demanded John Wilkes's attention, while Claree was lost in a swarm of ladies who buzzed about her as if she were coated with honey and they were starving bees.

Lucy was certain she could fling a bobcat into the center of the room and no one would observe that it was there. And not even the fiercest old dragon of society would notice if the ambassador's American guest were missing for a few hours.

Lucy peeked from behind the curtain of the alcove where she'd retreated after the last dance, her gaze traveling to the clock upon the mantle for the tenth time in as many minutes. She wished to blazes she could make the hands move faster by force of will alone.

But in spite of her impatience, she curbed the impulse to go charging off earlier than planned. She had worked too hard and waited too long to risk ruining her chances of escape tonight by growing careless.

She had planned this expedition with the precision of a general throughout the past week, while the rest of the house had been in an uproar preparing for the coming ball. Her bundle of masculine clothes had been tucked behind a pillar in the garden just that morning, ready to be snatched up at a moment's notice. And she had spent countless hours charting the movements of the grooms so she would know at what time the stable would be most deserted.

She considered it a heavenly gift that Claree had planned the ball for Thursday night—the appointed time she was to rendezvous with the mysterious stranger in the gaming hell. And although Lucy had failed in her mission last time, she was resolved that tonight she'd not allow even the devil himself to stand in her way.

The devil . . .

She felt a tingling awareness beneath her skin, something dark and enticing stirring inside her, as her memory filled with the image of eyes black as Satan's soul, a mouth tempting as sin.

The earl of Valcour's mesmerizing features danced like some sensual dream inside her mind. His face was cold and arrogant. His eyes were burning, intense. The carnal heat of his mouth seemed so seductive that Lucy had spent the past week wondering what it would be like to taste it.

It was absurd, this curiosity. A result of too many sleepless nights. And yet, even in his absence, the fascinating English lord had tormented her, taunted her, dared her—to *what,* she did not know.

Lucy drew deeper into the shadow of the curtain, raising trembling fingers to the exquisite likeness of Alexander d'Autrecourt she had pinned in the froth of lace at her breasts when she'd dressed three hours earlier. She had worn the ornament in vague hopes that one of

54

Claree's guests might recognize her father's face and comment on it. Of course, it had been ridiculous to hope that the English would stop peering down their noses long enough to remark on something so small and delicate.

Especially when they had such a deliciously fresh scandal to sharpen their teeth on.

Lucy nibbled at the corner of her lip, scraps of conversation she'd heard earlier that night echoing in her memory. She must have listened to a dozen accounts of what had happened in the now notorious "duel at the gates of hell." It had taken all Lucy's willpower to keep her own mouth clamped shut as each story grew more fantastic than the last, the truth lost in embellishments so ridiculous she was certain her baby sisters would not have believed them.

But, truth to tell, she could almost have been grateful for the flurry of gossip, since it provided such a convenient distraction to aid in her escape. She *could* have been grateful, if it weren't for the grudging sympathy she was beginning to feel for the earl of Valcour's brother, who was the butt of the constant jests.

Still, Lucy thought with grim determination, this wasn't a night to go crusading on behalf of some English boy she'd never even met. She had to keep her mind fixed on her purpose. To find the mysterious man who had disappeared into the twisted alleyways the week before. To discover the secrets that had been hidden in the vague, sorrowful blue eyes she'd glimpsed so briefly before Valcour had ruined everything.

She pressed her hand against the pocket hidden beneath her silver-tissue gown and heard the soft crackling of the parchment she had concealed there. But even this scrap of music he had left behind in the gaming hell saddened her. For when her fingers had tried to coax the melody out of the pianoforte, she discovered that whatever creative fire Alexander d'Autrecourt had once had

had vanished. Gone like the serenity that wreathed his face in the painted miniature.

"Pardon, Miss Blackheath." The sound of a voice at the edge of the curtain made her turn, and she saw a man with a ruddy face and lecherous eye sidling into her haven. "I would delight in claiming you for this dance."

"Please, go delight someone else," she said with a beatific smile. Then she hurried from the alcove, leaving the gentleman gaping. She glanced one more time at the clock, relieved to see that it was time to make her escape.

With great effort, Lucy restrained herself to a casual stroll toward the door, fully intending to make an exit without another interruption. But just as she rounded an urn full of roses, she glimpsed a crowd of raucous men, their laughter tinged with a nastiness that raked her nerves.

Lucy gritted her teeth, quickened her step. She might even have managed to pass them altogether if she had not caught sight of their quarry. A golden-haired youth near her age stood like a man facing his executioners, his face rigid, his cheeks as white as the froth of neckcloth tied beneath a boyishly smooth chin. But it was his eyes that pierced Lucy like a dagger thrust. They caught hers for a heartbeat—filled with abject misery—then flashed away as if the humiliation were too great to bear.

"I envy you, Aubrey!" said a sly-looking fool. "It must be very convenient to have a brother like Valcour."

Lucy missed a step, her gaze returning to the boy. Aubrey? Surely this couldn't be the brother Valcour had supposedly been defending. The boy was as different in appearance from the earl as sunshine to midnight. And yet at first glance, who would guess that Lucy and Norah were sisters?

She paused, pretending to rearrange the lace at her wrists while she stole another glance at the boy. He was young, but a man nonetheless. Old enough to make his own choices. No wonder his pride was so battered by what had happened. Lucy felt a swift jab of anger toward Valcour.

"Chalmers, haven't you heard?" A portly youth with a purple wig cuffed Patch on the back. "Valcour is like a mastiff trained to attack anyone who distresses those he is responsible for. Perhaps we had better warn that little opera dancer who rejected Aubrey's suit last week. Aubrey may set his brother on her for revenge!"

Lucy flinched in sympathy as two hot spots of color darkened the boy's cheeks. "I wanted nothing more than to match steel with d'Autrecourt," he snapped. "The instant Sir Jasper is recovered, I'll meet him. By God, I will."

"Sir Jasper will refuse to meet you after his tête-à-tête with the point of your illustrious brother's sword. D'Autrecourt may be a fool, but he's not suicidal."

"It is I who will fight."

Disbelieving laughter rose from the crowd.

"Of course you will, my treasure," Purple Wig chortled.

"I've told you a dozen times, I knew nothing of Valcour's plans until it was all over!" Aubrey said.

"That's not the way Filby told the tale," Patch sneered. "He said there was a blond gentleman at Valcour's side when he came to d'Autrecourt's table. Everyone knows how nearsighted old Filly is, but there can be little doubt it was you."

"Damn it to hell, it wasn't! There was a private party at Bridgeton's. I was there all night. Mirrivile can attest to it!"

"Your bosom friends? How convenient. We know exactly how objective they would be."

Swearing inwardly, Lucy charged into the breach. "It is as he says," she announced in a clear voice.

The men wheeled to face her, none more stunned than the Earl of Valcour's brother. Eyes that had been filled with fury and misery widened in surprise.

"A thousand pardons, miss," Patch said with such annoying obsequiousness that Lucy was tempted to loosen his teeth. "It's not our custom to discuss such inappropriate topics in front of a lady as lovely as yourself."

"I am unfamiliar with English customs, sir." Lucy peered up through thick lashes. "Is it considered appropriate for gentlemen to spread lies about an incident as long as there is *no* lady present to stop them?"

The patch quivered with anger at the corner of the man's thin lips. "Certainly, miss, you do not mean to infer—"

"I'm not inferring anything. I'm stating quite plainly that you are spreading vicious and unfounded rumors."

Lucy delighted in the man's cheeks puffing out, scarlet with outrage.

"You see," she continued, "I am intimately acquainted with the young gentleman Valcour dragged into his infamous duel. And I promise you it was not Lord Valcour's brother. The earl was acting on his own dictatorial impulses. I'm astonished you didn't guess as much at once. Surely you must know his despicable temperament better than I."

"Damned disrespectful way to talk of an aristocrat!" Purple wig sputtered.

"We have had a great deal of practice at it in Virginia." Lucy gave him her sweetest smile. "Tell me, can you think of a better way to describe such a high-handed interference in his brother's affair? He tore Mr. Aubrey's reputation to shreds with no thought of the man's honor. It seems to me you should be defaming Valcour's character for his inexcusable indifference to his brother. If any man behaved so abominably to me, I vow I would make him sorry!" Lucy tossed her curls.

The company gaped at her outburst, but Lucy didn't care. She had brought color back to Aubrey's cheeks.

There was a questioning light in his eyes. For an instant, his lips tipped in a vulnerable half smile.

"I must thank you for your defense, milady, though I'm uncertain how I came by it." He gave a courtly bow. "May I present myself? Aubrey St. Cyr. Your servant."

"St. Cyr?" Lucy echoed a little faintly. Her fingers strayed to the miniature at her breast. "Of Harlestone Castle?"

"I sincerely hope not," Aubrey said with a warm smile. "I fear it's in such bad repair that it's fit only to house the family ghosts at present."

"But someone must have lived there."

"At Harlestone?" Purple Wig scoffed. "It's nothing but a crumbling pile of rubble with a few tapestries for the mice to chew on."

"There are a few servants who still live there to oversee the lands, I think." Aubrey cut in. "And my brother, the earl, keeps a suite of rooms in decent repair for when he must visit the lands. But no one has truly lived there since I was two or three years old. Why do you ask?"

Lucy looked away. "I . . . have a bit of music that was supposed to have been written for someone there. I was curious."

"I'm sorry, but we St. Cyrs are a notoriously tone-deaf lot from all accounts. Not a one of us has ever played or sung a note to my knowledge." He shrugged. "I'd like to help you, miss, but I'm afraid I can't."

"Which should be no surprise," Patch interrupted in an annoying nasal drawl. "You'll find that Mr. St. Cyr can't even help himself, let alone someone else, my beauty. You are the ambassador's houseguest, are you not?" He tried to take her hand to kiss it.

Lucy snatched her fingers away as if he had the plague and favored Aubrey with her most dazzling smile. "Lucinda Blackheath," she said with a curtsy. "My friends call me Lucy."

Aubrey smiled back, raising her hand to his lips. "Then I shall call you Lucy too."

"It is the least you should do, St. Cyr," Purple Wig said in pompous accents. "Since the lady has charged to your defense, berating us about things she doesn't understand. Miss Blackheath, you can hardly be expected to comprehend how great a value we Englishmen place on honor, when you come from the wilds of America."

"We Americans understand the British concept of honor very well. You should also be aware that we don't shrink from pointing out tyranny when we see it."

"Tyranny!" Patch echoed, a round of gasps erupting from those around him. Lucy took deep satisfaction in the way their faces paled, their eyes widened. Aubrey looked ashen as well, but Lucy could not resist burying her verbal thrust to its hilt.

"Tyranny, sir," she enunciated in accents that would have done Patrick Henry proud. "The earl of Valcour is the most loathsome, arrogant, insufferable monster that I've ever had the ill luck to stumble across. Thankfully, we Americans have ways of dealing with tyrants."

The chiming of the clock brought Lucy to her senses. But she couldn't regret that she had stepped in, although it had cost her precious time.

She spun on her heels, fully intending to make good her escape. But she slammed headfirst into a solid wall of muscle, garbed in velvet. Hands caught her arms to steady her, but she couldn't raise her eyes from the disturbingly familiar diamond stickpin glinting up at her with mocking brilliance from her captor's neckcloth.

God, no! Not again! The fates couldn't be so unfair.

"Valcour." She squeezed his name through her lips and tilted her head back to meet dark eyes, their fierce intelligence all but concealed beneath narrowed lids.

He was magnificent: his sable hair unpowdered, caught back in a thin black ribbon, his broad shoulders covered in amber velvet with touches of rich gold about the collar and buttonholes. His waistcoat was the tawny color of a lion's mane, accenting his powerful physique. The scar on his face only made him more dazzlingly handsome, more intriguingly dangerous.

He might have been a pirate, or some reckless knight of the road, if it hadn't been for the aura of cold arrogance he wore like a mantle. For an instant Lucy couldn't breathe.

Some emotion darted like quicksilver across the earl's patrician features, but it was gone so quickly Lucy wondered if she'd imagined it. His lips curved in a smile that was unbridled mockery.

"I am waiting with baited breath to find out exactly how Americans deal with tyrants," he drawled. "Something distressingly primitive, I would imagine."

Suddenly Lucy wanted him to know exactly who she was. "I would be happy to refresh your memory, my lord," she said.

"That would be most unwise, little one," Valcour cut in silkily. "But, then, it is my impression that you aren't half so wise as you are . . . beautiful."

Lucy stiffened against a strange curling sensation in her stomach as those intense eyes swept from the white roses twined in her golden curls to the silver-gilt tip of the slipper that peeked from beneath the hem of her petticoat.

"Valcour, I'll not have you tormenting her!" It was Aubrey charging to her rescue, his eyes filled with defiance.

"I am merely all eagerness to renew my acquaintance with the lady, Aubrey. You see, my introduction to Miss Blackheath was the most singular one I've ever experienced from an . . . er . . . *female.*"

"There is a tale behind it, your lordship?" Purple Wig piped up. "Do tell!"

Valcour smiled with a barely veiled warning. "I am the soul of discretion, Willoughby. And I am certain Miss

Blackheath will reward me for my virtue by giving me the honor of this dance."

"It's quite impossible!" Lucy said with a wave of her hand. "I cannot . . ."

Lucy's words trailed to silence as her eyes locked on the implacable lines of Valcour's face. He said nothing, merely arched one dark brow.

Lucy wanted nothing more than to drive her slipper into Valcour's shin, to turn and flounce away, but there was a subtle threat in Valcour's hooded eyes that made her aware of exactly how disastrous it would be if Valcour revealed her part in the debacle at the gaming hell a week before.

No gentleman would do such a thing—but hadn't Lucy witnessed firsthand exactly how ruthless this particular nobleman could be?

Seething, she lifted her chin with the dignity of a queen and allowed him to lead her to the floor. She satisfied her raging temper by digging her nails as deeply as possible into the villain's forearm.

Valcour's eyes flicked to her hand. "Wasn't it you who told me that it is always unwise to react in anger, Miss Blackheath? Or should I say, 'Mr. Dubbonet'?"

"I don't get angry, my lord," Lucy said with acid sweetness. "I get revenge."

He swept her into the line of dancers and made her an elegant bow. "I am quaking with trepidation."

Lucy dropped into her most insolent curtsy. The strains of the minuet usually triggered Lucy's most romantic dreams, carrying her far away, until her partner faded into a misty haze, the man necessary but insignificant in comparison to the music.

But as she dipped and circled tonight, every nerve in her body sizzled with awareness of Valcour. Valcour's hand brushing hers, Valcour's lean, powerful body circling with predatory grace. Something earthy obliterated the airy sensation she'd always had in the dance before—Valcour's cold drawl building fires inside her.

She was reacting to him because of her anger, she reasoned, coming about to meet that ruthless gaze again. Anger at his intrusion, his insufferable conceit.

But she had felt anger with great regularity in her twenty years. And she had never felt like this . . . as if she were dancing on the edge of a precipice, waiting to topple in.

The sensation infuriated Lucy, and she glared up at the earl's impassive face. "Well? What the devil did you want to dance with me for?" she demanded. "And don't say it's because you think I'm lovely or want to renew our acquaintance or any other such rot. If you do I'll . . . I'll . . ."

Valcour's lips twitched. "Kick me?" he provided.

"It occurred to me." Lucy touched his hand as if it were a viper and circled gracefully. "Unfortunately, it's near impossible with all these petticoats getting in my way."

Valcour chuckled, a rich, husky sound that seemed to burrow into Lucy's chest. She was not the only one affected. His lordship's reaction created a sensation, the couples around them gaping as if he had just pulled the chandelier down upon their heads.

"All right, madam," Valcour said at last. "I am dancing with you because I have a marked aversion to surprises. And discovering that I had involved a lady in a duel—a duel in a most unsavory setting, I might add—is exactly the sort of surprise I detest the most. As if that was not distressing enough, I discover that this lady was not some street urchin but, rather, the guest of the new American ambassador. You can't blame me for being intrigued."

"You can go on being 'intrigued' until you're eighty, my lord. One would think you English would have learned your lesson after the War for Independence. People who go poking their aristocratic noses into a Virginian's business get them snapped off."

What amusement had shown on Valcour's face vanished. "You will tell me, girl. The whole story."

Lucy tossed her curls. "I'll tell you when I feel like it. You can't frighten me like you do your poor brother, my lord."

"Ah, yes . . . poor beleaguered Aubrey, tyrannized by his wicked elder brother."

Lucy managed a stiff smile at the Countess Maine and made a delicate dancestep with her slippered toe. "You humiliated him!" she muttered to Valcour under her breath. "Perhaps you've been too busy to notice, but people have been jeering at him the whole night!"

"You're quick to leap to the boy's defense. I wasn't aware you were such bosom friends."

"I suppose that you've never met someone and felt an immediate kinship with them?"

"I can't remember feeling—what did you call it? kinship?—with anyone."

For just a heartbeat there was something unexpected in Valcour's eyes—a shadow that might have been loneliness. But it vanished as quickly as it had come, leaving in its place his customary disdain. For some reason it left Lucy even edgier than before.

"I find your brother kind," she said, "and charming and handsome and amusing . . ."

"I would not be taken in by Aubrey's charm if I were you. It has a way of vanishing at the most inopportune moments. Truth to tell, I would advise you to stay away from him altogether, madam. I fear he is rather volatile at present, and . . ."

Valcour paused, his gaze sharpening on Lucy's face, his lips curling in something like amusement. "God knows, the thought of him joining forces with a little termagant the likes of you would be alarming to anyone concerned."

"You had better be the one concerned, my lord," Lucy said. "Your brother reminds me of a horse I once knew."

"Knew?" Valcour echoed pointedly. "I suppose you shared a special kinship with it as well?"

"I did." Lucy nodded. "He was a beautiful chestnut, with a glorious mane and wide, intelligent eyes. He belonged to the owner of a neighboring plantation, and the oaf had no time for the gelding. He'd climb on it once a month and expect the horse to do his bidding. When it did not, the man abused the animal, sawing at its mouth with the bit. One night the horse had had enough of such treatment. He threw the heartless bastard into a fence and broke his neck."

Lucy's eyes clashed with Valcour's. "Where your brother is concerned, my lord, I think you should prepare to take a nasty fall."

Valcour gave a cold grimace. "Your dire predictions don't interest me in the least, madam. The reason you were in that gaming hell does. You have until the next minuet to tell me. Otherwise I will go straight to your guardians with the whole tale."

"You wouldn't!" Lucy sputtered.

The music drifted into silence, and Lucy was aware of the other couples making their bows to each other. She stiffened her spine, glaring at Valcour. He said nothing. He didn't have to.

She cursed under her breath and started to spin away, but he caught her arm in a viselike grip to escort her from the floor.

"Miss Blackheath, I will be watching you. In case you were considering doing anything . . . more foolish than usual," he remarked, then he turned and walked away.

Lucy's hands clenched in her skirts, and she wished it were Valcour's throat beneath her fingers. Now what was she to do? She had no doubt Valcour meant what he said. And if John or Claree ever found out what mischief she'd been about, that would be an end to any more such nighttime adventures. Helplessness was a new sensation to her. It made her blood boil.

"Bastard," she muttered at Valcour's retreating back. "Cursed, dictatorial—"

She started at the light touch of fingertips against her arm and wheeled to see Aubrey St. Cyr peering down at her with a worried expression.

There was something almost shy, endearingly boyish about his face. "Miss Blackheath, I couldn't help but notice how upset you were. I hope my brother didn't distress you."

"Your brother *lives* to distress people. He *delights* in it. I only wish I could return him blow for blow."

Aubrey shot her an engaging grin. "I know exactly what you mean. Perhaps if we joined forces we could think of something appropriately infuriating."

"Join forces," Lucy echoed, delight surging through her. "Of course. That's it! If he was carrying you off in a huff he could hardly plague me, could he? Not only that, but with you to escort me, I could ride about town without worrying—"

Aubrey's brow wrinkled in confusion, a lock of lightly powdered gold hair tumbling across it. "I beg your pardon?"

Lucy dimpled and gave Aubrey her most dazzling smile. "My dear Mr. St. Cyr, I believe you have just fallen desperately in love with me!"

Aubrey's eyes went saucer-wide, and he tugged at his neckcloth as if it had just become too tight. "Miss Blackheath, you're very beautiful and—and I appreciate your defending me, but . . . we barely know each other."

Lucy gave a merry laugh. "You don't think I mean it—*really!* It would all be a game of pretend. The perfect way to avenge ourselves against the wicked earl!"

"The earl? But how?"

"Think of the possibilities!" Lucy said with fiendish glee. "Your brother dislikes me immensely, an emotion I intend to see grows deeper with time. And he treats you as if you were a child—ordering you about, interfering in your affairs. How do you think the earl of Valcour would react if his precious heir were to fall into a *grand passion* with an American girl who delights in nothing more than thumbing her nose at English society?"

"He would be . . . appalled." Aubrey's eyes twinkled, his mouth spreading in a slow smile. "By God, I might fall in love with you at that!"

"It won't be difficult at all, I promise you!" Lucy said, leaning close and giving him her most adoring look for dramatic effect. "You can be very useful to me, and I—well, I shall use all my skill at stirring up devilment on your behalf! Now, I have a secret appointment to keep, and not much time to get there. Your brother has threatened to keep watch on me and go tattling to my guardians if I so much as breathe in a way he does not approve."

"Pah! He would. There is nothing more loathsome than someone who carries tales."

"But if you take me out into the garden and become . . . impassioned beyond reason . . . I would wager that his lordship would forget all about tormenting me in his eagerness to snatch you out of my clutches and escort you home!"

Aubrey scowled. "I don't think I like that. Being hauled away—"

"He'll hardly drag you through the ballroom by the seat of your breeches," she cajoled. "After all, he has *his* precious dignity to consider, even if he doesn't bother about yours. The agreement is that I will help you infuriate your brother if you will be useful to me. And I need you to be useful at once."

Lucy lay a pleading hand on the sleeve of his coat.

"Please, Aubrey. I can't tell you why I need to escape him, but it's imperative that I do. I know this isn't the best scenario for you, but there will be plenty of other times you will get to come away triumphant. I promise you that my help in thinking up mischief to bedevil him will be well worth a few moments of discomfort now."

Aubrey regarded her for long seconds and then nodded. "I do believe you are right."

"Good!" Lucy said with an eager glance around the room. "Now take my arm and look all glaze-eyed and besotted, or no one will believe we're *enchanté* with each other.

Aubrey chuckled. "But I am *enchanté*, Miss Lucy. Your so beautiful eyes are like stars in the heavens. And your lips—I shall die of want if you don't allow this humble pilgrim to taste—"

"Ridiculous boy!" Lucy giggled. "No one can even hear us! You have to wait until your despicable brother is near."

"I'm just getting in practice," Aubrey said, his eyes taking on a most satisfactory glow, his mouth a soft smile.

He guided her through the room, her hand tucked in the crook of his arm and cradled like a treasure against his side. He dipped his golden head until Lucy's nose was bare inches from his, her fluttering eyelashes seeming to hold him in thrall.

As they neared Valcour, who stood talking to an elegant lady in saffron brocade, Lucy trilled out a laugh like silver bells and gazed up at Aubrey with blind adoration, moistening her lips with her tongue.

She had the satisfaction of hearing Valcour stumble over what he was saying. At that moment Aubrey had the brilliance to lift her other hand to her lips. But Lucy's eyes clung a moment more to the exquisite beauty. The woman wasn't touching Valcour, but there was a kind of possessiveness in her gaze, a sultry promise in her smile.

"Who is that woman?" she whispered as Aubrey led her through the wide-flung doors to the garden.

"Camilla Spencer-White. My brother's . . . er . . ." he stammered to a halt, flushing.

"His mistress?" Lucy provided, leveling at the woman a curious stare. She was stunned to feel an uncomfortable wave of something akin to jealousy sweep through her.

"You aren't even supposed to know such ladies exist!" Aubrey choked out.

Lucy crushed the astonishing sensation and made a face. "It would be hard not to, the way you men flaunt them."

"Not Dom. You'd think he'd want the whole world to know of the liaison. God knows I would! It would turn every man in my club green with jealousy. But no. He's above all—damnation, you got me talking about it again!"

"I only mentioned mistresses at all because I find your brother confusing. With a woman so beautiful as that hanging on his sleeve, you'd think he could find more interesting ways to spend his time than meddling in my affairs."

Aubrey guffawed. "You are the most extraordinary girl," he said. "Don't tell me you are the one woman in England who is immune to my brother's fascination."

"I barely notice him at all!" Lucy protested. "It will be a cold day at Hades's fireside when *my* head is turned by a magnificent set of shoulders," Lucy said, then paused. "*Or* a fine set of legs. And I suppose his eyes are rather remarkable. All dark and dangerous and—" Lucy stopped. "But none of that signifies when weighed against his monstrous arrogance, his tyrannical temperament, his—"

"I'm so glad you've barely noticed him at all." Aubrey frowned. "Before you go into further descriptions of attributes you haven't noticed, why don't you tell me where you would like the two of us to become impassioned."

"Near that lovely wall. My gown will stand out against it, and the light from that lantern will fall on our faces." She stopped, giving him a quizzical look. "I trust you *do* know how to kiss, don't you? I've not had a *great* deal of experience."

"I do well enough!" Aubrey laughed aloud, and Lucy was glad to see that the misery of the hour before had fled from his face.

They reached the wall, and Lucy slanted a glance toward the house. Valcour had wasted no time, already positioning himself near the window, and even from the distance she could feel his displeasure as if it were a physical thing.

Aubrey turned to her, his mouth quirking in a smile. "A captive audience already, eh, madam?"

Lucy made a great show of taking one of the white roses from her hair. She leaned forward until her breasts brushed the front of Aubrey's frockcoat and then drew the blossom across his lips.

"Ouch! Damnation, the thing has thorns!" Aubrey burst out.

"You're supposed to be dazzled," Lucy hissed.

"But I'm bleeding!"

"Don't be an infant! Take me in your arms at once!" Aubrey did so, a little awkwardly.

"Closer. Pull me closer and tip my face up to yours."

"You could teach my brother a few things about giving orders, I vow," Aubrey said, doing as she bid. "Steady, girl. He's watching."

With that, Aubrey clutched her against him so tightly her ribs were in danger of being crushed. His open mouth planted itself on hers with such force it drove her lips into the sharp edges of her teeth.

Instead of drawing him closer, she shoved at his chest.

"Let . . . go!" she struggled to say. "Can't . . . can't breathe—"

But Aubrey had warmed to his part as passionate suitor. He only clutched her more tightly, kissed her more energetically, his hands roving up and down her back, his breath coming in raspy gulps.

Lucy could only pray the earl of Valcour would come storming into the garden before his brother suffocated her to death.

5

*V*alcour glared across the dance floor to where Lucinda Blackheath stood, Aubrey leaning close to her as if lost in rapt enchantment. The boy was captivated. Laughing. The stoic misery that had been on his face from the minute they'd entered the room that night was gone, driven away by a pair of sparkling blue eyes.

If Aubrey had been distracted by any other woman present, Valcour would have been glad. Determined cheerfulness was exactly what was needed on an occasion like tonight.

But Lucinda Blackheath was disaster in hair ribbons, and letting her anywhere near Aubrey was the same as flicking a burning brand into a keg of powder.

"Valcour?" Just the sound of Camilla's voice was said to be more sensual than the intimate touch of the most skilled courtesan. Valcour barely noticed she had spoken. "You must stop scowling at poor Miss White." Camilla gestured to the gawky girl who was staring at Valcour with the frozen terror of a baby rabbit trapped in the gaze of a wolf. "I think the girl is going to cry."

"I'm not scowling at the chit," Valcour scoffed.

"I know that. You're scowling at your brother. Unfortunately, poor Miss White doesn't have the benefit of that knowledge, and she is standing directly in your line of vision."

Valcour gave Miss White a curt nod. But that only seemed to terrify the girl further. She spun in a cloud of puce satin and fled to her mama's skirts.

However, Valcour wouldn't have cared if the girl had summarily dived into the punch bowl at that particular moment. The earl was distracted by the sight of Aubrey taking Lucinda Blackheath's hand, the girl's infernal laugh trilling out across the room. She was obviously delighted. That knowledge alone filled Valcour with the same instinctive tension he felt when a particularly wicked storm was about to break.

But his irritation deepened further as Valcour's gaze flicked again to where Aubrey was touching the girl. Something about the sight of that feminine hand in Aubrey's and that bright smile the girl kept flashing knotted anger in the earl's vitals until he had to grit his teeth against the ridiculous sensation.

"The ambassador's ward is quite lovely, isn't she?" Camilla observed. "Very young and fresh."

"The girl is a curse," Valcour gritted.

"I . . . see." Valcour was aware of Camilla eyeing him intently. "Your dance was not enjoyable, then?"

"I didn't dance with her for pleasure." Valcour stopped, his brow furrowing as Aubrey led Miss Blackheath across the room.

She was looking at Aubrey as if she adored him, while Aubrey was so besotted Dominic expected him to trample over the other guests in their way. Miraculously, they managed to sail through the maze of people as if carried along on some mystical current they alone could feel.

Valcour watched them, his lips compressed, his gaze

flicking to the doors leading to the garden. No. Surely even Aubrey wouldn't be foolish enough to take the girl outside. He'd come to dampen an old scandal, not stir up a new one.

At that moment Lucinda tossed the golden curls that tumbled about that queenly little face, her fingers swishing the gown that shimmered like a river of silver. It clung to her tiny waist, cresting upward in waves of foamy white lace to embrace breasts that were delectably full.

Valcour felt a swift tightening in his breeches, a surge of heat in his blood. The girl was sweet temptation. But only a youth like Aubrey—wild, reckless, *insane*—would be fool enough to get tangled up in her snares.

But, then, considering Aubrey's performances of the past few months, there could be little question that the youth was a fool. Valcour caught a glimpse of silver petticoats fluttering out the doorway, Aubrey barely a step behind.

The earl gritted his teeth, certain he wasn't the only one who had noticed their exit. He caught a glimpse of the ambassador's wife across the room, her face puckering with worry. The "friends" who'd been giving Aubrey no peace earlier had also noticed the couple's clandestine departure, for they eyed the doorway with keen curiosity.

Damn Aubrey to hell, Valcour thought, glaring out the window. He was going to murder the fool.

Aubrey had wasted no time.

Lantern light picked out the silhouette of two ardent lovers turning to each other, catching each other in eager arms. The saucy hoyden of moments before seemed transformed by the moonlight into a sylph that whispered of fairy woods and enchantments, while Aubrey looked suddenly older. A man who wanted a woman.

Valcour's muscles went rigid. Of course, it was only his fury at Aubrey making a spectacle of himself that fired

Valcour's blood with such unaccustomed rage. It was only the fact that the ambassador's ward was clinging to Aubrey with a rapt attention that made Valcour's chest tighten, his hands knot into fists.

"Valcour?" Camilla's voice came to him as if from a distance. "Valcour, what is it?"

"I'm going to wring that boy's neck," Valcour snarled, then turned on his heels and stalked out into the night.

A cool breeze touched his cheeks, but his anger blazed hotly as he approached the two lovers. It was even worse than he'd suspected. Aubrey's hands were all over the girl, reddening her pale skin, rumpling her gown until it drooped over one creamy shoulder, revealing a glimpse of blue-ribboned shift.

Her hair was tumbling like a waterfall of gold over breasts whose tops swelled in plump mounds, crushed against the toile of Aubrey's frockcoat.

Valcour's eyes narrowed to slits as Aubrey's breathless moan was carried to him on the flower-scented air, in counterpoint to a pronounced whimper from the lady.

"If you intend to carry on much further, I'd suggest you retire to a bedchamber." Valcour's voice cut as hot ice through the stillness of the garden.

The two sprang apart, Aubrey flushed and glazy-eyed, as if the girl had just clubbed him over the head. The girl turned pink as a peony. But her eyes held a saucy light that made Valcour want to shake her until her teeth rattled.

"D-Dom!" Aubrey stammered.

The girl was gasping with breathy little sounds. Valcour wanted to clamp his hand over her kiss-reddened lips to stop them.

Aubrey drew the girl into the protective curve of his arm. "You have no right to disturb us."

"Perhaps you would like me to send out the servants with flambeaus, illuminate the entire garden so that everyone at the ball could witness your indiscretions, instead of making them a privy entertainment for those twenty or so guests closest to the windows."

Lucy glanced at the panes of glass, a little daunted to see a number of strange faces peering out with undisguised interest. Her cheeks burned.

"Damn," Lucy muttered. "I hadn't thought . . ."

"That anyone would see you?" Dominic finished for her.

"Not *any*one. *Every*one," Lucy flung back.

"Well, Miss Blackheath, let's just say that the guests at the Wilkeses' first ball now have something to discuss besides that infernal duel a week ago." Valcour leveled a glare at his brother. "Aubrey, I think it best if you take your leave. I'm sure Miss Blackheath will be heartbroken at the loss of your company. However, her guardians will be rejoicing that you are gone."

Lucy could feel Aubrey seething with stubbornness, his chin jutting at a pugnacious angle, as if he'd forgotten that the entire purpose of this little display had been to bundle both St. Cyr brothers into a homeward-bound coach. "No!" Aubrey said. "I refuse to—"

Lucy jabbed him with her elbow. "Do as he says, my love. He can only part us for a little while."

"My love?" Valcour sneered. "You Virginians fall in love rather precipitously, I fear."

"Exactly, my lord." Lucy tipped up her chin, remembering her father's words back at Blackheath Hall. "We careen into love like a runaway carriage hurtling over a cliff."

Valcour raised a brow. "That is perhaps the most apt description of love I've ever heard, Miss Blackheath. Especially if my brother is involved."

Aubrey trembled where he brushed Lucy's side, and there was a world of hurt beneath the anger in his voice. "What, Dom? You think it's impossible that someone cares for me? I'm a man made of flesh and blood, not of ice as you are."

"A *man* would not have exposed his lady to social derision by dragging her into the garden as if she were a demimondaine. Now you will take your leave, Aubrey, before I do something we shall both regret."

There was something frightening in Valcour's eyes, something that left Lucy flushed and breathless. Her hands quivered a little as she reached up to touch Aubrey's face. "It will be all right, my darling. Go now." It sounded exactly like the sugary kind of rot the heroine of a melodrama might spout.

Aubrey clutched her hands against his heart. It was pounding so hard Lucy prayed he didn't drop into apoplexies and ruin the entire performance. "Farewell, Lucy. For now."

He stooped to pick up a single bruised rose—the one she had brushed his lips with before they kissed. Closing his fingers tenderly around it, Aubrey strode away with astonishing dignity, considering the fact that his neckcloth was askew.

Valcour turned to glare at Aubrey's retreating back and Lucy smirked in triumph, waiting for him to follow his brother. Instead, the earl rounded to face her with the slow menace of a stalking wolf.

"Please go after him," Lucy said in her most pleading tones. "I know you're angry, but he's suffered so much—"

"He's suffered?"

Lucy gave a squeak of surprise as the earl's hand flashed out, manacling her wrist. But instead of dragging her back into the ballroom, he charged down the garden's overgrown path, deep into the shadows, where the moon threaded silvery fingers down through the leaves of the trees.

"Let go of me, you bloody oaf!" Lucy demanded,

trying to resist. It was like a nightingale attempting to free itself from the talons of a hawk.

With a flick of his powerful wrist, Valcour brought her around until she was pinned against the very pillar behind which she'd hidden her bundle of clothes earlier that morning.

His face swam before her eyes, dark and dangerous, fierce and infuriatingly seductive. Every nerve in Lucy's body tingled in response.

"The game is up, girl," he bit out. "Whatever game you are playing."

"I'm not *playing* anything, damn you! I—"

"What are you? Some sort of spy, poking around in gaming hells, bewitching vulnerable boys? Or have you set your sights on marrying an English title?"

"I wouldn't stay in this godforsaken country if I got a mandate from St. Peter himself!" Lucy scoffed. "In Virginia we don't give a damn about your titles! A man proves his mettle through his own wits and skill, not by what some musty old ancestor did three hundred years earlier. What did *your* ancestors do, my lord? Chop off some innocent queen's head so the king could wed his mistress? Starve out the rightful owners of a castle so the king could steal their treasure?"

"I have no interest in your opinion of my ancestors, girl. Only your interest in my brother."

"And the reason I was at the gaming hell. *And* God knows what else. I said it before. I say it again. Go to hell, *my lord."*

Valcour glowered down at her. "Tell me, damn you, or I'll—"

"You'll what? Drag me off, kicking and screaming to lock me in a tower?"

"I would never stoop to such crude methods to persuade you."

"Oh, no. You're a man of ice, just as Aubrey said! You

may possess the title, *my lord,* and the family wealth. But Aubrey is five times the man you are! At least when I kiss him I don't get frostbite!"

Valcour's eyes narrowed, that arrogant, sensual mouth curling in an expression she disliked. A flame flickered to life in Lucy's chest. She realized his intent in that heartbeat and tried to skitter backward. She slammed against the pillar with a force that made her see stars.

The stars exploded into a wild conflagration as the earl of Valcour jerked her into his arms, his mouth claiming hers with a sensual ferocity that made her bones melt, her heart attempt to beat its way out of her chest—and into Valcour's own.

She had been kissed by boys before, tentative gropings that had been uncomfortable and vaguely embarrassing, like her exchange with Aubrey.

Valcour was a man.

She could feel it in every sinew of his body pressed so intimately against her. She could taste it on his lips, a drugging passion that whispered of dark pleasures she had never explored. His hands seemed alive with power, as if he could dominate her at will.

Lucy snapped to awareness as if she'd been struck. Terror and fury raged inside her. Terror at her reaction to Valcour's kiss. Fury at the power he had held over her, even so briefly.

She fought like a wildcat to escape him. Her nails bit into one arrogant cheekbone, but he caught her wrist before she could slash downward.

"Let me go, you bastard!" Lucy raged. "I'll kill you, by God I will, if you don't!"

Was it possible for regret to touch such wintry eyes? Valcour's features seemed carved in stone, but he held her, trapped.

"Don't move," he said quietly. "We're tangled somehow."

Lucy tried to pull away, but she felt a tugging at her breast, heard a soft ripping sound.

"I told you to hold still!" Valcour gritted. "My lace has caught on your gown."

Lucy pressed her back against the pillar, struggling to keep her knees from buckling.

Long fingers went to the snag, Valcour's knuckles brushing the sensitive skin of her breast, dipping into the shadowy hollow of her cleavage. Lucy's flesh quivered at his intimate touch, her throat tightening.

She could tell he was trying to be as detached as possible, as if the kiss had meant nothing to him. And it hadn't. It had been a punishment for an unruly child. A lesson taught by the high and mighty earl of Valcour in the most expedient way possible. For some reason, the knowledge made Lucy's eyes burn.

She drove back the unfamiliar sensation by snarling between clenched teeth. "If you break my brooch, I'll—"

"I think we've both leveled enough threats for one night." Something about his voice made Lucy go still.

Valcour worked a few moments more, then stepped back, her miniature cupped in the palm of his hand, his tanned fingers closed over it. How many times in the past month had Lucy herself held the image of her father? It seemed as if she could draw from the smooth porcelain a little of Alexander d'Autrecourt's essence, a whisper of the dreams that had fashioned her precious "Night Song." To see Valcour holding it as if it were a worthless trinket wounded her somehow.

She tried to take her treasure back, but he whisked it out of her reach.

"Obviously you prize this brooch more than your reputation, Miss Blackheath," he said coldly. "Perhaps I should hold it ransom to guarantee that you comply with my wishes."

"You wouldn't dare!" Lucy hated the tremor in her voice.

"You have witnessed firsthand the lengths to which I will go in order to arrange things to my satisfaction. Absconding with a lady's trinket is far less strenuous than a duel. My wishes are as follows: You and Aubrey will conduct yourselves with discretion. There will be no more performances at social events. No more embraces in front of windows."

"Next time I'll have him drag me away into the garden as you did," Lucy said hotly.

"I wouldn't recommend it, madam. Nor would I recommend getting carried away by your . . . er, youthful passion. Perhaps in the wilds of Virginia it is accepted when a girl of breeding and a gentleman of good family act like a mare and stallion at breeding time. In England it is assumed that a young man will indulge in such potent pleasures. But the same pursuits have disastrous results for a lady."

A familiar wildness was surging through Lucy's blood, that blinding sensation that overcame her when her temper spun out of control. "I assume it was a man who made such an asinine rule."

"For the lady's protection, perhaps. After all, she is the one who swells with a bastard child if—"

"Maybe I have a dozen bastards littering Virginia already!"

"I much doubt it unless you began whelping them when you were five years old," Valcour snapped. Then, as if he suddenly realized the absurdity of the conversation, Valcour's eyes narrowed to slits.

"God help whatever man gets himself snarled up with you, madam. I suppose this miniature is a picture of the last one you made a fool of?" Valcour opened his fingers, his gaze flashing in mocking scorn at the object.

A stream of moonlight danced on the miniature, wreathing the image painted upon the delicate white porcelain in an unearthly light. Lucy tried to snatch the piece of jewelry, but her hand froze at the expression on the earl's face.

His skin was ashen, as if the miniature had sprung to life in his hand. His eyes, always so intense, were consumed with some emotion Lucy couldn't name. "Where did you get this?" he breathed.

Lucy swept the miniature out of his hand and clutched it against her breasts, searching desperately for some plausible lie. God knows, she didn't dare blurt out the truth.

"I'm devoted to—to music. I came upon some that this man had written. It was beautiful and . . . and my . . . father surprised me with the miniature as a gift."

"You lie." There was something in those handsome features that made her tremble inside. Fury and pain and . . . could it be *fear?*

"Did you know him?" Lucy asked, her heart standing still. "Have you—you seen—"

The words ended on a gasp as Valcour's hand shot out, knotting in the curl that tumbled down to her breast. He crushed the silken tendrils in those powerful fingers.

"I'll tell you this only once, girl." Valcour's voice sliced to her core like a blade of steel. "Stay away from my brother. I may be a blackguard, madam, but I protect my own. Remember that."

Lucy stood shaken as he stalked away, leaving her with only the smooth press of the miniature in her hand, the burning memory of his kiss on her lips, and the searing enigma of what he had seen when he'd looked into the miniature's painted face.

An hour later Lucy dismounted before Perdition's Gate, her palms damp with nervousness, her mind still haunted by the stricken expression on the earl of Valcour's face. In the week since she had last come to the gaming hell, she had attempted to convince herself that there could be no danger in the vague blue eyes of the enigmatic stranger. He had seemed so lost, almost child-like, as if a breath of wind could crumble him to dust.

But if the mere sight of Alexander d'Autrecourt's painted face was enough to get such an alarming reaction from a man as powerful as the earl of Valcour . . .

Lucy wiped sweating palms against the breeches she wore, feeling once again the sensation Pandora must have experienced when she opened her mythical box. She jammed her hands in the voluminous pockets of her frockcoat to hide their trembling from curious eyes, and to comfort herself with the smooth feel of her pistol and the worn parchment of the letter she had received in Virginia. Then she walked through the now familiar doors.

The establishment was much less crowded this night, with only a handful of patrons casting dice or playing cards. It was as if the place were half asleep, far different from the sizzling tension that had characterized it during the exchange between Valcour and Jasper d'Autrecourt.

Lucy had been vaguely uneasy that someone would recognize her after her part in the notorious duel, but it seemed that without Valcour poised like some great black hawk at her shoulder she was beneath anyone's notice.

She made her way toward the stairs, then up the risers to the second floor. It was even more deserted than below stairs.

One of the doors was ajar, its occupant repainting her mouth with carnelian.

Another door was shut, the enthusiastic sounds of those within penetrating the wooden panel.

The chamber that had been appointed for Lucy's meeting was open, the room empty, not even a fire on its hearth.

Just beyond it, a sultry prostitute was trying to entice a gentleman of advanced age into her room. The man had evidently been imbibing spirits so freely that he had made it only as far as a chair in the hallway. His head lolled back, his mouth sagged open as he began to snore. A familiar little boy was merrily pilfering the man's pockets.

At the sound of Lucy's approach, Natty Scratch turned his back to the stairway, stuffing a gold watch into his pockets and adopting an aura of total innocence. The harlot looked up and gave her a look of frank appraisal. "I think this one's dead. Want to come along with Josy, little man?"

The girl who had been painting her lips peered out and gave a throaty chuckle. "You'd have t' find the sugar stick in his breeches with a tweezers, Jo!"

Two spots on Lucy's cheeks went blazing hot as the harlot swayed over, her dark nipples bobbing above a rim of lace. "He may be a bit scrawny, but at least he's still moving."

"I'm not interested in . . . in . . . *that,*" Lucy said, looking studiously at a point over the woman's shoulder. Her gaze collided with the boy's shrewd one.

"Great balls 'n' garters! It's you!" Natty trilled in delight. "Josy, this was the man I was telling you about! The virgin who jumped out the window the night o' the duel! Did you come back for a sample of sweet Josy here?"

"No," Lucy said hastily. "I've come here to meet someone."

"Found someone you have, sweetmeat," Josy said, feathering her fingertips down Lucy's arm.

Lucy jerked away. "I came to meet a gentleman."

Josy's delicate brows arched. "It just ain't my night, is it," she lamented with a grimace. "We don't cater to that particular taste here. But if you come into Josy's bed-chamber I'm sure we can contrive some way to satisfy you."

Even Lucy's fingertips felt red with embarrassment. "I didn't come here for—for carnal pleasures. I came to find a gentleman who is supposed to be staying in that room over there, but he seems to be gone."

"You mean Mad Al—" Natty gave a squawk of pain as Josy dug her elbow into his ribs.

The harlot's eyes clouded with suspicion, and Lucy could feel her withdrawing. Under other circumstances, she would have been heartily relieved. "Natty, you know there's no man staying here," Josy said firmly. "Never has been."

"Natty, please." Lucy turned to the boy. "I saw him there just last week. He sent me a letter, asking me to meet him here. I have to find this man, whoever he is."

"Well, best of luck to you, sweetmeat. Last Thursday there was a duel here and the poor fellow ran off like the devil himself was after him."

"That's so," Natty supplied helpfully. "Climbed out of the window a few minutes before you did. Course, he came down a lot more careful like. You just jumped. But, then, if that dark-haired bastard who was bellowing at you had been chasing me, I'd have jumped straight into fire to get away from him."

Lucy swallowed hard. Valcour had seemed like menace incarnate, his shirt clinging to the powerful contours of his chest, fires of intensity seeming to blaze beneath his harsh features. His sword had beckoned like death's outstretched hand.

If Alexander d'Autrecourt had indeed clashed with Valcour at some time in the past, the mere sight of the earl that night would have been enough to drive off a gentle musician. Or had it been Jasper d'Autrecourt who had sent his brother fleeing into the night?

"Natty, do you have any idea where he went?" Lucy asked.

The boy tried to touch his nose with the tip of his tongue. "Got enough troubles o' my own. If I tried to keep track of every crazy person that came around here my head would explode."

"But he has to be here somewhere," Lucy insisted. "He took nothing with him. Perhaps I could look through his things."

"Took 'em the next day," Natty said. "Even if he hadn't, they'd have been filched by someone else by now. He had a right nice velvet frockcoat I had me eye on."

A niggling sense of defeat pressed down on Lucy's chest. She dug in her pocket, extracting the cryptic poem she had received in Virginia, staring at it as if it might somewhere hold the key to this madness.

"What's that?" Natty chirruped.

She hesitated for a moment, then extended it to the boy. He held it upside down and eyed it as if it were written in Greek, then he showed it to the woman. Josy scrutinized it, then looked up sharply and brushed one finger across Lucy's cheek.

Josy grinned. "I'll be tarred and feathered. You're a girl!"

"He ain't no a girl!" Natty squalled, looking as if he'd just swallowed a crate of lemons. "Girls don't jump through windows an'—"

"You must be the one," Josy said.

"The one?" Lucy echoed.

"The one he told me to watch out for. Jenny, isn't that your name?"

A shiver scuttled like icy mouse paws down Lucy's spine. "I'm . . . Jenny."

The harlot disappeared into her room. A moment later she returned, a bit of vellum in her hand. "He told me to give you this."

Lucy snatched the note, holding it to the candlelight to read it.

Dearest child,
It breaks my heart to leave without first seeing your sweet face, but I am in grave personal danger. There are those who would stoop to any villainy to

keep us apart. But do not fear them. Be strong and patient, my darling Jenny. I will find you.

                                                              A.

Lucy crumpled the note in her fist, acid impatience washing through her. She wheeled on the startled Josy, Natty's eyes rounding in astonishment.

"Damn it, I'm tired of this dancing with shadows! This tells me nothing about where to find him even if I wanted to! You have to think, both of you. Was there ever anything he said? Something he did that might give me some clue where to begin?"

"I don't have to do nothing 'cept keep my bed thumping and my belly full." Josy adjusted the neckline of her gown until only the tops of her nipples peeked over the tawdry lace. "I got business to take care of. Got to earn my keep."

Lucy rummaged in her waistcoat pocket and withdrew a handful of coins. "Here. I'll pay you even more if there is anything you can tell me."

Josy licked red lips, her pretty brow furrowed as if she was concentrating so hard it hurt. Her mouth pursed in irritation. "I just can't think of anything. He sat in there and scribbled music. Seemed a little queer in the attic, but kind of sweet." She waved her hands in exasperation, then her eyes suddenly lit up. "I don't know if this means anything, but he used to call me a name in bed, one that wasn't my own."

Lucy felt the heat of embarrassment flood up her throat and spill onto her cheeks. "I hardly think his pet names for you could be of any interest."

"He called me Emily."

Lucy felt as if she were going to retch. Her mind filled with images of her mother's heart-shaped face, those gentle hands that had healed the wounds of a defiant little girl and a rakehell bound straight down the path to destruction. Emily Blackheath's hands had always seemed more like those of an angel than of a mortal woman. Lucy knew that Ian Blackheath felt the same as she always had, that Emily was a gentle treasure to be shielded, protected.

And this mysterious man—whoever he was—had been calling a harlot by her name.

"What's the matter?" Natty's voice seemed out of focus somehow. "You look right green."

"I have to find him," she said faintly as Josy plucked the remaining coins from Lucy's hand.

There was a sound of heels clicking against the floor. A spindly little man with protuberant eyes and slack lips was approaching. One glance at Lucy and his froglike face fell in disappointment. "Josy, my angel, you already have someone to entertain, I see. I was so hoping we could play." He gave a nasal laugh.

"And so we shall, handsome." Josy started to sashay over to him, but Lucy caught the harlot's arm.

"Please, you must have some idea where I could start."

"You can start by getting your bum out of my way so I can get back to work. That is, unless you want to make a few coins yourself." Josy chortled. "There are customers who'd pay a fortune to take the first dip in your tup."

"A boy to play with too, Josy?" the frog-faced man asked, those round eyes peering at Lucy in a way that made her skin crawl.

Bile choked her as she wheeled and stomped down the stairs. She slammed out the door of the gaming hell and leaned against the wall, trying to steady herself. Her whole body trembled as she looked again at the note.

She heard the door open, then jumped at the sound of Natty's voice.

"Does it help?" The boy was regarding the note warily.

"The note? No, Natty. It doesn't help a damn bit."

She stopped, disgusted with herself as she looked down into the child's eyes. "I'm sorry. I'm just so damned frustrated. I feel so helpless."

"Makes a body right crotchety, I know. That's the way I feel when ol' Pappy Blood is beating on me."

The magnitude of the little boy's troubles in comparison to Lucy's own made her ashamed of herself. She knelt down until she was at eye level with the little rogue.

"Natty, I'm sorry."

"For what?" the boy asked, perplexed. "Not as if you darkened my daylights or anything. Course, I'll be damned if I'd ever hold still for being hit by a *girl!*" He looked up at her a little wistfully. "Are you sure you're a girl? I just can't seem to 'custom myself to the notion."

"I'm sure."

Natty heaved a heavy sigh. "I s'pose you can't help it, even if it is a disappointment to me. I just wanted to tell you that, well, that I'll keep an eye out for Mad Alex for you. You might not think it, but I'm a man o' some importance hereabouts."

"I don't doubt it a bit," Lucy said. Her mouth tugged into a smile, her heart wrenching with sudden homesickness for Norah. "I'll pay you well for any information you can find."

The boy nodded.

"Natty, even if you don't find the slightest clue about the man I'm seeking, you can still find me. If you ever need anything—*anything,* a place to sleep, or food, or just someone to hug you—I'll be at Ambassador Wilkes's townhouse. Tell them you are a friend of Lucy's."

"Hope I'm not some sniveling Nancy-boy who runs crying for help from a girl! A girl!" He gave her a mournful look. "I don't know if I'll ever quite get over my disappointment."

Lucy reached out, brushing back a tendril of carroty hair, then she fished in her pocket and took out a purse full of guineas. "Natty, give the gentleman upstairs back his watch and take this instead. I don't want you getting in trouble for stealing."

"Do it all the time. He'd never guess. And besides, I don't take charity. I told you that already."

"But you helped me escape a week ago, and now you're going to help me again. I consider it a debt of honor. Besides, then you can pay for a hackney cab to bring you to the Wilkeses if you should find anything out."

"Been traveling around this city since I was three years old and never once had to pay for the trip," Natty bragged. "I'll find you if I need to, Lucy. That is, if you're sure you want me to."

"Of course I do. I have to find this man."

"Do you?" Natty suddenly looked wise beyond his years. "There was a swell who came here once and dropped his stickpin under a step that was half mired in the mud. Dug under there until he found the pin, but something bit him. Maybe a dog. Maybe a rat. We never knew. Heard later he went crazy from it and died. Bet he wished he'd never started poking around after the pin at all."

Something in the boy's story made Lucy cringe long after she had mounted up and ridden away. Three times she almost cast the note into the gutter, certain that Natty was right.

She should never have come to England in the first place. She should have thrown the box of objects into the fire and burned them to ashes. She should have gone to Ian, told him everything. He would have known what to do.

She should have done anything besides taking up this insane quest as if a medieval gauntlet had been flung in her face.

But she wanted to know Alexander d'Autrecourt, the father she barely remembered. She wanted something tangible to add to her beautiful "Night Song."

And now she had it.

A crazy person who penned bad music and called a harlot by her mother's name. A haunting face that vanished like a will-o'-the-wisp whenever she got near enough to touch it. It seemed impossible that the man who had woven the dreams, the magic that was captured in Lucy's cherished lullaby, could be twisted into a pathetic madman wandering through the London stews alone.

And the only clues she had at the moment were the book tucked in her pocket and the enigmatic expression she had seen in Valcour's eyes.

Lucy reined her mare through the gate to the Wilkeses' townhouse, the windows still glowing with light, the confusion of the ball. Her eyes stung hotly as she rode to the rear of the stable, and she scrubbed the salty wetness away.

Damnation, what a fool she was. What had she expected? A reunion like something from a fairy story? To run into her father's arms and have him understand that hidden part of her that no one else could reach? The place where the music lived, swirling in her soul.

She grimaced. At least the fates couldn't torment her with any worse catastrophe after all she'd endured tonight, Lucy thought, dragging her fingers away from her eyes.

She was wrong.

The stable's interior drew into focus and she froze, her gaze locked with that of John Wilkes. He stood in the lantern light, his face wreathed with puzzlement and a very real disappointment, the silver-tissue gown Claree had chosen for Lucy with such loving care crumpled in his fist.

6

*L*ucy gripped the paintbrush so hard it threatened to snap, sweeping vivid colors across the vellum with the savage industry of a frontier general fending off a hoard of Iroquois on the warpath. Her enemies were the halcyon beauty that enveloped St. James Park, the swans that drifted, living clouds upon sky-blue water, and the unrelenting tension that clambered inside her until she felt ready to burst with coiling sizzling energy.

The whole blasted aura of civility that wreathed London snapped against her nerves like tiny whiplashes, a feeling only exacerbated by the Wilkeses' stoic kindness and the sorrowful expression and hurt in their eyes.

Lucy would have relished the Blackheath family tradition of a nice, predictable row: some angry bellowing, perhaps a little stomping of feet or a few rare tears, then the storm over, everyone's emotions aired.

But during the week that had passed since the fateful night of the ball, the whole incident lay there between them, festering, along with the memory of a moonlit garden and the earl of Valcour's ruthless kiss.

Lucy stiffened, the memory rising up yet again in her mind so clearly she could still smell the roses, still see the moonlight drizzling over Valcour's dazzlingly handsome face. She could still feel the imprint of his hard mouth, as if Valcour had only just lifted his lips from hers. And most distressing of all was the knowledge that she wanted to tunnel her fingers deep into the midnight hair at his nape and draw his mouth back to her.

Damn the man! Every time she closed her eyes to sleep she tossed and turned, feeling the flames he had loosed inside her lick at her skin. Every time she passed the ballroom she remembered Valcour's animal grace as they moved in the minuet.

She found herself searching for his broad shoulders and glossy black hair at the theater, in the park, and in grand carriages that flooded the London streets. She found herself listening for the slightest mention of his name. And she woke up after a night of dreaming, her skin steamy hot, her mind befuddled with dreams so vivid, so sensual, that even here in the park her cheeks burned like fire at the memory.

There was a simple explanation. She was going mad.

Mad with frustration as she waited for another communication from the mysterious stranger. Crazed at the strange emotions the earl of Valcour had unleashed in her with his kiss and with the odd reaction he had had to the miniature of her father.

With a muttered oath, Lucy slammed shut her paintbox, drawing a startled gasp from Claree. "Is something amiss, child?"

Only everything, Lucy thought, but she said only, "I just need some time to walk. The day is so lovely."

"Would you like me to join you?" Claree started putting away her drawing utensils.

"No!" Lucy burst out so hastily she could see a hurt light dart into the older woman's eyes. "I don't want to interrupt your pleasure in painting. And I'm afraid I'm quite a despicable, temperamental wretch at the moment. Not fit company for anyone."

"John will be back in a few moments. Perhaps you should wait for—"

"I'll just walk around the pond. What trouble could I get into here? Especially at such an unfashionable hour. The only people about are children and their nurses."

"That is why I like so much to come to the park now," Claree said a little wistfully. "Did you see those engaging little boys over at the other side of the pond a few moments ago? They looked quite delighted with themselves, wading in the water with lengths of hemp before their nurse chased them away."

Lucy stood up and shook out the folds of her gown. "Probably stirring up devilment of some kind. I'll stroll over and see for myself."

She walked along the pond's edge, the restlessness so hot in her blood she could barely stand it. Yet even in her current temper Lucy couldn't be angry with the Wilkeses. She knew that it would take only a word from her to change things back to the delightful camaraderie she had shared with them before the disastrous night of the ball. All she had to do was sit down with John and Claree and tell them everything, from the moment the box arrived in Virginia to her trip to Perdition's Gate and her clash with the earl of Valcour. Then they would understand.

She grimaced, remembering the painful interview with John Wilkes, the kindly man giving her every opportunity to get out of trouble gracefully. But there was no way Lucy could tell him where she had been, what business she had been about. If she had done so, Wilkes would have taken matters into his own hands. Most likely he would have written to Ian and try to find the person who sent the box himself. Lucy would be fortunate if the overprotective ambassador would even let her out of the house without an armed guard.

And as for any chance Lucy might have of meeting this mysterious golden-haired stranger who might be her father, it would be gone.

She had had no choice other than to allow the Wilkeses to believe she had just been a careless, headstrong girl who had raced off on a crack-brained adventure without worrying about the consequences to anyone else. God knew there were plenty of other people in Virginia who thought worse of the Raider's daughter. And only seldom did Lucy give a damn what people thought of her. But the Wilkeses were among those few whose good opinion she valued. It aggravated her no end to realize just how much.

A breeze tugged at her wide-brimmed bonnet, ruffling the blue ribbons that tied it in place. She passed a pair of girls who cupped their hands to their mouths, whispering and giggling, and a young mother and adoring father with a delightful toddler. The boy lay belly down at the edge of a blanket on the ground, a blade of grass clutched in his chubby hand. He eyed a rabbit blissfully nibbling clover, then attempted to copy the behavior.

Lucy smiled a little, remembering when she had caught Norah with a mouthful of oats out of her pony's feedbox. A lump of homesickness formed in Lucy's throat and she turned away, hurrying around the gentle curve of the pond. The blue water and white swans blurred before her eyes, and she blinked furiously in an effort to drive back the tears that stung.

She missed them all so much. Her mother's gentle smile, her papa's laughter, the nights they had spent in the nursery, playing games and telling stories and stealing cakes from the pantry. Other girls Lucy knew had been eager to be rid of their little brothers and sisters and get on with their own life, but Lucy had been denied the simple pleasure of a bustling nursery for so very long that she had often thought she would be content to stay at Blackheath Hall forever. She had never wondered about having a brood of her own, had never pictured little ones, the way Claree had obviously done.

Lucy closed her eyes, trying to imagine the new baby that must have already arrived in Virginia. But the child she pictured had night-black hair and eyes dark as jet buttons. "Of all the ridiculous notions! There isn't a pair of black eyes in the whole family—except when Norah takes it in her head to jump from the stable rafters!"

She had barely muttered the words when she caught a glimpse of the gaggle of boys hiding behind a shrub. Lucy was well schooled enough in devilment herself to read all the signs in the children's faces. Ruddy cheeks, parted lips, their eyes narrowed in anticipation. Lucy followed their gaze to where a swan and her fuzzy gray cygnet sailed toward the shore, scooping up crusts of bread floating in a suspicious trail atop the water.

She stopped to watch them, a strange sensation shivering to life inside her, a fragment of memory so faint she was sure she must have imagined it. She had so few memories of her life in England, and yet even as a child, she had remembered her "Night Song" that had comforted her, a fierce brass lion that had frightened her, and suddenly she was certain she had watched swans before, sailing across this very wisp of blue water.

She caught her lip between her teeth, unnerved at the vivid image: water and sunshine and her mother's laughter, swans that seemed like magical fairies she wanted to touch . . .

At that instant Lucy was shaken from her thoughts as her gaze locked on something strange beneath the surface of the rippling water. A web of hemp the boys had woven through a submerged branch. Lucy cried out in an effort to startle the birds into going the other way, but it was too late. A squeak of alarm came from the cygnet as it bumbled into the snare, the mama swooping to its aid. In a heartbeat the two were hopelessly tangled. Worse still, the baby's head was being dragged beneath the water.

Lucy heard a gruff masculine shout and glimpsed the boys scattering in abject terror. But she was already scooping up her skirts and plunging into the water.

She knew full well that the big birds could be dangerous, strong. The mama swan was already hissing and beating her wings furiously in an effort to protect her baby. But all Lucy could think of was the tiny ball of gray fluff drowning in the grip of the snare.

She reached them in a moment and tugged furiously on the hemp, but all she managed to do was get the gasping cygnet's head above water for a moment. A sharp pain stabbed her arm as the mama's beak found its mark, but Lucy didn't release the baby bird. A sob of frustration rose in her throat at the knowledge that she had nothing with which to cut them free. That she couldn't begin to untangle them while they thrashed about.

"Help!" she cried out. "Someone help!" But it seemed that no one else dared approach the swan, especially with the papa swan sailing toward Lucy in a fury, as if she were the one who had attempted to harm his baby and lady love.

"Get away! Lucy, you'll be hurt!" Claree cried in alarm, running toward her. But at that instant Lucy glimpsed a flash of massive equine shoulders thundering toward her and a dauntingly masculine figure flinging himself from the horse.

The mother swan struck again, and for an instant Lucy lost her balance. She fell in, shoulder deep, the ropes entangling her as well, but she couldn't worry about that as the little gray head dipped beneath the water again.

A splash of crystal-blue water in her face obscured the figure splashing toward her until all she could see were polished boots, form-fitting blue riding breeches, and flashing black eyes.

Lucy choked and sputtered, suddenly aware that she was now trapped as well. Just as she sucked in a mouthful of water, she felt a steely arm catch her across the breasts, hauling her upward as the rope that held her snapped free. Then another rope snapped and another. Lucy heard a black curse in a stunningly familiar voice as the cygnet sailed free, swimming off in a cloud of distressed little cries. A moment later its mama joined it, swooping to where the papa swan had just reached the cygnet. As if exhausted from its adventure, the cygnet climbed onto its mama's back and lay pillowed on the white down, shivering.

The stinging in Lucy's arms and the discomfort of her sodden skirts vanished as she watched them sail away. But at that instant, a strong arm curved beneath her knees and shoulders, and she was lifted against the earl of Valcour's iron-hard chest.

He splashed his way to the shore, then both of them collapsed onto the grass. Lucy stared down at the pen-knife Valcour had dropped on the blanket of green.

"You little fool!" he grated, looking decidedly shaken. "What the devil did you do that for?"

"The baby was . . . caught. It would have died."

"I don't suppose you considered that if you'd been pulled under you might have drowned yourself!"

Lucy stared up at him, amazed that he still held her. Amazed that she wanted him to. "I didn't think about it. I just . . . the baby was so tiny and helpless. I—thank you for helping. I can hardly believe that you—"

"That I didn't let you drown? Helping damsels in distress happens to be a weakness of mine. I try to cure it, but I suppose we all have our frailties of character. Now let me see that hand!" He took her fingers in his, examining the small bite. It was bleeding. He dabbed it with his handkerchief, then gently bound it up.

"What are you doing here at all?" Lucy asked in an effort to keep her mind off the stirring brush of his fingers against her skin, the bewitching contrast between his strong, darkly tanned hands against her smaller, paler one.

"I had come expecting the park to be quiet so that I could exercise a particularly skittish gelding." Valcour grimaced. "Of course, if I'd had any idea that you would be here, I would never have nursed such a delusion. The infernal horse is probably halfway back to the stables by now."

"Will he be hurt? Stolen?" Lucy asked, starting to scramble up, hampered by heavy layers of sodden skirts. "We have to go after it."

Valcour's fingers gripped hers, hauling her back down. "Chasing across London looking like drowned rats is hardly necessary, hoyden. Any man who attempted to touch that horse would find himself lighter by the weight of a few fingers. He's got the devil of a temper. Of course, his last owner gelded him, so I can understand his irritation with the world."

Lucy found herself smiling into that darkly handsome face. His shirt clung to his skin. Straggled dark strands of hair clung to the cords of his neck. Lucy watched, her mouth suddenly dry, as crystal droplets pooled in the shallow hollow at the base of his throat. She knew instinctively that the water would have cooled Valcour's sun-bronzed skin, but she was certain it would have done nothing to douse the melting heat of his mouth. Awareness sizzled through her, and she felt her cheeks heat.

"Your clothes are ruined," she said, excruciatingly aware of how the wet garments molded themselves to Valcour's powerful frame.

"A spoiled suit of clothes is a small price to pay, don't you think?" He was watching the swans. For a moment, Lucy saw something soft in those relentless features. A kind of wistfulness, almost yearning, as his thumb skimmed gently over her knuckles.

Lucy astonished herself by saying in a soft, confiding

voice, "Valcour, have you ever felt as if you'd been somewhere before? Somewhere you can barely remember?"

"No. But I've been plenty of places I've tried to forget. Why?"

"Because I feel as if I'd watched swans a long time ago, when I was tiny."

"Little girls have been flinging bread crumbs to swans since time immemorial. And there are a million ponds the birds can sail on in a million different places. However, knowing you, I'd wager you were casting rocks at them instead of crusts of bread."

"I never torment animals. Only people." She laughed, then glanced up at Valcour's face through the veiling of her lashes, feeling uncharacteristically shy. "I just . . . seeing the water the swans, the sky so blue . . . I felt as if the place I was remembering was—was here."

The change in him was so subtle she thought she had imagined it. The thumb that had been caressing her hand ever so slightly stilled. The dark eyes were shuttered. He angled his face away. "What? You've been to England before?"

"I was born here. I left when I was very small. It always bothered me that I never had any memories of it, or only the vaguest of shadows. But I remember this place. I remember." Her voice was so soft.

Suddenly she was looking into Valcour's eyes, remembering another time: a moonlit garden, the rasp of his breath as he captured her mouth with his. She was suddenly certain that when she was an old woman she would still remember that kiss. Remember it as she did the swans and the haunting melody of the "Night Song."

For a heartbeat, she wondered if Valcour felt that inexorable tug as well. His lips parted, his hand coming to curve beneath her chin.

She wondered what it would be like if he were to lower his mouth to hers—this Valcour with the slightest shading of vulnerability in his eyes, the astonishing tenderness in his touch.

Lucy started to lean toward him, her own lips trembling. But suddenly a shout made her spring away from the ear. Aubrey St. Cyr's carriage came rattling to a halt a short distance away. "What's happened? By God's blood, Dom? Lucy?"

She turned to see him springing from a ridiculous-looking curricle, his eyes regarding them as if they had both sprouted fish from their ears.

Valcour climbed to his feet as if he had been caught doing something despicable, his cheeks flushing a dull red.

Mrs. Wilkes reached them at almost the same time. "Your brother is a hero, Mr. St. Cyr," Claree supplied, bustling over with a robe from the Wilkeses' coach to wrap about Lucy's shoulders. "He plunged right into the pond to save a baby swan, not to mention our Lucinda."

Aubrey's eyes narrowed, his mouth curling in a way that irritated Lucy no end. "Getting soft-hearted in your old age, Brother?"

"I merely objected to all that splashing upsetting my horse."

Lucy saw Valcour's gaze flick to where Aubrey's hand was curved possessively about her shoulders. A muscle in Valcour's jaw tightened.

"I suppose I should thank you," Aubrey said grudgingly.

"Why? I didn't do it for you. Besides, you needn't strain yourself on my account. I am certain that in time Miss Blackheath will give me ample cause to regret the fact that I didn't drown her myself."

Lucy was stung by the harsh words, the sudden spark in Valcour's eyes.

"I would advise you to keep a close watch on your charge, Mrs. Wilkes. There may come a time when no one is present to pull the little fool out of danger."

Lucy sputtered with indignation and an odd sense of hurt at those cold words, but Valcour was already striding away.

A hundred men in London would have committed treason to be in Camilla Spencer-White's bedchamber that night. The renowned beauty lay draped across tumbled coverlets, her chestnut hair cascading across the most beautiful breasts in England. Her mouth was a scarlet kiss of temptation on a face only recently showing traces of her thirty years. Years Camilla had put to use perfecting talents that could bring a man to climax with the merest brush of her fingers.

But the man attending Camilla this night had little interest in her pleasure, and even less in his own.

Dominic St. Cyr paced the confines of the elegant bedchamber, oblivious to the pucker of confusion on Camilla's pale brow.

The black breeches he had put on when he'd left the luxurious bed clung like a second skin to his narrow hips, his naked chest still marked with a faint trace of lines from Camilla's eager fingers.

He had come here to forget. But even with Camilla draped like seduction incarnate on passion-tumbled sheets, even with the marks of Camilla's eager fingers still reddening his skin, Dominic had not found oblivion. He'd broken off the lovemaking before its completion with an abruptness that astonished them both, storming away from the bed still hard and aching. He had been agonizingly frustrated, his mind filled with the image of a golden-tressed hoyden setting free a baby swan, a defiant beauty seething with rebellion in a moonlit garden.

The coiling tension crushing his chest only tightened more ferociously than before as he recalled the weight of her against him, her soaked garments letting him feel every curve and feminine valley of her body, the precious heaviness of her breasts against his chest, the supple columns of her legs draped over his arm.

Two weeks had passed since the meeting at St. James Park. Yet every time Dominic closed his eyes, he still pictured Lucinda, her eyes glowing as the cygnet sailed away, her smile so beautiful his chest had ached at the sight of it.

Until Aubrey had ridden up. Aubrey—Valcour's mouth hardened at the memory of the boy silhouetted against Lucinda Blackheath's silver skirts, embracing her at the ambassador's ball, while at her pale breasts was pinned a portrait of the man who had shattered Valcour's life.

Every time Valcour had felt Camilla's talented mouth on his, he had remembered the wild, pulsing sensation that had shot through him when he had crushed Lucinda Blackheath's defiance with his kiss.

Night after night the infernal girl had invaded his dreams, his hands branded with the feel of slick satin as he molded her body against his own, his passions inflamed by the hot rebellion in those blue eyes—rebellion that had changed to astonished wonder, then outrage and fear.

Outrage because he'd punished her with his kiss. Fear because she had been unnerved by her reaction to that kiss. The same way the earl had been stunned by the hot rush of need that had jolted through him—a sensation unlike any he had ever known.

"Valcour?" The sound of Camilla's voice made his shoulders stiffen. Dominic stopped in front of the window, staring out into the starless night.

"I'm sorry, Camilla. I don't have the stomach for bed games tonight." The words were harsh, but Valcour had never been one to coat bitterness with sugar.

There was a beat of silence, then the soft rustle of Camilla slipping out of the bed. "I see," she said, and he glimpsed a flash of emerald satin as she drew her dressing gown over a body still lithe as a willow. "It seems to me that you haven't had much . . . stomach for bed games for some time now. In fact, you've barely touched me since the ambassador's ball."

"Occasionally more important matters take precedence."

She crossed to her dressing table and took up a silver-backed brush, stroking it twice through her luxurious hair. "Matters like . . . Lucinda Blackheath, I suppose," she said softly.

Valcour's jaw knotted, and he felt as if Camilla had somehow seen the intimate scenario that had just played itself so vividly in his mind. He made a curt gesture of dismissal. "What the devil does that girl have to do with anything?"

"She is the primary topic of conversation throughout the city of late. All London is glorifying the grand romance between the ambassador's beautiful ward and your brother."

"Of all the ridiculous prattle!"

"I don't consider it ridiculous. She and Aubrey have been inseparable since the ball. He hovers about her at every entertainment. In fact, I heard that he strode into Lady Norton's musicale without an invitation because Miss Blackheath was there. I've seen them three times in Hyde Park and taking in the entertainments at Vauxhall. The last time Miss Blackheath was rambling on in ecstasies over the trip he'd taken her on to the Tower of London."

"She would have enjoyed that, I'd imagine. The bloodthirsty little—" Valcour stopped abruptly.

"Valcour, there are those who say she might be Aubrey's salvation."

"Salvation? She'd drag him down to hell first." Valcour stalked to a table and poured himself a brandy. "I'll drown the boy myself before I let her get her hooks in him."

Camilla watched him intently. "Aubrey wouldn't be the first man to be redeemed by love."

"The boy would have a better chance of being eaten by a sea monster. Love is a pretty lie concocted by those too cowardly to face the hard reality that we are alone. Every one of us. From the time we are born until we die."

"If that is what you believe, I'm sorry for you," Camilla said softly. She drew the fall of her hair over one shoulder to brush it. The nape of her neck looked like a child's, pale and more than a little vulnerable.

Dominic grimaced, remembering Camilla as she had been the first night he met her, a dewy-eyed girl swirling out onto the floor in her debut cotillion, the first person who had dared to defy society and show the young earl of Valcour kindness.

Dominic had been a desperate youth then, grappling to save estates on the brink of ruin. A seventeen-year-old still reeling with pain and betrayal and so much guilt he thought he'd go mad from it.

Camilla had been lovely and charming and amusing, teasing the too serious Dominic and offering him friendship. He'd never forgotten. But that innocent girl had vanished, just as the agonized boy had been encased beneath layers of ice.

She had been changed forever—first by her arranged marriage to an aged duke, then by her grand passion for a fortune hunter who stole her legacy and left her a penniless widow, her reputation in tatters. Several disastrous affairs had followed.

Perhaps it had been only natural for Dominic to step in and become her protector. A man had needs. And with Camilla, there had never been a question of any inconvenient emotions like love.

"I found love once."

Valcour was startled by the pensive tones of Camilla's voice.

"Valcour, it was . . . beyond imagining."

"I don't need my imagination where the power of love is concerned. I've seen firsthand the devastation it can leave in its wake. With you and with . . . others."

He turned back to the window, other images creeping from the darkest corners of his mind.

His father, Lionel St. Cyr, the riding crop in his hand flashing out at Lady Valcour in a blind frenzy of betrayal and rage. Dominic's voice was roughened on the edges of that pain.

"Before God, I hope I have more sense than to tangle myself in an emotional noose from which there is no escape."

"When you are in love, Valcour, you never want to escape," Camilla said, a little wistfully. "You fit the noose about your neck with joy."

"And then you hang yourself with it," Valcour bit out. "My life is complicated enough without such madness as love. That is, if such a thing truly exists, which I doubt."

"But if you don't believe in the redeeming power of love and are totally set against a match between Miss Blackheath and your brother, why don't you forbid him to see her? From what I understand, he depends upon you for every penny he lives on. With one tug of the purse strings, you could put an end to it."

"And set up some Cheltenham tragedy to rival *Romeo and Juliet*? I think not. There is nothing Aubrey would enjoy more than a chance to play the beleaguered romantic hero. Especially since he knows that I have always had an aversion to the star-crossed lovers' theme. Every time I've been forced to endure watching that particular Shakespearean tragedy, I wished the two fools would both leap off the balcony in the first act and be done with it."

Camilla gave him an unsteady smile. "Valcour, you *are* heartless."

"Thank God for that. As for this nonsense with Aubrey, his fascination will pass. Miss Blackheath is far too headstrong. Aubrey will eventually tire of being led 'round by the nose. And besides, the girl will be returning to her precious Virginia in a few months at most. Then this grand passion will die a natural death."

"And if it does not?"

"I will take whatever measures I deem necessary."

Camilla raised her eyes to his, and he saw her tremble just a little. "What *will* you do, Valcour, if Aubrey continues down the path to ruin?"

Dominic stiffened, the restlessness that had tormented him all night tightening even more ruthlessly in his gut. "I come here to forget my problems, not dredge them out to discuss with my mistress." There was cruelty in the icy tones, enough to quell the most brash of men. Camilla flinched. But she did not look away from him.

"Dominic, I know you don't want my opinion—or anyone's, for that matter. But I care about you."

"That's not required."

"Perhaps not of a mistress. But it is of a friend. You've worked so hard to restore your family's estates. And what you've accomplished has been a miracle. But your brother—"

"I have said he is none of your business, madam."

"Perhaps not, but he is yours. Valcour, there is no need for you to surrender all you've worked for to a careless boy! If you would just open your heart a little, you could find a wife. Get yourself an heir—a little boy of your own with black hair and . . . and a brave smile."

"I'd make the devil of a husband and a worse father. From the beginning of time, the St. Cyrs would have been better off to be whelped like snarling dogs, their sires never to even look upon their faces."

"Dominic, this is not a jest. People are taking wagers on how many days you will be in your grave before Aubrey spends the last Valcour shilling on drink or gaming. After all you have suffered to salvage your inheritance from your father's reckless waste—"

"Enough!" Dominic's eyes blazed. With barely leashed fury, he yanked on shirt and waistcoat, knotting his neckcloth about his throat. "I will not tolerate anyone, even you, becoming embroiled in my family's business. Perhaps it is time for us to end our arrangement. The house is yours already, and I'll put a comfortable sum at your disposal."

Camilla paled. "It's not necessary to take such drastic steps. It wasn't my intention to make things worse. I just . . . you are a good man, Valcour. Better than you know. I can't bear to see that boy take advantage of you the way he does. I know you'd die before admitting that it hurts you, but I know it does."

"To feel that kind of pain I would have to have a heart. You, above anyone, should know I deadened it long ago. Aubrey and I have an arrangement every bit as civilized as is yours and mine. But if you try to saddle either of us with some pastoral familial scene, we would both of us laugh in your face."

"And your mother, Lady Valcour? Does she laugh as well?"

Valcour's eyes went dark, his voice low. "No. My mother never laughs at all."

He turned away and grabbed up one of his boots. He thrust his foot into it.

"Dominic, please." Camilla came to him and caught his rigid fingers. "I don't want you to go like this. There is something—something I need to say to you."

Valcour's muscles were rigid, his mind crowded with a dozen ghosts, familiar scenes that had been stirred into flight like unquiet spirits.

Camilla's eyes glistened, overly bright. Her face was very pale, a shadow of that vulnerable girl he had met so very long before.

"Valcour, that child I spoke about. That little boy. I . . . I could bear him for you. We get along comfortably enough, don't we? Nothing need change, even if . . . if I were your . . . wife. You could go your own way, with no entanglements."

Dominic stared at her as if a veil had suddenly been torn away. He wondered how long he had been blind to what lay behind Camilla's careless smiles. How hard had she had to work to conceal the emotion that flickered beneath her lashes now?

Regret burned inside him. "Camilla, there is nothing for you here." Dominic lifted her hand and flattened it against his heart. "There is nothing for any woman."

"You are wrong. Someday you will meet a woman you will love no matter how hard you battle to stop it. She'll set you free, Valcour, and even though it will break my heart a little, I think I will still be glad for you."

He raised her fingers to his lips. "Camilla, please understand. I can't visit you any longer."

"Because I . . . love you?"

"Because I can never love anyone. I'm . . . sorry." Valcour stood up, grateful for the ice that encased his heart. It almost saved him from feeling Camilla's pain.

He was just starting to walk away when a timid rap sounded at the door. Camilla recovered herself with great dignity, looking unruffled as she glided over to open the door. "What is it?"

An apple-cheeked maid from Cornwall bobbed a curtsy, her face washing scarlet as her gaze flicked to the disheveled bed.

"Pardon, miss, but . . . but there be a lady here to see . . . see his lordship at once. She looks desperate pale, miss, an' she's crying."

"Who the devil?" Valcour demanded.

"It be your lady mother, my lord. Lady Catherine St. Cyr."

Valcour paled. His mother? Here? The very thought of her tracing him to his mistress's residence was enough to make Dominic's jaw clench, alarm bells jangling in his head. He strode down the stairway and into Camilla's green salon.

Catherine St. Cyr paced before the fireplace, wringing her hands, her eyes like those of a doe run to ground. Her soft hair clung about her face, damp with rain. Her gown was soaked through. Whatever calamity had occurred, it was so upsetting she hadn't even stopped to grab a cloak.

He had seen his mother distraught before. He had seen her terrified and hurt and heartbroken. But only one other time in his life had he seen the wild grief and terror that was in her eyes at that moment. Then he had been a horrified boy. Now even though he was a man, he felt his heart race.

"My God, madam, what is it?"

She ran to him, sobbing, her shaking fingers knotting in his shirtfront. "You must stop them, Dominic! Sweet God in heaven, this is all my fault!"

Dominic grasped her by the arms, afraid she was going to collapse. "Of course I shall stop them if it distresses you, whoever they might be. But you must tell me what happened."

"It's Aubrey. He . . . Dominic, he's disappeared with that girl!"

Dominic's gut clenched, and he was stunned at the sensation that shot through him, a swift shaft of murderous rage and something akin to fear.

"Her guardian is crazed with fury. I'm afraid he'll— he'll do something drastic. One of the grooms overheard that they were heading toward Scotland in Aubrey's curricle. I think that they mean to elope!"

"Elope? Damn the fool to hell! Marriage to that

termagant is just what he deserves. It would serve him right if—"

The agonized sob that tore from Lady Valcour's breast chilled Dominic to the core. "No! No, you don't understand! He can't marry her. Dominic, you know the brooch she wears? The miniature—"

"May the damn thing burn in hell!"

Lady Valcour buried her face in her hands. "Jesus save us, Dominic. Lucinda Blackheath is Alexander d'Autrecourt's daughter."

If his mother had suddenly turned into poison in his arms Dominic couldn't have been more horrified. His fingers dug instinctively deep into her flesh. "No!"

"She told Aubrey it was so! He confided it to me this morning. I was going to tell you the moment you came home, but—but now it's too late, and—oh sweet God! Dominic, what are we going to do?"

Dominic's mouth curled savagely. "I'm going to find them."

7

*T*hick black mud sucked at Lucy's shoes and penetrated her stockings as she trudged along the country road, her stiff fingers gripping the leading reins of the limping gelding. Lightning flashed, turning the countryside a shade almost as sick as the hue of Aubrey's face beneath the makeshift bandage Lucy had used to bind up a gash in his forehead. And each additional crack of distant thunder reminded Lucy of the sound of the curricle wheel splintering, Aubrey's cherished vehicle catapulting into the ditch where they had abandoned it an hour before.

Lucy peered through a mist of rain at the blocks of light that grew larger and larger with each step they took. The Hound's Tooth Inn, the sign proclaimed, promised warmth and food and shelter from the rain. But Lucy eyed the stable that was half hidden in back of the Elizabethan structure.

"We're almost there, my brave boy," she crooned.

"I'm all right, Lucy," Aubrey said in his most noble accents. "It's not *so* bad."

"I was talking to the horse," Lucy said, giving Aubrey a

look of pure disgust. "After all, *he's* not the one who insisted on racing hell bent for leather down an unfamiliar road in the dark when it was already slick with—"

"Damn it to hell, we've gone over this a dozen times," Aubrey burst out. "You're making my head ache!"

"What I'd like to do is box your ears! I told you I could make this trip alone, but no. You had to play knight errant. Then we can't go on horseback as I planned. You must have your infernal curricle—that ridiculous contraption that's suited only for impressing milksop fools in Hyde Park! And then—"

"Thunder and turf, girl! Excuse the devil out of me for attempting to help you!"

"I didn't need your help!"

"Oh, no! You only had the ambassador so up in arms over your last little escapade that he all but manacled you to his wife's side the past three weeks! If I hadn't agreed to this mad pretense of pretending to be in love with you, you'd still be sitting at Madam Ambassador's feet painting swans that look like elephants."

The reminder of that fateful day at St. James Park only made Lucy more antagonistic than ever. Ever since the day Valcour had hauled her out of the pond, the slightest thought of the man made Lucy's blood heat with fury and something more. "The only reason John lets me go about with you at all is because of the high and mighty earl of Valcour. Because you're Valcour's brother, John thinks you're *respectable.*"

"My head aches bad enough without bringing up my blasted brother!" Aubrey objected.

And Lucy was dismayed to realize that she herself ached at the mention of Valcour's name as well. In ways she didn't dare admit, even to herself. She caught her lip between her teeth, the sting a futile attempt to banish the heat at the memory of Valcour's mouth on hers, melting her, bewitching her. She trembled just a little at the remembrance of his strong arms scooping her out of the water, carrying her to the grass as if she weighed no more than the cygnet they had rescued together.

Aubrey obviously sensed the source of her sudden silence. His brow darkened. "I suppose you're thinking that the earl would never have botched things the way I have tonight!" he snapped. "Damnation, I didn't overturn the carriage on purpose, you know!"

Lightning flashed, and Lucy could see his face, as petulant as a fractious child's.

Lucy turned her back pointedly on Aubrey and crooned nonsensical endearments to the injured horse.

"Perfect!" Aubrey swore. "I get flung headfirst into a tree and the one you're giving sympathy to is the blasted horse!"

"Perhaps that's because we won't have to shoot you if you don't mend properly, while my sweet beauty here . . ." She couldn't say anymore as a rain-dampened muzzle nudged her, liquid equine eyes peering at her in absolute trust. A lump formed in Lucy's throat and she was painfully aware of the exquisite animal's uneven gait.

"You needn't be afraid," she said. "I'll take care of you. There's a wondrous warm stable ahead with fresh oats and clear water. And I'll rub you down until you're warm and dry."

"For God's sake, I should have stayed in London!"

"I told you that before we left!" Lucy impatiently slapped away a fold of her sodden cloak.

"What kind of a man would I be if I'd allowed you—a helpless lady—to confront Sir Jasper d'Autrecourt alone? With no one to protect you? You haven't any idea what kind of man you are dealing with! And the rest of his family is equally despicable!"

"Sir Jasper is mean and petty and cheats at cards. He's a decent enough swordsman, but your brother is a better one," Lucy said in exasperation. "From the beginning, I've been planning to go to Avonstea, face down the d'Autrecourts in their own lair! I can't just sit about, waiting for Natty to come with news or for the person who wrote those notes to contact me. I feel like I'm going to blast into a million pieces!"

"It might have been more merciful if you had," Aubrey said. "In case you hadn't noticed, we're in the devil of a lot of trouble here. There's no way we can get back to London or to the infernal d'Autrecourts' tonight." He made a face. "At the d'Autrecourts' we'd likely be murdered in our sleep, but at least we'd be appropriately chaperoned while they were dosing us with hemlock."

"You're being absurd!" Lucy sniped. "They wouldn't dare hurt us—not with the memory of your brother's prowess with a sword so fresh in their memories. And as for being chaperoned, it is totally unnecessary. I can assure you that your virtue will be quite safe with me."

"It's not *my* virtue that will be in question, you little fool! *You* are the one who—"

"Perhaps you should lock your bedchamber door tonight so I won't burst in on you, carried away in a fit of passion."

Aubrey caught her by the arm, spinning her to face him. His face was flushed, his eyes over bright with disturbing emotions—hurt and a dangerous recklessness. "Damn it to hell, Lucy, for miles I've been trying to think of some way to put this into words without . . . without upsetting you."

"It would take a deal more than a few words to upset me after the day I've had. Just say it, for God's sake."

"Lucy, it's past midnight. And you are alone with a man who hasn't made any secret that he . . . he loves you."

"Who has *pretended* to be in love with me."

Aubrey's eyes flicked away from hers. "It doesn't matter anymore whether or not this began as a game. It's going to end in deadly earnest. Lucy . . . I'm going to have to marry you!"

Lucy gave a bark of disbelieving laughter. "You must have bumped your head harder than I thought! Aubrey, I'm soaked to the bone, worried about this horse, and I've got bruises on some very particular parts of my anatomy from the accident. I'm not in the mood for any of your stupid jests."

"It's no jest! Lucy, there is no other way out of this disaster. You're ruined, girl. I know you don't want me for a husband. But that's the only way to satisfy society."

"Thankfully, I don't give a tinker's snap about satisfying society. As for my being ruined, you haven't even kissed me since that time at the ball, and then we only kissed for Valcour's *pleasure.*"

Aubrey looked at her with eyes soulful as a spaniel's. "What would you say if I told you that I've wanted to kiss you since then? At Vauxhall. In the park."

"It wasn't necessary without Valcour—"

"Without Valcour to play audience?" Aubrey asked, his mouth curling in hurt. "Perhaps I wanted to kiss you for other reasons, Lucy. Because I . . . I . . ."

Lucy looked at Aubrey, suddenly wary. Surely the boy hadn't . . . hadn't what? Forgotten that their *amour* was all a game?

No, she wouldn't allow him any foolish misconception about her feelings toward him. She tossed her wet curls with a saucy smirk. "The moment we reach London, I will be happy to take out an advertisement in the *Gazette* proclaiming your innocence for all to see. We can tell the world all about our grand scheme to get the better of Valcour—"

The horse gave a startled snort as Aubrey grabbed Lucy by the shoulders. The lank strands of his hair clung about his face, the once jaunty plume on his tricorn drooped dejectedly over his shoulder.

"Listen to me! Maybe we didn't mean for this to happen, but people won't care. Do you think the ambassador is going to let a girl under his protection be ruined

116

this way? He'd be scorned by all England! And his wife . . . his wife will blame herself for not guarding you closely enough. You know it's true. And the rest of society will be happy to blame her as well."

Lucy felt a twist of guilt at the thought of the Wilkeses. Aubrey was right in this. Claree and John had barely started to trust her again after the disaster the night of the ball. How would they react to this wild new scheme of hers? If it did indeed spiral out into a scandal, the Wilkeses would once again suffer for what she had done.

Lucy cringed inwardly. She hadn't wanted it to be this way. Had never meant to repay their kindness with worry and shame. Before she'd left, she had penned Claree a letter of explanation and tucked it beneath her pillow. But after listening to Aubrey, Lucy doubted Claree would take much comfort in the letter now.

Please try to understand, there is something that I must do. I promise to explain everything when it is at an end.

"I'll simply tell John and Claree that we met with an accident. Apologize for worrying them, and—"

"I see. And exactly what are you planning to tell my infernal brother?"

"What does he have to do with any of this?"

"He's the earl. Head of the St. Cyr family. He'll feel responsible—"

"I take responsibility for myself." Lucy shivered as Valcour's implacable features seemed to swirl before her in the rain. "If he tries to interfere, I'll tell him to go to blazes. I've done so several times already. He should be used to it by now."

"Since he was fifteen, Valcour has been trying to crush any scandal attached to our family. He's not going to stand by and allow it to be said that I destroyed you. And I won't let it be said either." There was something almost desperate, vaguely pathetic in Aubrey's words.

"Aubrey, I can manage your brother." Lucy gentled her voice. "I know I've been lambasting you with my temper, but you *were* trying to help me. I'm sure His Royal Painness, the earl, can be brought to see reason."

"Reason?" Aubrey swore. "Every time I so much as mention your name, he looks like he wants to commit murder! He never says a word, but it's in his eyes. You know those damned devil eyes of his! And that day in the park, the way he looked at you!" Aubrey made a wild gesture. "By God, there were times I almost thought—"

"Thought what?" Lucy asked, the ribbons of her cloak suddenly feeling too tight about her neck.

Aubrey gave a weak laugh. "That he wanted you himself."

Little bursts of heat came to life beneath Lucy's skin as Aubrey's words echoed in her mind.

Even though the earl of Valcour had kissed her to bend her to his will in the garden, there had been something more hidden in the savage power of his kiss. Something in the way his hard, masculine body had branded itself into hers, all rock-hard muscle and intoxicating need. That fierce touch had raised a hundred questions inside her, questions that had only grown more compelling when she looked into those dark, predatory eyes, the lashes spiky with dampness, the strange expression on his face as he had watched the swans glide away.

Of course, most men weren't overly particular when it came to women. Their desires flamed over this pretty face one minute, this lovely ankle the next. Still, Lucy felt a clandestine thrill at the idea that she had awakened desire in a man as icily controlled as Valcour. There was a place inside her that wanted to tempt him again, push him over the emotional precipice she had teetered on while she was in his arms.

Lucy shook herself. What the blazes was she thinking of? She detested the dark-eyed earl. And at the moment she hated Aubrey as well, for stirring up such vivid fantasies in her head.

She would have been better off walking all the way to

the ducal seat of Avonstea—in bare, bloody feet—than to have embroiled herself with either of the St. Cyrs. At that moment she wanted to be alone more desperately than she'd ever wanted anything in her life.

"Aubrey," she ordered briskly, "take yourself inside and get us two rooms and a parlor, and I'll lead Ashlar here to the stable."

"I should take care of the infernal horse. You're the lady! How is it going to look if anyone sees—"

"It's going to look as if you are an insensitive, lazy, bullheaded clod whose brains leaked out when he bumped his head!" Lucy said through gritted teeth. "Blast it, get in there before you faint and I have to drag you inside by your boot heels! I would recommend ordering up a quantity of brandy. As long as you're going to have a headache, you might as well have a pleasant time before it hits you."

But instead of returning her quip for quip as had become their custom, Aubrey hesitated beneath the watery glow of a lantern, his face inexpressibly young and daunted. Suddenly Lucy was aware of what the boy had dared for her when he'd defied his formidable brother.

"Lucy, I am sorry. I've made a muddle of this hero business, haven't I?"

"You were going along swimmingly until the curricle overturned." Lucy forced her lips into a smile. "Don't worry. I'll take care of everything."

"There are some things that can't be fixed. But maybe . . . maybe it won't be so bad. Maybe . . ." Aubrey reached up one awkward hand. "Would you laugh at me, Lucy, if I told you that . . . that you're the most . . . marvelous girl I've ever known? And the bravest. And that I . . . I've been thinking for some time now that I—"

"Don't." Lucy pressed her fingertips against Aubrey's lips to stop the words, suddenly aware of the heartache her careless game of vengeance might cost this innocent boy.

"Tomorrow we'll hire two horses and we'll be at Avonstea before anyone knows what befell us. This will all be like a bad dream."

"It will be a nightmare all right," Aubrey moaned, trudging up the inn steps. "Valcour will know, and that will be the end of us both."

Dominic leaned low over the neck of his silver stallion, the rain driving through his cloak, the wind lashing at his face. He rode as if he were one with the storm, the raging of the heavens insignificant in comparison with the roiling emotions in his gut.

Jesus save us, Dominic, his mother's agonized voice echoed in his head, tightening his sick horror like the relentless pull of the rack. *Lucy Blackheath is Alexander d'Autrecourt's daughter.*

Dominic gritted his teeth against the savage fury and ruthless despair that had dragged him from his hard-won detachment and into the swirling pool of darkness that was his past.

Christ in heaven, was it possible? Possible that this girl was indeed d'Autrecourt's child? If there was any chance at all, he had to catch the two runaways, stop them before the unspeakable happened.

He ran his hand beneath the mane of his horse, speaking low, soothing words of encouragement to the massive beast, praying that the horse's incredible speed could overtake Aubrey's curricle.

For the first time, Dominic was grateful that the boy's ability for handling horses was nowhere near as well developed as his instinct for finding trouble.

But the boy had found trouble this time, by God. More than he could ever imagine.

Dominic cursed. How could he have been so blind where this girl was concerned? How could he not have seen the likeness of Alexander d'Autrecourt in Lucinda Blackheath's face? The straight, aristocratic nose, the blue eyes, gold hair. That sweet curve of her upper lip.

But there the similarities between father and daughter ended. Alexander d'Autrecourt had always seemed somehow wounded. Lucinda Blackheath met the world with clenched fists and a stubborn chin. Those blue eyes weren't filled with dreams but rather with defiance and vitality, courage and daring, and a kind of wild mischief.

And now, as Dominic raced down the night-darkened road, he knew why she faced the world with that saucy stubbornness, that regal tilt to her head. She was bastard-born.

That was the only possible explanation. Alexander d'Autrecourt's by-blow, a castaway child whose mother had fled to the new world, where no one would question her lack of a husband, her child's lack of a name.

Where she'd not have to endure jeers and whispers and the fury of those who felt betrayed.

Dominic's stomach gave a sick lurch. Hadn't there been enough people hurt by the musician without including this girl as yet another sacrifice? Hadn't the weakness that lurked like poison behind those dreamy blue eyes caused enough pain?

Dominic battled the sense of fury and helplessness inside him, his anger at Lucinda Blackheath becoming an almost savage protectiveness, mingled with the fierce resentment that he couldn't bar this fresh pain from his chest. He couldn't keep her locked away from those secret, hidden places inside him. Because now she was one of the shadows he would always see there, one more victim, a face, innocent and vulnerable. And even with her strength of spirit, Dominic doubted she could endure facing the truth about the man whose face was painted on her porcelain miniature.

Lightning flashed, sending his stallion skittering as a huge black beast seemed to rear up beside them. The muscles of his arms standing out like strips of steel, Dominic got the stallion under control, then looked at the object that had frightened the horse.

The curricle lay on its side, one wheel splintered, the jagged lightning that illuminated the sky trickling along gold lettering lost in an elaborate mural that had been painted on the equipage's door: A. St. Cyr.

Dominic's heart thudded in his chest, his gaze sweeping the area for any wisp that might be clothing, any glisten that might be dampened hair. But thankfully there were no bodies crumpled in the ditch and the harness of the curricle had been unfastened, the horse gone.

Dominic felt a surge of triumph. They must have ridden the animal to the nearest shelter. Most heartening of all, they would be stranded there, far from Gretna Green and elopements held over the anvil.

Stranded overnight at an inn, a voice inside Dominic suddenly whispered. A boy whose first passion would doubtless obliterate what little sense he had to begin with. Dominic could almost hear Aubrey's rationalizing taking Lucinda Blackheath to bed.

There would be no difference in the eyes of society whether they had decorously spent the night in their own separate beds or entwined in a red haze of passion. Either way, the girl would be ruined. Since they were already planning to be wed, wouldn't it be better to fortify themselves for the coming scandal by spending the night locked in one another's arms?

Desperation made Dominic tighten his knees around the stallion's barrel, urging the horse onward until he picked out the lights of a building near the road. He'd changed horses at the Hound's Tooth a dozen times on his travels to various St. Cyr estates. Though the accommodations had been rather spartan, they had also been clean, the food palatable, and the proprietor decidedly lacking in curiosity. He could only hope the man could be induced to be discreet now.

Dominic rode into the yard and dismounted, flinging his reins to a spindly groom. He flipped the boy a guinea. The lad grinned and trotted off toward the dimly lit stable.

Shaking the rain from the folds of his cloak, Valcour strode to the door and flung it open. The candlelit interior was such a contrast to the night that Valcour saw the room through a wet haze of gold, bright splotches of coats and dresses blurring before his eyes.

His hand swiped impatiently at his eyes, his gaze sweeping the room. A quick inquiry had the innkeeper ushering Valcour to the private parlor that a Mr. St. Cyr had secured a few hours before.

Dominic flattened his hand on the door and sucked in a steadying breath, uncertain of what he would find beyond the wooden panel. A scene of romantic bliss? Aubrey with Lucinda Blackheath in his arms, kissing her, touching her the way Dominic had in the moonlit garden?

Dominic's jaw tightened, and he shoved open the door.

A high-backed settle was situated near the fire, a table tucked beside the window. Candles glowed on two place settings, one pristine and untouched, the other holding the remains of a makeshift supper.

The room was deserted except for the lone figure sprawled in one of the chairs. Aubrey sat with his back to the door, guzzling brandy with the dogged fervor of someone determined to find oblivion. His fingers drummed restlessly on the table, and a handkerchief embroidered with the initials *L.B.* encircled his head.

From Dominic's vantage point, he could see one of the boy's eyelids drooping, his cheek a hot spot of color from the brandy he'd obviously consumed.

What could make an eager bridegroom just hours away from eloping with his lady descend into such a drunken spree? A lovers' quarrel? Or, more likely still, the awkward fumblings of an over-eager youth who had made a disaster of taking a virgin for the first time?

The relief Dominic had felt at the boy being safe was obliterated by a far darker emotion as he strode to Aubrey's side and grasped him by the shoulder.

"Dom?" Aubrey gave a bitter laugh, his eyes surprisingly lucid. "Don't know why the devil I should be surprised to see you! Heaven knows, you've always managed to find me whenever I was at my worst."

"I didn't come here to fight, boy. I came to stop you from doing something you'll regret for the rest of your life. Where is the girl?"

"She's in the stables, holding the horse's hand—or hoof, I should say. The animal got banged up pretty bad when the carriage overturned. I think she'd have carried the damned horse like a baby all the way here if she could have managed it."

"You left her out in the stable alone while you came in here and got drunk?" Valcour asked, his voice dangerous as black ice.

"Seemed like the logical thing to do at the time. Isn't that just like a woman? I all but get myself killed and she is out with the accursed horse!"

"You should be thanking God that curricle overturned before you got to Gretna Green."

"Gretna Green? You thought we were eloping?" Aubrey chortled.

Valcour scowled. "Where the devil else would you be going?"

"The d'Autrecourts'. Lucy wanted to clear up some infernal mystery about the English lord who is her father."

Dominic stared, incredulous. Was the girl mad? What

the devil had she intended to do? March up to the chamber where the reclusive duke stayed and say *Good morrow, your grace. I'm your illegitimate niece?*

"Then you never intended to marry the girl?"

"Oh, I planned to marry her in time. In fact, Dom, you should be elated. The continuation of the St. Cyr dynasty is assured."

"What do you mean, *is* assured?" Dominic squeezed the words through numb lips. "Aubrey, don't tell me there is a child—" Dominic reasoned ruthlessly through the wild clamoring in his head. There had not been time. The girl couldn't even know if she had conceived . . .

Valcour could see the ugly light in the boy's eyes, that familiar expression that meant he was spoiling for a fight. "Ah, I see. You're wondering if I already planted the eighth earl of Valcour in Miss Blackheath's womb, aren't you, Brother? It need not concern you. Even if she's not with child already, I promise you the instant she becomes my wife, I'll turn all my energies to impregnating her."

Bile rose in Dominic's throat, but he battled to keep his face impassive, resolved to hold true to the promise he had made so many years before.

Aubrey must never know the truth.

"Are you telling me you bedded her already?" Valcour asked carefully.

"You don't like that, do you, big brother?" Aubrey sneered. "The idea of me bedding *her*? And it's not because of any noble rot on your part, either. I've seen the way your eyes burn whenever you hear her name."

"That's enough." Valcour struggled for mental balance.

"Not this time!" Aubrey's voice broke on something suspiciously like a sob. "I know you think me a worthless fool. You and the rest of London! God knows, I don't have your brain or skill with horses or swords or . . . or the ladies. But damn it to hell, I do have my honor! Lucy Blackheath is ruined, Dom. And I'm the lucky bastard who did the ruining. She's mine, damn you!"

Dominic's fury wrenched into pain, poison from a dozen years before pouring through his veins as he stared at his brother's anguished face. "You don't know what you're doing."

"Yes I do. And it's more than the infernal St. Cyr honor I'm worried about. I think—Dom, I think love her."

"No."

"Why? Just because you aren't man enough to love a woman—with your heart, with your soul—you think no other man can? You think I haven't seen how Lucy affected you? You've been hot as a stallion barred from the mare he's wanted to mount ever since the night at the ball, and since you saw Lucy at St. James you've been worse still. And even the lovely Camilla hasn't been able to take your mind off it, has she? But I love the girl, Dom. The devil himself couldn't stop me from making her my wife."

Dominic stared at him, images roiling in his head: Catherine St. Cyr's desperate eyes, Lucinda Blackheath's regal face, and Aubrey on the brink of a hell he couldn't begin to comprehend.

In that frozen instant, Dominic knew what he had to do. "Perhaps the devil can't stop you," he said, the fierce accents of his voice undercut by pain. "But *I can.*"

With savage force, he drove his fist into Aubrey's jaw. The boy cried out in surprise, his head snapping back. Then with a groan, he crumpled to the floor, unconscious.

8

$\mathcal{T}$he swelling was going down.

Lucy ran gentle fingers down Ashlar's foreleg, feeling the tendons that ran like slender ribbons beneath the gelding's silky black coat.

She was exhausted. Her clothes still clung to her in sticky patches from the rain. Wispy tendrils of hair straggled about her face, the rest of her golden curls caught back at her nape with a scrap of hemp one of the grooms had found for her. Her shoulders ached, and her fingers were a mass of tiny cuts from the sharp leaves of the herbs she had crushed to put in the poultice she had been applying to Ashlar's injury the past four hours.

Lucy leaned her face against Ashlar's glossy withers, grateful that the animal was better at last. She only wished she could be certain that other hurts would be as easy to mend.

She closed her eyes, remembering Aubrey's face in the lantern glow, his fingers clutching at her hand. His eyes had been filled with emotions that had made Lucy desperately sad and terribly sorry.

Time and again the old biddy women around Blackheath plantation had shaken their heads, predicting that someday the Raider's daughter would get herself into a mess that she couldn't sweet-talk herself out of. Someday someone would be hurt.

But Lucy had laughed at their gloomy prophecies. She hadn't believed them. She had never even considered . . . what? That a lost and lonely boy might fancy himself to be in love with her? That John and Claree Wilkes would be tormented by gossip and censure because of something Lucy had done?

John Wilkes had lost so much on the battlefield at Yorktown, the wound he sustained there stealing away any hope of the children he and Claree had yearned for. But instead of allowing that bitterness and longing to overshadow the rest of his life, John had been determined to play father to the newborn country instead, nurturing it with his diplomatic skill and his unremitting courage.

That battle had proved to be as grueling as any of the ones he had fought in Virginia. One that had required him to gain the respect of the stiff-necked English, battling hatreds born of war and a subtle contempt for all colonials that had been nurtured far longer. The thought of that proud, kind man and his gentle wife paying the penalty for Lucy's reckless behavior was sobering at best.

And Aubrey St. Cyr . . . Lucy knew with painful clarity what he was feeling. During the childhood years she had been parted from her mother, Lucy had been lost and frightened, angry and hurt and unloved. She remembered the emptiness and pain enough to recognize it beneath the brash bravado in Aubrey St. Cyr's eyes. In the yard of the Hound's Tooth, Aubrey had reached out to her. Lucy knew how much courage that had taken. And how much pain he would feel when she turned him away.

Her eyes burned. God, she *detested* crying! Infernal

female weakness! But for the first time since she'd been a child, Lucy wanted to run to her mother, bury her face in Emily Blackheath's lap and confess everything, cry out her fears, her frustrations, her regrets. The threatening tears welled up, her throat a crushing knot of emotion she was battling to control.

"No," she berated herself fiercely. "There has to be a way to make this all right."

The gelding snuffled softly against her shoulder. "You'll see," she said to the animal. "Once I gather my wits, I'll find a way to make it seem like tonight never even happened."

"And exactly how are you planning to do that?" The sound of the low masculine voice behind her made Lucy wheel, staggering to her feet. "A secret potion? A magic wand? Or were you merely intending to kick fate squarely in its . . . tender parts?"

She gaped in disbelief as a face took shape in the stable's shadows, broad shoulders in a flowing roquelaure seeming to melt into the edges of darkness.

"Valcour," she gasped.

He stepped into the ring of light like some dark angel of legend. His shirt clung wetly to the powerful contours of his chest. Shadows, like black velvet, dipped into the corded muscles of his throat and lingered in the hollows beneath his high cheekbones, the thin white line of his scar just visible on that spellbinding face. Any sign of the man who had watched the cygnet with such quiet yearning in his dark eyes had vanished. The man of ice and steel from the night of the duel at the gaming hell stood in his stead, his face frighteningly pale and still.

"What . . . what are you doing here?" Lucy stammered.

"Rescuing a damsel in distress yet again. This is becoming a most disagreeable habit, Miss Blackheath." The words were more than a little bitter as Valcour unfastened his cloak and draped it over the stool, the droplets of rain that clung to his hair glistening like some kind of unholy aura in the lantern light.

"How did you even find out so—so quickly that I was in distress?"

"I was roused from a very pleasurable evening by your guardian and my mother," the earl said. "Both of whom were quite distressed that you were eloping with my brother."

"Eloping?" Lucy echoed, astonished. "With Aubrey? Of all the ridiculous assumptions!"

"Is it? You and my brother have been trailing about London like lovesick calves for three weeks. You suddenly disappear together, leaving a note saying you will explain all when you return. Coincidentally, you are headed in the direction of Gretna Green, the traditional site for such insane marriages. If you were a guardian, responsible for a rebellious, besotted boy and a reckless madcap girl, exactly what would you have thought under the circumstances?"

Lucy felt the blood drain from her cheeks. "I hadn't thought of it that way."

"After our last three encounters, I am convinced that you rarely think at all, madam, especially when it comes to considering the consequences of your actions."

Lucy bristled, stung by the truth in his words. "Well, all of you stodgy guardians can set your minds at rest. We are not eloping. We were never planning to elope. And as for the great love affair between Aubrey and I"—she gave a defiant toss of her curls—"the whole thing was all a game to irritate *you,* my lord. So there is no reason to get your aristocratic hackles up."

"A game?" Valcour's voice bit harshly. "You staged the entire debacle at the ball for my benefit, did you? And afterwards you paraded about London, flashing Aubrey that temptress's smile of yours, fluttering your lashes at him adoringly, letting him hold your hand and play the knight errant. And it never occurred to you in all this time that a foolish, inexperienced boy treated to that sort of flirtation might become infatuated with you?"

Lucy's cheeks burned. "I thought—I mean, from the beginning the whole purpose was to annoy you."

"Well, congratulate yourself. You have achieved your goal. I hope that triumph will be worth the price that must be paid."

Lucy hated him for raising up images of Aubrey and the Wilkeses in her mind, her own guilt grinding down on her. "I've never tried to escape the consequences of my mistakes."

"I'm relieved to hear it."

There was something so damned arrogant about his voice, something so scornful, that Lucy wanted to shove him back until he buried one glossy boot in a pile of manure.

"I accept responsibility for my mistakes, but I'll be damned if I'm going to listen to you raging at me. This is none of your affair."

"You made it my affair the moment you dragged the name St. Cyr into your scheme. Do you know what happens to girls who are ruined, Miss Blackheath? They are a shame to their families. Often disowned, cast out."

Lucy shuddered as he touched a chord of memory, the bittersweet story of her mother, a frightened vicar's daughter who had married a duke's younger son, only to have both of them barred from the only life they'd ever known, left to struggle and suffer with their tiny daughter. Until she was taken from them as well.

Her chin jutted up. "My parents would love me no matter what I had done," she said with absolute certainty. "They would never cast me out."

"Then you are fortunate. You can go back to your precious Virginia with no repercussions from what you have done here. You can forget this ever happened, or look back on it with fond remembrance of how you managed to . . . what was it? Annoy an English earl."

He was being far too agreeable. The fine hairs along Lucy's spine tingled in the instinctive way that had always warned her of danger.

"Of course, there are those who will not be so fortunate," Valcour continued in steely accents. "The Wilkeses will be scorned by everyone because of what you have done. They will be shamed and sneered at, whispered about and mocked. And as for John Wilkes's effectiveness as an ambassador . . ." Valcour gave an ugly laugh. "How will anyone be able to take him seriously? After all, how can a man mediate crises between two countries if he cannot even keep one American girl out of trouble?"

Lucy chewed at her bottom lip. "I'll go back to Virginia immediately. The scandal will die down."

Valcour chuckled, a harsh sound deep in his muscular chest. "The English have a distressingly long memory when it comes to scandals, my dear. I speak from personal experience. But I wouldn't trouble myself overlong about the Wilkeses. They will merely return to the colonies in disgrace, having failed in their mission. I'm certain they will get over it in time."

"Blast it, I didn't mean for this to happen!" Lucy burst out, stinging under the full impact of what she had done. "I said that I'm sorry."

"Sorry." Valcour mouthed the word as if it were the vilest of curses. "The single word that can magically erase any mistake. Make it seem as if it never happened. I'm quite sure that Mary Queen of Scots was heartily sorry for annoying Elizabeth. Especially in those moments just before the headsman's axe fell. Unfortunately, her regret changed nothing. There are equally permanent consequences to your actions, Miss Blackheath."

"I suppose you're going to cut off my head because I accidentally got trapped at an inn with your brother?"

"Don't be absurd. I'd never resort to such primitive methods." Valcour paced to the gelding and stroked its muzzle. Lucy watched the horse turn traitor, nudging with some affection the earl's hand. "Of course, these inevitable repercussions from tonight's events are nothing for you to concern yourself with, Lucinda. You'll be in Virginia making someone else's life a living hell by the time the . . . *axe* falls."

The flame from the lantern danced in the black irises of Valcour's eyes. Devil's eyes, Aubrey had called them. And as Lucy looked into those hypnotic depths, she wondered if the boy were right.

"What are you hinting at?"

"Just that it won't be so simple for Aubrey to escape the consequences of this night. He has ruined you, no matter how noble his original intentions were. No matter how naive he was to be dragged into your scheme. Perhaps in Virginia honor is insignificant. But I would sacrifice the last drop of blood in my veins to preserve the honor of the St. Cyr name."

Lucy swiped sweating palms against the dust-smudged blue damask of her petticoat. "What are you going to do, my lord? Challenge your own brother to a duel?"

"It would be swifter and more merciful if I did." His voice slid like splinters of ice beneath her skin. "However, it could hardly be considered honorable to shed the blood of one so much weaker than myself."

"How civilized of you." Lucy should have been relieved, but she was not. A creeping sensation of doom pervaded the stable, making it seem as if the walls were shrinking inward, as if Valcour were taking up all the air.

"Surely during the time you have spent with Aubrey you've noticed certain . . . shall we call them *weaknesses* in his character, Miss Blackheath? He's a scapegrace boy, addicted to expensive clothes, extravagant carriages, and horses whose hooves might be cast of gold they come at such a high price. Aubrey is constantly running afoul of his creditors. And you might be interested to know that I've rescued him from sponging houses on numerous occasions the past two years. You see, you are not the boy's only passion. He has an insatiable lust for hazard, an equally perilous game. But as his guardian, I have paid his gaming debts and furnished the other accoutrements he desires. Every shilling that jingles in Aubrey's pocket originates with me." Valcour paused, staring meditatively at the gold signet ring that glinted on his first finger. "How long do you think my brother would survive, Miss Blackheath, if I suddenly cut him off without so much as a guinea?"

Lucy's chest tightened with disbelief. "You wouldn't do that. You—you dueled to save his life."

"You mistake my motive. I dueled to save the St. Cyr honor. Imagine how embarrassing it would have been if Aubrey had been cut down by a miscreant like Sir Jasper d'Autrecourt."

"But Aubrey is your heir!" Lucy groped desperately for some way to deny Valcour's threat. "The estates are entailed. Even if you wanted to you couldn't keep them from him."

"Aubrey will inherit only after my death. And I intend to live for a very long time. Use your considerable imagination to picture what would happen to that fresh-faced, foolish boy you bewitched if he were subjected to years of grinding poverty. There is not a useful thought or a practical ability buried anywhere in that empty head of his. I doubt he could tie his cravat without a valet and three servants to assist him."

Lucy stared at the implacable lines of Valcour's face, her hands trembling. "What kind of a monster are you? Willing to fling your own brother to the wolves over something as worthless as honor! Honor means nothing in the face of real love!"

"Love is not an emotion that has ever troubled me overmuch, thank God. My honor, however, has come at a high price. I was a mere boy of fifteen when I began to scrape and claw my way out of the abyss of disgrace that was my birthright. I have shed my blood and the blood of other men to douse the fires of scandal. Believe me, Miss Blackheath, disinheriting my reckless fool of a brother would be easy in comparison to some things that I have done."

Lucy wanted to rage at him, but his features were unyielding as a mountain cliff, Aubrey's softer, gentler face rising up before her, tormenting her. "You can't do this," she entreated. "Aubrey didn't mean for things to go awry. It wasn't his fault."

"He chose to accompany you."

"He discovered I was planning to journey alone! He was worried that I would get lost or be hurt."

"I can't imagine why. I'm certain the d'Autrecourts would have welcomed you with open arms, considering the circumstances."

The earl's acid mockery burned Lucy to her very marrow. "Aubrey told you."

"You must forgive him his indiscretion. He had drunk a quantity of brandy. Of course, stone sober, my brother has never been known for his prudence."

"Perhaps, then, he is known for his generosity," Lucy fired back in Aubrey's defense. "He only meant to help me."

"The reasons for what he did are immaterial. He dishonored—"

Lucy's mouth twisted in loathing. "You can take your infernal honor, my lord, and thrust it up your—"

Lucy couldn't stifle a gasp as Valcour's hands shot out, manacling her arms in a ruthless grasp. "I would mind my tongue if I were you," he growled, his dark face mere inches from her own. "I was roused from my mistress's arms by my frantic mother. I rode in the pouring rain, at night, trying to find the two of you. I was greeted in the inn by my drunken brother, who was so belligerent I ended up slamming my fist into his jaw and knocking him senseless. Don't tempt me to do the same with you."

"I'm not afraid of you!" Lucy shot back, praying Valcour couldn't feel the traitorous quivering in her knees.

The earl's lip curled in derision. "You should be. I guarantee you, Aubrey has the wit to be afraid of me. He has had enough experience to know that I never make idle threats, Miss Blackheath. And I never cower from taking whatever unpleasant steps I deem necessary to achieve my goals."

"Even if it means destroying your own brother?"

Valcour sketched her a bow that reeked of insolence. "Even that."

"You are a monster."

"I am what life has made me. Now, if you'll excuse me, I must inform my brother that he is penniless. The brandy he was guzzling was, without doubt, the most expensive available. I wouldn't want him to run up a high ticket at the inn."

Valcour spun on one glossy boot heel and started to walk from the stable.

"No, wait!" Lucy flung herself in front of him. Her hands flattened on Valcour's muscular chest to detain him as she faced him with steely defiance. The damp cloth of his shirt was heated by his skin, his pulse throbbing beneath her palm. She wished she could rip his unfeeling heart from his breast.

"Aubrey did nothing!" she insisted, his buttons cutting into her hand as her fingers clenched in desperation. "There must be something I can do to make things right. I'll do whatever you wish if you'll just—just not destroy him."

Valcour looked down at her, a glitter that might have been triumph in his eyes, if it weren't for the roiling darkness that obscured it. "You aren't willing to let him suffer in your stead? How infinitely refreshing."

For an instant, Lucy felt as if the entire conversation,

from the first moment he'd walked into the dimly lit stable, had been building to this point. She was suddenly and excruciatingly aware of her hands on Valcour's chest, his stone-carved musculature brushing her knuckles. She released him, falling back a step. Even so, she had the sensation that she had been dancing on the edge of a precipice and had just jumped off.

Valcour's inky brow arched in consideration, and for a moment Lucy wondered if he was going to insist on some hideous primeval torture. The rack. The iron maiden. Either would have been preferable to being impaled by those devil's eyes.

"Perhaps there is one way you can save your errant knight from the dragon, Miss Blackheath," Valcour mused. "But I warn you, his ransom is high."

Lucy's hands knotted in her skirts. "Name your price."

"Become my countess."

"Wh-What?" Lucy staggered back, incredulous, horrified.

Valcour's mouth spread in a slow smile that sent shivers racing for cover at the base of her spine. "You might find it difficult to believe, but when I was a boy I was partial to worthless drivel like myths and legends. One of my favorites was the tale of Persephone, the beautiful young goddess who was carried down to the Underworld to be Hades's bride. If you are willing to descend into my domain, Aubrey will be spared."

Lucy's head swam with the image of the statue outside Perdition's Gate that first night she had met the dark earl. Never had she imagined that the rendition of Persephone's descent into the Underworld would be a foreshadowing of her future. She reeled beneath the weight of Valcour's words, Aubrey's claim echoing in her mind: *There are times it almost seems as if Valcour wants you for himself.*

"You can't possibly want to marry me!" she protested. "You don't even know me! I'll marry Aubrey if that will make things right. But—"

"Allow you and Aubrey to wed? I place more value on my sanity than that. No, Miss Blackheath, you asked my price. I have told you. The decision is yours."

Lucy's heart thundered painfully against her ribs, her stomach churning with desperation, fury. Marry this man with his riveting intensity? The dark fires that glowed like live coals in his eyes?

Marry this arrogant Englishman who was ruthless enough to disinherit his brother over a simple mistake made, not out of recklessness or cowardice, but, rather, out of kindness?

It would be madness. Insane to consider even for a moment binding herself to Valcour.

Lucy closed her eyes tight, seeing her mother's face, tender and loving and so understanding. Ian Blackheath's indulgent laughter, his eyes shining with unconditional love and approval. If she married this man, she might never see her family again. Never urge Norah in mischief, or look into the coming baby's unfocused eyes.

And yet, how could Lucy allow Aubrey St. Cyr to suffer for what she had done? How could she abandon him? Everything Valcour had said about the youth was true. Like so many of the aristocracy, Aubrey had been born to a life of idleness and plenty. He was little more than a spoiled child in spite of his seventeen years. Lucy doubted he could survive for three days without the wealth and power of Valcour shoring him up.

Lucy raised her eyes to Valcour's, feeling the crushing burden of inevitability settle on her shoulders.

"You want a wife who doesn't love you?" She attempted to reason with him one last time. "A wife who loathes you?"

Valcour waved one elegantly sculpted hand in dismissal. "I do not want a wife at all. But I will take you in order to preserve my honor and my foolish brother's inheritance. You see, I am not completely heartless."

"Yes you are." Tears of futility burned Lucy's eyes, but she would suffer the fires of hell before she would let them fall. "You're an unfeeling, cruel bastard and I'll hate you until the day I die!"

"I shall attempt not to be heartbroken at the prospect," Valcour said, negligently straightening the lace at his wrists. "Now make your decision. What will it be? Countess of Valcour or Aubrey taking up residence in a rat-infested garret on Fleet Street?"

Lucy's hands knotted into fists. There would be time, she assured herself desperately. Time to figure out a way to escape this insanity before it was too late. The banns would have to be cried, and then she could drag out the betrothal, find some weapon to use against Valcour. Anything could happen in the month before they could be wed.

"I'll marry you, damn your eyes," she conceded. "But I swear, I'll make your life the same hell that you've given to me."

Valcour's teeth gleamed white in a tigerish smile. "A most original wedding vow, my dear. But I've no objection. We'll start our wedded life with more honesty than most—no promises of connubial bliss or eternal passion. Just clean, clear hatred from the moment I slip my ring upon your finger."

That will happen the day England sinks into the sea! Lucy vowed inwardly. She fully expected Valcour to see the rebellion in her eyes, but the sound of coach wheels clattering into the yard made him cross to the dingy stable window. He swiped a hand against the cobweb-laced pane and peered out.

When he turned again to confront her, the hard satisfaction on that ruthless face sent tiny frissons of alarm racing through Lucy's veins.

"Who . . . what is it?" Lucy demanded.

"The bishop of Lothshire."

Lucy's brow furrowed in confusion. "What would a bishop be doing here?"

Valcour's eyes glinted like slivers of jet beneath hooded eyelids, the smile that spread across his face grim and predatory. "He's come at my request to bring us a special license, my dear. You see, I am a most impatient bridegroom. We are passionately in love, you and I, and cannot wait until the banns are cried."

"What?" Lucy shrank back, the hard reality of Valcour's words all but driving her to her knees. "You planned this from the beginning, didn't you?" she raged. "You planned to force my hand!"

"Let's just say that I make it a point to prepare for any eventuality. I sent for the bishop in case you could be brought to see reason. In case you could not, I sent a note to my solicitor, telling him that Aubrey would no longer be allowed to make withdrawals from my accounts until further notice."

"But I can't marry you right now!" Lucy protested, feeling as if she were being sucked beneath the current of a raging river. "I need time to—"

"To what?" His eyes were ebony fire, stripping bare the deepest secrets of her soul.

"T-To get a proper gown," she stammered, raking her fingers back through her disheveled curls. "To tell the Wilkeses of our betrothal. I'm certain they will—will want to plan an elaborate celebration. After all, a man with your monstrous arrogance wouldn't want to take a bride who smelled of the stables and had half a bale of straw tangled in her hair! You will want all of London present at the wedding of the great and glorious earl of Valcour. You appearing the grand seigneur, with me trussed up in some preposterously expensive gown."

"And the entire time the seamstresses were stitching on that preposterous gown, you would be scheming to find a way out of this marriage, wouldn't you, my dear? Searching for any skeleton in the St. Cyr family crypt that you could use as a weapon against me?"

Lucy felt the blood drain from her face, certain her expression had betrayed her.

Valcour was smiling, that sensual twist to his lips that made her think not of ice but of the fire that hooded gaze seemed to ignite beneath her skin.

"You say that I don't know you," Valcour said, low. "But I know enough." He was close, much too close, taking up all the air in the stable. And hot—he was making the room seem so hot and dark and . . . intimate. "I know that you have the devil's own temper, Lucinda. That you're brave to the point of madness, and that you gasp with pleasure when I touch you . . . here." His finger dipped into the hollow at the base of her throat and traced a delicate line along the fragile bow of her collarbone.

"Don't do that!" Lucy jerked away as if he'd slipped a live ember into the bodice of her gown. She was stunned by how much the mockery in his caress had hurt her.

"You needn't fear, madam. I have heard that all brides are nervous on their wedding night. Or . . . should I say, prior to the ceremony. Now, there is a lovely church three miles down the road. You will marry me there at once. Or there will be no bargain to save Aubrey from being disinherited. What is it to be, Lucinda?"

Lucy trembled with helpless fury. "I'll make you regret this."

"I am quaking with trepidation. Answer me, girl. Now. I have an aversion to Cheltenham tragedies, and if Aubrey awakes, he'll rival any performance that ever graced Drury Lane. I'd not mind thrashing the boy again, except that my knuckles are still tender from the last time I hit him."

Lucy swallowed hard, imagining Aubrey's pain when the sensitive boy discovered the disaster that had befallen her. No, better to have it over with before he came rushing to her rescue, risking even more on her behalf. God only knew what the reckless boy might do.

She lifted her chin with regal hauteur in spite of the twine that bound back her hair. "I'd prefer the blow of a headsman's axe to exchanging wedding vows with you," she said fiercely. "But since you have brought the bishop instead, let's get my infernal execution over with at once."

Valcour sketched her an arrogant bow, shadows dancing in the planes and hollows of his austere face.

He had won this battle, Lucy thought, seething with hatred. But she would make certain it was the bitterest victory the earl of Valcour had ever known.

There had never been a more defiant bride.

Valcour stared down at Lucinda Blackheath with a surprising twist of tenderness in his heart. She stood with her chin thrust belligerently at the bishop, her hair straggling about her face like a milkmaid just returned from a tumble in the meadow. Her gown was wilted about her slender body as if she had worn the infernal thing since Christmastime.

And yet even with twine straggling down that graceful neck, even with a smudge of dirt on that aristocratic nose, she looked like a hostage queen being forced to wed a villainous churl.

And as Valcour stared down into those rebellious aquamarine eyes, he felt every inch the heartless bastard she had named him.

Even the bishop was intimidated by the sizzling waves of tension consuming the bride and groom before him. The old man squirmed as if Satan's fires were heating the altar stones beneath his very feet. He spoke the wedding ceremony with the awkwardness of a boy reciting ill-learned lessons, stumbling over phrases he must have read three hundred times and wincing at his mistakes as if he expected to feel the cut of the willow switch. Valcour's mouth hardened with satisfaction at the knowledge that, in spite of the bishop's discomfiture, the holy man would never dare defy the mighty earl. Much as the bishop might like to intervene, he was decidedly lacking in courage.

Lothshire's sausagelike hands fidgeted with the exquisite prayer book, the ring on his finger, as if hoping for some heavenly intercession that would give Lucy time to reconsider her rash marriage, or the earl of Valcour time to redeem his sin-scarred soul.

But it was far too late for that.

Dominic St. Cyr had looked straight into the pit of hell, and the images he had seen there would be reflected forever in his eyes. The scars left in his soul would always form a barrier as impenetrable as the legendary Queen Morgawse's invisible wall, Valcour's solitary existence serving as both a prison and a haven that no one would ever breach.

"Do you, Lucinda Blackheath," the bishop stuttered, "take this man to be your husband?"

He dropped his prayer book in alarm as Lucy bellowed, "I wouldn't be standing here like an idiot if I didn't!"

The bishop, unused to such assaults on his priestly dignity, turned scarlet and scrambled to retrieve his book. "Do you promise to—to love him, honor him, comfort, and—and obey him as long as you both shall live?"

Valcour felt a grim smile tug at the corner of his mouth. The old curmudgeon looked as if he were poised to dive beneath the altar cloth at a moment's notice. Truth to tell, the bishop would be far safer hiding himself there.

"Do you promise to love my lord Valcour, honor him, comfort—" the bishop began again, but Lucy cut him off with a wave of her hand.

"I predict that my lord will need a great deal of comforting in the future," she said, her eyes slits seething with malice.

"I—I take it that means yes?" the bishop queried unsteadily.

"Yes, you infernal fool!" Lucy blazed.

The bishop's jowls wobbled as he swallowed hard. "And you, my lord Valcour, do you take this woman to be your wife? To have and to hold from this day forward? In sickness and in health until death do you part?"

"I do."

"The—the ring. Have you got a . . ." The bishop glanced from one to the other as if he expected a box on the ears. "I mean, often in these hasty affairs, one forgets such—such trivialities."

"I have no ring." Then Valcour paused, the glint of the bishop's ruby stirring a vague memory. "Wait just a moment."

Dominic dragged his watch from his waistcoat pocket. He felt Lucinda's anger-hot eyes on his fingers as he fumbled with something attached to the fob. A gold disk fell into his cupped palm. Candlelight danced in the petals of what looked to be a wreath of roses, the hearts of the tiny blossoms each glowing red with a perfect ruby.

Of their own volition, Dominic's fingers curled over the ring, as if it were something to be ashamed of, some sign of weakness he had to hide. In that frozen moment, his mind filled with the remembrance of his mother on his twentieth birthday. For years he had not considered the day of his birth an occasion to be celebrated. That day he'd forgotten it entirely and had been laboring over some shipping interests that had reached a crucial point.

Lady Catherine had come to him with that hopeful, hurting softness in her eyes. She had curled up on a stool near his feet, looking as fragile as a lily battered by a storm. The ring had been gripped in her hand.

"Dominic, life is so uncertain, we cannot know when

the angels will claim us. And I wanted to make certain that you have this someday when you are ready to take a wife."

"I have told you, I've no intention of saddling myself with a marriage."

She had winced and looked away. "You cannot blame a mother for hoping that you will change your mind in time. This ring is a love gift that has been passed on for generations. A chevalier from Anjou first fashioned it for his lady, Angelique, before he went to fight in the Crusades. Angelique's father would not allow her to marry her love until he proved himself in battle. It was a bitterly painful parting, but the knight rode off, determined to win his lady love. Nine months later, Angelique received word that he had been lost in a crushing defeat that no Englishman survived. She was at the altar, being forced by her father to wed a man of his choosing, when her knight strode through the church door. He said that in the heat of combat he saw the ring shimmering all around him, shielding him from the scimitars of the infidels. And when he had awakened after the battle, he was safe, drifted down on English shores. Since that day, the ring has been said to fit only the finger of the giver's true love. And once it is in place, that bond can never be severed."

Her cheeks had flushed at the hard cast to Dominic's face, and the quiet pain had returned to her eyes. "I know that you think such talk of magic ridiculous, Dominic. But the ring is lovely, don't you think? It would be beautiful on your own lady's hand one day."

Dominic had been damned uncomfortable. But the ring had seemed to mean so much to his mother that he had fastened it to his watch fob. He'd thanked her, fighting to keep the impatience out of his voice. But she had known what he was feeling. It had been one of the great tragedies of Lady Catherine's life that she had always known. . . .

He wondered what his gentle mother would think of him if she could see him now. Forcing his troth upon an unwilling girl, innocent of any crime save dishonoring the St. Cyr name. This was no tender love match, no desperate passion the like of Angelique and her knight. And Dominic could only thank God for that.

"My lord?" the bishop's voice shook Dominic back to the present, and he was aware of the holy man's questioning look, and Lucinda's rebellious one.

"Having second thoughts, *my lord?*" the girl asked with an acid bite.

"Not at all," Dominic said, the ring seeming to almost pulse in his hand. "I am only preserving this tender moment in my memory."

It was ridiculous. But he felt a sudden stark reluctance to slip the ring on Lucinda Blackheath's hand. His jaw clenched as he took the gold circlet, sliding it to the first joint of her finger, holding it there, the gold smooth and cool, her fingers overly warm, trembling just a little.

"With this ring I thee wed," he repeated after the bishop.

"With my body I thee worship." They were words, only words. They meant nothing. Then why did an awareness sizzle to life beneath the tips of Dominic's fingers, fingers that brushed the facets of the small rubies and the ivory satin of Lucinda Blackheath's skin?

His voice was damnably unsteady as Dominic finished the vow: "With all my worldly goods I thee endow."

Almost by instinct, Lucinda curled her fingers as if to keep the circlet of gold from being slid into place. A ring that was not a love token, but the final blow of the axe blade she had feared. For a moment, Valcour felt regret. His shoulders tensed as he forced the ring into place. A momentary stab of astonishment pierced him as the ring fit her slender finger to perfection.

"You are now man and wife, my children," the bishop

said, mopping his brow with obvious relief. "Go in peace."

"Not bloody likely," Valcour muttered, grateful to retreat behind his shield of acid wit.

"Pardon me, my lord?"

"I said, I am vastly in your debt. You have shown yourself a friend to the St. Cyrs yet again. I will not forget."

The bishop looked into Dominic's eyes, and for a moment the blithering fool of minutes before took on an expression that was disturbingly wise. "I can only pray that this child will help you to do so, my lord."

9

*T*he sweet, dew-misted air played about Lucy's heated face as she stepped out of the church at Hound's Way and into an uncertain future.

She stared down at the ring on her finger, her throat thick with the tears she had walled in behind her belligerent facade during the endless wedding ceremony. She was the countess of Valcour. Never to be plain Lucy Blackheath again.

Lucy, who had climbed trees in the midst of storms and frightened bullies by playing at ghost. Lucy, who had dashed through Blackheath Hall like a whirlwind of pure mischief, secure in her parents' love.

Lucy, who had taught her sisters how to slip despised bits of vegetables beneath the tablecloth to feed to their father's hounds. The Raider's daughter, who had ridden secret missions for the bold patriot Pendragon, was now the wife of an enigmatic stranger.

Lucy's lips trembled at the memory of that night she'd first decided to race off to England on this "grand adventure." She had never seen Ian Blackheath look so stricken. *You belong here,* he had raged. *With us.*

I'm not trundling off with "prospective bride" marked on my forehead, Papa, she had said, so certain in her own power. *All I want is to take a holiday . . . for a year at most . . .*

I don't understand, Lucy, he had said. *Help me to understand. . . .*

But Ian Blackheath would never understand this.

No, that was wrong. He would understand only too well the recklessness that had driven her into the middle of such a disaster. Most likely he had expected her to become embroiled in some kind of debacle from the moment she cajoled the Wilkeses into bringing her to England.

Lucy bit her lip until it bled. There had been real fear in her father's countenance that night. Even Emily's teasing hadn't driven it from his eyes.

Are you afraid some dashing English rogue will carry her off to his castle and we'll never see her again?

Oh, God, Mama. Lucy felt the wrenching agony in her chest. *What have I done?*

She wanted to fling herself upon the bishop's chest, beg the holy man to ignore the vows she had spoken. She hadn't meant them, hadn't wanted to make them. But it was too late.

Anxious to be quit of the whole affair, the bishop was lumbering into his coach, leaving Lucy alone with the man who now stood as a dark silhouette against the first mauve ribbons of dawn.

Valcour's back was to her, and she was struck again by the imposing width of his shoulders, the long, muscular length of his thighs. His hair was liquid silk, caught back with as much precision as her own curls were tumbled in disarray.

Since the moment he had stalked into the stable, Valcour radiated power, ruthlessness. But now, as he stood with the fingers of the dew-kissed morning breeze threading through his hair, there was a curious hesitancy about him, almost as if he were uncertain what to do next.

Lucy swallowed hard, his taunting words about the wedding night echoing in her mind. Her only hope was that he'd continue to stare off into the mists of the newborn morning for all eternity.

"So, it is done," Valcour said at last.

"Yes."

"In spite of all that has gone before, I will try not to be too reprehensible a husband to you. You will not find me an exacting master, Lucinda."

"I will not tolerate you being my master at all." Her chin bumped up a notch despite her melancholy.

Valcour's face angled toward her, and she was suddenly aware of dark circles beneath the earl's eyes, the faint lines that bracketed his mouth. "Would it be possible to lay down our weapons for a little while?" he asked. "Not surrender, by any means. A negligible truce. No more than that."

She didn't know what to say. God in heaven, she didn't know the man at all. "I suppose," she allowed. "But I'll keep my hand on the swordhilt just in case."

Valcour smiled a little. "I don't doubt you will." He walked past the coach he had hired to bring them to the church and leaned against a stone fence that meandered along the road. A baby duckling paddled blissfully in a miniature pond last night's storm had created in a particularly deep rut. The little creature reminded Lucy poignantly of those few moments she and Valcour had been in harmony, watching the cygnet and its mama swim away.

"I will need an heir," Valcour said at last. "I will make no other demands on you."

That demand alone was enough to make the blood rush to Lucy's cheeks, images of how he would sire that heir playing with disturbing vividness in her mind.

Instinctively, Lucy crossed her arms over her tingling breasts.

"I—I have hardly had time to get used to being a wife. Surely—"

"Lucinda, I am very selective in my villainy. I hardly intend to fling you to the ground and get you with child at once. You will have whatever time you need to . . . accustom yourself to the idea of me coming to your bed."

Lucy sucked in a shuddering breath at this unexpected consideration on his part, but she didn't dare show such a formidable adversary any weakness. "I suppose you expect me to thank you for that?"

"That would hardly be fair, would it? Considering what I've put you through the past few hours?" Valcour dragged one bronzed hand through his dark hair and rubbed at his eyes.

"Is there anything else you require of me?" Lucy demanded, hating the sensation of empathy she was beginning to feel toward him.

"Honesty. I have a great aversion to lies."

"That may be difficult. From the time I was a child I've been a most accomplished liar."

The hard edge was back in Valcour's voice. "You're not a child anymore, Lucinda. You needn't fear any repercussions as long as you are honest with me. Once our son is born, you may conduct whatever affairs you wish with impunity, as long as you exercise an appropriate amount of discretion."

Lucy's cheeks stung with outrage. For God's sake, the man had just forced her to marry him because of some crazed notion of honor, and now, before an hour had passed, he was giving her permission to sleep with half of London as long as she didn't flaunt her actions.

His impatient words in the stable replayed themselves in her memory: *I was roused from my mistress's arms.* . . . Thunder in heaven, the woman's bedsheets probably hadn't even had time to cool. A prickly knot of something Lucy couldn't name bubbled up in her chest.

Shadows from the past drifted through her mind: Celestia Blackheath, Ian's sister and Lucy's adoptive mother. A frivolous, petty woman who so thirsted for the attention of her lovers that she'd locked up the pianoforte that had given Lucy so much joy. It was the only way the woman could be certain that no man would be distracted from her beauty by the magic of Lucy's music.

Lucy might bow to giving Valcour a child. Heaven knew, she'd been terribly lonely without her own family, and the babe might fill a part of the empty space their absence would leave in her heart. But the thought of her husband—even a husband in name only—being entangled with another woman was something Lucy could not endure.

"You have laid out your demands, my lord. Now I will give you my own."

Valcour's brow slid upward in silent query.

"I will not take another woman's leavings."

"Pardon me?"

"If I am to bear you a son, I will not tolerate you coming to me with your lips warm from another woman's kisses. I know this is not a love match, but I would find it humiliating."

"Lucinda, a man has needs. I'm no different from any other." He paced toward her. Lucy stepped backward, bumping up against a tree.

She stiffened as his hand came up to catch her chin, tipping her face to his. "You are beautiful, Countess."

He reached out to touch a tendril of hair that straggled across her shoulder. "You have a tantalizingly ripe look about you. Your lips full, like berries ready to burst in the sun. Your breasts perfection, pale as milk, with that tracery of blue veins like ribbons beneath the petals of a white rose."

She had never expected such praise from Valcour, intoxicating phrases in that husky, seductive voice.

"As long as your bed is open to me," Valcour said, "I won't find it a hardship to abandon all others."

His thumb skimmed her lower lip, as if testing its texture. His gaze heated, as if he were anticipating tasting something sweet.

"Don't look at me that way, my lord," Lucy protested, uncomfortable with the tiny bursts of excitement the mere brush of his gaze was igniting in her breasts, her lips, and other places more secret still.

Valcour braced his hands on either side of her, trapping her against the tree with the sinewy circle of his body. "I'm your husband. Call me by name."

"I can't," Lucy said, the absurdity of it all making a nervous smile tug at the corner of her lips.

"Don't be stubborn, girl."

"I *can't*," Lucy repeated. "I don't . . . know your name."

Valcour chuckled, a sound like whiskey warmed in the sun. "Dominic. Dominic Braxton St. Cyr, sixth earl of Valcour. Say it." His mouth was a breath away from hers. If she trembled she would touch it, taste it.

"Say it," he urged again.

"I—I can't," Lucy stammered. "I can't remember past the first two!"

"A woman should know her husband's name, to whisper it in the darkness, to cry out when he buries himself inside her."

She raised her gaze up to his, felt herself falling into something so compelling she couldn't stop it.

"Dominic," she murmured.

Those fire-hot masculine lips brushed hers, tantalizing, tempting, then left her needing.

Of their own volition, her fingertips touched the hard wall of his chest, felt the unsteady beat of his heart. "Dominic," she said again, her voice quavering.

He rewarded her with another kiss, the moist heat of his mouth lingering a moment longer before he drew away.

Lucy's head whirled, her breasts heavy and aching, her center soft with a heat that made her squeeze her thighs together, long for Valcour's hands to touch . . .

For a heartbeat Lucy wanted more, to explore those illicit fires of seduction that had dizzied her in the Wilkeses' garden. But the next moment reality crashed in about her, reminding her exactly how much this man had just cost her.

As if reading her thoughts, Valcour pulled away from her, his fingers curling into a fist. "I have said I will give you time, and I shall keep my word. As you shall keep yours, Lucinda."

Lucy would have flung back a suitable retort, but she was still struggling to breathe.

"The first matter I demand your complete honesty in is this: You will tell me exactly what your purpose was in traveling to the d'Autrecourts. Everything, girl. To the last detail."

"I thought that Aubrey had—"

"The boy gave me some garbled mash I could barely decipher. I know that you were going to the d'Autrecourts, and I know that the miniature you wore the night of the ball wasn't some trinket to amuse you. It was a picture of your father, Lord Alexander d'Autrecourt, third son of the duke of Avonstea."

Lucy's cheeks burned, her eyes flickering away from Valcour's. The idea of confiding any of this to him was daunting. How would anyone believe such a wild tale? She could scarcely believe it herself, and she had opened the box of Alexander d'Autrecourt's belongings, seen the misty-eyed face above the stairs in the gaming hall.

"Lucinda." There was real gentleness in Valcour's usually strident tones. His fingers took up hers, the new wedding ring glinting against the edge of his thumb.

"Don't be afraid. I don't hold it against you. I figured out the truth before I even got here, while I was riding on the road."

The man had deduced that her father—who had supposedly been dead for seventeen years—was alive and had been living above a gaming hell? No wonder Aubrey was more than a little afraid of his brother. No, she was being ridiculous. Valcour couldn't know.

"It doesn't matter to me, Lucinda. I am a man of some arrogance, I know. But I hope I am not such a monster that I blame the helpless for other people's sins."

Now she was totally confused. "Other people's—I don't understand."

"I just want you to know that it matters not at all to me. The fact that you are . . . baseborn."

Lucy almost laughed aloud with relief. "You think me a *bastard?*"

Valcour's brow furrowed. "I tell you it is immaterial—"

"I'm no bastard, my lord. I'm Lord Alexander d'Autrecourt's true-born daughter."

Valcour drew back, his eyes flashing, every muscle in his body seeming to reverberate with warning. "His only true-born daughter died when she was three years old, and he died with her. I've warned you that I've no tolerance for liars."

"I'm not lying. My mother was the daughter of the vicar on the d'Autrecourts' estate. She and my father grew up together, best friends. When my mother's family tried to force her into marriage with a cruel squire, my father rescued her. Married her out of hand. They were disowned and came to London, where my father worked as a music teacher and composer. I was born a year later, and—"

"No!" Valcour hissed between gritted teeth. "I saw the grave."

"By the time I was three years old they were a whisper

away from debtors' prison. My father was desperate. He was walking in the rain, Mama says, and . . . and got sick. She took him to his family, hoping they'd take care of him, and of me. They took the two of us, but my mother . . . they wouldn't even let her in the door."

Lucy's voice cracked, the image of Emily alone and desolate, one of the few that could break Lucy's heart. "When she came back to get me, they showed her the grave."

"Sweet Jesus."

"I don't think Jesus was listening to either my mother or me. She was insane with grief. And I was terrified, alone. It seemed the d'Autrecourts didn't want any inconvenient reminders of their son's mésalliance. The duke gave me to a sea captain to carry away from England forever. I was never even to know my own name."

"How did you ever discover the truth?"

"My mother heard me singing the melody my father composed for me when I was a baby. No one else had ever heard it." The tears were threatening again. Somehow telling the tale to the earl of Valcour was leaving her raw and aching.

"My God, how could Avonstea do such a thing to his own granddaughter? A helpless child?"

"That's partly what I was going to Avonstea to find out." For an instant she considered telling Valcour the rest, pouring out the truth—that Alexander d'Autrecourt might be alive. But Valcour gripped her shoulders, the intensity in his eyes suddenly terrifying.

"You planned to go confront them *alone*? With no one—not even the Wilkeses—having the slightest idea where you had disappeared to?" Blue sparks of fury lit his dark eyes. "Do you have any idea how much danger you would have been in if you had succeeded in this crazed escapade and arrived at their door? The instant the d'Autrecourts knew who you were you would be at their mercy. If they did something so villainous to dispose of you before, who knows what they'd be capable of doing to hide such a heinous deed now."

"I'm not a helpless child anymore, my lord."

"No. You're a fool. A beautiful, brave little fool."

His hand skimmed over her straw-spangled curls, his harsh features filled with something she had never seen in them before. A savage tenderness, fierce outrage. And guilt. Lucy's brow furrowed in astonishment. Why would Valcour feel guilt?

His hands were trembling just a whisper. She felt it to the core of her soul.

"You are my wife now," Valcour bit out, smoothing her hair back from her cheek. "You are the countess of Valcour. They cannot touch you."

It was as if this man—so fiercely arrogant, ruthlessly powerful—were seeking reassurance not for her but, rather, for himself.

He drew away from her, rubbing his fingertips against his eyes. "My God. An empty grave . . . when all these years . . ."

"My lord, did . . ." She paused to suck in a steadying breath, almost afraid to ask. "Even in the Wilkeses' garden the night of the ball, when you saw my father's face, it was as if you had seen it before and it caused you pain."

Valcour turned away from her, and she could feel him drawing deeper into the closed places inside himself.

"Valcour, did you know my father?"

"There was a time I believed that I did."

The cryptic answer made Lucy's fingers tighten their grasp until the ring cut deep into her tender skin. "Tell me. Please. Anything about him. I . . . I can't remember him at all, except through his music."

"He was my music teacher for a time." Lucy sensed

that Valcour was giving her only the barest answers, so much more lying hidden in his simple words.

"It was you! The music was for you. Of course!"

"What?"

"I received a box full of my father's things while I was in Virginia. The miniature, his pocket watch, and a musical score he had written for a Master St. Cyr of Harlestone Castle. It was a gift for your tenth birthday."

"My birthday." Valcour walked to the stone fence, resting one hand on the rough surface. "I remember. In the end, he gave me a far different sort of gift." Bitterness, edged with the echoes of remembered pain.

"Valcour, please. I can tell this is upsetting to you, but since I was a child of ten I've been trying to find the father I lost. You must know something of him that you can share."

Valcour's fist knotted on the wall, and Lucy was stunned to see a smear of blood on his knuckles.

"You've hurt yourself," she said, crossing to where he stood. She took his hand in hers. A sharp edge of stone had bitten into his skin, leaving a small but rather deep gash. Valcour looked as though he didn't feel it at all. Why? Because she had let loose far deeper pain?

A cold veil of foreboding settled about her heart. "Tell me," Lucy demanded. "Whatever it is—"

"Your father is dead, Lucinda. You are alive, by some miracle. Alive. You have his music. Let it be enough."

"I did what you wanted. I married you. I've even agreed to bear a child. Don't you think that you owe me the truth?"

"The truth?" Valcour wheeled on her, the uncharacteristic tenderness she had sensed in him earlier having vanished, leaving the harsh earl made of ice she had known before. "Your father was a mediocre composer at best, with a few rare sputters of brilliance. He was a fool, unable to look in the mirror and see what everyone else knew. That he was as substantial as mist, as naive as a babe in its cradle, and as full of grand delusions as any madman in Bedlam."

Lucy flinched at the venom in his voice. "No. I don't believe you."

"Feel free to dismiss everything I said. After all, you can hardly think that I would be privy to the secrets of a lowly music teacher. Your father's marriage had effectively banished him to the bare fringes of society, while I was the heir to Valcour. The son of one of the most powerful noblemen in England. What possible gateway could an outcast like Alexander d'Autrecourt pass through to enter so deeply into my world?"

His contempt filtered through Lucy's veins, poisoning the fragile empathy she had shared with this man so briefly before. Worse still, his words cut to the quick of her own doubts about her father, left her with raw images of the man in the gaming hell, the stories of the harlot Josy.

Valcour's dismissal of d'Autrecourt as weak blended far too well with the notion that he could still be alive, and the far more unthinkable notion that he had allowed his wife to believe him dead all these years. That he had abandoned his tiny daughter. Why? So that he could retreat once again to the wealth and security of the duke's household?

No. That idea was absurd. Even if Alexander d'Autrecourt had wanted to surrender to his parents' will, erase all memory of his former mistakes, he would not have staged his own death. He could never have entered society again. He would have had to stay hidden away so that no one would discover his guilty secret.

It made no sense. But did an empty grave make any sense? A child cast to the winds of fate? Did the arrival of the mysterious box make any sense, especially after so many years without a single word from England?

Lucy's head throbbed, and she was stung into rising to the defense of the father she had dreamed about for so many years, that figment of her imagination who had been as beautiful inside as the "Night Song" he had left behind.

"My father was a genius in his compositions," Lucy burst out at Valcour. "You were just too much of a blockhead to appreciate his music! Some dolt of a boy dragged to the pianoforte by the scruff of his neck, kicking and screaming. I wager teaching you anything was pure torture."

Valcour's mouth tightened. "Since it is evident that you know everything regarding your father, and regarding me, there is no further need for us to discuss the matter. Except for this: You will not, under any circumstances, contact the d'Autrecourts without my knowledge. Is that understood?"

The tension that had been building inside Lucy from the moment she'd entered the gaming hell that final time was bubbling inside her, all her doubts, her fears, her frustrations dangerously near the surface. "I understand you completely, *my lord*. Please be informed that I am going to Avonstea the instant I can hire something to ride."

"The bloody hell you are."

"What are you going to do? Skewer me the way you did Sir Jasper? Knock me senseless the way you did Aubrey? Your knuckles are tender, remember? And murdering your bride half an hour after the wedding could prove rather awkward to explain."

"You don't have the slightest idea the kind of people you are dealing with."

"Don't I? I was the one stolen away from my mother! I was the one cast aside like a pair of slippers that pinched! There is a grave in their family cemetery with *my* name on it. I'll be damned before I let those sadistic, selfish, pompous sons of Satan sit in their accursed castle and pretend that I never existed!"

There were years of anguish in those furious words,

and pain that Lucy thought she had buried long before. Her fists knotted, and she wanted to hit something— anything. Preferably the man standing as stony and implacable as cliffs beaten by a raging sea.

He was silent for a long moment, his gaze so hot, so intense, it seemed it must melt her flesh away.

"So be it," he said at last. "But when you confront your demons, it will be as the countess of Valcour, with me at your side."

Dominic stared into her dawn-kissed features, features more bold and courageous than those of any man he'd ever faced across a dueling field, more lovely than spring's first violet, cupped in a white lacing of snow.

And he wondered if his new bride could possibly know that she hadn't just cast forth her own demons to be purged. She had flung open the portal to the earl of Valcour's private hell.

10

*B*utter-colored slats of sunlight pierced the windows in the private parlor at the Hound's Tooth, glittering on the remains of Dominic's half-eaten breakfast. He grimaced, acknowledging that it was damned difficult to fill your stomach when you were about to break a seventeen-year-old's heart.

Aubrey stood on the other side of the room, looking as if he'd been dragged down Fleet Street beneath his horse's belly. Lank wheat-colored hair straggled about his puffy face, his skin the color of dirt-smudged paste. There was a decidedly greenish cast about his lips, and his eyes were feverish pools above the clumsily tied cravat.

But in spite of the evidence of last night's drunken spree, there was a certain quality of maturity about Aubrey that Dominic had never seen before. As if the boy had been able to muster all that was best in himself in order to champion Lucinda Blackheath. No, Valcour corrected himself. Lucinda St. Cyr, wife of the earl of Valcour.

Dominic took a drink of scalding hot coffee, his gaze studiously avoiding the purpling bruise that shadowed Aubrey's jaw. He gestured to the chair opposite him. "Sit down, boy, before you fall down."

"I prefer to stand." Aubrey's bloodshot gaze skittered with pure revulsion across the remains of runny egg yolk swimming in a pool of steak juice. "I only came down here to tell you that nothing has changed since last night. I still intend to marry Lucy as soon as possible."

"That may prove a trifle difficult," Dominic said slowly, turning the coffee cup in his hand. "You see, the lady in question is already wed."

"Wed?" Aubrey echoed hoarsely. "What the devil?"

"It seems she preferred becoming a countess to being the wife of a scapegrace boy."

Valcour thought he had prepared himself for the expression on his brother's face. The reality was far more disquieting.

"You didn't!" the boy cried in disbelief. "Lucy wouldn't have . . . have married . . . She despises you! I know she does!"

"She would not be the first woman seduced by a title."

"I don't believe you! I'll see her at once!" Aubrey wheeled, obviously intending to charge out the door.

"That would be rather awkward, brother. My countess is currently making her toilette for our bridal trip. I would assume she is in the bath I ordered up for her an hour ago. Of course, she might be able to flash her ring at you above the rim of the tub."

"You can't be wed! There wasn't time! Barely eight hours have passed since you arrived!"

"It is astonishing what an earldom can do to reduce such minor complications. The bishop of Lothshire was only too happy to accommodate me with a special license. And of course, officiating at the wedding of the earl of Valcour is a great honor."

The boy was ghost white. "Why, Dominic? Why would you wed her when I told you . . . I *told you I loved her, damn it!*"

"From all reports, you were in love with a French opera dancer a month ago," Valcour said, flicking an imaginary crumb from the lace at his wrist. "The fortunate thing about adolescent hearts is that they are astonishingly resilient. I predict you will forget Lucinda before the month is out."

"Forget her?" Aubrey was trembling with rage. "She's mine, damn you! Mine! You can't have her!"

"Aubrey, we are not children squabbling over some plaything."

"Don't you dare mock me! I won't let you make her miserable! She's far too fine and brave and beautiful for a cold-hearted bastard like you!"

Valcour's fingers tightened around the cup. "You are right in that. She is far above my touch. But there are times even we cold-hearted bastards get more than we deserve. She is the countess of Valcour. There is nothing you can do to change that."

"I can make her a widow, by God!" Aubrey's eyes were wild, desperate, as he fumbled with the dress sword at his side. The blade rattled as he stripped it from the scabbard. "Damn your hide, Dom, you *will* fight me! Draw steel!"

Valcour took a meditative sip of coffee. "The only weapon I have at the moment is a rather bent fork. I think it would be a most inglorious way to die."

With a cry of rage, Aubrey flung a chair out of his way, the steel tip of his sword brushing the frothy lace of Dominic's neckcloth. The lethal point trembled, tearing the delicate web.

Valcour's gaze locked with Aubrey's desperate one, not so much as an eyelash betraying the fact that a blade was mere inches away from his heart.

"Are you going to kill me, boy?" Valcour asked softly.

"You betrayed me! You forced Lucy to wed you! I know that you did! The world will be well rid of you!"

"Then plunge the blade home. Think of the hero you'll be, saving a beleaguered heroine from your wicked brother."

The weapon was shaking more wildly, tearing at the linen of his shirt. Dominic made no move to lean away from the point of the sword. His eyes never left Aubrey's tortured face.

"I hate you!" the boy almost sobbed.

"I know. But are you capable of driving that blade through my heart?"

Sweat trickled down Aubrey's temples, his breath coming in harsh gasps. "You deserve to die for what you've done!"

"You have my permission to send me to hell." Valcour's gaze never left Aubrey's face. The boy's lips were quivering, ragged sobs rising in his chest. "Do it, boy," Valcour murmured.

Seconds spun out into eternity—an eternity of agony in Aubrey's eyes, an eternity of watching him battle inside himself only to discover that he hadn't the will to drive the blade home.

After a long moment, Dominic took up his napkin and dabbed at his lips. "I don't mind being murdered in the middle of breakfast, as long as it is done expediently. However, you know how impatient I am with delays. I'm afraid you will have to kill me some other time."

He reached out, pushing aside the blade with the wadded-up piece of linen. A sob racked Aubrey's whole body as Dominic disengaged the weapon from his hand.

The earl placed it on the table.

"Aubrey." The mockery was gone from Valcour's voice. "I know you won't believe me now, but driving the blade home would not have made you more of a man. Lucinda is my wife. This whole miserable affair is over."

Valcour rubbed the stiff muscles in his shoulder,

feeling jaded and weary and old beyond his years. "I have put the finest coach available for hire at your disposal. I would suggest you go to London by way of Lord Norton's estate. It is widely known you've had your eye on the team of matched grays he has been bragging about. Feel free to purchase them at once. Tell Norton I have no concern about their price."

"You think you can just dangle a new trinket in front of me and I'll forget her?" Tears were running down the boy's face. "I'll never forget! Never!"

"Long memories have always been the curse of the St. Cyrs," Dominic said quietly. "Why should you be spared?"

It was an hour after Aubrey's coach had rattled out of the inn yard that Dominic found his new countess, not in her bath, or taking air in the inn's garden, but in the stable, crooning over Ashlar.

Dominic watched her from the shadows, where she couldn't see him. The mask of defiance was stripped from her lovely features; the wild hoyden girl, so brash, so reckless, looked distressingly vulnerable, where no one but the gelding could see her.

She was dressed in a simple gown of white muslin, touches of rose embroidery along the neckline of the bodice seeming to have stolen all the color from her cheeks. The smudges had been scrubbed from her flawless skin, and her hair had been washed and brushed until it shone like a coronet of gold. Her hand glided down the horse's black nose, the light filtering through the window making the rubies in her wedding ring glow like fire.

But it was her eyes that made Dominic's heart trip. Eyes filled with grief in an unguarded moment of quiet despair. Could he have expected anything else?

He had told Aubrey there were women who could be seduced by a title, and God knows, Dominic had met more than his share of those who would have bartered away their soul to be countess of Valcour. But this young woman, as proud and strong and brave as the goddess Athena herself, cared nothing for the prestige his name could bring her. Cared nothing for him at all.

Why was it that the knowledge twisted something tight about Dominic's heart?

"The people here will take wondrous good care of you while I'm away," Lucinda said to the beast, laying her cheek against its glossy neck. "I've told the groom that you are to have nothing but the finest oats to eat, and that he is to put the poultices on your poor leg every three hours. I know you dislike the smell of the herbs, but they will take the pain away."

The gelding nibbled at the end of one of her ribbons.

Dominic's throat tightened as the sunlight revealed a sheen of moisture in those incredible blue eyes. "I'm a countess now," Lucinda said in a choked voice. "Everyone must do as I say."

There was something heart-wrenching in those simple words. She didn't bemoan her fate or rail about the circumstances that had brought her to this pass. Dominic wanted to cross the straw-strewn space between them and draw her into his arms. Tell her that she could ask to put a diamond collar about the moon and he would see that it was done, if it would only drive the shadows from her eyes.

Instead, he moved soundlessly backward, then, after a moment, reentered the stable, making so much noise they probably heard him a county away.

It was a far different Lucinda who faced him as he strode toward her. Her neck arched proudly, her lips firm, her blue eyes frosted like winter-kissed meadow flowers. "I wanted to be certain the horse would be cared for. The servants said that Aubrey left before I had finished my bath. He must have forgotten all about Ashlar."

"He was on his way to look over a new team of grays. If it would please you to take this horse off his hands, I doubt he would raise much objection."

"And what objection did he raise to my becoming your wife?"

Her gaze was unforgiving, and Valcour squirmed inwardly, feeling as if the ugly scene in the parlor was reflected in his eyes.

"He was not pleased. But I trust he will recover in time."

She said nothing.

"Lucinda, there is a coach waiting to carry us away from this place. I have an estate called Harlestone a day's travel away from here. It will be a suitable place for us to stay while you rebuild your strength."

"You agreed to take me to Avonstea."

"I can see no reason to go charging off—"

"I could see no reason we should marry. But here I stand, wearing your ring."

"I will honor my promise to take you to the d'Autrecourts," Valcour said. "I just think it would be wise for you to wait a little while, recover from the . . . excitement of all that has happened the past day."

"I've been waiting to confront the d'Autrecourts since I was ten years old. I'm not willing to wait any longer. Valcour, I want this first meeting with them over with. Can you understand?"

Dominic closed his eyes, remembering a fifteen-year-old boy who had left his father's fresh grave to challenge the enemies of Valcour.

He was silent, long minutes that seemed to spin out for much longer. For the first time that he could remember, the earl of Valcour bowed to the desires of someone other than himself.

"It shall be as you wish," he said.

* * *

From the time Lucy was ten years old, her nightmare had had a name. Avonstea. The ducal seat of the d'Autrecourts, the grand mansion to which her desperate mother had gone to plead for help for her dying husband and starving child.

A hundred times Lucy had tried to dredge an image of the grand estate from the dark recesses of her mind. But it was forever lost to her, like the sound of her father's voice, the image of his face. She had filled in the gaps in her memory by picturing the grand estate in her head, imagining it to be some dark, hideous place. Grim stone walls, mortared with the ground-up bones of any who dared defy the mighty aristocratic dynasty. A carriage drive of sharp rocks that led to walls guarded by grotesque gargoyles, and hollow-cheeked servants with their tongues carved out so they couldn't tell the d'Autrecourts' evil secrets.

But as Lucy stared out the coach's window to where Avonstea rose in palatial splendor, it hardly seemed possible that such a beautiful place could be the lair of a villain.

Lucy swallowed hard, her gaze flitting suddenly to the massive bronze lion that stood guard beside the d'Autrecourts' door. Slivers of memories pierced her, echoes of her childish screams reawakening inside her. She had been terrified of the lion's fangs, the feel of someone's arms dragging her away from her mother. She could hear her mother sobbing as she stumbled down this very road, leaving Lucy behind.

I'll come back for you . . . I'll come back . . .

But her mama hadn't come back. Lucy remembered waiting and waiting, her face pressed against the window. She had screamed all night. Screamed and screamed until her throat was raw and her eyes felt like fire from crying. A woman had come then, her face like carved ice above a gown glittering with jewels. Lucy could remember that face staring down at her with loathing. She could feel the crack of the woman's hand against her cheek, the bite of a ring cutting Lucy's tender skin.

You'll never see her again! the woman had vowed. *She'll not have even the smallest part of my son.*

Lucy shuddered, stunned by the clarity of the memory, all the emotions of the terrified child she had been pulsing through her with a power that made her tremble, made her throat close.

She had expected to march up the stairs to Avonstea like a conquering warrior, haughty, scornful. She hadn't expected her stomach to be threatening rebellion, or her mind to be suddenly struck with a craven impulse to turn the coach around and flee down the road faster than she'd come.

She curled her fingers into the folds of her dress in an effort to steady herself, but at that moment the image of the bronze lion was blocked from view by Valcour astride his magnificent stallion. For hours the earl had ridden as if he were a pagan god of thunder astride the fiercest storm, his cloak streaming out behind him, his sinewy thighs flexing about the stallion's gleaming saddle.

She had been grateful beyond belief when he'd chosen to ride instead of make the trip in the close confines of the hired coach with her. But much as she hated to acknowledge it now, she was also glad to see those stalwart shoulders, those fiercely intense eyes as she teetered on the brink of her mystery-shrouded past.

The door opened, but it was not the postilion who offered his hand to help her down. Her new husband reached into the coach, his hands spanning her waist as he lightly drifted her down onto the ground.

Lucy kept her gaze fixed on the diamond stickpin in his neckcloth and tried to keep her knees from knocking together.

"You're ash pale," he said, crooking his finger beneath her chin and turning her face up to his.

Lucy gave a sick little laugh. "I suppose that's to be expected. After all, I am a ghost."

"You're no ghost, Lucinda." His voice was as bracing as a blazing fire after wandering lost in a blizzard. He rubbed the tips of his fingers against the ridge of first one cheekbone, then the other, as if trying to coax color into the skin. "You are a strong, brave, beautiful woman who has come to confront the people who tried to destroy you. Remember how helpless you were, Lucinda. At their mercy. Remember what they did to you. As God is my witness, I'll not forget."

Lucy was stunned by the fierce protectiveness in those ebony-lashed eyes. Never in her twenty years had Lucinda Blackheath leaned on someone else's strength. Now Lucinda St. Cyr slipped her hand into the crook of her new husband's arm as they mounted the stairs.

A footman in scarlet livery opened the door, his gaze flicking over Lucy with patent scorn before he glanced at Valcour.

The sight of the earl affected the servant as if a tidal wave had just crashed over the man's head. "M-My lord Valcour," the servant stammered. "You are not welcome here."

"My wife desires to be presented to his grace of Avonstea and his mother, the dowager duchess."

The servant tugged at his neckcloth. "The d-duke? He is something of a recluse, as you know. And at present, he is—is . . . unavailable. As for her grace, the dowager duchess cannot be expected to tolerate the company of the man who nearly murdered her son."

"The devotion and family loyalty of the d'Autrecourts has always been a source of . . . amazement to me," Valcour began, but Lucy stepped forward, her chin held high.

"The dowager duchess will receive me."

"Who are you?"

"Her granddaughter."

"Her grace has no living grandchild."

Lucy allowed a chill smile to play about her lips. "Then I must have risen from the dead. Tell her grace that Jenny has come home."

The servant glanced from Lucy to Valcour's implacable face, then cleared his throat. "I will inform her grace of your arrival, but I cannot guarantee that she will see you. If you would care to wait in the silver drawing room." He gestured for them to follow. Lucy stepped into the chamber indicated.

Sunshine illuminated French wallpaper on which shepherdesses had been painted, their crooks dangling from elegant fingers, while sheep frolicked about their feet. Porcelain candlesticks carried through the theme, ruddy-cheeked boys playing flutes for their ladies, rapt smiles painted on their china faces.

She stepped over to touch an exquisite gold box that was lost among a dozen other trinkets on a small table. "Do you know that the value of this box could have kept my parents warm and safe and fed for more than a year? I can't imagine what it must have been like for my mother to come here, to beg . . . beg in an effort to save my father and me."

"I am certain it was the most difficult thing she had ever done," Valcour said.

"No. The most difficult thing was the moment she walked away from me. Left me here, while she . . . she wandered away with nowhere to go, no means to feed herself. She was willing to sacrifice all for me."

"It is one of the great tragedies of all mothers, I think," Valcour said quietly.

"I prefer to consider it a triumph. My mother is the most gentle person I have ever known. And the bravest. I always wanted to be like her, but . . ." Lucy shrugged. "I don't have the strength to meet adversity with her quiet courage. Instead I kick it in the teeth."

"If you aim for adversity's teeth, Lucinda, I can say from personal experience it should consider itself most fortunate." Valcour hesitated for a moment, his eyes flicking impatiently to the door.

Lucy paced into the block of sunshine shaped by the window, an alcove partitioned off from the remainder of the room by a blue velvet curtain. Instinctively, Lucy glanced behind the fabric partition, her breath whooshing out in a gasp as she caught a glimpse of something half hidden in the shadows.

Her hand whisked back the curtain, the light spreading in a glistening pool over the polished wood surface of a pianoforte.

A crewel-work chair embroidered with the three muses was positioned as if begging someone to sit down, while the keys of the instrument drew Lucy's fingers as inexorably as the poisoned spindle had tempted the fingers of the sleeping beauty in the fairy tale.

Had this been the instrument at which her father had picked out his first awkward notes? At which he had first been struck by the beauty of the pianoforte's soul and been compelled to try to release it so that others might hear that beauty themselves?

Lucy could feel Valcour's eyes upon her, but she couldn't stop herself from sliding into the chair, her fingers curving over the keys, touching them gently, lovingly. A misty, melancholy sound rippled out.

She hadn't touched an instrument since leaving left Blackheath Hall, and the music was like the caress of a long-lost lover, the warm embrace of a trusted friend.

The tiniest sound made Lucy freeze, turn to see Valcour watching her, a terrible stillness in his face, his eyes holding the silent torment of a man feeling the ropes of the dreaded rack tighten about his wrists and ankles.

She had entered this house with a hundred childhood

fears clustered around her. But she was far more frightened by the expression on Valcour's face at this instant.

"Wh-what is it? Valcour, I . . ."

Her stammered query was lost in the sound of the drawing-room door opening, the footman standing aside with a flourish. "Her grace, the dowager duchess of Avonstea."

Lucy had always imagined that the unspeakable crime the dowager duchess had committed would somehow be inscribed on her face—harsh lines and thin lips, narrow eyes and a squat neck. But the woman enthroned in an invalid's wheeled chair seemed as if she had cast dice with the devil himself and won eternal youth.

Flawless skin was pulled with astonishing suppleness over a bone structure that would have done a Grecian statue proud. Her eyes were disconcertingly like those Lucy saw in the mirror every morning, except that where Lucy's were filled with restless energy, the duchess's were filled with cool disdain.

Her grace of Avonstea waited until the footman had shut the door behind her, then she turned to Lucy, the fury in her eyes a living thing. "Who are you, and what do you want?"

"I am Jenny d'Autrecourt, Alexander d'Autrecourt's daughter," Lucy said. "Your granddaughter."

"Jenny d'Autrecourt has been dead for seventeen years! You are a craven impostor! If you've come to cause trouble, I vow to you the might of Avonstea will crush you!"

"Perhaps you might have been able to do so yesterday, your grace," the earl's voice cut in icily. "However, I would not recommend distressing the lady further unless Avonstea cares to cross swords with me."

"You—you who cut down Jasper!"

"I spared his life. But I promise you that if there are any further attempts of violence against this girl, I will show no mercy." Even Lucy was stunned at the virulence of his words. "She is the countess of Valcour," the earl said. "My wife."

Wife. The proprietary emphasis he placed on the word "wife" filled Lucy with an odd sensation of disappointment. Of course he would care for his wife, in much the same way he would care for his horses: see her fed and housed with a good measure of grain and given the respect due one connected to the mighty earl.

"This woman has played you for a fool, Valcour," the dowager duchess accused. "She is nothing to me. Not a drop of d'Autrecourt blood runs in her veins. I swear it, or may Satan himself take my soul."

"An interesting prospect," Valcour said. "However, in my estimation, your spirit is so vile that even Lucifer would shun you. To steal a child from her mother. To cast aside an innocent girl because of your own selfish pride is the most despicable crime imaginable."

Blue veins stood out starkly against the dowager duchess's pale skin. "How dare you accuse—"

Lucy stepped forward, meeting the old woman's gaze with her own. "My mother found me in Virginia twelve years ago, where she married the patriot Raider Pendragon."

The dowager duchess's eyes widened.

"I'm certain you remember, Grandmama. You were trying to have her murdered at the time, so she could never discover your treachery."

The old woman gasped, her lips curling back from her teeth in a feral snarl. "How dare you come here spouting your lies?"

Lucy met her gaze levelly. "I come by invitation."

The dowager duchess's fingers clenched about the wheels of her chair. "You're mad!"

"Am I?" Lucy watched her intently. "Someone sent me a box filled with my father's belongings three months ago. Someone wrote me *this.*"

Lucy slipped her hand into her reticule and extracted

the cryptic poem she had received in Virginia. The noblewoman imperiously snatched it from her hand.

"Lucinda," Valcour's voice cut in. "What the devil—"

"I received a box with the miniature in it, a watch, and some music my father had written. I told you—"

"You told me you had received a box of your father's things. I assumed your mother had given it to you, that they were some keepsakes she had saved."

"My mother had nothing left of my father's. She'd pawned everything in an effort to feed us, didn't she, Grandmama?" Lucy's voice dripped with loathing, her eyes never leaving the duchess's face.

The woman's gaze slashed dismissively down the elegant script, and for a moment Lucy expected her to crumple the page up and throw it away. Instead, those blue eyes widened in shock.

Georgianna d'Autrecourt's hand trembled. "Where did you get this?"

"I have told you. It arrived three months ago in Virginia. It was directed to Miss Lucinda Blackheath on the outside of the package. But inside . . . inside were notes to Jenny d'Autrecourt."

"No. I don't believe . . ." The dowager duchess turned away, shaken. "He could not have . . . have sent . . ."

"He? Who is *he?* My father?"

"Your father is dead!" Valcour let fly a disbelieving oath and snatched the missive from the duchess's fingers.

"People have a strange way of coming back to life in this family," Lucy flung back. "Now Grandmama, I want to know who sent this to me."

"Surely you can't believe it was anyone here! You are supposed to be buried in the family crypt! That Blackheath person who found you threatened to expose the whole tale of your abduction if we ever dared approach you again! After all these years, why would we attempt to contact you?"

"I don't know. All I know is that I did as the letter instructed. I went to the gaming hell to meet with this . . . this man, whoever he was. I saw him there. But circumstances were such that I didn't get a chance to talk to him. Now he's disappeared, and I don't know where to find him."

"Find him . . . yes. Someone must . . ." The dowager duchess seemed to forcibly steady her hands. "He is a dangerous madman masquerading as my son."

"My God." It was Valcour's voice, almost sickened with disbelief. When he raised his face to Lucy's, what she saw there made her stomach twist into knots. "Damn you, girl, I expected the truth! Why didn't you tell me—"

"This is my affair. It's none of your concern."

"You're my wife! Being stalked by some insane maniac posing as your father!"

"He might *be* my father."

"No! Alexander died of fever," the duchess said. "I buried him in his blue frockcoat, the one he wore when he was presented at court. We slipped his signet ring from his finger, and the watch that I had given him on his sixteenth birthday . . ."

"This watch?" Lucy withdrew the timepiece from her pocket and dropped it into the duchess's lap. The woman's fingers closed convulsively about it.

"Dear God, he must know . . ." She cut off her statement, her eyes chilling, her face falling into icy lines.

"Know what?" Lucy demanded. "Tell me—"

"Philip!" the dowager duchess cried out, the footman racing in at her command. "Take these . . . these people away from me! Take them away!"

"No!" Lucy dropped to her knees before the old woman and clutched her birdlike hands. "I'm not leaving until you tell me what you know! Is my father alive? Blast it, is he—"

The duchess tore at Lucy's grasp, trying to free herself,

when suddenly the old woman's eyes locked on Lucy's hand, the glittering circlet of rubies gleaming on her finger.

"Why don't you demand your answer of *this?*" The duchess twisted the ring until Lucy gave a gasp of pain. "The legend says that it can tell you all you need to know."

"Legend?" Lucy asked. "What . . ."

"The legend of the magic ring. Surely that empty-headed mother of yours must have told you. It has been the mystic love token of the d'Autrecourts since the Middle Ages."

"There must be some mistake. I didn't receive it from my mother. Unless she pawned it and . . ." Lucy glanced at Valcour, her heart stopping at the expression on his face.

It was as if she were staring into a shattered mirror, reflecting horror, anguish. Stark betrayal.

"Valcour, I . . ."

"You will see the earl and his . . . countess out," the duchess commanded the footman. "They shall never be allowed to enter this house again."

Lucy started to protest, but Valcour stalked to where she stood, his hand closing in a bruising grasp about her arm.

"No! Let me go! I have to find out!"

Valcour all but dragged her out into the wide entryway and down the stairs. He flung her up on his stallion, then mounted behind her, his arms like steel bands encircling her as he drove his heels into the horse's sides.

Lucy struggled for a heartbeat, swearing, clawing at him, but as the stallion raced at breakneck speed across the countryside, self-preservation won out over her fury.

The hills blurred, stone fences became wisps of gray beneath the stallion as he leapt them effortlessly, in spite of his heavy load.

Lucy's chin bumped the steely muscles of Valcour's

arm and she bit her tongue, tasting blood. The whole world seemed a whirling mass of color and emotion, fury and confusion. When the horse was suddenly reined to a shuddering halt, Lucy felt as if she were still hurtling through space.

Valcour shoved her from the horse, and she stumbled, grabbing the nearest solid object to regain her balance. Thorns sliced her palm, as velvety petals were crushed between her hand and a rough-carved block of stone.

She fell to her knees before it, her eyes focusing on a crude yet beautiful angel etched into what looked to be a tombstone lost in a tangle of rose vines. She pulled away a mass of blossoms to read the inscription.

Jenny d'Autrecourt, sleep, beloved angel . . .

Lucy couldn't keep from staggering to her feet, backing away. She slammed full force into Valcour's solid chest.

"Damn you, are you insane?" Lucy rounded on him, sick horror reverberating through her.

"Only temporarily. I should have known better than to trust a d'Autrecourt. But I'll not be deceived another moment. You will tell me everything! Every goddamn thing you know about this madness. Alexander d'Autrecourt—alive? Alive!"

For a heartbeat Lucy was truly frightened by what she saw in his face. "I don't know anymore than what I told you and the duchess back at Avonstea," she said, groping for something, anything, to use to regain her mental balance. "But perhaps we should ask my wedding ring for the answers, *my lord*—this legendary love token of the d'Autrecourts."

For an instant, Lucy thought Valcour would strike her.

"Take it off," Valcour snarled.

"It's my wedding ring, remember? The one you forced onto my finger? Exactly how did you come by it, *my lord?* And why does it make you look as if you want to murder me."

"You're not the one I'm tempted to throttle."

"Then who is?"

Valcour slammed his fist into the more impressive monument that rose up behind Jenny d'Autrecourt's small marker. "A ghost. A goddamn ghost that will give me no peace!"

Lord Alexander d'Autrecourt, Lucy read the letters carved in stone. *Died of fever . . .*

"Damn him!" Valcour raged. "Hasn't he taken enough already? I'd sell my soul to the devil to be free."

Lucy stared into eyes that were black pools of agony, a face as tormented as that of Lancelot when Guinevere was sentenced to the flames. But what flames were searing the earl of Valcour now? Torturing him until Lucy was certain he would gladly have exchanged them for the devil's own?

And why did she feel as if she were being sucked down into the inferno at his side?

11

$\mathcal{T}$he crofters called Harlestone the Castle of Sorrow, claiming that it was haunted by a Saxon lord who had laid a curse on the bold French chevalier who had stolen his land.

But Dominic had always believed that there was a far more logical reason for the castle's dismal history. One that had nothing to do with ghosts or curses.

Rather, it had to do with the corrupt nature of the St. Cyrs themselves. Arrogant, greedy, with a pronounced streak of cruelty, they had brought sorrow down upon themselves by their own actions, generation after generation.

Somehow it seemed fitting that Dominic had brought his new bride here, to spend their wedding night among a hundred silent reminders of other St. Cyr disasters.

For despite the battle Dominic had waged to escape the St. Cyr legacy, he had added his own chapter to the tradition of infamy by forcing this unwilling girl to be his wife. But Lucinda had had her own revenge. For through her Alexander d'Autrecourt's hand had reached out from the grave, dragging Dominic toward the past he had buried so long before, and there was nothing he could do to stop it.

Dominic raked his fingers through the dark masses of his hair, his eyes gritty with exhaustion as he sat at the desk in the dim study that lay in the deepest reaches of the castle.

At Avonstea, Dominic had threatened the dowager duchess with the might of Valcour. Now that daunting might would be turned to another task: searching out the hell-spawned bastard who had written the letter to Lucinda and sent her the mysterious box. The madman who believed he was Alexander d'Autrecourt.

Dominic capped his inkwell and shoved the chunks of sealing wax aside. He had done everything possible tonight. He had placed Lucinda in the capable hands of Harlestone's housekeeper. Then he had barred himself in this room. He had worked for hours, drafting letters, sending the swiftest messengers he could find to carry those letters to London to alert his most trusted hirelings to the problem. He had let the dowager duchess know that any attempt to harm Lucy would result in calamity for the d'Autrecourts. He had instructed his solicitor to spare no expense in searching for information at Perdition's Gate.

He had confronted this crisis with the same determined resolve with which he had faced a dozen other challenges in his life. The one thing he had not done was face the possibility that Alexander d'Autrecourt might truly be alive.

What a hellish possibility. If there were the remotest chance that it were true, wasn't there one more letter Dominic should write? One more person he should alert to the possibility?

He closed his eyes, picturing his mother as he had last seen her, half out of her mind with worry in Camilla's drawing room. Lady Catherine's delicate features had been savaged by her anguish. Her hands had shaken, clutching Dominic's shirtfront, as if pleading for strength.

How could he send a letter to the Valcour town-house in London? Tell her . . . what? That the security he had worked so hard to give her had been an illusion? That their secret was no longer safe? If Alexander d'Autrecourt were alive, he could destroy all that Dominic had fought for. Destroy Aubrey, his mother, and the beautiful, innocent young woman who was even now waiting in the great bedchamber for a husband who had forced his ring upon her finger.

No, not *his* ring. Bitterness seethed inside him, a fierce sense of betrayal surging through his body. Even that circlet of rubies was tainted by d'Autrecourt's poison.

And she had known. His mother had known.

Dominic sat down again and took up the quill. *Tell her all*, a savage voice inside him said. *She deserves to suffer with the truth after what she did.*

Valcour dipped the point of the pen into the ink, then wrote: *My lady, Alexander d'Autrecourt may be alive, a circumstance that might prove rather awkward for you, considering the fact that his ring is now on my bride's finger.*

Dominic rended the paper to bits, then stalked to the fire and hurled the scraps into the flames. How could he condemn his mother to such an agony of uncertainty, no matter what she had done?

There was no way of knowing for certain if Alexander d'Autrecourt was alive. No way of being sure that the grave on the windswept hill was empty. Unless . . .

Valcour stilled, his eyes flashing to the window. The stars were just beginning to appear, bloodless wounds in the underbelly of night. And for a heartbeat, it seemed as if the shadows themselves were waiting, testing the earl of Valcour, to see how far he had fallen from grace.

Valcour's jaw tightened. How could he even contemplate such an act? He had battled so hard for his honor, had struggled to hold it through countless storms. And he had done so, damn it! He had.

But how could he risk not knowing what lay inside that grave? Images swam before Dominic: Lady Catherine's features, so bruised by sadness. Aubrey's tear-streaked face at the inn, anguished, broken. And Lucinda, facing her cruel grandmother with such regal courage. The visions were thrust away by another, more vivid one—that of a fifteen-year-old boy, lashed by rain, a sword clutched in his hand while he faced the man he had trusted, cared about . . . the man who had betrayed him.

Blue eyes haunted Dominic, stricken, agony-filled eyes. God, how he had wanted death to close them forever. To see those eyes, robbed of flesh, vacant sockets staring into nothingness. To see the hands that had glided over the pianoforte's keys with such grace, now tiny bones, crumbling to dust. How could he face that?

Dominic's fists clenched. How could he refuse to do so? He had to make certain the nightmare begun so many years before was over. The unspeakable act he would commit tonight was necessary, damn it. Inevitable.

He shoved himself to his feet and stalked from the study.

A bright-eyed footman sprang to attention in the corridor. "May I be of service to my lord?" the youth asked with great eagerness.

"You are new here, are you not?"

"I'm Randolph Jarvis's son, my lord. Worked here since my pap's died three years ago. Sure'n you must remember you hired me an' my brother Tim, my lord? Saved us all from the poorhouse, my mama said. Course, you've not been to the castle since, so I could thank you myself."

"Do you know how to keep your mouth shut, boy?"

"I be the soul of discretion, my lord. You can wager your last groat on it."

"I am going to make a far greater gamble than that. I have a most important errand to accomplish, and I need two strong, trustworthy men to help me."

"Randolph Jarvis's sons be ready to help you, my lord."

"Then fetch your brother and get a brace of spades. Meet me by the stable in half an hour."

"Spades? I don't understand."

"You will continue to be baffled, from the beginning to the end of this escapade, and beyond. It is my wish."

The youth shrugged. "Whatever you say, my lord. I'd dig clear down to the devil hisself to repay you for what you did for us."

"You won't have to dig quite that far," Valcour said, then watched as the boy hurried down the hall.

Valcour watched him go, then drafted a quick note.

Lucinda,
   You shall be spared my company at dinner this evening. The castle is in ill repair. You will remain in the suite of rooms assigned to you.
                   Dominic St. Cyr, Earl of Valcour

He found a ruddy-cheeked maid and pressed the note into her hand. "You will give this to the countess at once."

"Aye, my lord." The girl regarded his cloak. "I know it's not my place to be warning you, my lord. But have a care. There are brigands about."

"It would be a relief to match swords with a brigand," Valcour muttered. At least then he would have a chance to best his enemy with the clean, fierce clash of steel.

It would be far more difficult to defeat the foe he was confronting tonight.

For no matter what Dominic found when he pried open the lid of the coffin, his actions would quite possibly be testimony that Alexander d'Autrecourt had triumphed over him at last.

Lucy wandered the deserted corridors like a restless spirit, her nightshift flowing in ghostly ripples to skim the bare arches of her feet. The branch of candles in her hand nipped at the shadows, backing them into the corners as she passed.

Midnight had fled, chasing the last of Valcour's servants to their own feather ticks. But the elegant bed designated as Lucy's own might as well have been made of thorns for all the rest she had found upon it.

She had been so tired. Yet every time she'd closed her eyes, images had risen to haunt her. Valcour's face, tormented, enraged. The duchess's eyes, filled with hatred. Lions with bronze teeth bared. And a crude angel hidden beneath the rose vines Lucy's grieving mother had planted so long before.

She had battled the anguish those images stirred up inside her, had chafed at the curt, dismissive note Valcour had sent to her earlier that evening, commanding her to remain in the rooms "assigned" to her.

God knew, she should have been relieved that he was leaving her alone for the time being. The last thing she wanted to face right then was spending a wedding night in the arms of her husband. Or was she fooling herself?

Lucy couldn't stifle the tiny thrill of anticipation at the nape of her neck. Valcour was all but a stranger to her, and yet he was also the most fascinating, enigmatic man she had ever met. A man who had kissed her until her bones turned molten, her breasts had ached, heavy, needing. A man whose dark eyes simmered with passions, the hottest of sensual fires trapped behind a sheet of ice.

He was her husband. Their joining was inevitable, necessary to get the heir he needed. Yet she would be lying to herself if she didn't admit that the idea of sharing Valcour's bed lured her thoughts, time and again, like a moth to flames.

Beneath Valcour's skilled hands there would be no room for doubts or fears. He would drive away everything, Lucy sensed, immersing himself in the woman he was pleasuring with the same primal intensity that radiated from every muscle in his hard-sculpted body.

This was insane, Lucy thought, dragging her thoughts away from images of Valcour's sun-bronzed body against white sheets, his sinewy hands skating over her pale skin. She didn't really want him . . . need him that way. She was just naturally curious. And she had always been desperately impatient when it came to surprises, peeking beneath wrappings, searching through clothes presses and under beds for gifts at Christmastime.

It was no wonder that she viewed the consummation of this marriage the same way. Her mother had always insisted that the consummation of a relationship with someone she truly loved was the most beautiful experience a woman could have. That it was nothing to be ashamed of or to fear. That it was to be savored, delighted in.

Yet Lucy did not love Valcour. And the earl had made it quite clear that she was an unavoidable annoyance, upsetting his well-ordered existence. It was best if she remembered that.

Lucy grimaced. Why was she even thinking of such things at all? Only because she felt out of balance after the confrontation at the scene of her childhood nightmare. It had left her raw and vulnerable and aching. Desperately in need of something to divert her thoughts. But there were far safer distractions than thinking of the marriage bed. A bracing argument would be delightful, or a biting exchange of wits to remind her that she had left helpless Jenny behind on the windswept hill and had found brash Lucy once again.

When she could endure tossing and turning no longer, Lucy had climbed from bed and gone to the exquisite desk in the corner of the chamber, where she found the writing supplies she needed. There she had tried a dozen times to compose the letter she knew she must send to Virginia.

Dearest Mama and Papa, I am a countess now . . .

But no matter how she tried to phrase the news of her marriage, no matter how she attempted to hide her misery, every stroke of the pen reminded her of the hard truth that Blackheath Hall would never be her home again. She would never slip into her blue drawing room in the middle of the night to play a song she had dreamed of upon her beloved pianoforte. She would never climb out her bedchamber window and perch in the crook of her oak tree's branches to watch the sun come up.

Mama, I miss you so much. Papa, I'm sorry . . . so sorry I've made such a mess of things. . . .

No, she couldn't burden them with the truth of her situation. The tale of Pendragon and his lady was still one of the most renowned romances in all Virginia. How could two people who had risked everything for love understand what Lucy had done?

They had never wanted anything but her happiness. Had never attempted to mold her into anything except what she was. They had delighted in the fact that she was as unique as the exotic bird one of Ian's captains had once brought Lucy as a pet.

But in time the bird's bright plumage had grown drab, its eyes resigned, as if it were pining for its tropical home. Lucy had planned to send it back by the next ship, but the bird died before the ship could sail. She was certain it had died of a broken heart, missing everything it had ever known.

Now Lucy understood the bird's sorrow more vividly than ever before.

When Lucy had spoiled her fifth attempt at a letter by wetting it with hot tears, she flung down the quill and took up the candlestick, wanting only to escape the pages that were a silent reminder of the family she had lost.

The stones beneath her feet were cold, the drafts from the castle ruffling the delicate fabric of her nightshift. But she was glad of the physical sensations that drew her mind away from the painful squeezing of loss about her heart.

This was her home now. This crumbling English castle with its suits of standing armor, sentinels of another age.

She pushed open a heavy carved door, and light spilled from her candles into a long, narrow gallery leading to another part of the castle. Her footsteps echoed in the tunnel-like room. Small puffs of dust stirred by her passing tickled the insides of her nostrils. She sneezed but walked on, examining portraits of St. Cyrs from the time of gallant knights on.

Warriors in chain mail were hung lackadaisically on ill-aligned pegs. Ladies in elegant farthingales and stiff ruffs were leaned against the wall, moisture from the floor creeping up their painted skirts. Bold cavaliers, their ebony eyes laughing at the world, stood upside down, as if balanced on their dashing plumes. Some industrious mouse had gnawed at a corner of one of the frames.

The painted images stared out from their gilt-edged prisons as if disgruntled that they had been shoved into this ignominious corner of the castle they had once ruled. And they had been shoved aside, Lucy realized, swept from view, as if the current earl had wanted to wipe the evidence of his ancestry from his sight.

It made no sense. A man as arrogant and proud as the earl, abandoning this record of his family's legacy of power to the mice and spiders. One would think Valcour would have such portraits hung in the most conspicuous places, with plaques beneath them citing every glorious achievement the family had made.

Sir Melchesidec St. Cyr cut down three hundred infidels in the name of Christian charity.

Lucy made her way to the end of the gallery, where a holland cover draped some objects, hiding them from view. Curious, she lifted the edge of pale cloth and held the candle flame closer to the portrait she revealed.

It was far more recent than the rest. A gentle, dreamy-eyed girl sat beside a man who had Valcour's dark eyes and rugged features. Valcour's intensity was in the man's face as well, but it was edged with a certain wildness, recklessness. Beside them stood a boy of about seven, his eyes bright as new buttons above a gap-toothed grin, his hand on the back of a fawn-colored mastiff.

Lucy stared at the painting for a moment, stunned, her gaze scanning down to where the artist had inscribed the identities of the people in the painting. Lord Lionel St. Cyr, the fifth earl of Valcour; Lady Catherine, his wife; and Master Dominic St. Cyr, seven years old.

Lucy crouched down, her fingers numb as she pressed them against the cheek of that delightfully mischievous little boy. A child that seemed worlds different from the man he had become.

There was no haughty superiority in young Dominic's face, no hard disdain nor tyrannical temper. There was an openness about him, a certainty that life was an adventure to be savored.

Only the woman in the portrait seemed out of place among generations of fiery-eyed St. Cyrs. Dominic's mother peered out at the world a little fearfully, as if expecting the dreams in her eyes to be stripped away.

Why was Lucy suddenly certain that they had been?

She stood up, brushing sticky cobwebs from her fingers, and went to the door that led onward through the castle. She grasped the heavy iron ring bolted to the door and pulled, but the wood had warped, and it stuck.

She braced herself, grasping the ring with both hands, then tugged. Hinges screeched in protest, the wood panel resisting, but at last the door swung slowly open.

Lucy hesitated, holding the candle closer to the soft darkness beyond.

The castle is in ill repair, Valcour had written. *You will remain in the suite of rooms assigned to you.* Was there some crumbling pit she would fall into? Some teetering balcony up these stairs that would send her plunging to her death? Or were there other reasons the powerful earl of Valcour had not wanted her to roam through his castle?

Did he keep the moldering bones of some ancient prisoner dangling in medieval torture devices? Or did some other darker secret lurk behind a forbidden door?

He had ordered her to stay in her room like an unruly child. And nothing had ever infuriated Lucy more than orders flung at her with no explanation.

She squared her shoulders. From the moment she met the earl of Valcour, he'd been bullying her: ordering her to be his second in the duel, practically dragging her into the Wilkeses' garden by the hair, and, last of all, demanding that she marry him. And not just demanding. He had been far viler than that. He had blackmailed her into becoming his wife, using the most loathsome weapon at his disposal—his own brother's vulnerability.

Valcour would have to cherish that triumph for a very long time. It was the last time the infernal earl would best the Raider's daughter.

Dominic St. Cyr was entirely too used to getting his own way. If he thought his new bride was going to leap whenever he snapped his fingers, he was going to have an unpleasant surprise!

No, Lucy thought, taking another step into the stairwell. Better to start this strange marriage the way she meant to continue it.

She peered upward, her gaze tracing the ascending spiral of stone steps that led to one of the mighty castle towers she had seen when she arrived at Harlestone.

Candlestick held before her, Lucy made her way up the stairway. Arrow slits from ages gone by let tiny slivers of moonlight filter in. She flattened her other hand against the rough stone wall to help guide her as she wound her way higher and higher.

Damp patches chilled her fingertips, cobwebs snagged at her fingers, and Lucy remembered countless tales of ghosts and ghoulish horrors she had woven for playmates in Virginia.

She half expected to find a madwoman shackled to the walls, or a witch's lair with vacant-eyed skulls and poisons brewing. At the very least a phantom in spectral armor.

Even her wildest imaginings couldn't prepare her for what awaited her at the top of the stairs.

Lucy stepped through a stone archway into a circular room far too enchanting to house a ghost.

The oppressive layer of dust and decay that had shrouded the other places she had explored was gone, this room pristine and bright, as if its owner had slipped out the door moments before.

Tapestries depicting maidens and unicorns covered the walls. The narrow castle windows had been widened, letting blocks of night peek into the room. A work basket sat beside an elegant chair, and a piece of linen stitched in tiny primroses trailed out from the container, a bright needle thrust through the unfinished embroidery. Exquisite leaden soldiers were set up in mock battle array behind a fortress constructed of books, the miniature army seeming to await the commands of its child general.

Was this beautiful chamber the secret that Dominic St.

Cyr had not wanted to share with anyone? Even his new bride? Why?

Lucy touched the embroidery, as delicate and lovely as any she had ever seen. What woman had made these tiny stitches? Surely not some servant. Was it possible that it was someone Valcour had wanted to hide? Or to protect?

Lucy felt her considerable fancy take flight.

Could the embroidery belong to one of Valcour's lady loves? Some poor village girl who had been seduced by the mesmerizing lord, then left to bear the child who had played with the toy soldiers? A woman and child who had to be hidden because of the earl's monstrous pride?

She shook herself fiercely. She was being absurd. Ridiculous. Valcour was so stiff-necked and arrogant that he would never house his bride beneath the same roof as his mistress. Still, it was as if Lucy could sense some unseen presence in this room, hear laughter that had long since faded.

She turned to look at the other side of the room, and she reeled back, thunderstruck, as she stared at an instrument enthroned upon a dais on the far side of the room.

She crossed to where it stood, a pianoforte polished to the brilliance of a treasured jewel. The instrument was so cunningly fashioned that Lucy could scarce believe its beauty. Silhouettes of ladies and gentlemen dancing the minuet were inlaid into the wood, while angels cavorted above them.

Her fingers stroked the keys experimentally once, twice. Almost miraculously, the notes rang true, crystal-line, flawlessly in tune.

Who could have tracked through the dusty, neglected gallery? Waded through the dirt and the spiders and the gloom to keep this instrument in perfect repair? Almost as if the room were a shrine.

The top of the instrument was littered with parchment, disturbingly like the one that had arrived in the box in Virginia what seemed a lifetime ago.

Lucy reached out, taking up the ink-smudged page nearest her. Music. Notes splashed across the page, as if the melody were racing out of the composer's head faster than he could get it down on paper. Measures were scrawled out, then reshaped into even more lovely phrases.

Lucy's fingers trembled. Her father had been Dominic St. Cyr's music teacher. Surely these must be his compositions. A shiver scuttled beneath the thin cloth of her nightshift. It was as if her father were everywhere, some omniscient presence, waiting for her, always taunting her, then darting back into the shadows just when she reached out to touch him.

Still, Lucy sat in the chair before the pianoforte and set her candlestick on its glossy surface, angling the light so that it spilled over the music rack.

She took up the composition and set it where she could see it. Her eyes skimmed over the blotted music, her hands coaxing it from the exquisite instrument.

As a child she had always insisted that pianofortes had a soul that had to be taught to sing by someone who loved them. If that were true, this piano had been taught to sing by an angel. There was a richness in the tones that flowed through Lucy like sugared cream, thick and sweet. There was an ethereal mistiness about the sounds like the whispering of moonbeams. There was a joy and a sorrow that made Lucy's fingers tremble, her throat close.

It was every bit as beautiful as her "Night Song." Maybe more so. It was as simple and lovely as a perfect meadow flower, sprung up between the paving stones of a crowded street. It was as haunting as the reflection of a fairy nymph in a silver stream.

It wooed her, beckoned her, seduced her, deeper and deeper into the mists of music, until suddenly, in midmeasure, it stopped so abruptly Lucy felt as if the floor had suddenly dropped out from under her and she had slammed to the stones three floors down.

"There must be more," Lucy said, desperately rummaging through the mass of pages on the pianoforte. "How could he have stopped when it was so beautiful? If I were penning something so perfect, I wouldn't have left the pianoforte if the whole castle were in flames."

But there was nothing. Only snippets of other melodies. A rollicking country dance that made Lucy want to tap her bare toes. A minuet that made her want to laugh, a subtle mockery in the music's stately strains.

There was another piece inscribed *To the most wonderful mama in the world, with my deepest, most sincere love.* Lucy swallowed hard. Had Alexander d'Autrecourt written this for his mother, a gift to attempt to mend the rift caused by his marriage to Emily? When had Alexander entered this room? Played at this pianoforte?

Lucy chewed at her fingernail, trying to piece the puzzle together. She had been born a year after her parents' marriage. Alexander d'Autrecourt had died when she was three years old. Surely his father, the duke, would never have allowed his son to stoop to giving music lessons. Alexander d'Autrecourt must have haunted this tower room sometime during the four years he was an outcast. Years he had spent trying to bludgeon music into the skulls of blockhead students like Dominic St. Cyr, in order to put bread on the table in the tiny apartment in London.

Her lips trembled, and she hoped that her father had found some little happiness here.

Lucy scanned the lines of script, so different from the elegant penmanship on the letters she had received. Obviously, Alexander had been in a rush, intending to copy the piece of music over. But there had never been time. Why? Had he been struck down by fever before he could return to the piece? Had he somehow offended the proud St. Cyrs, so they had driven him from his position here, not even giving him time to collect his precious compositions?

There was something so tragic in the unfinished music. Lucy took the first melody she had played and began again, letting the music draw her deeper this time, farther. Every fiber of her being reached out into the night, trying to grasp the thread the composer had lost when he had set the piece aside. With all her strength, Lucy listened for the magic, the haunting strains that seemed to dance in a rose-hazed mist all around her. Measure by measure, note by note, it curled through every pore in Lucy's skin and sank into the marrow of her bones, to lay, heavy and pulsing, in the soft, secret center of her spirit.

Again and again she played what her father had written, each time probing deeper, staying longer in the half world of magic he had woven.

All the longing, all the loneliness, all the fear hidden inside her rose to lodge in her chest, burning there in embers of need. Joy and hope sparkled, tantalizing, just out of reach, promising fulfillment if she but had the courage to reach out, take it.

Take what? Lucy wondered dizzily, her eyes closing, the music now as much a part of her as the tiny crook in her smallest finger, the flash of temper in her eyes, the shimmering gold of her hair.

The music was possessing her in ways that summoned up the grief she had been fighting for so long, the nameless yearning that ate inside her. She didn't feel the tears run down her cheeks as her pain flowed through her fingertips and was given flight in the music. She didn't see the first rays of dawn drizzle pink and mauve patterns upon the window ledges.

She was so lost in the glittering web of music that she would not have known if a dragon were attacking the castle walls.

She didn't notice the sound of footsteps echoing on the ancient stone stairs. She didn't hear the anguished sound of denial that rose in the throat of the man who stood framed in the stone entryway, his boots mud-spattered, his eyes filled with silent agony, as if she had just torn away the last piece of his soul.

12

*D*awn was tinting the sky with the most delicate paintbox colors of rose and violet when the earl of Valcour trudged wearily through the castle door. It was over. He was certain he'd remember for the rest of his life the hellish vision he had seen when the Jarvis boys pried the lid from the dirt-encrusted coffin.

As a boy, Dominic had concocted a hundred grisly fates for the musician who had betrayed him: fierce duels with sword and pistol, tortures worthy of the Inquisition. But tonight, staring down into the sunken, empty sockets, the frayed remains of a neckcloth tied about Alexander d'Autrecourt's fleshless throat, he had felt only a numb relief.

His nemesis was dead. There would be no whirlwind of scandal, no fresh pain for Lady Catherine, no danger to Aubrey. And for Lucinda, there would be no reunion with her father.

Valcour felt a momentary stab of empathy for the girl who lay in the bedchamber above. But he quelled it ruthlessly. She was better off this way, never having to meet a father who could only disappoint her. Never having to face ugly truths that would scar that brave, brash heart of hers, bring shadows into those bright blue eyes.

It was likely that she had spent the entire night tossing and turning, fretting over this mysterious stranger who'd contacted her in Virginia. A stranger who was obviously some scheming bastard embroiled in a plot Valcour couldn't figure out as yet. But he would be damned before anyone harassed the countess of Valcour. He'd be damned before he allowed anxiety to dull Lucinda's eyes.

Resolved to end her suspense as quickly as possible, Valcour strode up the bedchamber assigned to her, meaning to rap on the door and tell her all that had transpired that night. He arched a brow in surprise at the partially open door.

"Lucinda," he said quietly, not wanting to startle her. He started toward the curtained bed but stopped at the small desk that sat beneath the window. The first rays of sunlight illuminated writing supplies that were scattered across the glossy surface.

Valcour's gaze was snagged by one of the pages, and for an instant he half expected some dramatic letter telling him that Lucinda had run away. As he read the page, he almost wished she had fled. Fled so he could be angry instead of feeling a grinding sense of pain and despair as he read what she had written.

Dearest Mama and Papa,

You know how much I have always delighted in concocting surprises for you and the girls. This time, I must say, I have outdone myself! I am countess of Valcour, mistress of a grand castle. I dare say Papa believes such a title will cure me of my mischief and make me quite dignified, but I assure you that when you come to see me in England, I will be the same scapegrace Lucy I have always been.

My only regret is that I shall miss seeing the new

baby, Mama. Norah will have to play the role of big sister now to all the girls. But even at six years old, I was quite accomplished at fomenting disaster, and I'm sure with practice she will be a deliciously naughty child. If she is in need of any advice as to such, tell her to write me a letter.

You must take care of yourself, Mama. You know how Papa worries about you in your time of travail. He uses up the entire family measure of distress so that none of the rest of us can say how much we worry about you and love you without sounding redundant. But I do love you, Mama. I pray for your safe delivery every day.

Papa, you must not plague yourself with anxiety over me for one minute. England is not such a dastardly place after all. And being a countess has its advantages. I can order people about as much as I please, and they must do as I say.

The writing was flowing, delicate, but splotched where tears had obviously fallen to wet the page. Valcour felt an odd squeezing sensation in his chest, not because of what Lucinda had written, so much as what she had left unsaid.

Not a word was spoken of the frustration, the anger, and the fear she must feel. Nothing was said of her loneliness, or his ruthlessness in forcing her to marry him.

There was no blame or scorn or pleading for rescue from home. Yet there was a peek into the Lucinda that Valcour had not bothered to know. Another life, an ocean away. She had a father who obviously adored her. A mother who was about to give birth to a new babe. That mother would receive this letter, telling her that this golden-curled hoyden of a daughter was virtually lost to her across an ocean divide. And there was a little sister, one Lucinda had taught devilment, who would barely remember her in time.

Not to mention the fact that this new babe would never know its eldest sister at all.

Had Lucinda sobbed herself to sleep, racked with the grief of losing everything she had known? The thought made his throat swell.

He turned to the next page and read on.

As for my husband, he is more wonderful than anything I have ever dreamed of. Brave enough to ride with Pendragon's raiders. Dashing and bold, with fierce dark eyes and black hair. Papa, do you remember the stallion you gave me for my eleventh birthday? The one everybody said would break my neck? That is what Valcour reminds me of. He is arrogant and stubborn and seems untamable, and yet I love him so much that when he is with me he is the most tender of men.

Mama, being in love is every bit as wonderful as you promised me. I am sure, in time, I will not miss all of you so much.

Valcour's chest burned, his fingers clenching on the page he held. Never had he felt more like the ruthless bastard so many had named him. Salvaging his honor had been so blasted important he'd been blind to anything else. He hadn't even listened to Lucinda's claim that her parents loved her so much her mistakes would not matter, that they wouldn't care about society's conventions. He had been so certain he was doing the right thing in marrying her. Taking the only possible course of action. But now, reading the words Lucinda had written to comfort her loving parents, Valcour knew a bitter surge of regret.

He was no dashing, bold hero, able to shower Lucinda

with love. He was no man to cherish her, as her family had. He couldn't give her the kind of future she had written about in the letter. But he could stop being so damned harsh with her. He could find some gentleness inside him to repay her for all he had taken away.

His voice was roughened by uncharacteristic tenderness as he crossed to the bed and drew back the curtain. "Lucinda, don't be alarmed. It's Valcour. I—"

The words died in Valcour's throat as a shaft of light from the window pierced beyond the curtain. He stared down at twisted coverlets and tumbled pillows, but there were no golden curls tousled across them, no tear-stained face buried in the cottony mounds. The bed was empty.

Valcour swore, his jaw tensing. The sympathy that had flowed so briefly inside him was replaced by a simmering anger. Where the devil had she gone? He'd told her to remain in her rooms. She must be somewhere nearby. By God, she wouldn't dare defy . . . Valcour stopped, arrested by a sudden certainty that his new countess would be exactly where he told her *not* to go. Blast the infernal woman!

His gut twisted with unease. He made quick work of lighting a candlestick and started down the corridor, calling her name. The gallery door was open, and he flinched at the idea of Lucinda pawing through these portraits, images that gave him nothing but pain. The painting in the corner, stripped of its dustcover, made Dominic's chest ache. He stalked toward it, intending to yank the covering back on, when suddenly he heard it. Music drifted down from the tower like the most illusive of sorceress's spells.

Dominic rushed up the stone stairs, his chest feeling like an open wound, his throat closed in spasms of memory, as the haunting music drew him closer to the chamber high above.

Agony flowed through Dominic's veins as he crested the stairs and stood in the doorway he hadn't entered for sixteen years. It was as if he had never left it. Everything, to the smallest detail, was exactly the same as it had been. Except for the woman who sat in the light of guttering candles, her hair flowing in loose skeins of gold down her back. Lucinda's lithe body was bent over the keys, her head tilted just a little as if listening to the directions of angels.

Angels, or the most subtle demons in hell.

The music was a delicate whipcord biting into Dominic's soul. Each wisp of the melody brought to life by Lucy's gifted hands sliced inside him like fragments of something shattered—no, some*one* shattered.

The boy who had come here to dream and to laugh and to sit at that instrument and try to translate the tumult of emotions in his breast into music. The boy who had longed for his beloved father, far away on a diplomatic mission for the king. The boy who had listened eagerly while his mother read hastily scrawled letters from mysterious places like Turkestan.

It was as if Lucinda had torn out his heart and held it, agonizingly exposed. It was as if she had trespassed not on his property but in his spirit. And yet, somehow, there was a promise of release—a release such as he'd never known.

He was so damned confused. He wanted to shake her, wanted to go to her and drag her into his arms. He wanted to bury himself in her courage, her beauty, the wild sweetness that he'd tasted so briefly on her lips in the garden. He suddenly wanted to spare her from what he had found on the windswept hill of the graveyard.

But he stood silently as the music built to a crescendo, carrying him higher, flinging him farther into emotions he had tried so long to deny. The sensation was painfully vivid, like a candle flame thrust close to his eyes, or plunging through thin ice into a raging winter river.

It would have been so easy to release what little hold he still had on his feelings, let out the passion, the pain, the desperate, soul-searing need to reach out, touch her, tell her . . . That she was exquisite? That she was music incarnate? That never in his life had he been moved as deeply as he was by the sound of her hands caressing the pianoforte's keys?

But some dreams were too beautiful to survive the ugliness of the real world. He dared not let her music fill up the winter-cold void that was his heart. The realization stripped away the magic Lucinda wove through her song, leaving Valcour as bereft and angry as a starving man led into a banquet he could never taste.

It had been the devil of a day: the wild ride to the inn, the forced marriage, the battle with the d'Autrecourts, and, later, the grisly task of digging up Alexander d'Autrecourt's grave. All he had asked of Lucinda was that she stay in her chamber, where they would both be safe from the ghosts that entwined their pasts. All he had wanted was to ensure her peace of mind, put her at ease.

But she had to barge into places that were like an open wound to him. She had to sit like some golden-haired enchantress at the pianoforte and make it sing as if possessed by angels. She had to send out her music to burrow into the secret reaches of Dominic's soul.

Damn her to hell! He didn't have a soul anymore. Didn't have a heart. He had deadened it, ruthlessly and thoroughly. He wouldn't have this accursed woman breathing agonizing life into something he had battled so hard to kill.

Something burst inside him, tearing a snarl from his chest. "How dare you!"

Lucy leapt up as if the pianoforte had bitten off her fingers, her knee bumping hard against the wooden edge of the instrument. She gave a choked cry of pain, then stood there, frozen, one hand pressed to her breasts, the guttering candles shining orange-gold light through the thin fabric of her nightshift, turning it nearly transparent.

Dirt smudged her small naked feet, and there were dried tracks of tears along her cheeks.

She'd been crying. Crying over the letter he had found in her room, crying over the music she had been spinning with the mastery of a sorceress.

She looked like a sleepwalker wakened too suddenly. She looked like a fallen angel, her full breasts delectable swells beneath the cloth of her shift, her throat graceful and delicate and white, her legs so perfectly shaped Dominic's hand burned to touch her. But to touch her would be the most dangerous risk Dominic St. Cyr had ever taken.

"I ordered you to stay in your rooms." Each word was heavy as stone.

He could see her gathering her wits, driving back the misty dreams that had been pouring from her fingertips and mustering her courage in their place. She shook back the tumbled gold curls, her chin lifting in that now-familiar gesture of defiance. "I came here *specifically* because you forbade me to."

"You're my wife. You'll do as I say."

"I'm the countess of Valcour. If I want to dance naked on top of the parapet, I will, and there is nothing you can do to stop me." Those blue eyes shimmered at him, defiant, lovely. "You had my father's things and you never told me," she accused.

"There was nothing of your father's here."

"Then what is *this?*" Lucy grabbed up the parchment and thrust it toward Valcour.

Valcour looked down at the ink-blotted music. He crossed his arms over his chest, refusing to touch the pages.

"It's fit for nothing but the rubbish heap."

"You said my father was a mediocre musician. This is brilliant. But, then, what would a man like you understand about passion in this music? You who have no feelings at all?"

205

Feelings? Sweet Jesus, how long had he labored to deaden the roiling emotions inside him? The only possible way to kill the ferocious pain? What could this girl know about what it had cost him to construct the wall of ice that kept him separate from the world that had all but destroyed him? And how could she guess that the pages in her hand had opened countless wounds he had hidden for so long?

With an oath, Valcour snatched the pages from her hand and thrust them over the candles that glowed in the branched candlestick on the pianoforte.

Lucinda shrieked in pain and fury as the paper ignited. She dove for the music, all but setting her golden curls aflame as she battled to reach it, but Valcour held the music high above her head, his arm rigid, tiny sparks showering down his hand, burning small holes in the white linen of his sleeve.

"You bastard! Give them to me! Give them!" She was sobbing hysterically, clawing at his arm, kicking at him, fighting like a hellcat. But the flames devoured the pages, eating them down to the tips of Valcour's fingers.

He grasped Lucinda's arm with his other hand, holding her away from him. Then he dropped the charred remains of the music to the floor and crushed out the glowing orange that rimmed the blackened pages with the heel of his boot. The music crumbled into ashes, like the dreams of the boy he had once been.

Lucy fell to her knees, scrabbling for the few scraps of unburned paper, tears flowing down her cheeks, her fingers blackened with soot. She pushed herself to her feet, her eyes seething pools of hatred.

"I might have forgiven you for forcing my hand in marriage," she said in a terrible, measured voice. "I might have forgiven you for being a cold-hearted bastard. But I will *never,*" she said, her voice quavering, "*never* forgive you for this!"

"Perhaps next time you will do as you're told."

"Go to bloody hell, *my lord!*" She spun around and started to bolt from the room, but Valcour grabbed her. Her skin was silken beneath her thin gown, a wild pulse beating in the hollow of her throat. Valcour's mouth went dry at the feel of her, the scent of her, cinnamon and rebellion, honey and defiance. The need to crush those berry-red lips with his own made Dominic's head spin.

Unnerved by his need, he gritted his teeth, clinging to the red haze of his fury. "I've already visited hell tonight, Lucinda," Valcour said. "I found your father there."

"What?" She shrank back as if he had slapped her. The globe of one breast brushed against Valcour's rigid forearm, the nipple a dusky rose just visible through the thin material of her nightshift.

"Your father is dead." Valcour forced his voice into steely accents. "I am certain of it."

"No! You saw the duchess's face. She was terrified when I showed her the letter I had gotten. My father is—"

"He's a pile of moldering bones in a worm-eaten frockcoat, just as the dowager duchess said." The words were deliberately cruel. The only way Valcour could keep himself from dragging Lucinda into his arms, delving his hands into her hair, and kissing her until everything vanished: the room, the specter of her father, his own overwhelming sense of foreboding.

"How do you know he is dead for certain?" she flung back at him, her eyes glittering pools of denial. "How do you know that the man at Perdition's Gate wasn't my father?"

Valcour hesitated a heartbeat. "Because I opened his grave."

"You *what?*" Lucy fell back a step, her eyes flicking with unabashed horror to the mud that flecked Valcour's boots.

"I opened his grave. It was the only way to be certain. You will put this madness behind you now, Lucinda. It is over."

"I see! The entire thing is decreed madness by the great and powerful earl of Valcour, so of course, I'm supposed to kiss your accursed feet and thank you for tidying everything up for me!"

"Lucinda, I know this is difficult. But believe me, it's best this way."

"Best! And you know what's best for me, don't you, you pompous, interfering son of a bitch! Far better that I be forced to marry you than do something crazed like go home to the people I love! You practically break my neck, racing on that accursed stallion of yours to the graveyard, because you're furious that I didn't show you the letter I brought to Avonstea. Of course, you don't have to tell me a damned thing you don't want to! You still shroud everything about my father in mysteries and riddles and answers that tell me nothing! You all but lock me in my bedchamber while you go out, without a word to me, and desecrate my father's grave!"

"If your father had been alive, *as you believed,* I would have desecrated nothing."

"You had no right! You had no right! It's no wonder peasants want to chop off the heads of you aristocrats! By God, if I had an axe—"

"I know *exactly* where you'd aim!" Valcour grabbed her, her skin petal-soft under his fingers. "Listen to me, girl. If you're going to survive this marriage, you will abide by a simple set of rules. I'll not tolerate—"

"*I'll* not tolerate being ordered about like some . . . some blasted dog! Sit, Lucinda. Heel, Lucinda. Curl up by the fire and lick my bloody feet, Lucinda!"

"You are my wife. You—"

"Believe me, I haven't forgotten! I wish to God I could!" She gave a bitter, broken laugh. "This was supposed to be my wedding night, wasn't it? The night where my husband claimed me for his own? This is the night my mother told me about, as if it were some sort of . . . of magical dream."

Valcour tried to ignore the tiny catch in her voice. "We agreed there would be no consummation."

"And you're all so damned civilized here, aren't you! I suppose I'll have to get used to English customs. In Virginia, the wedding tradition is to steal the bride's slipper to trade for a bottle of liquor. Apparently, in England the bridegroom trundles himself out to rob graves instead."

There was something wild in her eyes, as if the strain of the past days had stretched her nerves to the point where they were about to snap.

Valcour caught her chin in his hand and tried to steady his voice. "Lucinda, I am going to take you to your room. You will get some sleep and calm yourself."

"What are you going to do? Sew my blasted eyelids shut?" She yanked away from him, driving one fist hard against the wall of his chest.

Valcour's jaw clenched. "I'll do whatever I have to do to make you see reason."

"You can't make me sleep! You can't make me calm myself! You can't even make me stay in my room unless I choose to!"

Valcour stared down into that defiant, lovely face, her cheeks flushed, the neck-edge of her shift gaping low over one moonlight-pale breast. The edge of her nipple was a rose kiss, a sinful temptation peeking out at him, taunting him with the driving need that centered in that part of him that made him a man.

And in that moment, Valcour was aware of just how far this woman had pushed him. She had shattered his well-ordered life, inflamed the temper he had prided himself on keeping under control. She had charged into this room—this accursed room—and made him face a torment more exquisite than any torture master could have devised. And now she had his own body turning traitor. His loins raged out of control, as if he were a green lad. His hands shook where he touched her. His head was filled with erotic images of what he'd like to do to her, with her.

He wanted to draw out her pleasure until she begged him for release. Wanted to conquer her on the sensual battlefield of that lovely body, inch by supple inch.

Sweet God, he wanted to possess her so completely he could forget everything, everyone. . . .

No! He had to end this—before it was too late.

With an oath, Valcour swooped her off her feet, flinging her belly-down over his shoulder. Lucy gave a shriek of outrage, her fists hammering at his back, her legs kicking out as she twisted and writhed, trying to free herself.

Valcour's arms ached with the effort of restraining her, but he did so, carrying her down the spiral stairway, through the dusty gallery, while she all but deafened him with her curses.

When he reached her bedchamber, he kicked open the door with one booted foot. The maid he had seen the night before was hunkered down by the fireplace, obviously come to stir up the embers. The servant squawked with alarm as Valcour stalked to the bed and flung Lucinda down upon it.

"You will leave the room at once," Valcour barked at the maid, but the girl was already bolting as if he were shooting poisoned arrows at her backside.

"No!" Lucinda shrilled. "Don't leave! You don't have to do what he tells you!"

Valcour slammed the door shut behind the girl and stood there, his breath rasping in his chest, his heart pounding against his ribs like a blacksmith's hammer on an anvil.

"Go to sleep," he enunciated clearly.

"Go to hell," his wife flung back.

"Get in that bed. Now. And stay there. Or . . ."

Lucinda stalked to where the washbasin stood and grasped the handle of the pitcher. For a moment, Valcour thought she might surrender, might be ready to wash her face, calm herself.

Instead, she wheeled on him like the huntress Athena and, with precise aim, hurled the contents of the pitcher into his face.

Cold water splashed his chest, his face, his neck, making the fabric of his shirt cling to his skin, the flap of his breeches outlining with even more painful clarity the purely physical effect the woman was having on him.

The idea that she should know how blasted vulnerable she had made him infuriated Valcour beyond imagining. With a roar, he grasped her by the arms and forced her backward until her delectable bottom slammed up against the edge of the bed. He jammed her back until she lay on the pillows, every muscle in her body straining, fighting him, as she arched her back, struggling to escape. But her arching thrust her breasts up against Valcour's chest, and the edge of the shift caught beneath her, tugging to expose most of one pale mound.

In that instant, Valcour wanted her so badly that he didn't give a damn what it would cost him. Later, much later, he would pay whatever forfeit was demanded of him. But now she was his wife. His wife, damn her! And he had felt swift rivers of attraction pouring through her as well, felt it sizzle between them like lightning.

Valcour grasped both her wrists in one large hand and pinned them over her head. His mouth came down on the belligerent curve of her lips, and he tasted his own defeat.

13

*L*ucy struggled to free her hands from Valcour's grip as his weight bore her down into the feather tick, but his rein-callused hand was unyielding as iron, intoxicating as mulled wine. She felt swallowed up by his big body, conquered by the sensations he loosed inside her like a firestorm.

Never had she felt anything so primitive as the response that exploded through every fiber of her being as Valcour's corded muscles branded themselves into her breasts. He flung one granite-hard thigh over her hips to restrain her, dragging her tighter into his body. The wetness from his shirt soaked through her thin nightshift, melding them together, until she could feel every sinew of his chest, the hardened points of his nipples.

She had always seen him as a man of ice, but the heat their bodies were creating was so intense, Lucy half expected to see wisps of steam simmering up wherever he touched her.

She was furious at him, so blasted angry, and yet, as Dominic St. Cyr's mouth traced hot, drugging kisses from her mouth and down her throat, she arched her head back to allow him better access.

"D-Damn you," she choked out on a gasp as his teeth nipped with tender ferocity at an exquisitely sensitive place on her neck. "Don't make me want you!"

"Do you, Lucinda?" Valcour growled. "Do you want me?"

She wanted to deny everything she was feeling, wanted to fling out words of disdain, wound his insufferable arrogance. He had hurt her so damn badly, in ways she would never allow him to know. Ways a man like Valcour could never understand.

"Why should it matter what I want? You've been ordering me around from the moment I met you. I'm your wife."

"It matters." Valcour's free hand slid up her ribcage to where her nightshift lay twisted beneath the globe of one breast. His palm cupped the fluid weight as if molding it into a more perfect shape. His gaze touched the delicate shell-pink nipple, a dark inferno raging to life in his eyes.

"Lucinda, I may be the devil of a husband in many ways, but I promise you, you'll never have cause to regret that I am the man in your marriage bed."

No, Lucy thought with a strange tightness in her throat. *I'll only regret that you don't care about me.*

She looked into those ebony eyes, fierce yet wary, uncannily like the stallion she had tamed as a child. A stallion whose life had been filled with cruelty and hate. She sensed in that moment that if she pushed Valcour away, it would wound him on some level she might never be able to reach again.

It would have been the perfect vengeance, leaving him to stew in the wild desires that were consuming him. But for once, Lucy didn't care about avenging past wrongs.

"Lucinda," he repeated, his voice low, rough, sending tingles into the secret place between her thighs. "Do you want me?"

He was giving her a choice, this fiercely proud man, leaving himself open to rejection. He was also forcing her to take some measure of responsibility for what was about to happen between them. She wished he would just kiss her again, that he would put his hot palms on the places where she was dying for his touch. But he just peered down at her, his dark lashes low over eyes that promised heady seduction, his hard mouth still damp from kissing her, his breath rasping in his broad chest.

She could feel his heart thundering in counterpoint to her own raging pulse. Most intriguing and intoxicating of all was that part of him pressed against her thigh, a delightful mystery, a sensual promise. . . .

Lucy moistened dry lips and looked straight into her husband's passion-darkened face. "I want you, damn your eyes to hell."

For a heartbeat, one corner of that unabashedly male mouth ticked up, in something like amusement—but the amusement vanished under a shower of intense need as Valcour dropped a kiss at the lower curve of her breast. "A countess . . ." He stroked his lips higher. "Doesn't . . . swear."

"This countess does." Lucy could barely squeeze the words from her throat as Valcour's lips burned against skin that had never been touched by another man. He pressed hot kisses in a circle around the edge of her nipple, his loose hair a delicious contrast, cool and silky, pooling in the cleavage between her breasts. The sensation was so exquisite, she felt as if one more grain of pleasure would be more than she could bear. She twisted, writhed, a shuddering moan tearing from her chest.

"You're so damn beautiful," Valcour whispered hotly against her skin. "And you're mine. Mine."

The words proclaiming ownership should have inflamed her fury, but they weren't filled with Valcour's usual cold tyranny. Rather, there was an undercurrent of astonishment in them, something almost like awe, as he drew the hardened rosette of her nipple into the hot, wet cavern of his mouth.

Lucy cried out in response, arching her back to deepen Valcour's erotic kiss. She had seen her mother nursing the babies a hundred times and had eavesdropped on more than her share of bawdy stories around the camp-fires of the soldiers under her father's command. But never had she suspected that an almost painfully intense pleasure could be centered in such an innocuous-looking place. Valcour suckled her with tender ferocity, the rough, wet point of his tongue toying with her in ways that made her whimper. She struggled against the grasp of the hand that still held her wrists, wanting to touch him the way he was touching her. And suddenly he released her.

She shoved against his shoulders, almost desperate to tear away the layer of cloth between them. She heard Valcour's groan of protest, but he drew away. And Lucy saw in that moment he thought she had changed her mind.

"Don't be afraid of me, girl," he rasped. "Don't be afraid."

Tenderness, from a man so unyielding Lucy had thought him made of stone. A rough plea from a man more proud, more arrogant, than any other she had ever known.

In that instant, she wondered what it would be like to be loved by a man like Valcour. The thought was bittersweet in its impossibility, bewitching in its power.

She drowned in the heat of those eyes one long moment, then raised her fingers to the fastenings of his shirt.

Her intent inflamed Valcour further, and he yanked the garment over his head, revealing planes and hollows carved of muscle, gilded with a web of dusky hair.

Beneath his ribcage, his stomach was a mass of ridges bisected by a feathered silky ribbon that disappeared beneath the straining fabric of his breeches.

A primitive thrill shot through Lucy. The man who hovered over her was the incarnation of every secret fantasy she had ever had. She let it show in her face, let him see how much she wanted him, needed him.

Valcour's hands delved into her hair, a cascade of gold tangling about long, bronze fingers. His mouth came down on hers with such savage fervor it made the world spin crazily off its axis. Lucy reveled in the ferocity of his kiss, her jaw clamped hard against whimpers of need.

He seemed to want something, his mouth so insistent, but she didn't know what.

At last he traced kisses down her cheek, caught the lobe of her ear gently between his teeth. "Lucinda, open your mouth."

"M-My . . . mouth? You're always telling me to—to close it."

A low chuckle rumbled from Valcour's chest, and even through the haze of her desire, Lucy was stunned at the beauty of the sound. "I want to kiss you, hoyden."

"You *were* kissing me so—so well it's a wonder the bedsheets didn't catch fire. And don't think it doesn't cost me to say that. You're arrogant enough as it is."

The chuckle turned into a low, caressing laugh. "I'll try not to let your flattery turn my head, hoyden, if you will do as you're told. Now open your mouth. I want to kiss you inside, treasure. Deep."

"It sounds . . . disgusting," Lucy said faintly. And it did. To someone halfway rational. But the thought of Valcour exploring any part of her was sweet intoxication.

"I think you'll find the sensation amazing."

"You've amazed me . . . already," Lucy said. But she raised her lips to his experimentally, first inviting another hot kiss, with her lips barely parted.

But when the very tip of Valcour's tongue swept along

the seam of her lips, she sucked in a shuddery breath, then allowed her mouth to soften, to open.

She hadn't known what to expect, but it wasn't the liquid arousal caused by Valcour's tongue stealing deep, possessing her mouth in the way he would soon possess her body.

The sensation of his deep kiss was honeyed fire. It bedazzled her, melted her as his tongue toyed with hers, acquainting her with male passion.

Lucy kissed him back, following his lead, testing, trying what he taught her. She couldn't have known that the questing of her untutored mouth and inexperienced hands were more sensual than the lovemaking of the most skilled courtesan the dark earl had ever possessed.

Lucy arched her hips against his, his kisses seeming to have created a yawning void inside her, waiting to be filled.

Valcour drew back, his eyes flashing to where one exposed breast trembled above the ribboned neckline of her shift. The petal-soft mound still bore the faint pink blush of his caresses, her nipple glistening wet from his suckling. The sight of her seemed to push him higher, harder.

His fingers knotted in the neckline of her nightshift, but the drawstring was hopelessly tangled. With an oath he tugged at the snarled blue ribbon, but the fabric ripped beneath his impatient fingers.

He glanced up at her, starting to release her, but Lucy cried out in protest. She closed her hand over his knotted one, imprisoning the wadded-up cloth in his fist. At her silent goading, the last vestiges of civilization vanished from his countenance. He levered himself to his knees above her, then he rended the garment down the middle, as if it were made of nothing more substantial than moonbeams.

Sunlight drizzled butterscotch patterns over Lucy's nakedness, the garment looped about her arms, and pooled on either side of her, framing her peach-glossed skin like petals framing the heart of a rose.

Valcour's fingers went to his breeches, and there was something excruciatingly erotic about his long fingers unfastening the flap, stripping away the black fabric that clung to his muscular thighs like a second skin.

In a heartbeat he was naked. Magnificent. Indomitable. And Lucy wondered if having such a man as her lover wouldn't be some consolation to the fact that she would never have a man who adored her.

She couldn't breathe as Valcour's eyes swept over her body, fierce and savage. It was as if in that instant he possessed her soul, a soaring hawk, ready to claim its mate. A stallion, preparing to mount his chosen mare.

Always when Lucy had envisioned her wedding night, she had imagined darkness to cover her nakedness, hide the flush of embarrassment, the awkwardness that would come from her inexperience. But Valcour could see everything about her—from the tiny freckle beside her navel to the dark blond curls that glistened at the apex of her thighs. A place that felt heavy with yearning, liquid with anticipation, pulsing with a craving that she didn't fully understand.

A muscle at the corner of Valcour's jaw ticked as he lay down beside her again, his mouth a hard line, as if he were trying to keep rein on the desire that glowed like embers in the deepest reaches of his eyes. Then he touched her.

A thousand bright-winged creatures seemed to take flight inside her as he splayed his big hand on the slight swell of her stomach.

"I'll take care of you, Lucinda," Valcour said. "Tonight. Always."

It was a promise far different than the fevered vows of love most brides dreamed of on their wedding night. But there was something in Valcour's voice that made her throat ache as if he had murmured tender love words.

After a moment that seemed to stretch out forever, he slid his hand lower, to the uncharted place beneath her navel, then to the edge of golden curls.

Every muscle in his body stood out rigidly against his sun-bronzed skin, a fine sheen of sweat dampening his face, his chest. One finger traced the *v* of her inner thigh, while the rest of his hand cupped the mound of her femininity.

Lucy saw his jaw clench as he threaded his spread fingers through her curls and dipped down to where she was damp and hot and restless.

Curls parted, his callused fingertips finding sleek, satin petals. Lucy jumped at the intimate contact, a shock wave sizzling to the core of her being. She squeezed her thighs instinctively together, but instead of closing Valcour out, her legs only drew him deeper into the secret place he had touched.

"Open for me," Valcour urged, kissing her neck. "Open and let me touch you. It will feel wondrous. Magic. I promise."

Magic. The word seemed so strange yet so right coming from his lips. Lucy caught her lower lip between her teeth and slowly, ever so slowly, parted her thighs.

A groan of appreciation rumbled in Valcour's chest. "You're so lovely, Lucinda. Here." His finger circled on a hidden nub, making her cry out. "You're beautiful . . . everywhere. I don't deserve . . . don't deserve . . ." She ached for him to finish his sentence, sensing pain in him, a chink in his armor she would never have believed existed.

But instead, Valcour began a sensual assault on her body, on her spirit, that was as devastating and as magical as the mortal Leda must have felt when the king of gods, Zeus, mated with her.

Hot, probing fingers explored, a wondrously skilled mouth made her his slave, inch by torturous inch. Low groans and words of praise seduced, while her own body writhed in response, her own fingers clenching on his shoulders, her legs twisting against his hair-roughened ones, as if trying to draw him closer.

He smelled of wind and rain and musky male arousal. He felt hard and hot and dangerous. Lucy shivered in response as he submerged her in a rainbow-shaded haze of desire, sinking her deeper and deeper into a world of his creation.

Sparks scattered through Lucy's body as his fingers toyed with her most sensitive secret places, then dipped into the damp, quivering sheath that was aching for him to fill it.

"You're small," Valcour groaned. "Tight as a fist. My God, I don't want to . . . hurt . . ."

Lucy arched her hips toward the tormenting caress of his hand, wanting him to caress her more deeply, mount her and drive himself deep. She insinuated her hand between them and touched the pulsing shaft between Valcour's hard thighs.

He convulsed as if she had burned him, a pained groan tearing from deep in his throat.

"Does it hurt?" she asked, snatching back her fingers.

"I've never been in such accursed agony," Valcour ground out. "But, then, you've always delighted in paining me there. Lucinda, Lucinda . . . what sweet vengeance you have worked against me." He stunned her by grasping her wrist and pressing her open hand against him again, tighter, harder.

Lucy's hand closed around the shaft, and Valcour arched his head back as she fingered it delicately. It was velvet-sheathed steel, hot and throbbing with need. And Lucy was awed that she could have such an effect on a man like Valcour. Her fingers skated over the velvety tip, learning the feel of primitive male arousal.

Valcour was shaking, his breath rasping like a dying man's. A groan hissed between his clenched teeth, and he drew her hand away. "Lucinda, don't. I'm trying to hold back, damn it. Have to keep control."

"Why?"

"You're a virgin." It was as if Valcour were trying to remind himself of her innocence. "I won't take you like a stag in rut. I won't hurt you."

"It would take more than a stiff-necked, tyrannical English lord to hurt me. Virginians are made of sterner stuff." She tried to jest, then stopped, moistening her lips. "Valcour, you already hurt me, infuriated me, frustrated me. You've ordered me around for days. For once, do what someone else tells you to do. Make love to me, Valcour. Now."

With a groan, he hooked his hand under her knees, drawing them apart, then positioned himself between her legs.

"Damn, you're an obstinate woman," Valcour breathed. "Stubborn, infuriating, you never goddamn do what you're told."

"I opened my mouth for you to kiss me. Kiss me like that again, Valcour. Hot and hard and deep, when you take me."

Valcour groaned. "Call me Dominic. Call me Dominic and I'll kiss you until your bones melt, your body shakes."

"Dominic. Dominic, Dominic, Dom . . ." Lucy's words were stopped by Valcour's mouth on hers, fierce, so fierce. She felt that part of him that deemed him a man probe the dewy cleft between her legs.

Valcour braced himself on his elbows to keep from crushing her, and Lucy turned her gaze away, her cheeks heating, her breath unsteady with anticipation. She didn't want him to see that she was suddenly frightened —not by the breaking of her maidenhead, but at the thought that she would expose her own ignorance, that she would be awkward, ungainly, in this new erotic dance.

"Look at me, Countess," Valcour demanded, his mouth trailing over her cheeks, her chin, as he pressed himself against the petals of her femininity. "I want to see your face when I make you my own."

Valcour entered her just a little, an unaccustomed heaviness, a delicious pressure that promised so much more. He withdrew, then eased himself deeper. Lucy opened her eyes, feeling herself drown in liquid midnight, heated muscular flesh. She flattened her hands against Valcour's broad back, her fingers hungrily exploring the ridges of his spine, then the hardened curves of his buttocks.

Valcour groaned, his arms shaking where they braced him above her, his face sheened with sweat. "It will hurt for but a heartbeat, my little rebel." Then he kissed her, so hard, so hot, that the pleasure of it drowned out the sudden pain as he thrust his hips forward.

Lucy gave a choked little cry, then felt only Valcour, inside her, deep, so deep, a part of her. She wanted him to lose control, wanted so much for the passion to carry him away, carry them both away. But no matter how hungrily she touched him, how her lips swept over his chest, his face, no matter how desperately her hips rose up to meet his measured thrusts, there was something restrained about him, careful.

He bracketed her hips with his hands, still keeping most of his weight from crushing her as he taught her the movements of the dance of passion.

The heaviness between her thighs grew more insistent, more exciting, Valcour's hard body carrying her along with him in the currents of a wild river she had never known existed before this night.

Lucy gasped, arched, and he filled her again and again, his mouth lavishing her with kisses, fragments of praise, his hands building wildfires in every fiber of her being.

Valcour lowered his mouth to her breast, taking her nipple in his mouth with a tender savagery that made

Lucy's body convulse, the pleasure center between her legs heating to a raging inferno of need.

She whimpered, writhed, as he teethed the excruciatingly sensitive bud gently, ardently. Her fingers clawed at Valcour, trying to draw him even tighter into her body. She battled desperately to catch the sensation fleeting as quicksilver that tantalized her from the tips of Valcour's fingers, the sweet, hot questing of his mouth, the powerful thrusting of his manhood deep, so deep.

When she couldn't bear another moment, he reached between their bodies to where they were joined, his fingers seeking out that part of her that felt like a sizzling ember of need. The callused pad of his fingers stirred it, seduced it until Lucy quaked with the building of pleasure, arched against him faster, gasping, pleading for that magic that drifted in a shower of silver just beyond her reach.

Then he gave it to her.

With a flick of his skilled hand and a heavy, dizzying plunge of his powerful body, it seemed as if Valcour had driven himself into her very soul.

Lucy cried out as the sparks of pleasure burst inside her, engulfing her, empowering her, making her head toss on the pillows and her legs tangle around Valcour's hips, holding him there as the contractions hurled her into oblivion.

He prolonged her pleasure as if it were some holy quest, his face contorted, almost as if in pain, his eyes filled with some emotion she couldn't identify.

Then he surged into her with all the might of his magnificent male body. A groan that was almost agony tore from his chest as Lucy felt his essence pulse against the mouth of her womb.

Lucy had dismissed so many romantic fancies as a hoyden girl, certain that eternal passion was reserved for beautiful angels like her mother. But as Lucy lay in her husband's arms, newly made a woman, she felt a sudden yearning, a gnawing regret. What would this night have been like if Valcour had come to her with the same fierce adoration Ian Blackheath had for her mother? If Valcour were a far different man, freed of his icy shell, and she were a bride, blushing with eagerness, ecstatic as she entered a world of love and trust and passion? What would it have been like if Valcour had wanted her so badly, he hadn't been able to master his passions, keep them under control? What would it have been like if she could have pried loose his grasp on the real world and hurtled him into pleasure so wild, so intoxicating, the mighty earl of Valcour had vanished and only Dominic, Lucinda's lover, had remained?

She was stunned at the tears that welled at the corners of her eyelids, trickling free. She turned her face against the pillow, wanting to hide them.

Valcour braced himself on one elbow, gently stroking the web of hair back from her brow. "It will be easier next time, hoyden."

Easier? To have Valcour take her physically, knowing that neither of them felt the love that would have made their union pure magic? To know that Valcour had created these same sensations in his mistresses, and that she was no different to him? A woman to pleasure himself with, a pretty toy to tantalize and torment with the skill of his hands, his mouth.

She corrected herself. She was far different from the other women who had taught Valcour to be such a talented lover. She was his countess. She would carry his name, produce his precious heir. But he would never love her. As a child, stolen from her mother, Lucy had been starved for love, felt that need gnawing inside her like the most brutal hunger. Now, in this bed, with this enigmatic man beside her, she wondered if that hunger would return, along with the feelings of anger, despair . . . worthlessness.

Valcour's voice, uncharacteristically gentle, shook her from her thoughts. "It always hurts a woman the first time a man takes her, Lucinda. And I . . ." His face twisted with regret. "I wasn't as gentle as I wanted to be."

Lucy dragged the frayed remnants of her nightshift about her, groping for the belligerence that had always served as a shield against too much vulnerability. He had been gentle with her body. But her spirit . . . He must never know how bruised she felt there.

"I didn't know what to expect from the marriage bed, my lord, but I hardly anticipated gentleness since I shared it with you."

Valcour drew back, lines carving between those straight black brows. "I see."

"You needn't be offended by my observation," Lucy said, climbing from the bed and crossing to the dressing table. "After all, I can hardly be expected to hold any sentimental delusions about your character."

She picked up a comb and stroked it through her hair. "You fling me over your shoulder like some Celtic barbarian, your boots still encrusted with dirt from my father's open grave. You hurl me into bed, and—"

"I didn't force you, Lucinda," Valcour said, a terrible stillness in his face. "You said you wanted me."

"I suppose I did. You are, after all, quite a magnificent specimen of a man. Of course, I haven't much basis to make comparisons. I suppose I'll remedy that lack in my education in time."

She glanced into the mirror, catching Valcour's reflection in the silvered glass. His jaw seemed cast in iron, his features very pale.

"When you set forth the conditions of our marriage, you did say that I could do as I wished, as long as I was discreet," she reminded him.

"Once my son is born," Valcour growled.

"*Your* son? He won't be your property. He'll be mine

225

as well. I'm certain that by the time I conceive, you'll be more than relieved, anxious to get back to entertaining —what did Aubrey say your mistress's name is?— Camilla. Lovely name. I'm certain she'll be heartbroken at your defection."

There was a flash of some emotion across Valcour's face that twisted in Lucy's vitals like a knife.

Valcour grabbed his breeches, jamming his legs into them with barely restrained fury. "I'll not discuss this with you, Lucinda. A mistress and a wife are not of the same world."

"But you are so civilized about such matters here. I have heard that some great men have their mistresses and wives become the best of friends. All quite amicable." She pursed her face in mockery. *"My dearest Sally, shall we cast dice to see who gets into Barrington's breeches tonight?"*

"Enough," Valcour said, snatching up his shirt. He dragged the still-damp linen over his shoulders.

Lucy tossed her curls, her whole body vibrating with anger and pain. "You shall have to tell Camilla your separation is only temporary, of course," she taunted. "That once the exalted Valcour heir is thriving in my womb, you will be able to return to her with a clear conscience. After all, the English aristocracy is hardly expected to cling to any tiresome values like fidelity."

"What Camilla and I had was ended before I made you my wife." Valcour shot out of bed, crossing the room in three quick strides. He grasped Lucy by the shoulders, spinning her around to face him. "What the devil is the matter with you?"

Lucy wished to God she knew. Wished she understood why she felt so broken, so battered, so bereft. She should have been comforted by what she had just experienced in Valcour's arms. She had been awed by the power of it, the wild sweetness of his passion. Yet she had only felt more vulnerable, more powerless. His touch had only taunted her with fleeting images of the love she would never have a chance to know.

Valcour's voice softened, one finger hooking beneath her chin. "I thought we did remarkably well together in bed, Lucinda. In time—"

"What? I can prove a tolerable substitute for your demimondaines as long as necessary?" She jerked away from his touch. "After all, I'm a mere receptacle for the cherished Valcour heir. If I will follow your instructions, everything will be wonderful, won't it? I suppose I should be thanking you. After all, you made some effort on my behalf. I would guess that heirs can be gotten more expediently, and I am certain there are few bridegrooms who would spend the night excavating graves on their bride's behalf."

"We are back to that again, are we?" Valcour turned away, dragging one hand through his hair. He suddenly looked unutterably tired. "Lucinda, this marriage can be as tolerable or as miserable as you choose to make it. I know we began badly, but in time we can grow to know each other better. In time, we will have children to fill the place of your little Norah."

"Norah? How do you know about Norah?" Lucy felt a sick tensing in her stomach, horrified realization dawning inside her. Valcour's cheeks stained dark, his eyes flicking, almost as if by their own will, to the letters she had all but broken her heart to write hours before.

During the barren, lonely years the d'Autrecourts had banished Lucy to Jamaica, she had learned to keep the vulnerable part of herself protected. Even basking in the love of Emily and Ian, she had been unwilling to share that tender, fragile part of her with any but those few people she trusted most. To know that Valcour had seen beneath her tough facade made her feel furious, violated.

"You read my letters!" Lucy choked out. She waited for him to deny it, but he met her gaze squarely, his answer in his eyes. "How dare you!" she raged, mortified that he had seen her weakness. "They were mine! Mine! You had no right!"

"I suppose we can count ourselves even, then, madam. You had no right to be prying in the tower room."

"Oh no, Valcour. We're not *even* by a long way. You have worked three times the villainy on me that I have on you. But I warn you, the score will be evened. I promise you will pay for every piece of devilment you have done to me."

"And exactly what is on your list of my crimes? That I saved you from that gaming hell? That I rescued you from the disaster you and Aubrey had gotten yourself into? That I married you to save you from social ruin and then opened your father's grave to make certain you would be safe?"

"Safe? From what? Are you telling me that my own father was supposed to be a danger to me if he had been alive?"

"Someone is stalking you, girl. Taking great lengths to lure you into some mad dream that your father lives. Did it ever occur to you that this person might be dangerous? Hell, whoever is stirring up this insanity would have to be unbalanced to concoct such a scheme in the first place."

"Did it ever occur to *you* that the corpse you unearthed might *not* be my father at all?" Lucy flung back.

"What the blazes? Of course it was d'Autrecourt."

"How can you be so certain after seventeen years?" Lucy demanded, her fists clenching in the torn cloth of her nightshift. "There couldn't have been much left of his face. It could have been anyone lying in that coffin, rotting."

Valcour's gaze narrowed, but not enough to wholly conceal the sudden unease in his eyes. "What are you saying?" He sneered. "That the d'Autrecourts murdered some poor helpless bastard, dressed him in Alexander's clothes, and buried him beneath a headstone with Alexander's name on it?"

"Is that so inconceivable considering everything else they've done to protect their family name?" Lucy demanded, so close her bare toes brushed the tips of Valcour's own. "I wouldn't be surprised if there were the bones of some poor child in the coffin that was supposed to be mine. Maybe you should trundle yourself out again with your spade and dig that up as well, to make certain *I* am not dead."

Valcour's jaw squared, and she could see a vein throbbing in his temple. "Don't be a fool."

"Why shouldn't I be? I certainly wouldn't want you to change your estimation of my character, after the tender little scene we just played out. Of course, I can understand why you might be reluctant to go graverobbing again so soon, my lord. Maybe *I* will go out and exhume the coffin. Quite a unique experience, I would imagine, digging up one's own grave. It should make quite an intriguing tale for the new countess of Valcour to share over the tea table. Unless, of course, I can dredge up a more interesting skeleton in the St. Cyr family history."

"The St. Cyr family skeletons are a dangerous lot, Lucinda. Tampering with them would be the biggest mistake you ever made."

"Obviously you have no knowledge of my distinguished career. I've made a great plenty blunders, my lord. I'm not afraid to add another. This castle seems fairly bursting with secrets. Imagine the fun I could have, ferreting them out, displaying them to the world. I was a mere child when I discovered the secret that Ian Blackheath was the dread patriot Raider Pendragon. I even dressed up in his mask and cloak. It was quite entertaining."

Valcour's face was ice-white, hard as stone. "I am certain you would find it so. Unfortunately, your entertainment at the St. Cyrs' expense will have to wait. We are leaving for London as soon as the coach can be brought 'round."

"London?" Lucy couldn't keep the astonishment from her voice. "But we just arrived here."

"In case you've forgotten, there are a great many people who are quite worried about you. I have it on high authority that John Wilkes was ready to slay my brother and Claree Wilkes was all but hysterical with worry and remorse. After all, your parents entrusted your safety to them."

His words sliced through Lucy's carefully erected wall of belligerence, wounding her. She'd be damned before she let him see how deeply.

"And then," Valcour continued ruthlessly, "there is Lady Catherine St. Cyr, who was distraught over all that had happened."

"Lady Catherine?"

"The unfortunate woman who bore me. She needs to be told that all has been arranged satisfactorily."

"Satisfactorily?" Lucy snorted. *"That* depends on your perspective."

"I suppose Lady Catherine will take comfort in the fact that I have produced a daughter-in-law for her at last. I am certain she had despaired of me ever providing her with one." There was something about Valcour's face that belied his biting humor. "You will do nothing to upset her, girl. Do you understand that?" he said. "Hate me, revile me, curse me if you will. But distress her, and I vow, I will deal with you so harshly you'll regret you were born."

"I'm trembling with fear."

"Do not mock me. Lady Catherine will be told nothing of this madness—nothing of your father's supposed resurrection. Nothing of opened graves or mysterious letters."

"Or else what, my lord? You'll banish me back to Virginia? Lock me in the forbidden tower?"

Valcour's mouth twisted with a savagery that took Lucy aback. "You wouldn't be the first woman a Valcour imprisoned there." He was potent danger, pure ruthlessness, towering over her. "Defy me where Lady Catherine is concerned, and I promise you this, my rebel bride: You will regret it for the rest of your life."

Lucy laughed, tossing her curls. "I think it far more likely that *you* will be the one experiencing regret in the future, my lord. Regret that you forced me to marry you."

Valcour spun her around, his hands closing with savage delicacy about her throat, his face a mask of cold fury. He didn't tighten his fingers, merely curved them about the fragile cords of her neck, making her aware that with the smallest flick of his wrist he could crush the breath from her body. Lucy didn't flicker an eyelash. She faced him, her eyes blazing defiance.

"Before you decide to match wits with me, girl, you might want to remember the night of the duel at Perdition's Gate," Valcour said silkily, running his thumbs from the base of her jaw down to the fragile hollow where her pulse seemed to be trying to beat its way through her skin. "I have had a great deal of practice dealing with people foolish enough to show themselves as my foes. I am as gifted in exacting pain from an enemy as I am at pleasuring a woman. Challenge me in this, and I'll not be overly concerned about which sensation I evoke in you. Do we understand each other, Countess?"

Lucy had been bred in rebellion from the time she was three years old. She glared into Valcour's eyes, a hundred plans for outright mutiny simmering in her mind. "I understand you perfectly, my lord," she said with venomous sweetness.

Valcour released her and took up his boots, then

walked from the bedchamber, his features cold, his jaw set. But the instant he shut the door behind him, the earl leaned against the wall of the corridor, his dark head arching back, his eyes shut tight, as he tried to block out the roiling images, the fierce emotions, that still reverberated through him.

But all he could see was Lucinda's face, full of witchery and sedition. All he could feel were the fiery trails she had blazed across his shoulders and upon his chest with those hands that had woven such magic over the keys of the pianoforte.

She had been so damned beautiful, the edges of her nightshift white about breasts full and crying out for his mouth, her waist impossibly narrow, her hips a lush cradle that made a man want to bury himself deep. And her legs—they'd seemed to go on forever, slender and shapely, supple and seductive, wrapping about his body, dragging him fiercely against her.

She had been quicksilver in his arms, wildfire beneath his mouth, the wide range of emotion Lucinda gave to her fury, her righteous indignation and her temper had flowed into passion and desire like a river bursting its banks. Valcour had felt himself being swept away to places he didn't dare contemplate.

And after a climax more shattering than Valcour had ever known, he had nearly been ready to release himself to that wild, uncharted world, seduced by the knowledge that he was the first man to have delighted in that lovely body. The first man to possess her.

Even as a youth, Valcour had considered feminine virginity to be not a precious gift but, rather, an obstacle he had no patience for overcoming. He had wanted women who were well schooled in the ways of male passion. Women who knew what they wanted in the bedchamber and were not afraid to take it.

But he had never suspected until he had seen Lucinda tumbled in his arms how astonishingly beautiful innocence could be. How bewitching it was to watch dark-lashed eyes widen in astonishment, berry-red lips quiver with pleasure, gasping as he dipped into that place no man had ever explored before.

He had never known that a virgin would give him back some fleeting wisp of his own innocence, remind him of the wonder of discovery.

And Lucinda had been wild with that discovery, greedy and bedazzled, generous and elated. She had given without fear, taken without shyness, opened herself for Valcour's plundering with a courage and a passion that had almost made him forget.

And then she had surfaced from the power of their climax, only to be jolted from the waves of honeyed pleasure and thrust again into reality and an emotional pain that dulled the star-bright luster of her eyes.

Valcour had watched the transformation from passion-tossed angel to heartbreak, his own chest raw with the awareness of what he had done to her.

He had wanted so damned badly to reach out to her, promise her anything to bring back the fragile yielding that had been in her face, the astonishment, the joy.

Only her outrage over her pilfered letters had saved him. Saved him from making an even bigger mistake than he had made in taking her to bed.

And her threats to reveal St. Cyr secrets had sent Valcour crashing back to reality—back to icy masks no one could penetrate, back to walls that kept pain out and imprisoned a hundred haunting demons of regret and guilt, betrayal and hopelessness. Back to the earl of Valcour and the hell he had built for himself brick by brick.

Valcour's jaw knotted, his fingers still tingling with the silken feel of her throat, his gut twisting with disgust that he had even so vaguely threatened a woman.

But it had not even been the threat to tell Lady Catherine that had pushed him over some unseen edge.

It had been Lucinda herself, delving into places Valcour had never allowed any woman to go, touching emotions in him he hadn't believed existed anymore.

Never before had he even been tempted to let anyone peek inside the walls that held him apart from the world. Never before had he forgotten that wall's existence, even for a little while.

He had forgotten it in Lucinda's arms. Forgotten it, only to have it slammed into his face again with the force of a morningstar mace—and with as devastating results.

Valcour jammed trembling fingers through the tangled masses of his hair—hair that Lucinda had caressed, kissed, delighted in. Whatever the depth of pleasure their physical joining might hold, he must never again let himself slide so deeply into oblivion. He must never again let down his guard.

For allowing Lucinda to see into his own private anguish would not heal him. The walls of pain would merely close her in as well, suck her into the black abyss that had twisted Dominic's life. And, like the most subtle poison, it could destroy them both.

14

Lucy sank onto the gilt bench in the entryway of Hawkvale House, feeling as if she had made the journey to London manacled to the axle of the traveling coach rather than inside it. Her joints were frozen knobs of pain, her neck crooked at an odd angle, and her stomach was snarling with all the refinement of a pack of starving wolves. Every inch of her body felt bruised by the bone-jarring jolting of the coach, Valcour having set a pace more hellacious than any even the impatient Lucy had ever endured.

It was all she could do to keep from crumpling into an ignominious heap on the marble floor in exhaustion. But she would cheerfully have stepped into a bath of boiling oil before she letting Valcour know how close she was to collapsing.

It was her own stubborn fault she was in this state, she was forced to admit grudgingly. Valcour had said that they would set whatever pace she desired. Any time she felt the need to stop, she only had to signal, and everything would be done to provide for her comfort.

Unfortunately, he had finished this chivalrous offer by making the fatal observation that ladies were, by nature, not such stalwart travelers as men.

The words had no sooner left his mouth than Lucy had resolved she would die a slow and torturous death before she cried enough. She had informed Valcour that the swifter the pace the better she would like it. That she never traveled fast enough to suit her.

But, then, Lucy thought grimly, she had never traveled with the earl before. The coach had seemed a heartbeat away from overturning as it barreled down the road, Valcour riding on his infernal stallion beside it. The wind had been in his face, the sun shining overhead. It had added insult to injury, the fact that the arrogant aristocrat was the most magnificent horseman Lucy had ever seen, controlling the spirited stallion as if they were some mythical entity joined by the gods themselves.

Lucy had passed the grueling hours imagining the earl at her mercy and plotting all sorts of tortures to inflict on him. But as the trip wore on, the most diabolical vengeance of all seemed to be locking him in a jolting coach while he battled against calls of nature until he felt ready to burst.

Through it all, she had remained determined that she would never be the one who precipitated a break in the journey. And in the end, she had triumphed. But it had been an empty victory. The moment Valcour opened the door of the coach, he had let fly a string of oaths, scooping her into his arms and carrying her up the stairs and into the entryway of the townhouse. Lucy had made a feeble effort to resist, but in the end she had only been relieved when he'd plunked her down on a gilt bench tucked in a shadowy alcove.

She sat bleary-eyed and numb, while servants in midnight-blue livery bustled around her, taking her cloak and bonnet and Valcour's roquelaure. The footmen's faces were blank, no sign of curiosity evident, as if their master arrived home at four in the morning with a runaway countess in tow every other Saturday of the year.

Yet how could it be any wonder the servants were so restrained, when their master looked for all the world as if he had just arrived home from a night of hazard at Whites?

Valcour was as perfectly groomed as Lucy was unkempt. The wind that had made her hair look like a ravaged straw stack had only tousled his dark tresses like the fingers of a lover. The sun had deepened the bronzed gloss that defined the planes and angles of his face. The tiny creases at the corners of his eyelids were faint, pale starrings that made his eyes more intriguing.

Only the slightest whitening at the corner of his mouth betrayed the fact that the past three days had been a grim ordeal.

"Grayson." Valcour's voice shook Lucy from her thoughts. "You will awaken Lady Catherine's maid and have her attend the countess at once. My wife will reside in the bedchamber linked to my apartments. Her smallest wish will be granted as if it were my own."

Lucy glanced up at Valcour, wondering what significance the location of her chamber had. Would he visit her bed that night? From the day of their marriage, Emily and Ian Blackheath had slept together at Blackheath Hall. The huge tester bed with its crewel-worked curtains provided a serene haven from the outside world for Lucy's parents. In that bed, Emily Blackheath had brought forth her babes to lay in her husband's arms. In that bed, the wounded Pendragon had been nursed through injuries sustained during the War for Independence. And it was on those pillows that Lucy had found her mother crying out her fears for him when he returned to the front lines of the war.

Now Lucy was herself a married woman, and yet there was no devotion, no love between her and the man who had taken her to wife in the church at Hound's Way. Despite the passion that had raged between them, he was still a stranger to her. An enigmatic, intriguing, infuriating man, who made her feel things she didn't want to feel, made her do things she didn't want to do. Made her a fool who had all but killed herself on the journey to London just to spite him.

At the church, Valcour had offered to give her whatever time she needed to become accustomed to the physical side of their relationship. But now that the marriage had been consummated, she couldn't imagine he would feel there was any reason for further restraint. The thought was both disturbing and alluring.

"I shall see to the lady's comfort at once, sir." The footman's words shook Lucy out of her thoughts. The servant bowed to her. "My lady, if you will follow me?"

"Dominic!" The sound of a voice from the top of the stairs made Lucinda look up so swiftly a sharp pain stabbed into the base of her neck.

A woman who looked to be about fifty years old raced down in a flurry of primrose bedrobe, her soft gold hair falling about a heart-shaped face. Delicate features were ravaged by worry and sleeplessness, her beautiful eyes lost in great bruised circles. But Lucy knew in a heartbeat that the woman was the dreamy-eyed girl who had touched her heart from the abandoned portrait. Valcour's mother. Or, as the earl had said, the unfortunate woman who'd born him.

Despite the woman's obvious distress, not so much as a muscle in Valcour's face moved. He didn't brush her touch away as she clasped his arm, nor did he seek to comfort her.

"Aubrey? Aubrey is safe?" she choked out.

"I told you I would make it right, madam," he said. "And so I did. The boy is on his way to squander my coin on some prime horseflesh, I believe."

"Thank God! And the girl is safely back with her

guardians? I was so terrified! After you all spent the night unchaperoned!"

"It is permitted for a bride to spend the night with her new husband, is it not?"

"H-Her new husband?" Delicate cheeks went white. "But you said Aubrey was safe!"

"Felicitate me, madam. I have provided the house of Valcour with a countess at last."

"A countess?"

"I was stricken by paroxysms of passion and married Lucinda Blackheath out of hand."

The woman staggered back, her hands clenched against her breast as if Valcour had thrust in a dagger. "No! Dominic, tell me you did not—"

"That is hardly the kind of reception due my wife. You shall attempt to do better, madam." Valcour went to the bench where Lucy sat and took her hand, drawing her to her feet. "Lady Catherine St. Cyr, dowager countess of Valcour, may I present the former Lucinda Blackheath, now my wife?"

Lady Catherine's eyes were huge pools of misery as she regarded Lucy. Excruciatingly aware of her unkempt appearance, and the almost horrified fascination in the older woman's face, Lucy stiffened.

She knew enough of aristocratic pride to discern that Lady Catherine must be aghast at her son's mésalliance to a woman society would consider scarcely worthy to kiss his exalted boot. Lucy had seen the high price that had been extracted from her mother for committing such a crime. The anger that rose inside Lucy was not so much for herself but for the young Emily d'Autrecourt, abandoned, alone.

"Lady Catherine," Lucy said, with all the dignity she could muster, "you'll be relieved to know that the thought of mingling my blood with that of some accursed noble family is as repugnant to me as I am to you."

"Repugnant? How could such a marriage be otherwise

to you?" Lady Catherine asked. "Or to you, Dominic? You know nothing of each other!"

"We know enough," Valcour interjected. "Lucinda knows that I am ruthless in getting what I want and I know enough to have a healthy respect for the toe of her boot."

"Wh-what is that supposed to mean?" Lady Catherine's hands knotted in the folds of her bedrobe. "Merciful God, Dominic, you've gone mad."

"It would hardly be the first time a beautiful woman had driven a Valcour to madness, would it, madam?"

Hot spots of color stained Lady Catherine's cheeks as she glanced up at Valcour's impassive face.

"I just . . . there must be some way for you both to escape this!" Lady Catherine looked into Lucy's face. "You must forgive me for being so blunt, child. But you cannot blame a mother for being dismayed at this whole affair."

Lucy winced, suddenly jolted by the image of her own mother, the stricken look that would have been on Emily Blackheath's face if she had been present at the announcement of this most unexpected marriage. The sudden stab of homesickness and grief must have been reflected on Lucy's face. Lady Catherine's voice filled with sympathy.

"Listen to me, prattling on, and you all but dead on your feet. Poor lamb, we will have the chance to make things right in the morning. Dominic should be ashamed of himself, dragging you about at such an hour. But the Valcour men have never been a patient lot, especially when traveling, and—"

Dominic interrupted. "Forgive me for pointing out that you continue to—how did you say it, madam?— *prattle*. Perhaps you could enlighten my bride as to the traditional vices of Valcour in the morning?"

Lady Catherine seemed to wilt as if his voice was a killing frost. Lucy was surprised to find herself bristling on Lady Catherine's behalf, but Lucy was so weary, she could barely muster her usual defiance.

"I am very tired, my lady," she said. "And you look as if you have not slept in days. I am sorry for any distress I caused you."

Lady Catherine raised trembling fingers to her soft hair. "I am certain things can be made right somehow, Miss Black—"

"Lucy," she interjected quietly.

"Lucy." There were shadows in the noblewoman's eyes: secrets, as if a dozen colored veils hid something from Lucy's sight. Lucy's heart twisted at the unhappiness that lurked behind that sweet heart-shaped face.

It was all too obvious that the source of the lady's sorrow was her tall, dark-haired son, resentment barely hidden in the chill reaches of his eyes.

Suddenly Lucy wanted to shelter the older woman from that coldness. "I am well schooled in mounting insurrection, but I haven't the slightest idea how a countess should behave. Perhaps you could help me learn."

"I will do anything in my power to help you, child." The noblewoman's lips moved as if forming words, soft, so soft. "For *his* sake."

Half an hour later, Valcour stood in front of the mirror in his bedchamber and dipped chill water from the washbasin with his cupped hands. He splashed the water over his face, as if to cleanse away the weariness that had seeped into his very bones. But he doubted the fabled Fountain of Youth could have rejuvenated him tonight.

From the moment the Valcour coach had rumbled away from Harlestone early that morning, Dominic had maintained a veneer of icy detachment. During the breakneck trip back to London, he had adopted an aura of frigid calm.

No one had suspected that the earl, astride his midnight stallion, had his gut in knots of roiling emotions he couldn't even name, let alone control. No one had guessed that his eyes traveled time and again to the coach window to catch glimpses of his bride. Or that his mind was filled with images of his hands on the bodice of her rose- and cream-striped gown, unfastening the lacings, delving under the fabric to find more sensual textures beneath.

No one had guessed how much Valcour had wished he could just turn his stallion the other way and ride away from Hawkvale, the Lady Catherine and his truculent brother. How much he had wanted to take his rebel bride to some distant Valcour estate and try to make something good out of this disaster. Lucinda had faced the journey like a prisoner of war, determined to defy her conqueror to the bitter end. And Valcour had known exactly how much that pride had cost her. For she had seemed utterly dejected in the confines of the coach when she thought he couldn't see her.

God knew, Valcour felt equally morose. But nothing had prepared him to face the scene that awaited him inside Hawkvale's doors.

His mother's face was shrouded with a depth of torment he had only seen one other time as a frightened boy. Tonight her eyes had been the same, wide and wounded, when he'd told her Lucinda was his wife.

He'd expected relief, astonishment. He had not expected Lady Catherine to gape at him as if he had made the girl his whore.

Valcour delved into the water again, holding it against his beard-stubbled cheeks. For Christ's sake, the woman had wanted him to fix things, hadn't she? And there was no other way to make Lucinda Blackheath right in the eyes of the world except to give her his name.

He had done what was necessary, what was expected of a gentleman of honor. What he hadn't expected was that Lucinda would stir such a fierce protectiveness inside him, make him feel raw, somehow, by touching him deep in the hidden reaches of his heart.

She had barreled into his life only a month before, turning it upside down with her insane mischief. She was the apocalypse that had shattered his hard-won peace. But she was so damned brave, so damned defiant in the face of disaster. There was such strength in her, such fierce determination.

Through those traits, she reminded him of the boy he had once been, sword clutched in his trembling hand, confronting crushing odds, heartbreak beyond bearing. But this time Valcour was playing the villain. He was the one forcing her to bend to his will. Valcour, and that mysterious madman who had brought her to England with his lies for some devious purpose the earl couldn't even begin to contemplate.

Valcour unbuttoned his shirt, his jaw set, hard. No one would hurt Lucinda, no one would break her, the earl resolved. Not even Valcour himself.

Valcour closed his eyes, remembering Lucinda in the bed at Harlestone, the elegance and grace of her supple body, the eagerness in her fingers as she touched him.

God, how he wanted to open the door between their rooms right now and drive away her misery with his kisses. Bury his own pain at the betrayal of the ruby ring by losing himself in Lucinda's beautiful body.

God, how he wanted to forget.

Valcour swore under his breath. The girl had looked ready to collapse despite the brave front she'd put up. He might be a bastard, but he wasn't enough of a beast to ease his own tension by bedding a woman so exhausted she had barely been able to stand. Better to get into the bed his valet had hastily prepared for his use and try to sleep, forget.

He was stripping his shirt from his shoulders when he heard a soft rap upon his door.

Valcour froze for a moment, his pulses taking a sudden

wild leap at the thought it could possibly be Lucinda. The thought of his countess seeking him out, coming to his bed, was more arousing than he could ever have imagined.

"What is it?" he called out, his voice strangely tight.

"Dominic?"

Lady Catherine's voice.

Valcour's jaw knotted. "I would prefer to be left alone, madam," he began, but the door was already swinging open. An ashen face was illuminated by the single candle clutched in Lady Catherine's birdlike hand.

Valcour winced as the light revealed reddened eyes, swollen from crying. She was painfully thin, drowning in a bedrobe of primrose satin. He wanted to press sweetmeats into her hands, to sit in the garden and have the sun kiss roses back into her cheeks. Instead, he pictured the tower room at the castle and the ring of ruby fire that would taunt him forever from his new wife's finger.

"Dominic, I—I have made certain the child is settled in the rose room."

"Lucinda is no child, madam. She is my wife. The bishop himself presided and all was conducted quite respectably." Valcour arched one brow. "I should think you would be delighted."

"Delighted? How could you even think such a thing?"

"The St. Cyr bloodline will be assured. You will have feminine company." Valcour crossed to where a decanter of Madeira stood on a table at the far side of the room and poured himself a glass. "By God, I could almost believe you are stunned by what has happened."

"Stunned? I am that. And horrified. My God, is this some kind of twisted vengeance? A way to make us both pay for sins long past? Do you truly want to condemn us to spending the rest of our lives seeing Alexander's daughter every day? Do you want to share a bed with her? Have children with her, when every time you see her face, you must remember—"

"God's wounds, you're being as overly dramatic as Aubrey about this infernal affair. Lucinda, Aubrey, and I were stranded overnight. She would have been ruined. She could not wed that idiot boy. You must have known what action I would take."

"I *should* have known what would happen! Should have guessed!" Lady Catherine set the candle down on the desk tucked in the corner of Valcour's room. "But it never occurred to me that you would do such a thing! I know there have been other women who attempted to trap you into marriage. You evaded them so easily that—"

"Lucinda was hardly trying to ensnare me, madam. I all but had to haul the girl to the altar trussed like a partridge."

"Why would you take her to the altar at all? Especially if she didn't want to marry? Dominic, it makes no sense!"

Valcour turned away, hating the gnawing uncertainty that ate inside his gut at her words. What had his motives been? He didn't know any longer. It had all happened so fast—the scene with Aubrey, the confrontation with Lucinda in the stable. He had been so damned determined to take her to wife he'd barely had patience for the bishop to go stammering through the wedding vows.

He told himself he had acted to preserve his honor, and to save Lucinda from ruin. That it was a marriage of grim necessity.

But it wasn't duty that had made him think of her time and again during the weeks since he'd kissed her in the garden. It wasn't a feeling of responsibility that had driven him into Lucinda's arms last night. It wasn't a sense of obligation that inflamed him, drove him to take her, knowing in his heart that by possessing her body he was shattering the last, faint hope that the marriage could be dissolved.

Resentment welled up in Valcour toward Lady Catherine, who stood there, forcing him to confront feelings he had tried so damned hard to deny. How dare she look so accursed broken when he was the one bleeding inside?

"Oh, sweet Jesus, why did I send you after them?" Lady Catherine choked out. "I should have gone myself!"

"You have great delusions of your own abilities. I would never have allowed you to distress yourself that way."

"No." Lady Catherine gave a sick laugh. "You'd not let Aubrey fight a duel. You'd not let me be distressed. You'd not let this girl be ruined. But you would sacrifice yourself in marriage to a girl you did not love. A girl who could do nothing but remind you of—"

"It is done, madam. There is no point in tearing yourself apart with regret. As earl, it is my responsibility to—"

"To what? Pay eternally for other people's mistakes?"

"To protect my own."

"There is still time to avert this disaster! You barely knew the girl. Despite the cold facade you show to the world, I know you, Dominic. You are a good man. Gentle. Surely you did not consummate a marriage to a frightened girl. Get an annulment and she could go back to her family."

"I took Lucinda to Harlestone and claimed her as my wife in the most physical sense of the word. With some effort, you will be dandling the Valcour heir on your knee by next Christmas." His lips firmed, a burning sensation in his chest. Why was it that the thought of Lucinda ripening with his child filled him not with a sense of duty accomplished but, rather, with a kind of yearning he didn't dare examine?

"Don't you realize the fate you've condemned yourself to?" Lady Catherine raised a trembling hand to her face. "The rest of your life, without love, without hope . . . for you could never love her, no matter how brave and beautiful she is. You could never forgive her for being Alexander's daughter."

"I have forgotten it already." Dominic snapped his fingers in dismissal. "Alexander d'Autrecourt is dead. She is Lucinda St. Cyr now. And as for love, I have never desired to be torn apart by the emotions that destroyed my father."

"What have I done to you, Dominic?" Lady Catherine's voice broke. "I never intended to hurt you."

"Didn't you, madam?" Valcour drained the glass of Madeira, then crossed to where the fire licked hungrily on the hearth. "If you did not mean to hurt me, why, pray tell, did you give me that ring on my twentieth birthday?"

"What?"

"You remember. The rubies. The legendary love token you said was steeped in romantic tradition. The ring that could only fit the finger of the giver's true love."

Lady Catherine stilled, a haunted light in her eyes. "I gave it to you because it was precious to me."

"I used it to wed Lucinda. Imagine my surprise when we stopped to visit her villainous relatives at Avonstea and the dowager duchess demanded to know how my wife had gotten hold of the fabled love token that had been in the d'Autrecourt family for generations."

Lady Catherine flinched. "Dominic, I . . ."

"You what, madam? Thought it would be a pretty jest that I used as a wedding ring some trinket from a man I hated?"

"You adored Alexander d'Autrecourt."

"I was a boy. A blind, foolish boy who knew no better. But he taught me well, did he not? A lesson I have never forgotten."

"You will not let yourself forget! People aren't perfect, no matter how much we might want them to be. Call me a fool, but I believed in the magic of the ring. I wanted so much for you to."

"And I suppose the tower room at Harlestone was preserved for my benefit as well? Fitted out like some infernal shrine? My God, madam, do you know what it was like for me to go there, to see it?"

A shimmering, desperate light shone in Lady Catherine's eyes. "Dominic, you—you went to the tower room?"

"My bride had gone prying about. I had to drag her away from the pianoforte there. I ordered that room locked years ago. By God, I should have had everything inside it piled in the center and burned."

"You didn't," Lady Catherine begged faintly. "Tell me you did not."

"I burned enough. The music left there. Lucinda was playing it when I found her."

"You destroyed the musical scores, then?" Lady Catherine asked faintly.

"More of my twisted vengeance against you, no doubt," Valcour said bitterly. "What did you expect me to do when I discovered the chamber intact? Rejoice?"

"I don't know. I just . . ." She turned away and walked to the window, so forlorn that Valcour's anger wavered. "I lost you there, Dominic. Perhaps I hoped I might find you again someday."

"The boy who played in that tower died the night his father placed a pistol to his head."

Lady Catherine spun to face him, her eyes meeting his. "Why don't you say it all, Dominic? What you truly feel? That I am the one who pulled the trigger. I am the one who murdered my husband, my son."

"I am alive."

"Are you? The Dominic I knew vanished. I cannot find him."

"I would never say it was your fault, madam."

"Of course not. You never spoke a word of reproach to me. Never told me how you felt. There was a time when I shared all your most precious secrets. Do you remember?

You would bring me pretty stones and feathers you found in the meadow. You would cry on my lap when your father was harsh. You would sing for me, and play——"

"Enough!" Valcour roared.

Lady Catherine swayed, like a blossom battered by a horse's hoof. She stood there, bruised and trembling, and Valcour could see how hard she fought to keep back the tears.

Valcour tried to gentle his voice. "You have another son. He can give you what I cannot."

"Children are not interchangeable, Dominic. Much as I love Aubrey, he does not dull the ache of grief inside me. He doesn't make up for the fact that I lost you."

Valcour sucked in a deep breath that burned his lungs. "I would not want you to lose any more than you already have, madam. If there is anything you wish to retrieve from the tower chamber, I would advise you to travel to Harlestone and do so within the week. I left orders for it to be dismantled and everything destroyed that you have not claimed. It will be as I wish."

"Will it? I wonder."

"What is that supposed to mean?"

"Only that I can't believe you will destroy everything. It would be as if you were destroying the last vestiges of your soul."

"I have no soul. I have made certain of that. Now, will you go to Harlestone?"

"Yes. As soon as I see Lucy settled."

"Agreed. Now, if you will pardon me. Between racing to find Aubrey and the girl, the difficulties of a somewhat ill-timed wedding and providing my new countess with a bridal night, I am somewhat tired."

"Dominic——"

Valcour turned his back to her, not wanting to risk her seeing the emotions he knew were simmering far too close to the surface. "Goodnight, madam," he said stonily.

Lady Catherine hesitated for a moment, then she slipped out the door so quietly he almost failed to hear the tiny, watery sound of her stifled crying.

Valcour's fists knotted, but he turned and stepped out into the corridor, watching his mother melt into the shadows.

"Madam?"

She turned, her face wrenchingly hopeful. For an instant, she was the beautiful young mother who had read him fairy tales when he was ill with a fever. She was the dreamy-eyed woman who had sat in the tower room, stitching.

Valcour stared at Lady Catherine's face, suddenly so young in the candlelight. "Madam, I am not worth a minute of your grief," he said softly. Then he returned to his bedchamber and shut the door.

The earl of Valcour walked slowly to his bed and sank down on it, his mind filled with faces: His mother's, still ravaged from pain long past. His new bride, angry and hurt, defensive, defiant. Deprived of her loving family, her sisters, her mother, the father who adored her.

The earl wanted to open the door that led to Lucinda's adjoining bedchamber. Wanted to lose himself in the passion, the fire of her body, drive away the shadows that threatened to consume them both.

But Valcour closed his eyes, remembering a boy of twelve who had suffered the same separation, crushing loneliness, and had no way to stop his own pain.

How could he be expected to stop up the wounds of anyone else? Even his mother seemed appalled that he had taken Lucinda to wife—and to his bed. *You are a good man, Dominic. You would not consummate a marriage with a frightened child.*

He had made love to a woman, his wife, his countess at Harlestone. He had spilled his seed inside her and had lost some small, guarded part of his inner self. He had even dared imagine Lucinda swelling with his son, the heir Valcour, destined to inherit . . . a legacy of villainy, hate, weakness? A mother, desperately homesick, trapped into marriage by the stiff-necked nobleman who had forced her hand? A nobleman who had never wanted a son, never wanted to experience that link that proved his own destruction?

Lady Catherine had all but begged Valcour for an explanation for his actions. Had challenged everything he had believed about himself.

Now her question echoed mercilessly in his head. Had he truly married Lucinda out of some twisted thirst for revenge? Or to punish himself forever for what had gone before? Or had he married her because she stirred him in places no other woman had ever reached? Because he had wanted her with a ferocity that had stunned him from the first moment he realized she was a woman—a bold, brave, beautiful woman he had wanted to touch, to take? Had he looked into Lucinda Blackheath's defiant face and fallen beneath the spell of an enchantress with sapphire eyes and a mouth lush and sweet as sun-ripened berries? Or had he been entranced by a fire maiden racing off to rescue a baby swan?

He had always been so carefully detached, so emotionally distant. Was it possible he'd wanted the hotheaded American beauty so badly he hadn't given a damn how he got her in his bed?

If that was true, wasn't he every bit as much of a monster as . . . Damn it, maybe it wasn't too late to free himself from the uncertainties that were tearing him apart, to stop this painful quickening in his chest. Maybe there was still time to save Lucinda from himself.

But if he decided to do so, he could never kiss her again, never run his palms over her silky skin, find the secret places that made her gasp, cry out. Never fill her with his seed and risk the danger of his son or daughter taking root in her womb.

Only then could he do what was necessary—send her

back to her family where she belonged. Valcour expected to feel a sense of relief at the prospect. Instead, bleakness settled over him, cold and undeniable.

He closed his eyes in an effort to drive it away, but images danced across his dark lids: a tiny golden-curled hoyden of a girl wrestling with a bevy of dark-haired brothers, Lucinda teaching the child how to aim her blows toward their tender parts.

It would be mayhem. Insanity. Worlds away from the dignified existence Valcour had always anticipated for himself. Why did it suddenly seem far too appealing?

Valcour gritted his teeth, banishing the image from his mind. For over twenty years he had cultivated a wall of solitude, cut off anyone who could hurt him. He had dug an unbreachable chasm to separate him from anyone who might see past the mighty earl's facade to the vulnerable man who lay buried beneath.

Such strong needs couldn't change in three short weeks. Couldn't be obliterated by one taste of a woman's mouth, one deep, delving thrust into her welcoming body. Could they?

But as Valcour stared at the door separating his rooms from those of his rebel bride, he couldn't stop the fierce yearning inside him. The mighty earl of Valcour faced the most frightening truth he had ever known. For the first time since the disaster that had changed the course of his life, he did not want to be alone.

15

*L*ucinda stared down at the matched team of grays that danced like living poetry in their traces, and she wished she could snatch the reins from Valcour's hands and steer the curricle away from the townhouse that loomed ever larger against the morning sky.

She had raced up the stairs of the Wilkeses' London house a hundred times since her arrival in England, teasing Claree about her handsome husband, chattering about balls and soirees and dreams for the newborn country they had left behind. Even the specter of Alexander d'Autrecourt had not been able to dim Lucy's bubbling enthusiasm for long in the face of this adventure.

But as Valcour drew the horses to a stop in the circle before the Wilkeses' doorway, Lucy knew that facing Claree and John Wilkes this morning would be the most difficult thing she had ever done.

They would feel as if it were their fault that Lucy would never return to Virginia again. They would have to face their dearest friends with the news that their daughter was lost forever.

Lucy had always thought she was so infernally brilliant in her mischief, magically able to extract herself from any dilemma. For the first time, the Raider's daughter had embroiled herself in a disaster from which there was no escape, one that had snared countless innocent people in its coils and dragged them down with her.

Her hands knotted together in her lap as the grays came to a halt and a groom bustled forward to take the lead gelding by the bit.

"Lucinda." Valcour's voice was soft, bracing. "Remember, you are a countess. It's not as if you had run away with a stableboy."

Lucy gave a broken laugh as she regarded her husband, resplendent in an emerald velvet frockcoat and bone-colored breeches. "Eloping with a stableboy would be far easier to explain, especially to my father. You forget, he risked his life to gain freedom from the English aristocracy. I can't think John or Claree or any of my family will be pleased to hear that I have become the enemy."

Valcour's fingers gently caught Lucy's chin and turned her to face him. "The war is over, Lucinda. We aren't enemies any longer."

"Aren't we?" Lucy looked up at him, and for a moment she wondered what it would be like to be arriving at the Wilkeses' flushed with happiness and passion for the man she had married.

A solemn light touched Valcour's eyes. "I would have us be . . . allies." He took her hand gently in his own warm, strong one.

No vow of eternal love, no claim of adoration. And yet, the words made strength seep into Lucy's limbs, made her chin tip up just a little.

She reached up and stroked a ribbon of night-dark hair from Valcour's brow. "Thank you for coming with me today. For being . . . kind."

One corner of Valcour's lips quirked. "I'd advise you not to become used to it, hoyden. I am everything you judged me in the past. Ill-tempered, impatient. Arrogant."

"Perhaps we have something in common after all," Lucy said.

Valcour squeezed her hand, then swung down from his seat. He waved away the footman who was hastening over to help Lucy descend from the equipage.

The earl's big hands encircled her waist, warm and firm and strangely bracing as he swung her lightly down to her feet.

Already people were staring: the footmen, the gardener clipping a yew hedge, and other eyes Lucy could feel somewhere behind her. She turned to catch just a glimpse of ragged jacket, a boy's dirty yet oddly familiar face. Then he vanished so quickly she could scarce believe he had been there at all.

She wished that she could turn and chase the vanishing child, like she had chased butterflies when she was small. But there was no way to escape what lay before her. Better to get it over with as swiftly as possible.

Lucy sucked in a deep breath, the trip to the Wilkeses' drawing room like that of a felon to the gallows. The censure in the butler's eyes was quelled by one haughty lift of an eyebrow from Valcour. The housemaids skittered away despite their curiosity as the earl leveled them a chill glare.

Delivered to the drawing room, Lucy paced the comfortable chamber where she had spent many pleasant evenings, John puffing his long clay pipe full of Virginia tobacco, Claree dithering over whether to place a knight above an honorable at the dining table.

Lucy bit her lower lip to keep it from trembling and strained to hear the sound of footsteps in the corridor beyond. When she did, she was tempted to bolt out the window into the small garden below. The door opened, and Lucy's hands knotted in the folds of her skirts.

Lucy's worst nightmare about this confrontation

couldn't have prepared her for the sight of the Wilkeses' faces. Claree was haggard, her eyes filled with self-blame. John Wilkes's appearance was even more alarming. The eyes that had made English generals quake in their spit-polished boots were seething with an anger that superseded his relief.

"Girl, I should acquaint you with the end of a willow switch for what you've put us through!" John growled.

"I would not advise it," Valcour said softly. "I'm afraid I would have to take exception to my countess being treated like an unruly child."

"*I* take exception to this whole cursed marriage, but you didn't give a damn about that, did you, my lord? I'd wager you think I should thank you for sending word that you were married before you posted a notice in the *Gazette!*"

"I know this marriage is a shock to you—" Lucy began.

"A shock!" Wilkes cried, wheeling on her. "Four days ago you were making calf's eyes at Aubrey St. Cyr and mocking Valcour so perfectly you sent us all into fits of laughter."

Lucy's cheeks were feverish red. "Aubrey couldn't make me a countess."

"You expect me to believe that Pendragon's daughter sold herself in marriage to become 'my lady'? Your father all but gave his life so you could be free of English tyranny, and you come to England and embrace one of the very men who oppressed us!"

"Strange," Valcour's voice cut in, almost lazily, "I thought you had come to England to bury the hostilities between our two countries."

Wilkes spun on Valcour. "I'll thank you to mind your own accursed affairs. I am this girl's guardian in her father's absence."

"And I am her husband. I will not tolerate anyone— even you, Mr. Wilkes—distressing my wife."

Lucy felt a shaft of fear, the duel at the gaming hell playing out before her eyes. John Wilkes was beyond fury, and Valcour's code of honor would endure no insults. "Please, it is over. Both of you. There is nothing to do but accept—"

John sputtered a string of curses. "You expect us just to shrug and excuse your behavior? From the first time I met you, girl, I heard the tales about Ian's indulgence of your every whim. I dismissed them as rubbish. By God, I wanted to coddle you myself after all you had endured. But it seems the gossip mongers were right! You are insufferably spoilt, selfish!"

"The fault in this debacle lies more with me," Valcour cut in.

"That is one judgment I don't doubt!" John snapped. "You steal the girl away from your own brother, then send us an infernal note informing us she has married you! A man we know she despises! Don't tell me you discovered some grand passion somewhere between London and Avonstea, Valcour!"

"I wanted her. I took her. It is done," Valcour said stonily. "You need have no fear for her welfare. The wealth of Valcour will be at her disposal. She will have everything her heart could desire."

"I see." John snorted in disgust and turned to Lucy. "And I suppose you don't desire to see your father and mother ever again, girl? I suppose you can forget Norah and the other little ones?"

Lucy felt as if her chest were going to burst with pain. "Valcour's honor demanded that—that we marry."

"Valcour demanded?" John stared into her face, as if he had risen from the haze of his anger and was really seeing her for the first time. "You don't give a damn about British notions of honor, do you, girl? You don't give a damn about this English cur?"

"Wilkes, that is enough." Valcour's voice was like tempered steel as he encircled Lucy in the crook of his arm. "I understand your shock, even your anger. And I take full responsibility for what has happened."

"I'm not surprised. What did you do, hold a dagger to the girl's throat to make her wed you?"

The barest tick of a muscle in Valcour's jaw made Lucy's knees quake with foreboding.

"What is the girl to you?" Wilkes charged. "She has little fortune of her own. She's no aristocrat with ancestors reaching back to the accursed William the Conqueror."

"You forget, her father was a d'Autrecourt."

"Her father is Ian Blackheath. An American patriot!" John raged. "He nearly died fighting against tyranny! And I lost all hope of ever—" John stopped, but Lucy knew the sacrifice that was like a burning brand in the man's chest. An eternally empty cradle. The knowledge that he would never be a whole man again. "Do you think that you can just storm in and take an innocent girl from her family? And because you are an earl, no man will dare to stop you?"

"Your anger will change nothing, Wilkes. Lucinda is mine. I will do right by her, I swear it."

"I'll take your oath and ram it down your throat with the point of my sword!" John grappled for the dress sword affixed to his waist.

"No!" Lucy cried out, diving in front of Valcour as Wilkes's steel hissed from its scabbard. "John, he is a master swordsman! Valcour, you cannot hurt him! I have enough to answer for already."

The earl's hand closed about her arm, moving her out of his way. "This is between Wilkes and me." The earl's gaze never wavered from the American diplomat's face.

"Please, for the love of God! Don't do this," Lucy cried out as Valcour slowly drew the lethal length of steel that had nearly sent Jasper d'Autrecourt to the devil.

Valcour held the sword before him, one hand on the hilt, the other fingering the tip. "Wilkes, I have killed men who have dared challenge my honor. I have wounded many more. But I have never cut down anyone for speaking the truth."

"I'll have your blood for this! Damn you, I——"

Lucy cried out, Claree shrieking as Valcour's sword flashed in the morning light, a loud, ringing crack shattering John's furious words as the earl slammed the blade against his own raised knee. The magnificent sword snapped in two.

Valcour took the pieces and placed them on a mahogany table. "I will not be responsible for a good man's death, John Wilkes. And I cannot let you kill me. I've done Lucinda enough harm, without cutting down someone whose friendship she cherishes. It's true that I don't . . . love her." He hesitated over the words. "But I will protect her. And make her happy, if it is in my power."

"If you make her unhappy, by God, I'll see you dead. I don't give a damn if you're the bloody king!"

"I will write to her parents myself, Wilkes. Explain everything. Perhaps they will not be so grief-stricken by Lucinda's mésalliance once they know that she will be the wealthiest countess in all England."

"You think you can put a price on a man's daughter?"

"No. I know Lucinda well enough to be certain she is a rare jewel. Brave as well as beautiful. Loving if somewhat hot-tempered." Valcour smiled, a little wearily. "You are the second man who has attempted to murder me in Lucinda's behalf, Wilkes. Such a hard-won treasure would have to be cherished, don't you think?"

John met his words with a stony silence.

"Now, we had best go," Valcour said, offering Lucy his arm. She slipped her hand onto his green velvet sleeve, drawing strength from the warmth that seeped into her palm from his muscled forearm. "Mrs. Wilkes, if you could have your servants pack Lucinda's trunks, I will send someone to fetch them tomorrow morning."

"Of course." Claree turned tearful eyes to Lucy. "Child, no matter what happened, John and I still love you. And so will your mama and papa."

"Claree," Lucy said in a shaking voice, "I didn't mean for things to go awry."

"Of course you did not, my precious. I—I only wish I had been more vigilant in guarding you. Your papa warned me of your escapades, but I didn't believe him. You have an angel's face."

"But I was always called the devil's daughter." Lucy turned away from her dejected friend and hastened out of the drawing room, down the corridor. Tears stung her eyes as the sunlight struck her face. How dare it be so glorious a day when her life was crumbling to ashes all around her?

Valcour said nothing as he swept Lucy up into the curricle. He circled around to his own seat, and Lucy felt the curricle rock beneath his weight as he settled himself, then took up the reins.

Lucy glanced at the townhouse window, seeing Claree there, sad and hurt and alone. Lucy knew that the shadows in the older woman's face would remain there a long time, the legacy of Lucy's willfulness and stubborn pride.

The curricle lurched, the horses skittering nervously in their traces, catching Valcour off guard. But he calmed the animals with a murmur and the flick of his hand. Both Lucy and the earl were both so lost in their own silent misery that neither saw the shadowy figure dart from the yew hedge and catch hold of the curricle's back brace. Neither saw the figure slip beneath the curricle's box and cling to the underpinnings, just as the carriage veered into the London streets.

Valcour gave Lucinda the gift of his silence during the ride back to Hawkvale, and after. He pressed one kiss to her hand, then let her go.

She dragged herself wearily up the stairway and into the beautiful rose bedchamber with its cream-colored and gilt furnishings. Then Lucy sank down on a stool beside the window and buried her face in her hands.

How long she stayed thus, she didn't know. Only that her muscles were stiff when she finally heard the soft movements of Valcour in the room beyond. He was pacing. Back and forth, with the restlessness of a peregrine on a tether. Lucy wondered why the icy earl should be so unsettled. She wondered if it were possible that the scene at the Wilkeses' had left him so.

She stood up, wanting to thank him for his kindness, for controlling his anger at John Wilkes's challenge.

I have never killed a good man, Valcour had said. Perhaps when Lucy had first faced the nobleman who was now her husband, she hadn't known the kind of man he was. Perhaps she had been wrong about him, as she had been wrong about so many other things.

She heard Valcour's footsteps hesitate before the door that joined their rooms. The door-latch rattled softly, then was still, as if he had started to open it, then thought better of intruding.

Suddenly Lucy wanted to see that strong, stubborn face more than she'd ever wanted to see anyone in her life.

"Valcour?" she called softly.

After a moment, the door swung open. He had stripped away his frockcoat and waistcoat, his neckcloth more disheveled than she had ever seen it. His ebony hair was tousled, as if impatient fingers had raked through it time and again, and his shirtsleeves had been shoved up muscular forearms.

The look on his face told Lucy all she needed to know. Harsh lines carved between his dark brows, bracketed his hard mouth. Those hawk's eyes, so intense, fixed on her as if to strip away any pretense and dredge out whatever feelings were warring inside her.

There had been a time—was it only a day before— that she would have cut her own throat before she called out to him for comfort. Now she wanted only to curl up against the hard wall of his chest, hear the steady, reliable sound of his heart beating. But she couldn't bring herself to reach out to him with anything but her voice.

"Valcour," she whispered. "Did you know you married a coward?"

"Hoyden, you have more courage than any man I've ever faced across a dueling field." He smiled that bittersweet, tender smile. "And I have faced a great many men with my sword, as you well know."

"I am a coward," Lucy insisted, walking to the window, pressing the palm of her hand against the cool pane of glass. *"And* I'm a liar. And worse. I all but browbeat Claree and John into bringing me along to England. I used their kindness and their friendship to get what I wanted. And once I was here, I caused them nothing but worry and hurt and for what? I told myself I came here searching for my father. But Alexander d'Autrecourt was only a shadow I barely remembered. And only then because of my "Night Song." My father is at home in Virginia, teaching Norah to ride her pony and bringing blue ribbons to my mother to tie up her hair. My father is making certain my favorite mare is groomed and exercised and ready for when I return, and he's telling Mama and the girls every night that only a few more months must pass before . . . before I sail into the harbor. But I won't be going home, will I, Valcour?"

"You would have left your family soon anyway, no matter how much you loved them all. You were a woman born for what we shared in the bedchamber at Harlestone—passionate by nature and so lovely. If I had not taken you to wife, one of your Virginian rebels would have."

Outside, twilight was tipping the tops of the trees with dusty purple, the groom was polishing the curricle, and in the street beyond children laughed. Lucy's fingers curled into a fist against the glass.

"Do you know that my father didn't want to let me come here from the first? He said I would be a loose cannon in England. That I would probably start another war."

"Did he?" She turned to see Valcour's lips curve into a smile that was shatteringly tender. "Your father must be a wise man."

"My mother teased him, saying he was afraid I would meet some dashing Englishman who would carry me off to his castle, so Papa would never see me again." Lucy stopped her throat swollen shut. "He dismissed it, all anger and scorn. But I know he was really afraid. I had never seen him so afraid, Valcour."

"He must love you very much."

"From the time I was dumped on his doorstep, all belligerence and rebellion and so much hurt, he was my hero. The brave Raider Pendragon. The patriot that men throughout Virginia exalted for his courage and cunning. I never had another hero, Valcour, until . . . until you broke the sword over your knee."

"I'm no dashing hero, hoyden. But you almost make me wish I was."

Lucy came to him, then stopped, not quite touching him. The scent of wind and dark spices, desire and regret emanated from every taut muscle in his body. "You would make a fine hero, Valcour. A bold gypsy count Iago, with midnight hair and eyes like black fire. And this . . ." She traced her finger down the scar on Valcour's face. She saw him wince as if the faint white line still pained him. She wondered why it did.

Lucy gave a feeble laugh and turned away, pacing to the stool where she had spent so many miserable hours. She sank down on it, linking her arms about her knees. "I suppose the truth is that any hero in his right mind would take one look at me and run the other way."

She felt small, somehow, lost in a sea of loneliness, regret. She started when Valcour sank down before her on one breech-clad knee, his palm curved upon her cheek. "I'm not running, Lucinda." He ran his thumb tenderly across the lower curve of her lip.

"Valcour, will you do something for me?" she asked, her eyes glistening with tears she would not shed.

"Anything, Countess."

"Would you hold me again? The way you did at Harlestone?"

Valcour wouldn't meet her eyes, his fingers toying with the ends of her sash. "I don't think that is a good idea, little one. I'm not a man to settle for holding you, when I really want to make love with you."

"But that's what I meant. I want you to . . . to make me forget, the way you did on our wedding night." Her voice caught on a broken sob. "Please, make me forget for a little while."

Valcour groaned, every resolution he had made not to touch her again vanishing like mist before the blazing heat that shimmered through him, the crushing, unfamiliar tenderness that wrenched his gut at the sight of her lips trembling, her cheeks still stained with the salty tracks of dried tears.

He wanted to see her brave and bonny again, tossing her curls in defiance, and laughing at him as if she were an empress. He would have gladly endured another kick to his tenderest parts if it would change her back into the bold hoyden who had challenged him at the gaming hell.

Valcour scooped her into his arms and carried her to the bed, then drifted her down on the coverlets as if she were some rare and fragile treasure. He framed her face between his palms, threading his fingers back through the sunlight-silkiness of her hair.

Make me forget. Lucinda's plea echoed back from the deepest reaches of Valcour's own soul. He lowered his mouth to hers, let his lips melt, hot and searching, into the yielding sweetness of hers.

With every fiber of his being, Dominic tried to drive the shadows from her eyes. His mouth was ruthlessly compelling, his hands unsteady with his own savage need.

And when he braced himself above her and plunged deep, there was nothing between them. No shadows, no ghosts, and—for a moment, just one shimmering moment—no regrets.

16

Something growled. Lucy wanted to take her pillow and smother whatever was making the disturbance. She was warm and safe, curled like a treasure in Valcour's strong arms, and she wanted to stay there forever. Safe from a hundred nagging doubts, safe from guilt and remorse. Safe from the doubts that tugged at her like starving children whenever she saw the icy detachment Valcour fought so hard to keep in his ebony eyes.

But whatever was making such an infernal noise wouldn't be quieted, an odd gnawing sensation in her stomach the final straw that prodded her awake.

She pressed her hand to her stomach and smiled against Valcour's chest. She had never been a lady of birdlike appetite. God knew, it took food aplenty to fuel her boundless energies. And after last night it was no wonder she was in need of fortification.

Her cheeks heated at the memory of what had passed between her and her husband. Slowly, she sat up, carefully loosening Valcour's fingers, which were tangled in the cascade of her hair. She looked down into Valcour's face, a face that had always been bewitchingly handsome, yet harsh as a cliff beaten by a storm.

But the man who lay sleeping beside her was like a stranger. He dozed, peaceful as an archangel at heaven's gate. His bronzed chest was sculptured with the virile perfection of a Greek god's, one long-fingered hand splayed across it. An artist's hand, Lucy noted in surprise, touching one finger gently with her own.

His cheek was buried against the pillow, concealing the scar that marred his face. His hair fell across the white linen, midnight against snow. His lashes fell in thick fans on his cheekbones, and those heart-stoppingly sensual lips were parted, as if he were tasting something sweet.

For a moment, Lucy wondered if she had ever seen anything more beautiful. She was just reaching out a finger to touch him when her stomach let out a growl that would have done a hunting tiger proud. She jerked her finger away from the sleeping Dominic and grimaced. It was little wonder she was starved. Neither she nor Valcour had eaten much at all the day before. Breakfast had been an appetite-crushing affair, with Lady Catherine looking as if her son had contracted some deadly disease rather than married. And after the scene at the Wilkeses', neither Lucy or Valcour had had the energy to taste anything. Until they'd feasted on each other.

He would be as much in need of sustenance as she was once he awoke. Or was *awakened* . . .

An idea formed in her mind, making her lips curve into a smile. Did she dare act so boldly? She nibbled at her lip, then shrugged. After last night she could hardly play the shy and frightened virgin.

Suddenly delighted with herself, Lucy slid out of bed and donned her bedgown. With a last glance at Valcour, she crept into the corridor. She could hear the servants downstairs moving about. With stealth gained on hundreds of other such raids, Lucy made her way to the dining room and peeped into the chamber. Several footmen were busy laying out slavers full of muffins and beefsteak, oranges and tea, muttering about the fact that their master had never been late at his breakfast before.

The moment the room was empty, Lucy stole in and purloined the most delicious morsels of food, bundled them in a napkin, then raced back up to the bedchamber, where her husband was still sleeping. The door gave an unexpectedly loud thud as she closed it, a heartbeat before the upstairs maid rounded a corner.

Lucy was certain Valcour would wake, but he only murmured something sleepily, his hand making a half-hearted search for her across the bed. Then he stilled again, his palm still extended, his fingers curled and empty.

Lucy went to the bed and snuggled up again beside the solid warmth of his side, then opened her bundle of food. She selected a section of orange dripping with juices, then rubbed it in a seductive path along Valcour's parted lips. The earl awoke slowly, turning to face her. The wrinkles in the pillow casings had pressed creases into his beard-stubbled cheek, his sleep-misted eyes haunted with confusion and a wariness that Lucy understood all too well.

A moan rumbled in Valcour's chest as he raised up on one elbow and glanced at the window bright with morning sun. Beyond the panes, street criers' voices were a faint cacophony of warring melodies as they urged people to buy fresh oranges, violets, and tallow candles.

Valcour's gaze shifted from the window to the napkin full of treats in Lucy's hands, and his brows dipped in a feigned scowl.

"Tell me you didn't go out adventuring this morning, hoyden. I've no desire for a bevy of disgruntled street vendors to be pounding on my door, accusing you of thievery."

"I stole this from beneath the very noses of your own servants, sir," Lucy said, letting her eyes dance at him.

Valcour's mouth softened into a drowsy smile. "I am much relieved."

That sleepy, mind-shatteringly sensual smile made Lucy tremble. She moistened her lips, her voice husky with need. "Reward me, then."

For a heartbeat, Valcour's gaze locked with hers. Then he caught her wrist in a tender grasp and drew the fingers that held the bit of orange back to his mouth. His eyes heated as he sucked the sweet fruit into his mouth, then his lips closed over the tips of Lucy's fingers, the rough heat of his tongue spearing primitive desire into the place still tender from his loving assault the night before.

Lucy thought he had showed her every facet of passion, but the Valcour who seduced her now was more potently sensual than ever before, enticing her deeper and deeper into pulsing sensation and heady delight.

He stripped away her bedgown and laid her down across the tumbled bedcovers, then he took cinnamon-laced muffins, still warm from the oven, and broke them, feeding her bits of the spicy warm cakes, cleaning the crumbs that fell on her skin by nibbling them away with his teeth.

He burst the translucent membranes of the orange sections between his fingers, letting the juices drizzle onto the hardened coral tips of her nipples, then laved away the moisture as if touching her had made it the nectar of some pagan god of passion. Lucy moaned and trembled, wanting to touch him, kiss him, but Valcour held her prisoner with nothing but the intensity in his eyes.

He explored her more intimately than ever before, savoring her most secret places until Lucy sobbed with the force of emotions he unleashed.

Stunned at the sensation, Lucy was unable to wait a

moment more. She dragged his mouth to hers, kissing him desperately, hungrily, moans forming in her throat, mating with his own groans of pleasure as their tongues warred and tasted, plundered and feasted.

Their bodies, still sticky, moist with sweat and desire and oranges, seemed to melt together, and Lucy pushed Valcour until he gave in to her impulse. He rolled over until she was atop him. Lucy kissed his cheeks, his throat, nibbling kisses down his chest to give his hardened nipples the same loving attention he had given hers.

Every muscle in Valcour's chest was rigid, his face contorted almost as if in pain, his breath rasping, broken by moans of pleasure. But when her mouth trailed lower along the dark ribbon that bisected his stomach, Valcour stilled as if he'd been turned to stone. Lucy hesitated for a heartbeat, then gave Valcour the same unselfish gift he had given her. For long minutes, Valcour held himself still, his fingers delving into the golden curls that lay in silky skeins on the hot flesh of his stomach. Lucy could feel him shaking, hear his groan of complete surrender.

With an oath, he grabbed her arms, rolling her beneath him and mounting her with one mighty, soul-searing thrust.

Lucy reveled in his primitive passion, dazed at the wildfire they had built between them. Valcour thrust, once, twice, Lucy crying out as the pinnacle crashed over her again. With a keening animal groan, Valcour drove one final time inside her, as if he could bury himself in her very soul.

He lay there for long minutes, his face pressed against her hair, the soft sheath of her body still clinging to him, holding him. Lucy longed to say something, tell him . . . tell him how magical it had been. How much she . . . what? Had lost herself to this man, torn open all of her vulnerabilities and held back nothing in his arms?

As if Valcour didn't already know. But he had given

her the taste of an unrestrained passion so potent she knew it would change her forever.

She swallowed hard as Valcour drew slowly away from her. "Lucinda, I . . ." He looked as if he'd survived some disaster, as if he were stunned that their loving was over, that he was still whole.

Or was he? Was she?

They were both so damned rigid in their strength and independence, fiercely controlling any situation that came to them. But there had been no controlling the maelstrom that obliterated the cold detachment from Valcour's eyes and the mutiny from Lucy's own.

She didn't know which of them was the most eager to escape the bed and the shattering intimacy they couldn't deny there. Valcour turned coward first. He climbed from the bed, gloriously naked, smelling of oranges and uncertainty. He scooped up his shirt and then took his leave of her, muttering something about never having been late to a meeting with his solicitor before.

She watched him stalk from the room, but at the doorway he paused for a moment and looked back at her, his eyes saying things his lips could not. He left.

Lucy drew the crumb-dotted coverlets about her, her body still tingling with remembered pleasure. Then Lady Catherine's maid, Millie, knocked on the door, offering to help Lucy with her morning toilette. Lucy tugged her robe about her and stole from the bed, feeling oddly shy, as if every kiss and caress, every shudder of desire and moan of pleasure, had been engraved on the sheets for the whole world to see. But the maid was the soul of servant discretion. Without so much as a word, she dressed Lucy's hair and got her into a gown of cloud-colored muslin, embroidered with thread of gilt. A shimmering scarlet stomacher was laced into place, gold bunches of ribbon fashioned into rosettes at the edges.

But as the maid surveyed her work, giving Lucy's

petticoats one last tug, the woman smiled. "It seems married life has put color back in your cheeks, my lady. I wish you and my lord much happiness."

Lucy stared at the vision reflected in the gilt-framed mirror, her lips curving into a dubious smile as she peered at the image of a stranger.

The golden curls were Lucy's own, scarlet ribbons woven through the tresses like the heated paths of Valcour's eager fingers. The lace that edged Lucy's bodice was the pattern Emily had lovingly tied for her for her eighteenth birthday. Even the haughty little bump on the reflected nose and the stubborn jut to the chin were those of the Raider's daughter.

But nothing else about that face was the same. The eyes that had always been sharp and keen, the almost painful blue of a summer sky, were big and soft and unsure beneath thick lashes. Her cheeks bloomed a delicate rose color that Valcour's passion had put there. Her lips were slightly puffy, warm and red, still tasting of Valcour's kisses.

But the most startling transformation of all was buried in the center of Lucy's chest. A heavy, joyously aching knot had formed there. A knot very like the one that had pulsed inside her when she was an emotionally battered child taking her first tentative steps toward allowing herself to love.

But then she had been reaching out to her gentle, compassionate mother, and to Ian Blackheath, who obviously adored the little girl who had brightened his barren life. Now she was reaching out to a man with scars Lucy was beginning to suspect ran even deeper than her own.

What would it be like to see Valcour's dark eyes without the clinging shadows, without the secrets and the pain that cut him off from the rest of the world? What would it be like to see him fling back his head and laugh, rich and unrestrained?

What would it be like to run and fling herself into his arms, confident that he would catch her up and kiss her?

The image made Lucy's fingers twine together, the places Valcour had explored earlier tingling again with remembrance.

She glanced at the sunshine-glossed window and felt the press of buildings beyond, the noise and bustle of the city. She would just as soon wait in her bedchamber all day, hoping Valcour would return to bed her again. But though that prospect was more alluring than she'd care to admit, she doubted she could manage again so soon, with the tenderness so much lovemaking had left between her thighs.

What *should* she do with the rest of her morning? Valcour was locked up in his study, neck deep in business dealings, no doubt. She smiled, hoping that he was dreadfully distracted, trying to concentrate on rows of numbers and messages from various estates but being taunted by images of their passion the night before.

Shopping sounded dreadfully dull after the night she had spent in Valcour's arms, any thought of making calls equally unappealing. Lucy nibbled at the edge of her fingernail. This bride rigmarole was confusing at best. The girls of Lucy's acquaintance who had married when she was still in Virginia had fairly burst with their eagerness to take charge of their new husband's home: tallying up silver, examining furnishings for signs of the housekeeper's neglect. Patience Chartley had gone into greater ecstacies over Thomas Chartley's chests full of linens than she had over poor Tom himself.

But Lucy wouldn't have cared if Valcour had table-cloths of spun gold tucked away somewhere. Her gaze flicked out the window at the rear of her room. The sound of a horse's whinny below made her race over to the casement. She might have no interest in linens, but she suspected her husband's stable was a veritable treasure trove.

Satisfied with her idea, she hurried down the sweep of hallway, intending to indulge her passion for fine horses, when suddenly a soft voice called her name.

Lucy stopped, trying to keep her face from falling as she saw Lady Catherine, framed in the doorway of what seemed to be her own suite of rooms. Valcour's mother was garbed in dove-gray satin, a white lace cap framing her face. She clutched a lace-edged handkerchief in her fingers, the delicate square crumpled as if she had been twisting it between nervous fingers.

"It's late," Lady Catherine said. "You must have had a . . . fatiguing night. I didn't sleep well myself."

Tiny flames seemed to ignite in Lucy's cheeks as she remembered the cries and groans, whimpers and wild urgings that had driven her passion and Valcour's. Was it possible Lady Catherine had heard them?

Lucy swallowed hard. "I slept very soundly."

"I'm glad. I have been hoping for an opportunity to speak with you. Get to—to know my . . . new daughter. There are some things that I need to say to you."

Lucy wondered what they could possibly be. An apology of sorts for the reception she'd given Lucy the first night? More likely it would be something far worse. A recounting of the myriad reasons she was not fit to be a countess. Lucy shrugged and said, "I have always felt it better to get such things into the open at once."

Lady Catherine gestured to the room at her right. Lucy walked into a lovely chamber of pale blue and white. Dried flowers stood in a vase, fragrances of summers long past drifting from the fragile petals. The portraits in this room were worlds away from the neglected ones at the Valcour castle. Miniatures of all different shapes and sizes were tucked on tables and candlestands, the whimsically carved mantle and the curio shelf beside the blue satin-covered settee.

It was as if Lady Catherine had gathered up pieces of her life here, making it into her own special world. Lucy reached out to touch a portrait of a fresh-faced girl, obviously the young Catherine herself, in a flower-draped pony cart, led by a sandy-haired man who looked as if he had yet to face his first shaving razor.

"My brother, Robert. He died at sea off the coast of the West Indies."

There was a wistful quality in Lady Catherine's voice that made Lucy's own throat tighten with sympathy. "I'm sorry."

"So was I. You see, from the time we were children, we had been inseparable. But we were estranged at the time he died. Had been for a very long time. From the moment I married Dominic's father."

Lucy had never been one to pry into people's private lives. She had too many hidden places in her own. She said nothing, but Lady Catherine went on.

"Robert was certain that I would be unhappy as Lionel St. Cyr's countess. He said he couldn't bear to see me miserable. But I wouldn't listen. I was so certain I could change Lionel, soften him, gentle him. Why is it we women are always so confident in our powers?"

Lucy nibbled at her lower lip, uncomfortable as Lady Catherine's words echoed her own thoughts of earlier that morning—that Lucy herself would be able to probe past Valcour's steely facade, reach the man buried beneath. She didn't want to change what was there. She only wanted to have him open himself, let her see beyond those intense eyes, that closed smile. "My father—adopted father—in Virginia was the most notorious rakehell in the colonies until he fell in love with my mother," she said. "Everyone said the change in him was a miracle."

For some reason, the mention of Lucy's mother made Lady Catherine wince and turn away. "There were no miracles for me. Robert was right. Lionel was wild and reckless, so handsome the demimondaines all but shed blood to get him in their clutches. He had the notorious

Valcour thirsts for danger and women and gambling. I was a dreamy child, the cherished baby sister that delighted my older, doting brother. Nothing in my life had prepared me for what it would mean to be Lionel St. Cyr's wife."

"If he was so dangerous, why did you marry him?"

"Lionel was a magnificent match for me, titled and wealthy, handsome and much sought after by match-making mamas. His attention to me was like a first sip of champagne: It turned my head, made me dizzy with excitement. My own parents were loving but stolid, Robert serious and responsible. Lionel was the antithesis of everything I'd ever known, something almost exotic and intoxicating. I'm still not certain why he fancied himself in love with me. But he was not . . . the type of husband I needed. And once his passion for my beauty faded, I know Lionel was disappointed in his choice of wife."

Lucy squirmed inwardly at Lady Catherine's revelations. Half of Williamsburg trucked themselves off to Emily Blackheath's door, confiding everything from their husband's latest drunken binge to financial woes to broken hearts to the compassionate mistress of Blackheath plantation. But such heart-rending confessions had always made Lucy run the other way.

Even if she hadn't already had that tendency, Lucy was having enough trouble sorting out her own relationship with Valcour at the moment. She didn't know if she could endure delving into heartaches that had happened so many years before to the earl's mother.

"I'm sure you didn't invite me here to spin out a story for me." Lucy tried to set the conversation on a different course. "You said you had something to discuss."

"I want to discuss my son with you, Lucinda. Tell you . . . some things you need to know." Lady Catherine took Lucy's hand and led her to the settee. She sank down on it. "I saw Dominic this morning when he left his chambers. There was something changed about him. A shadow of the Dominic I once knew was in his face. I don't know what passed between you. But I can't help but hope . . ." Her voice trailed off, as if that hope were too fragile even to voice aloud. "My son was not always as you see him now. He is what . . . pain and disappointment, loss and betrayal have made him."

"Everyone has pain and disappointment. We all have scars," Lucy said softly, remembering her own.

"Not like my Dominic's. The world sees him as the invincible earl of Valcour, cold and ruthless, fierce and strong. A man with no heart. They don't know that his heart was crushed a long time ago. I am the one who destroyed it."

Lucy climbed to her feet, restless. She wanted so much to know Valcour, understand the enigmatic man who was her husband. But she was feeling so raw right now, fragile in ways she hadn't felt since a child. "My lady, I—"

"Please. I know that there is no love between you and my son as yet. But what I have seen today, on his face and, yes, child, in your own, makes me hope." Lady Catherine's voice fell, hushed. "I was in love once. I've not forgotten how it felt, how it made me new and frightened and . . ."

"With Dominic's father?"

"No. Would to God I had been able to love him. But our infatuation with each other burned away, like dew seared from the grass by the morning sun. When it did, only Dominic was left to join us together. He was the single good thing in my life, Lucinda. Brave and sensitive, kind and caring. He was brilliant at his studies. And with his music . . ." She stopped and looked away.

"For a time it seemed as if Dominic would succeed where I had not—save Lionel from the excesses that had blackened the Valcour title for three hundred years. Lionel cared enough about his estates to keep them in decent repair for his heir. He wanted to bring the Valcour name back to some semblance of respectability, so he became a favorite of the king, went on diplomatic missions for him, staying away a year or more at a time. I was lonely, child, though not for my husband. Dominic was sent away to school, my parents were long since dead, and my brother Robert . . . though I'd written letter after letter, had never forgiven me."

There was such sadness in Lady Catherine's voice that Lucy found herself returning to the settee and taking up the older woman's hand. "But I don't understand. If you both loved Dominic, even though you did not love each other . . ."

"It was not our lack of marital bliss that changed Dominic. It was . . . something far more damaging. Lionel had just sailed for the Netherlands when an epidemic broke out at Dominic's school. He was ill, and they did not send me word until it was almost too late. I . . . cannot tell you what it was like to come so near to losing him."

Lucinda imagined the boy she had seen in the portrait, the eyes that twinkled so brightly dulled with fever, his mouth parched. The thought of that child so ill made her wince inwardly, want to reach out and comfort.

"I brought Dominic home to nurse him," Lady Catherine said. "It took him time to gain back his strength. And then I was selfish, Lucinda. I decided not to send him back to school at all until Lionel returned. I told myself it was because their negligence had almost cost Dominic his life. That Lionel would find some safer place to send him. But the truth was that I couldn't bear to give him up."

Lucy caught her lower lip between her teeth, remembering the desolation in Ian Blackheath's face as her ship had sailed from the harbor in Virginia. He had followed along the shore, limping as fast as he could, waving to her with his plumed tricorn. But nothing had hidden the desolation in every line of his body at the thought of surrendering his Lucy, even for a little while.

How had Dominic St. Cyr and his mother lost each other in the years that came after? How had that little boy, obviously adored and cherished, turned into the implacable, wary man who battled so hard to wall everyone out of his heart?

"Did Dominic resent being kept from school? Did he—"

Lady Catherine laughed, a gentle, musical sound. "He was a boy, my dear. He delighted in his holiday. He rode his pony, swam in the pond, built a wooden fortress out in the glen near the castle. He played his pianoforte and practiced dancing the minuet with me. I knew that he would soon be grown and gone. Twelve years old and already so tall and . . . and handsome a lad. It was the happiest time of my life. I had my Dominic. And I had . . . someone else as well."

Rays of sunlight caressed Lady Catherine's face, her cheeks still smooth, only the faintest signs of age touching her features, like a fine layer of dust covering an exquisite living statue.

Lucy stiffened, certain she knew where Lady Catherine's confidences were taking her. "My lady, I don't think . . . I mean, your affairs—" Lucy winced at her ill choice of words. "Your affairs aren't my concern."

"Do you want to understand my son, child? To be able to reach past his wall of ice and warm him?"

"I don't know," Lucy confessed.

Lady Catherine smiled and took Lucy's hand. "Let me only tell you this: The man I fell in love with was sensitive and kind, struggling with his own unhappiness. We . . . comforted each other but never acted on our love for each other. We didn't want to hurt anyone. We only wanted to spend time with each other. Talk and dream and . . ." She stopped as if she had said too much. "We might have been safe, except that Dominic idolized this man as well. Idolized him second only to his father."

A knot of dread formed in Lucy's gut, a premonition of what was to come. She closed her eyes, imagining Dominic's pain. "He discovered the two of you, didn't he?"

"We had battled so hard to keep our feelings from him. But then I received word that Robert's ship had been lost. There was a letter he had left at his solicitors to be delivered to me if he should die. In it he begged forgiveness for his pride and pleaded with me to find some happiness despite the mistake I had made in my marriage. The agony was so terrible I thought I would die of it. Dominic had always been mad about horses, and our groom had taken him to a fair to buy a new team for the carriage. My . . . lover came to comfort me, Lucinda, and we . . . we couldn't fight our feelings anymore."

Lucy's eyes stung and she ached, for the boy, reveling in horses while his life fell apart. For the woman, needing love so badly she had risked everything to take it. Even for the lover, who had fought so hard, yet had been there to ease Lady Catherine's pain.

"I'm glad that he was there for you, my lady," she said with heartfelt sincerity. She was stunned as tears welled up in the noblewoman's eyes and trailed down her cheeks.

Lady Catherine clutched the handkerchief in white-knuckled fingers, as if she were trying to crush all the pain inside her. "You are good to say so." She sucked in a steadying breath. "My lover and I couldn't stop . . . once we had been together. We knew it was wrong, were both in agonies of guilt and dread, and yet I loved him, Lucinda. Dominic suspected, but I know he couldn't believe his instincts were right. He trusted us both, you see. Then I started to swell with my lover's child."

"Aubrey," Lucy gasped. Of course. That explained the

differences between the two brothers, the bitterness, the anger. "No wonder they loathe each other."

"No. Aubrey doesn't know the truth. And Dominic has tried to—to do his duty by his brother."

"I don't think Aubrey wants him to do his duty. I think Aubrey wants Valcour to love him."

Lady Catherine nodded. "Exactly. For years I have watched them and wished things could have been different. Perhaps they would have been if . . ." She shrugged. "What is done is done. I suppose that a woman with any sense of self-preservation would have rid herself of the baby in my place. But how could I kill the child I wanted so desperately? The child of the man I loved? I kept my baby, Lucinda. And as time passed, I watched my other son change from a happy, loving boy to a withdrawn youth whose eyes were hot with betrayal and fear and distrust. He blamed himself, you see, for adoring this man so much he'd not . . . protected me."

"It must have been hideous."

"It was. My husband returned to England a month before I was to deliver. He was crazed with fury. The honor he had worked so hard to regain for Dominic was shattered by my bearing some other man's bastard. Valcour would be a laughingstock again, scandal laden and disgraced. He wanted to know the name of my baby's father—was willing to beat the information from me with his riding crop if he had to. Dominic leapt between us. The crop slashed his face when it fell."

"My God." No wonder Valcour flinched whenever she touched the faint white line. It was the pale legacy from wounds that had cut far deeper.

"Dominic's screams shook Lionel from his mad fury. Lionel loved Dominic as much as the boy loved him. Lionel cared for Dominic so tenderly, I thought . . . prayed that the worst was over. But once Dominic was well, Lionel again demanded to know who had been about the castle, to know who had defiled me. Dominic refused to tell him. That betrayal drove Lionel more savagely than anything I could have done. Raging that he had no son, he left for London and hurled himself into an orgy of drunkenness and gaming, whoring and excess."

Lucy could imagine Dominic watching the father he adored riding neck or nothing down the road to hell. The helplessness, the guilt, the crushing sense of responsibility the boy must have felt. For Lucy knew from her own personal anguish that when children observed cruelty or pain, faced rejection or betrayal from the adults they adored, always the children examined their own fragile souls for ugliness, for fault. Always they believed that if they had behaved better, worked harder, demanded less, the ills of the world could be cured.

"Lionel told no one Aubrey was not his son. There were some whispers, but I pretended we had visited earlier that year. For some reason, Lionel allowed my lies to stand. The estates he had tended for Dominic he let fall to ruin in his agony. Then, two years later, he sent for Dominic to join him in London."

Lucy began to have some small hope. "Did they reconcile? Did they—"

"Lionel asked Dominic one final time who had fathered my child. When Dominic didn't answer, Lionel put a pistol to his head and took his own life before Dominic's eyes."

"Sweet God, no." Lucy felt sick, her trembling hand pressed to her mouth. "How could he do such a thing to a child he loved?"

"I don't know. I only know that since the first moment Dominic discovered I was carrying my lover's child, he began to take pieces of himself and hide them where no one could reach. When Lionel killed himself, he destroyed what little of my bright, loving Dominic remained. The boy who became earl in his father's place battled just to survive the destruction left in the wake of my love affair and his father's suicide."

Lucy knew how much strength it must have taken for the boy to wade through the morass of pain, fight the mockery, the hate, when he was broken inside, everyone he loved torn away from him by death and betrayal. She pictured the earl of Valcour as he was now. Strong, fierce, protecting those weaker than himself. But never allowing anyone to reach out to him, heal the scars that still seethed with poison twenty years later.

"He all but drove himself insane attempting to rebuild the Valcour estates," Lady Catherine said. "And his honor was the life-blood that kept him fighting, trying, breathing."

"That was why he insisted on marrying me," Lucy said softly. "Because of his honor." But honor had seemed only some cold, empty catchword then, clung to by an arrogant English aristocrat, reeking of wealth and power and tyranny. Now Valcour's words changed in Lucy's mind, a desperate vow coming from a battered, soul-weary knight errant. Her heart squeezed at the image.

"It was strange," Lady Catherine continued. "Where Lionel had failed, Dominic seemed determined to triumph. It was as if his success were the final gift he could give his father—since he had been unable to give Lionel the truth he really wanted. Dominic dueled countless men who insulted me or dared to mock Lionel. Men far older and more skilled with a sword. Dominic's hatred and pain drove him like demons. And his demons always brought him victory."

The vulnerable place in Lucy's breast was aching, pulsing with an empathy such as she'd never known. Images of a little girl pouring her pain out through her music mingled with those of a desolate boy, driving back dragons of betrayal with the point of a sword. *Valcour,* she thought with a kind of tender wistfulness, *we are more alike than you could ever imagine.*

"Do you know what I have missed the most as the years have passed? What I have longed for more than anything else?" Lady Catherine hesitated. "The day Lionel came to carry him off to London was the last time my son ever called me 'Mama.'"

Lucy reached out and squeezed the older woman's hands in both her own. Tears burned in Lucy's throat, but Valcour's grief was one too wrenching for something so commonplace as weeping.

"Lucinda." Lady Catherine's eyes were huge and pleading. "Do not let Dominic suffer the fate Lionel and I did—a loveless marriage, a cold bed, emptiness, so much emptiness."

"I don't know what I can do, my lady. When you and Valcour's father began, you had infatuation. Valcour and I haven't even got that."

"Don't you? I saw my son this morning, rushing from his bedchamber." Lady Catherine's lips tipped in a tender smile. "His neckcloth was tied as awkwardly as a ten-year-old's, his hair was unruly. And his eyes were filled with confusion and there is no other word to say it—fear. I have not seen that expression on my son's face since the day Lionel St. Cyr was laid in the Valcour crypt. Child, I think he is falling in love with you."

A tiny thrill of hope shivered through Lucy's veins. She sprang to her feet and paced away, remembering the fervor in Valcour's hands and mouth, the tenderness that had stunned her, bedazzled her. She closed her eyes, remembering a hundred fairy stories, legends of princesses captured in towers, waiting for princes to release them. Perhaps this time it was the prince who waited, barred in the tower by pain and pride, arrogance and agony. Waiting for her to release him.

She turned to Lady Catherine, who seemed to have shrunken somehow, through the tale she had told, weighed down by shame and regret decades old.

Lucy realized what a torture it must have been for the gentle woman to expose her secrets, the courage it must have taken to leave herself open to the possible scorn and mockery of a daughter-in-law she barely knew. Not to mention inviting the wrath of the son she so obviously loved. For Lucy knew instinctively that Valcour would be enraged if he ever suspected that Lady Catherine had made such a confession, had shown Valcour's secret anguish to someone else.

Lucy crossed to Lady Catherine and knelt before her, catching the woman's birdlike hands in her own. "You love Dominic very much, don't you?"

"More than my life. You will take care of him for me, won't you? You will save him where I could not?"

"How could I possibly—"

"Love him, Lucinda." Lady Catherine's voice broke on a sob. "Please, please love my Dominic."

Love Valcour—a man who was like a shattered jewel, so many facets, shimmering, impossible to catch and hold and understand. Impossible to make whole again. A man who suddenly seemed not hard and cold but so very alone.

Lucy caught her lip between her teeth, her own long-buried fears mingling with the pain that Lady Catherine's story still rippled through her soul. How could the gentle noblewoman understand that Lucy was so much like her son, a heart still carrying scars from her past? Wary as a spirited horse battered by a cruel master, it was still difficult for Lucy to trust, in spite of her parents' love, in spite of years of their adoration. Shadows still lingered: her cruel stepmother, the wicked duke and duchess who had buried the soul of the child she had been in the grave with the tiny carved angel.

To take such a risk, to reach out to Valcour, knowing he could very well shove her away. To love, with the chance of being rejected . . . The very thought made Lucy cringe inside. Did she truly have the courage to try?

She rose and stroked Lady Catherine's hair, a gesture very like one of Emily Blackheath's own. "My lady, I am going to be lonely too here. Missing my sisters, my father, my . . . mother so much. I would like it if . . . if I could love you in their absence."

Lady Catherine smiled, and Lucy saw a shadow of the beautiful, dreamy girl who had charmed an earl and made another man love her in spite of any cost.

"I would like that, child, more than you can imagine," the older woman said.

Lucy kissed her cheek. "You should rest now. I will come later and we can sew." Lucy gave Lady Catherine a teasing smile. "My favorite stitching is still attaching buttons. When I first arrived at Blackheath Hall, I used to snip them off my father's clothes, just so I could put them back on. Perhaps I should visit Valcour's clothes-press."

She was rewarded by a weak laugh. "You are like a ray of sunshine, child. Brightening this house that has been dim as a tomb for so long. I only hope . . ." The clouds were back, dartings of dread in Lady Catherine's eyes. "I only hope that nothing ever happens to change that."

Lady Catherine released Lucy's hand, and it was as if the older woman were withdrawing, as if she were suddenly afraid.

"I never wanted to hurt Dominic," Lady Catherine said softly. "Please know this, child: I would never want to—to dull the light in your eyes either."

Lucy left the chamber, feeling like a sleepwalker who had awakened in another world, where nothing was as it seemed. A world laced with mysteries and tragic love stories, tower rooms and fathers who returned from the dead.

And knights errant with black eyes and tortured secrets locked in their hearts.

17

*L*ucy stepped into the fresh morning air, the breeze kissing color into her cheeks and toying with the golden curls that wreathed her head like a halo. London rose up to greet her in a cacophony of sound. Street criers called out their wares, cartwheels clattered, their drivers shouting out ill opinions of the other travelers on the crowded roads. Horses whinnied to each other in passing, while dozens of voices rose higher and higher, each trying to speak louder than the surrounding din.

An entire world seemed held at bay by the bastion of Hawkvale's vine-covered garden walls. She circled around the townhouse to where the stable stood, intending to begin her exploration with Valcour's beautiful grays, already kicking up their heels in a paddock that was better kept than most people's formal gardens. Lucy smiled, anticipating the soothing pleasure of stroking velvety noses, sleek necks, feeling the horses' insistent nudges against her as they demanded attention.

Before she had been returned to the loving care of her own mother, Lucy had poured out her loneliness and love through her music and in her adoration of any animal she could find—dogs and kittens, clumsy work-horses and lovely blooded mares. She had been more heartbroken by the loss of a nest of kittens at the Jamaican plantation where she had spent five miserable years than she had been at the death of her shallow adoptive mother.

She had always had a way with wounded creatures, had been able to reach out to them with the trust and confidence she'd been unable to offer all but a few trusted people.

When she was thirteen she'd found a peregrine, its wing broken, its body torn as it fought off a pack of circling hounds. She had swathed the injured bird in her petticoats and carried it back to Blackheath plantation to nurse it. She still had a faint scar on her arm where its talons had torn the skin. And yet, by the time the magnificent hawk was ready to take flight, it had been tamed to Lucy's hand.

What would it be like to tame Valcour as she had the hawk? The prospect was mesmerizing, alluring. Frightening. The talons of Valcour's pain wouldn't tear at mere skin, so easily healed with time. Rather they would tear at Lucy's heart.

She caught her lip between her teeth, Valcour's compelling face rising in her mind, his eyes so fierce, so cold, and yet, black fire when he caressed her naked body, uncertain when she had reached beneath his passion, and touched him . . . in that far more vulnerable place, his heart.

He would be her Hawk. The Hawk of Valcour. She grinned, delighted at a sobriquet as vivid as Pendragon, the one her father had used for so many years.

Her musings were interrupted by the sudden sound of shouts in the stable, horses neighing in fear, hooves striking at stalls. Lucy scooped up her skirts and ran to the open door of the structure, expecting fire or thieves or some other calamity.

But at that instant a small figure barreled headlong into her midsection, knocking her off her feet.

She tumbled to the ground, a flailing, ragged little bundle kicking and struggling to escape her grasp as desperately as if she were dangling him over the jaws of a lion.

"There he is!" one of Valcour's grooms bellowed as he raced from the stables with a pitchfork clutched in his hands. "Unhand me lady before I skewer ye, ye sewer rat."

Lucy shook the hair from her eyes, glimpsing carroty hair and freckles on a face blotched with horrible purple bruises. Natty. She clutched the child to her. "Stop this at once!" she ordered the groom.

"He's dangerous, me lady! A thief. For all he's a babe he's probably cut a hundred throats!"

"He's done nothing of the kind!"

"His lordship would hurl him to the authorities, he would!"

"He would do so over my dead body. This young gentleman is a friend of mine, aren't you, Natty?" Lucy loosened her hold on the boy. Natty scrambled to his feet, his breath rasping in his throat. He offered Lucy his hand to help her up, as courtly as any knight of the realm. Then he glared at the groom through one eye, the other swollen shut.

"I been of service to milady before, you curst oaf! She said if I were ever in trouble, to find her. So I did!"

"Then what were you doing in the stable? Plotting to steal my lord's horses?"

"I was jest catching my breath afore I went to find her." He pointed at Lucy. "By the by, milady. There be a prime mare in the last stall. Bet she could kick the piss outta any horse in St. James."

The groom drew back, looking from the raggle-tag street urchin to the new countess of Valcour. Lucy wiped grimy hands on her petticoats, trying to look as dignified as possible. "Go back to your tasks," she ordered the groom. Then she turned to Natty. "If you would give me your arm, sir?"

The child drew his dignity about him in a delightful manner, then did as she asked. They walked to the gardens, feeling the eyes of every stable hand on them the entire way.

"That was prime, milady!" Natty said with a triumphant skip as they reached the garden. "Showed that bloody bastard—"

But the moment they were beyond the shelter of the nearest hedge Lucy abandoned her dignified retreat and fell to her knees before the child, horrified at the sight of him so brutalized.

"Natty, what on earth!" She reached out, touching the edge of a bruise that was almost black, and noticed that his freckled little nose was crooked where it had not been before. "Who did this to you? Who hurt you?"

"It's nothin'. Happens all the time. Usually when Pappy's been guzzling Blue Ruin. Take exception to him breaking me nose, though. I was a handsome divil 'fore he did."

The boy's cockiness wrenched at Lucy's heart more deeply than any childish sobs could have. "By God, I'll find that cowardly cur myself and break every bone in his body!"

"No!" Natty shrank back in horror. "You want to make it so's I can't show me face on the street again! A *girl* running out to defend Natty Scratch? Me reputation would be in rags!" He made a face, then winced, as the battered muscles pulled. "I liked you the blazes of a lot better when you was a boy, y'know."

"If you think I'm going to let you go back to that monster, you're mad!" Lucy's brow furrowed with fierce resolve. "You can stay with me in the big house. There are plenty of rooms. I'm sure Valcour won't even notice you are about—" But even as the words came out of

Lucy's mouth, she was imagining her husband's reaction if she were to parade Natty into the grand townhouse.

Her apprehension on that score was interrupted by Natty's indignant cry. "What do you think I am? A beggar or something, living off charity? Got me pride, I do. And don't you be suggesting I muck out stables or turn a kitchen spit for a few crusts of bread, either. I'm a working man, I am. Got a right thriving business. I just gotta find some other place t' work *from,* somewhere Pappy Blood can't come and get me." Natty eyed the walled garden a little wistfully. "Now this place, ol' Pappy wouldn't dare come poking his nose about here."

"Then this is where you'll stay." Lucy glanced around, her eyes alighting on a tool shed in the far corner of the garden. She took Natty's hand and they wound their way to it. There was a trap door at the foot, a storage area for broken tools. From the thick dust in it, Lucy doubted the gardener had entered it for years. "I'll rummage about the house for whatever you might need. Candles and food, blankets."

"I could live like a king here," Natty chirruped. "Nobody could find me!"

"It wouldn't surprise me if you were king! Clever boy! How did you ever find me?"

"Waited around at the house you told me about at the Gate—those American people. I was kind of hoping they'd have a red savage around to entertain me. But . . ." He shrugged. "Found out you were gone and waited. Saw you drive up with that 'ristocrat man who near flayed out Sir Jasper's liver. When you left, I caught onto the carriage and climbed underneath. Had to hold on like bloody hell though. From the ride I got, would'a thought the bastard was aiming for every pothole in London. Tired me out, it did, so's I curled up on the hay, meaning to stay jest a minute, and ended up snorin' away like a drunken sailor 'til yer groom came greeting me with his pitchfork."

"You mean you've been hurt, waiting for help for days?" Lucy asked, with a sting of remorse.

"Help? Be a cold day at Satan's fireside when Natty Scratch whines for help! I'm not a baby, you know!"

"Of course not." Lucy tried to keep her face serious, her admiration for the little boy growing by leaps and bounds. "Then why did you go to such trouble to find me?"

The plucky expression on the boy's face changed to a troubled one. "Got something for you."

Apprehension enveloped Lucy like the coolness in the shed's cellar. "I don't understand."

The boy dug in the front of his grimy jerkin and pulled out a crumpled square of vellum, the sealing wax broken. Lucy stared at it for a moment, as if it were a living thing.

"Got it from the crazy man at the Gate. I told you if a soul alive could find him it'd be Natty Scratch. Mad Alex said it was important to get this letter to you. And he did give me a guinea."

Lucy forced herself to take the note, her memory filled with Valcour's face, furious, fearful, his boots still stained with the dirt of an opened grave.

From the time she left Virginia, she had been seeking Alexander d'Autrecourt, the mysterious father she had all but forgotten. But now she was beginning to hope she had found a far different treasure in the husband the fates had chosen for her. Perhaps the past was best forgotten.

"Thank you, Natty," she said, stroking the boy's carroty hair. "You shall have another guinea from me."

"Natty Scratch don't take coin from them as is his friends, milady," the boy said grandly, then his brows puckered. "It be as a friend I tell you this. Be careful. I don't think . . . well, people who's not right in their head can be . . . ." His warning trailed off. "You know what I'm saying."

She needed to be alone. "I'll be careful, Natty," she

said. She took the missive out into the sunlight, but she was suddenly cold to the marrow of her bones. She slowly opened the letter, her eyes scanning lines that were scrawled in a way that made her nape prickle with apprehension.

We are destined to be together! How could you betray me thus, marrying some accursed nobleman! After all I have done to find you again, make you mine, as you were meant to be! Jenny, you betray me! You break my heart!

Lucy's hand tightened on the page, crumpling it. No. Her destiny was not in this twisted, confused man who had brought her to England on a quest she no longer wanted to complete.

Her destiny was inside the townhouse, his dark hair tempting her fingers, his eyes haunted, yearning. His mouth so tender.

Lucy crumpled the note and shoved it into the pocket beneath her gown. The old life, Jenny's life, had no power to haunt her anymore. She had dealt with the duchess of Avonstea. She had found passion in Valcour's arms. It was time to put an end to this mad mission of hers. Let go of the old life and embrace the new one that shimmered, with such fragile beauty just beyond her reach.

Resolute, Lucy returned to the house, fully intending to tell Valcour everything. For the first time in her life, the Raider's daughter was going to ask someone to help her.

The solicitor who had served Valcour for the past twenty years often bragged that his master was so single-minded and intense while at work that London could be ablaze and the earl would not know it until his breeches were afire. Valcour attacked the mountains of work inherent in running his vast financial holdings as if he were Henry V facing Agincourt. For the earl had come too close to total ruin to ever forget the sense of gut-deep panic that condition engendered in him or the danger that ruin would have posed for his mother, his brother, and all the people on the Valcour estates who depended on the earl for their livelihood.

But this morning, the notorious Valcour concentration was as fragmented as a porcelain figurine hurled against a fire grate. The gift for tallying sums that dismayed the unscrupulous men who had tried to fleece a grieving boy out of his fortune had vanished. Valcour could not seem to add any mathematical equation greater than one plus one.

For every time he dipped pen into ink, he remembered the petal-soft blush of Lucinda's skin. Every time he scratched the quill across paper, he could hear the winning sound of her laughter, the husky urgings of her voice as she taunted him, tempted him.

Valcour swore, balling up the sheet of vellum he'd been laboring over for two hours, and hurled it into the flames where the rest of his morning's work already lay in ashes.

He'd never had a woman affect him this way. He'd regulated his sex life with the same rigid control he had dealt with everything else. An appropriate mistress, a regular night when he came to her bed. Fierce concentration between the sheets in order to facilitate her pleasure and his own. Then he returned to his work, closing the door on that facet of his life until the next appointed night.

It had been so damned simple, so reasonable. But there was nothing simple about the woman who fed him spice cakes in bed and asked for his loving with that brave little lift to her chin. There was nothing reasonable about the woman who burrowed past so many defenses, breathing agonizing life back into places he was certain he'd deadened so long before.

His gut felt raw. His head throbbed unmercifully with visions of a tumbled wood sprite facing him in the gaming hell, her slender legs encased in preposterous breeches, her eyes flashing with recklessness, daring. A vulnerable beauty in a lantern-lit stable, crooning words of comfort to an injured horse, when her own life was falling apart around her. A cool golden goddess, her hair like a crown, facing the duchess of Avonstea. And a sorrowful muse, spun of magic, bending over the instrument that was the most treasured thing Valcour had ever owned.

Valcour threw down his pen and jammed himself to his feet, stalking to the window.

Any fool would think he had feelings for the girl! Any fool would think he—

Valcour doused the sudden thought as if it were a flaming brand. He'd have to be mad to leave himself vulnerable to that kind of pain. He had learned in the most brutal way possible that love did not glorify the person who gave it. It made one weak and helpless, vulnerable and insane with jealousy. It made people lie and betray trusts and . . .

Valcour slammed his knotted fist against the window ledge in frustration. No, blast it, he wouldn't let her inside those secret places he'd fought so hard to keep safe. He wouldn't let her reach past the earl of Valcour and into Dominic St. Cyr. Dominic, the dreamer, who had closed his eyes to everything but beauty until it was too late.

His jaw clenched as he caught a glimpse of scarlet ribbon and creamy gown, golden curls capturing the sunlight as Lucinda wandered toward the stables. There was something almost pensive about her, something fragile and beautiful and so tempting. For an instant Valcour was tempted to shove the mountains of work from his desk and follow her. Where, though? To a place he could be hurt again? Destroyed? A place where the tiny piece of himself he'd been able to save would be crushed beneath the weight of his emotions?

Calling himself three times the fool, Valcour stalked back to his desk. He would have to fight to keep his distance from the girl, battle the imps of mischief that twinkled in her eyes, the stubbornness that clung about her delectable little chin. He'd have to fight the innocence, the passion that glossed her lips, and the courage that was evident in every line of her supple body. Most of all, he would have to shield himself against the Lucinda who had reached out her arms to him last night—a sorrowful angel, who made him want to keep her safe in his embrace forever.

Valcour had faced countless men on dueling fields, their swords but a whisper away from his heart. But already he could feel the weapon Lucinda wielded against him slipping past his guard, plunging to the hilt, leaving him wounded in a way he had never been before.

A soft rap at the door made Valcour start, and he turned to see a gawky young footman in the entryway. "My lord, you have a visitor."

"I don't give a damn if the whole of England is at my door. Send them away."

"But sir, it's Master Aubrey, and he . . ."

Christ, as if Valcour wasn't being tormented by enough demons. The last thing he'd expected was for Aubrey to press for a confrontation after all that had happened. Always before, Valcour had practically been forced to drag the boy into his presence, as if Aubrey were a felon awaiting a death sentence. But this would not be like all those other meetings.

Everything had changed between them forever during those frozen moments when Aubrey had held his sword point one flick of his wrist away from Dominic's heart.

"You will send Mr. St. Cyr in at once."

The footman bowed. After a moment, Aubrey came through the door. All signs of the scapegrace boy who had driven Dominic to madness were gone. His neck-cloth was immaculate, tied soberly beneath his chin. His blond hair was caught sleekly back in a ribbon at his nape. Even his frockcoat was a sober dove-gray. But it was his face that made Valcour's chest ache unexpectedly. The boy was gone. The man who stood before Dominic had been altered forever by heartbreak and betrayal. Heartbreak and betrayal at Dominic's hands.

Valcour rose and gestured to one of the wing-backed chairs before the fireplace. Aubrey clasped his hands behind his back. "I prefer to stand."

Valcour shrugged, taking the chair himself, trying to gather up the icy detachment that had always served him so well, keeping everyone at a distance, even his only brother. "As you wish."

"I've come to tell Mother goodbye."

"Goodbye?"

"I've joined the Eleventh Hussars. I leave for my post within the week."

"The Hussars? The devil you have!" Valcour bolted from the chair. "If I'd wanted my brother in the damned army I would have bought you a commission."

"It is not your decision to make, sir."

Before, Valcour would have diffused into cold fury, brushing the words aside as a boy's dramatics. But he only glared at Aubrey's resolute features, feeling damned helpless.

"What is this? Some foolish romantic notion about getting your head blown off because of unrequited love?"

"I've just decided that it's time to discover what I'm made of."

Valcour started to bite out a retort but was stopped cold by the fierce resolve in Aubrey's eyes, a quiet determination like nothing Valcour had ever seen before.

"If you want to follow the drum, I'll buy you a commission. You can begin as an officer."

"That is not necessary, sir. For years you've made it

clear to all of London that I'm a millstone around your neck, and I've done nothing to change their opinion, acting like a weak-spined wastrel. But I'm not destroying myself in order to spite you any longer. I relieve you of all responsibility for me."

Valcour stared into his brother's face and saw a reflection of the boy Dominic had been—saw the icy mask settling over Aubrey's features, sensed the withdrawal. The idea of this boy retreating into the chill reaches where Valcour himself had found haven was more disheartening than anything the earl had ever seen.

The boy turned and started to walk away.

"At least let me give you money," Valcour said. "Enough to begin on."

Aubrey stopped and turned. "No."

Valcour struggled to hold on to his temper, keep his voice even. "You've taken money from me before. This is no different."

"Everything is different now. You see, I never realized how much you hated me until you married Lucy."

"Hate you?" Valcour echoed, stunned. "You think I married Lucinda because I hate you?"

Aubrey's eyes were stone cold, reminding Valcour with chilling clarity of his own. "What other reason could there possibly be?"

The earl's chest filled with fury at a situation neither of them could control. An enmity that had been almost inevitable from the time Aubrey was laid in the St. Cyr cradle, a living symbol of all that Dominic had lost.

"I asked what other reason there could possibly be for what you have done," Aubrey repeated in frigid accents.

The blood drained from Valcour's face and he grabbed the edge of the chair to brace himself, his fingers crushing the cushions. "I can't explain. Just believe me when I tell you I married Lucinda, not because I hated you, but because I care about you."

"Do you know how much it would have meant to me

to hear that when I was five or ten or twelve?" Aubrey said. "Then I might actually have believed it. But I'm not a child anymore, listening to fairy stories and waiting for happy endings."

"You have to believe me in this," Valcour insisted. "Wedding Lucinda would have been a terrible mistake for both of you, one beyond your imagining."

"Why? I love her. You don't. Make me understand."

Valcour was only now beginning to understand the depth of pain he had caused this boy, the earl's eyes having been opened by a hoyden mischievous as the devil's own.

There were scars from a thousand subtle rejections in the boy's face. For seventeen years Dominic had driven Aubrey away from him by whatever means necessary. He'd ignored him, scorned him, dismissed him as a fool. And all the while, Valcour had hidden behind the lie, claimed he was trying not to cause the boy pain. Could the truth hurt Aubrey more than what Valcour had already done?

The truth? That he is a bastard? That the mere sight of him was agony for me, because it was as if I were staring into the eyes of the man who betrayed me?

Valcour's mind filled with the image of Aubrey, a golden-curled moppet toddling toward him, arms open, an adoring smile on his face. *Let me start over, Brother.* The plea was a ragged cry from Dominic's soul. *This time I won't turn away.*

But it was too late to begin again. The only reason to tell Aubrey the truth now was a selfish one—Valcour's attempt to salvage what little relationship he had left with the boy.

He roiled with self-loathing. He didn't deserve another chance after all the pain he had caused Aubrey. Aubrey, the one true innocent in the morass of pain and betrayal that had been spun out at Harlestone Castle so many years before.

Valcour turned from his brother, his shoulders sagging with soul-deep weariness and regret. "You are right, Aubrey," he said, covering his face with his hand. "I can never make you understand."

Aubrey said nothing for long minutes, and Valcour heard him start toward the door, but at that moment the portal swung open, a familiar feminine voice making Valcour wheel and Aubrey stop where he stood.

"Dominic?" Lucy called, hastening into the chamber, a pinched look about the corner of her mouth. "Something has happened, I need to tell you—Aubrey." She froze, her gaze darting from Valcour's face to Aubrey's and back again. The worry in her face deepened, the rich blue of her eyes filling with compassion as if she could peel away the chill facades on both men and put her soft palm upon the pulsing source of their pain. "What a—a surprise."

Every word seemed to twist a knife blade of pain deeper into Aubrey, and Valcour could see that the boy's hard-won dignity was crumbling at the sight of Lucy's animated face. The boy swallowed convulsively, his broken heart in his eyes. "Lucy, are you well?"

There was tenderness, sympathy in Lucy's face, a kind of softness about her smile. "Yes. I'm better than well. I'm truly happy."

Valcour stared at her, stunned. She crossed to Valcour and slipped her hand into the earl's own. Warmth throbbed through him, comfort from the feel of her fingers, touching him, holding him.

"I know that you're still getting over your heartache, Aubrey," she said softly, "but this has all worked out for the best. You see, I care for your brother in a way I had not imagined before. I promise you, there is no place I would rather be than at my husband's side."

Could she know the fiery pain she had dashed across the boy's battered heart? Could she know the astonishment, the wonder that now enveloped Valcour's own? The earl reeled from the force of emotions so different, so painful, so headily wondrous. A maelstrom of emotions where there once had been none.

"I'm certain someday that you will find a lady you will love far better than you believe you loved me."

Did Valcour imagine it or were Aubrey's eyes glistening with tears? "Then I suppose there is nothing more for me to say except goodbye." Aubrey took her hand and kissed it.

Lucy watched him go, feeling suddenly shy, strangely unsettled. Valcour was regarding her with hooded eyes. "I'm sorry," she said. "I didn't mean to intrude."

The corner of Valcour's mouth ticked up in a weary smile. "Aubrey and I had said all there was to say. Lucinda, it was good of you to tell the boy things that will help him forget. Even if they were untruths."

"Untruths? But when we married, you told me you required two things of me. One was that I told the truth."

She met his gaze, saw the quiet panic in it, the trembling sense of yearning.

"Dominic, can you guess the most harrowing experience I ever had?"

"Harrowing? Since I met you in a gaming hell in the worst stew in London, I can't begin to imagine."

"I was only eight years old. I had been alone for so long. Thought that—that I was so wicked and ugly inside that no one would ever love me."

Valcour cupped her cheek in his hand. "Poor little hoyden."

"You see, when I was dumped in Virginia no one wanted me, not even Pendragon. Children can be dreadfully inconvenient in a nest of sedition, you see."

Valcour's mouth tipped in a tired smile. "I can imagine."

"I stole a doll to love. A fashion baby from a millinery

shop. I didn't realize English spies were using them to pass messages. I didn't realize that the shop was the station through which the messages passed."

"I would imagine that made things somewhat interesting."

"The vicar says that sin will be punished and virtue is its own reward. But you see, my mama was the lady who owned the shop, though I didn't know then that she was mine. She came chasing after the doll and fell in love with Pendragon—the very Raider the English were trying to catch. If I hadn't been the naughtiest child imaginable, they never would have found each other."

"It is a lovely story, Countess."

"Anyway," Lucy continued. "I adored this doll, you see, kept it to love. But a doll doesn't love you back, Valcour. Especially when it's contraband, hidden in an apple barrel."

The earl chuckled, a hoarse, sad sound. "So what happened to this seditious stolen doll?"

"One night I mustered all my courage. I wrote a message to Pendragon and I slipped into his bedchamber and left the doll and the note for him there. I've never been so frightened, before or since."

"What of, angel?"

"You see, I told him he could have the doll back. I had decided to love him and my mama instead."

Valcour's dark eyes brimmed with tenderness and a kind of desolation. "You were very brave, little one."

"Valcour?"

"What, hoyden?"

"I just want you to know that—that I have decided to love you too."

Valcour's features went still, his eyes awash in sentiments so raw and new that Lucy felt herself sinking deep into something she dared not name. "No, hoyden. You mustn't," he said in a gravelly voice. "I'm not a man with a clean heart to give you. I have nothing—"

"You have a great skill with oranges," Lucy said, glancing up at him through the fringe of her lashes. "And you are gentle and tender and brave and . . ." *Tortured*, a voice cried out inside her. *Hurting so badly it breaks my heart.* "I know you are hurt, and afraid, and . . . and that you think there is ugliness inside you," Lucy said. "But there is so much beauty, if you would just let me show you."

"Even a wood sprite like you couldn't find beauty in this place." He drew her hand over his heart. "It's empty. Been empty far too long."

"If it were empty, Dominic, it wouldn't hurt so much right now," Lucy said softly.

She leaned forward to press a warm, sweet kiss against Valcour's chest, let her love pulse through him, a silent pledge. Then she turned and left him alone.

In the corridor, she flattened her hand against the note concealed in her pocket. She had fully intended to share the message with Valcour, enlist his help. But how could she add more worry to that pain-ravaged face? How could she force him to battle her demons when he was still so raw from the confrontation with Aubrey, so stunned by her declaration of love?

After all that had happened, she couldn't bear to bring any more worry to this man who had stolen her heart.

She would slip out tonight and find some way to finish this entire matter the way she had so many other adventures: alone. It wasn't as if the stranger she had seen at the gaming hell could hold any danger for her. She was the Raider's daughter. She had been neck deep in intrigue and skullduggery while other girls were still stitching samplers at their mama's knees. She would put an end to this mysterious haunting that had begun when she opened the box in Blackheath Hall. And then she would begin the greatest challenge the Raider's daughter had ever faced.

Teaching the Hawk of Valcour to love again.

18

V alcour struggled with his work until well after dark, not even bothering to stop to eat. He had told himself it was imperative he finish what he had started, complete the necessary tasks. But in that place buried in his gut, where he couldn't lie to himself, he knew that the dread earl of Valcour was being a coward, hiding from a slip of a girl with golden curls and eyes blue as a fairy stream. A woman who had pressed soft lips to his chest and murmured words that had wounded him, defeated him, entranced him.

I have decided to love you. Just like that, with a snap of her fingers. Without doubts or fears or any inkling of the heartache she had opened herself to. Without any idea that she had just made the most devastating mistake of her life: giving her heart to a man without the courage to love her in return.

Always, Valcour had faced his own shortcomings with the same ruthless clarity he did everyone else's. He didn't cringe from the knowledge that he was ruthless, cold. That he was unforgiving and sometimes cruel. But he hadn't expected that there was another shortcoming lurking behind it all: cowardice.

But the truth was that after Lucinda's confession of love, even his library was not far enough, not safe enough a haven for him to hole up in. No, he was damned certain he should go upstairs, have his valet dress him, then go off to one of his clubs. Spend the night in one of those familiar male bastions, as far away as possible from Lucinda's magic. Her silky seduction, not woven of her generosity beneath the coverlets, but rather the heady seduction of being loved, of being needed. Of letting go of all the shields, all the defenses, and being not Valcour the ruthless, the cold, but Dominic—a man who needed this woman who loved him.

Valcour swore, then stood and took up the single guttering candle. He paced up the stairs and into his own room. But before he could rouse his valet, he heard a sound. A soft moan drifted from where the door between the earl's chamber and that of his bride stood ajar.

"Lucinda?" Valcour called softly, his brows lowering as he flattened his hand on the panel and shoved it open.

"Dominic?" Her voice seemed so faint, so fragile, Valcour's heart plummeted. Candlelight spilled across the pathetic figure huddled in the big bed. Her face was flushed and warm above the lacy edge of the shift that rippled beneath her chin. Her eyes were half closed in the faint light of a single candle, while a hot brick wrapped in flannel was cuddled close to her middle.

He had seen his countess enraged and spouting defiance; he had felt her tenderness, her anger, and her scorn. Never had he seen this vibrant, animated beauty look so listless.

"Lucinda, I'm going to summon up Mrs. Bates at once. She has some skill at physicking—"

"No!" Lucinda cried out, looking alarmed. "No, please don't! It would be so humiliating. I will be fine, Valcour. I promise you."

Valcour sat carefully beside her on the bed. "Ho now, Countess. There is nothing humiliating about being ill." He stroked back a silken strand of her hair, felt it cling to his fingers the way her loving curled about his soul. "I insist that you—"

"No!" Her lips quivered, and Valcour felt a wrenching in his chest.

"Countess, let me help you. At least . . ." He stumbled over the words. "Perhaps it would be comforting if I were to lay down beside you? Hold you?"

"You can't! You mustn't! Oh, do go away!"

For a woman who had just been making tender declarations of love, she seemed rather unobliging. Valcour couldn't fathom why her words stung so badly.

"Blast it, girl, I'm worried about you! You were fine a few hours ago, and now—now you look as if you're at death's door! I'm not leaving until you tell me what the devil has happened to you!"

She levered herself up on one elbow, glaring at him with some semblance of her old defiance. "I'm *not* at death's door! But you may be if you don't leave me alone! I'm *not* sick and I'm *not* sad. I'm . . ." Her cheeks went pink as peonies. "I'm having the Curse of Eve!"

"The . . . oh!" Valcour swallowed convulsively, feeling his own cheeks burn. Thunder and turf, he wasn't some green boy to be aghast at such feminine mysteries. Why was it the girl was making him feel as if he'd been caught peeking beneath her skirts?

"Now *will* you leave me alone?" Lucy demanded, flinging her head back onto the pillow for emphasis. "I'm sorry I'm such a monster, Dominic. But this makes me exceedingly ill-tempered. I don't want to see anyone— not you, not my maid, not anyone—until this first day of misery is quite over."

Valcour had intended from the first only to bid her goodnight and stay far from her bed. Why was it that knowing it was forbidden to him made him feel as crotchety as his bride was evidently feeling. "As you wish. Is there anything else that can be done for your comfort?"

"Just don't let anyone so much as open my door until morning, or I vow I'll become violent!"

"No one has greater respect for your violence than I, Countess. I shall leave word that anyone who disturbs you does so at risk of life and limb." Valcour stunned himself by leaning down and brushing her forehead with a kiss. For an instant he saw something flicker in Lucinda's eyes, something like quicksilver, leaving unease in its wake. Then it was gone.

Valcour strode from the room to prepare for an evening at White's faro table. He was dead certain his luck would be as abysmal as was the prospect of being banned from his countess's bed.

The night had always been Lucy's friend, a cloak to hide her mischief, a haven when all the Blackheaths had curled up in the salon, chattering and laughing, quarreling and making music. She'd always loved the darkness. But tonight, as she traveled London's streets, it was as if some unseen presence were waiting for her in every shadow, lurking behind every dim, ragged figure that shuffled along in the grinding poverty that surrounded Perdition's Gate.

The only soul who even knew she had gone was Natty—her partner in stealing a horse away from Valcour's stable. The boy had been delighted when he had first seen her slipping from the townhouse's garden door, garbed in breeches, frockcoat, and a jaunty tricorn with a scarlet plume. He had come to raid her pockets, hoping for sweetmeats or spice cake or some other rare treat. And he had shaken his head in a way that might have amused Lucy greatly under other circumstances as he confessed that he was still not able to get over his disappointment that his benefactor was not a boy.

However, the instant Lucy told Natty that she planned to go riding in the night, the little rogue had turned jittery as a colt in a hailstorm, his usual brashness oddly subdued.

"It's an ill night to be abroad, milady," Natty had said. "See the ring of red about the moon? Pappy Blood says that be the gateway to hell, glowing when the devil sets the damned souls free to torment us."

"I can't believe you give countenance to such faradiddle."

"I *did* think it was nonsense, until I noticed that things happen on such nights. Bad things, milady. Drowned bodies float up on the Thames. Not suicides, you know, but people who are murdered. Houses catch on fire and the men who go up to see the whores at the Gate are so mean they leave marks on 'em. I know it sounds mad, but it's not. Surely you believe . . . believe in omens an' dreams, milady. Believe that some nights the world is full of hauntings."

"If that is true, this should be the perfect night to find a ghost," Lucy had assured him. "That is, if you can tell me where to begin my search."

With great reluctance, the child had told her all he knew about the location of the man who had given him the note. But Lucy had seen real fear in the urchin's eyes. "I wish you'd let me go with you. I be a good man in a fight."

Lucy had brushed her fingertip gently across Natty's bruised face. "I think you've had quite enough fighting lately, my fine sir. The moment I return, I'll bring out a whole plate of sticky buns and tell you the entire story, beginning to end. I promise it will be a grand adventure."

Then Lucy had ridden away, hating the unease Natty's words had spun about her, hating the guilt she felt every time she thought of how she had deceived Valcour.

The earl would not be amused when he discovered what his bride had done, but the entire affair would all be over by then. There would be nothing he could do but rage and sulk and lambast her with that delightfully tyrannical voice of his. But Lucy was certain she wouldn't have to endure his fits of temper for long. If she put her mind to it, she could find another deliciously sensual way to distract him.

She reined the horse into a twisted lane of gin shops and rookeries, taverns and brothels. The dregs of humanity littered the street like horse dung, ragged, stinking bundles with sly eyes and bone-thin bodies.

When Lucy reached the building Natty had directed her to, she was half tempted to spin the horse around and ride the other way. But she steeled her courage and dismounted. Her fingers felt numb as she tied her horse to the post, doubtful it would still be there when she returned. Then she shoved open the door to a gin shop disgusting beyond description.

The stench alone nearly flung her against the wall, and the crowd of customers looked as if they would like nothing better than to steal everything she owned, including the teeth from her mouth.

Lucy feigned a bored arrogance and paced to a toothless old hag slopping Blue Ruin into tankards. "A thousand pardons, milady," Lucy growled in a masculine tone. "I am searching for someone. A gentleman—"

"If you be looking for a gentleman, you come to the wrong place, laddie," the woman cackled. "Nothing but layabout bastards here."

"I would be willing to pay anyone who could help me find him. I'm a generous laddie."

The crone's eyes glittered like jet buttons in the loose folds of skin. "How am I to know one man among all these others?"

"He is tall and slender, with pale gold hair and eyes that are vague. He spends his time scribbling music. Some think him mad, but he seems gentle enough."

The crone's eyes disappeared into slits, and she sucked

her lips over toothless gums. "You be looking for Mad Alex, do you, laddie? I can't say that it would be a good idea to go barging in on him right now. He's been a trifle beside himself the past week. Ever since he found that notice of an earl's marriage in the *Gazette*."

Threads of unease uncoiled in Lucy's middle. "Can you tell me where to find him?"

"Sure'n I can. He's got a room out back, ever since his brother chased him from Perdition's Gate. Sir Jasper be hunting him down—you don't be working for that bastard, do you? Maybe I should have ol' Dickwilly there slit your gullet just in case."

"No," Lucy said hastily. "The truth is, Alex has been searching for me."

"If you're lyin' to me, I got a dozen men who would murder you cold for the price of one tankard of me finest."

"I understand."

"Who should I tell Mad Alex is calling?"

"Tell him I bring him word about Jenny."

The woman scowled. "Jenny? Is that one of those whores he has visiting?"

Lucy cringed inwardly. "No. Just tell him. He'll know what it means."

The crone returned moments later, eyeing Lucy with patent curiosity. "Go on back. He's pure perishing to see you. Last door on the left."

Lucy started away, but the old woman stepped in front of her. "Just to be safe, you can leave your sword with me. Mad Alex is a good-paying customer, and I'd take exception to losing him."

Lucy wanted to protest, but she saw two burly men close ranks with the crone. Slowly, Lucy slipped her sword from the scabbard and handed it to the woman.

"Pistol too. Now, laddie."

Lucy set her teeth, then gave up the weapon. She was going to see a man who claimed to be her father. An

310

impostor, no doubt. A weakling attempting to extort money from her, or involved in some other mercenary scheme. If he had wanted to do her harm, he would have come to Virginia himself, found her there, and . . .

Plotting out the most reasonable course to her own murder did nothing to keep at bay the prickles of foreboding that slid like slivers of ice beneath her skin. Lucy drove away the thoughts and made her way through what seemed almost a rabbit warren of close, foul-smelling chambers littered with straw, stray cats, and starving children. When she reached the appointed door, she knocked.

"Come in."

His voice. It was faint, a little grating. Frightening in a way Lucy had never expected. She lifted the latch and opened the door. Her vision was blurry from the dark, the blaze of candlelight making the figure before her shimmer and ripple like the surface of a stream stirred by her hand. She swiped her fingers across her eyes, then opened them again.

From the moment she had left Virginia she had been working to this end—to confront this mysterious person face to face. But as she stared into the features of the man before her, a tightness began to close about her heart.

He was the man in the miniature. Could there be any doubt? Soft blond hair threaded through with gray framed a dreamy face. The mouth was less defined, the chin far weaker, but then the painted image had been that of an optimistic boy. This was a man on whom the passage of time had laid heavily.

Yet as Lucy stared into the man's features, she couldn't help but remember how miserable she had been as an abandoned child, how close her mother had come to burying her sorrows in the muddy current of the Thames.

"Who are you and what news have you?" the man demanded.

Lucy crushed the brim of her tricorn between her fingers and swept the hat off, a wealth of golden curls cascading down to frame her face. "I am Jenny d'Autrecourt."

Even if Lucy had still clung to any doubts about the man's identity, his reaction would have banished them forever. A fevered light came to those vague eyes, like a licking tongue of blue flame. The bony fingers trembled as if stricken with palsy.

"Jenny? You are my Jenny?" The man crossed to her, cupping his quaking hands about her cheeks. "Child, it is your papa."

Lucy had always hated the thoughtless caresses some strangers seemed determined to lavish on anyone they passed. Every touch of affection was far too precious in her eyes to be flung out carelessly, without any love behind it.

But this was supposed to be her long-lost father. Why was it that each fiber of her body pulled whipcord taut, and she had to fight the urge to pull away from him? He was so close to her. She could smell the faint sourness of his breath, she could see the odd emptiness beyond the irises of his eyes, feel the surprising sinewy strength within his thin fingers.

Tears spilled down his face. "Jenny, don't you remember me?"

She stared into his features, searching for any scrap of memory, but there was nothing except the haunting strains of her "Night Song." Still, she didn't want to hurt him. "I was only three years old the last time I saw you," she said, "but my mother has told me many stories about you."

"Your mother. So beautiful. Gentle little Emily with her eyes like violets and an angel's smile. She is well?"

Lucy's cheeks heated. She looked away. "Mama is very happy. She fell in love and she has been wed for twelve years now to the most wonderful man, who adores her and takes care of her and loves her. After all that she suffered—losing me, and believing you dead, and . . . being cast out by your family—she deserves some joy, don't you think?"

Alexander's brow puckered. "Can Emily find joy in being an adulteress?"

"She didn't do it on purpose! You were supposed to be dead! How could she have known? And now, after all this time, her whole life is in Virginia. She has a husband, children she adores. She has already suffered so much you can't—can't mean to take that away from her."

Alexander seemed to consider for a long moment. "You are a good girl to defend your mama that way. Still, it is distressing to think of her sinning and sinning every time she goes to her lover's bed. Emily would not like to sin. She was a vicar's daughter, you know. I am certain I could find some way to remedy her dilemma if I put my mind to the task." His eyes clouded, his lips tipping in a thoughtful smile. Then he caught a glimpse of Lucy's face.

"Now, now, child," he tsked. "You almost look afraid —afraid of your own papa? Silly goose! As long as I have you, my own little girl, Emily need never know that her other babes are bastards, that she is not wife but concubine to the man who shares her bed."

Why was it that those words of reassurance only heightened Lucy's unease? "No. She's not a . . ." Lucy began, then stopped, sick with the knowledge that this man's very existence made those horrible charges true. "Papa, promise—you must promise me that you won't hurt her."

"Hurt her? I would never harm to Emily. Even when she was a girl, I wanted only to take care of her. But I failed. I failed, I failed, I failed . . ." His voice droned, sing-songy, off key. Then his fists knotted. "I will not fail this time, I vow. Now that I have found you, my Jenny, I shall guard you like a treasure, where no one will ever be able to take you from me again." There was a disturbing twist to the man's mouth, a curl to his lip that reminded Lucy all too clearly of Sir Jasper.

"I don't need to be guarded," Lucy began, but the man wasn't listening; his eyes were glazed, his nostrils flaring.

"They say that I am mad, you know. Insane. Yet what father would not go mad if he was locked in a secret room for sixteen years? No sun on my face, no fresh breezes to suck deep into my lungs. Locked away without knowing what had happened to my daughter, my wife."

"The d'Autrecourts held you prisoner?"

"Do you think they could have kept me away from you any other way? They locked me in the attic at Avonstea, guarded night and day by a man who could have shattered stone with his bare hands. I begged them to release me, pounded against the doors until my hands bled. Oh, God, child, can you even imagine what it was like for me? Knowing what they had done to you? Believing that you were lost to me forever?"

Lucy closed her eyes, remembering her mother the day they had been reunited in Blackheath Hall's garden: Emily weaving the tale of her despair, her heartbreak, her grief over the loss of her tiny daughter, while Lucy sobbed out how she had felt—unloved, unwanted, alone. Yet it had ended in triumph, reunion. They had found each other, and it had seemed a miracle.

Would the gentle musician from her mother's many stories of England feel any less bereft at the loss of his child? Wouldn't he have been broken by helplessness, despair, fury at his family's betrayal?

Lucy swallowed hard, empathy welling up inside her for this man—the pathetic shell of the young musician who had rescued her mother so many years before. "Oh, Papa, what have they done to you?"

"Do you think it matters anymore? I have you back again, my Jenny." Alexander smiled, and an eager blue flame seemed to lick in his eyes. "Those idiots thought they were far more clever than I, but I fooled them, Jenny. Do you want to know how ingenious your papa was?"

"Tell me, Papa."

"After a time, I calmed my hysteria. It was futile, hopeless. I realized that if I were to escape, they must think me harmless, a man lost in a gentle trance. Bit by bit I wheedled my way into my keeper's good graces. I fed him the wine they brought for me, gave him the best tidbits of food. What did I need it for anyway? I was sustained by the need to find you."

He chuckled lowly. "It was Jasper who gave me the means to escape them. Jasper always was a fool. His favorite pleasure was to come into my cell and taunt me. I used to sit, rocking in my chair, tears pouring down my face, as he told me that if it weren't for me, he could be duke . . . if it weren't for me."

"I met Jasper at Perdition's Gate. He was a horrible man."

"At the gate? You were there the night Jasper came? I didn't see you! I was keeping watch, always watching, hoping."

"I was dressed like this." Lucy waved a hand at her breeches. "I got caught up in the duel. By the time I came to your room you were gone. You never returned again."

"It was because of my brother, Jasper, stalking me, hunting me as if I were an animal. He would love nothing better than to lock me back up in that attic room and nail the door shut forever."

Alexander chuckled. "What he doesn't realize is that he is the one who opened the cell door for me. Once when he was about, tormenting me, I was able to steal the keys from him. He was always losing things. Didn't have any idea where the keys had got to. From that time on, I was able to rove Avonstea at will, taking anything I wished."

He licked his lips, an almost impish smile making

Lucy's scalp prickle. "The first thing I took was the sleeping potion my mother often used to drive away the guilt-spawned nightmares that have tormented her since she condemned herself to hell. Then I could lace the guard's cherished wine with the drug and creep about without fear of being discovered."

He gave a low chuckle. "I could have killed them all, you know," he continued. "Murdered them for what they did to us. Three times I held a pillow poised above my mother's face. She looked so tormented by the evil she had done us, it would have been an act of mercy to lower the pillow to her face, hold it there until she was at peace."

Lucy's head swam at the horrifying image, the calm, almost sweet tones of her father's voice, as if he were talking about tucking the blankets tenderly about his mama's cold feet.

From the time she was eight years old, Lucy had loathed the duchess, one in the cast of villains who had separated her from her mother. And yet Alexander d'Autrecourt's words made Lucy feel ill.

How many times had she sat at the pianoforte and dreamed of this man? A young god of music, a kindred spirit who shared that secret magical world of melody and harmony, notes that rippled and took shape into dream worlds so few could explore.

But he was not the idol she had made him. He was no longer even the simple, kind boy in the story her mother told, Emily's dearest childhood friend, who had saved her by taking her in marriage.

"You needn't fear, my Jenny, love," he crooned. "I didn't kill her. I kept thinking of you, child. Do you remember how you put your hands on mine so we could play the pianoforte together? That is the way we shall put my mama to sleep. And Jasper and the rest of those who tried to destroy us. Your hand curved so soft upon mine while we force the pillow down over their faces."

"Stop it!" Lucy shuddered, unable to keep the revulsion from her features.

A wounded expression flashed across Alexander d'Autrecourt's face. "Jenny, you are angry with me?"

"Angry? Papa, you're talking about committing murder—" The words were hard, but Lucy couldn't stop them.

"Murder? Jenny, you distress me," he said in a flat voice. "You know that they are eaten alive with guilt, like a cancer, burning and burning inside them. I am going to put out that unquenchable fire. I am going to save them from themselves."

"No, Papa. You're sick. And no wonder, after all that has happened."

Alexander's eyes widened, the sparse lashes starting out at awkward angles, accenting the blood-red veins that lined the whites of his eyes. "That is not what I want you to say. You are to be overjoyed. You see, we are reunited beyond the grave, you and I. You are my Jenny again, to care for and love. And I am your papa. I will play on the pianoforte, and you can dance."

"I'm not a little girl anymore, Papa. I'm going to bring you to Hawkvale with me, try to help you. You'll like it there. I'm the countess of Valcour now."

"Valcour? Again they spread their poison! Poison you against me!" The sudden virulence of his fury made Lucy fall back a step. He swept up a length of silk cord that lay coiled on the table and twisted it about his fingers in near frenzy. "What did St. Cyr tell you? Lies? Did he tell you that I—"

He stopped, his gaze sharp on Lucy's face. It was as if the blue flame were licking up through his mind, consuming him. Yet was it any wonder he was so unbalanced? Imprisoned all these years, then fleeing to hide in hideous places like this, hunted like a mad animal?

"Papa, I can't stay in this place, and neither can you. I want to help you. I do. But I love my husband."

"He cannot have you," Alexander said in a strange voice. "You can only be happy with me!"

Lucy knew she was helpless to change his mind. "I have to go back to Hawkvale, even if you choose not to come. If you need anything you'll know where to find me." It was hard, so hard to turn and walk away.

She expected protests, expected anger. But never did she expect the sudden hissing that sounded near her ear.

She started to wheel around, but a cord snaked about her throat lightning fast. For one disbelieving moment, Lucy groped for the cord. My God, what was he doing? It tightened.

Lucy fought like a demon as the cord bit like a circlet of fire about her throat, searing into the fragile skin with a diabolical delicacy, as if he were trying hard not to hurt her.

Not to hurt her? She thought wildly, struggling as her lungs screamed for air and the world spun crazily around her. He was strangling her. Cutting off all air with a mad tenderness.

Oh, God, what had she done? How had things gone so awry? She had a fleeting image of her pistol and sword tucked beneath the hag's gin barrels. She had a flashing picture of Dominic in his study, that frozen instant when she decided not to tell him Alexander had contacted her once again.

She could see the earl in her mind's eye, the moment he was told—what? That she too had betrayed him? Lied to him?

That she was dead?

Valcour! Her mouth rounded in a silent scream.

"Don't be afraid, Jenny, love," Alexander d'Autrecourt crooned in her ear, tightening the noose about her neck. "Sleep, now. Papa will take care of you."

The last sounds Lucy heard before darkness claimed her were the offkey strains of a child's lullaby.

19

$\mathcal{V}$alcour tossed and turned in his empty bed, cursing himself as a fool. He had never spent such a miserable night. From the moment he strode through White's doors he realized he had made a tactical error. Instead of finding a refuge where he could put his new countess and the feelings she inspired in him into perspective, he had opened himself to dozens of congratulations, veiled queries, and speculations about the woman who had finally managed to get the elusive earl to the altar.

Countless toasts had been drunk to Lucinda's health, and glass after glass raised in anticipation of the wealth of sturdy sons that would doubtless follow. From the time he was a boy, Valcour had schooled himself never to display emotions—neither anger nor embarrassment, uncertainty nor despair. But the entire time he had spent, lounging in a chair with his hand curved about his glass, he hadn't been able to disguise the feelings rushing through him.

He felt like a sulky boy, deprived of some cherished holiday, because he was banned from Lucinda's bed. He felt like a selfish beast, ill tempered toward the entire world, because of some unavoidable feminine ritual. A ritual that had made his vibrant bride look listless and petulant and forlorn.

Valcour was beginning to feel the same. He swore under his breath. Never before had the monthly inconveniences of his various lights-o'-love disturbed him. He had merely dismissed the matter and gone on with his life with no particular impatience, until the next week. But tonight, Valcour's hands burned with the need to feel his countess beneath them. His mouth tingled with the memory of how it felt to crush Lucinda's soft lips beneath his, to tease her, to toy with her, coaxing her deeper and deeper into the seductive dance of passion.

Valcour felt himself harden and ache beneath the coverlets. He jammed his fist into the pillow with all the force of his frustration. Damn it to hell. He wanted her. Not just to bury himself inside her, but just to be with her, to feel her nestled against the hard wall of his chest, to feel her breath, so soft, so sweet and moist against his skin as she lay dreaming. He wanted to lay in the first faint rays of dawn and watch her sleeping, a tumbled angel in his arms.

Valcour's chest constricted, a dull pain throbbing at the image his fantasies had woven. Hellfire, when had this happened? This infernal weakness, this desperately dangerous weakening in the walls he had constructed about his heart? When had he started to care for this woman? This lovely rebel who had tempted him, tormented him, mocked him, and then offered her love to him so sweetly she had broken his heart?

But the earl of Valcour had no heart. He had labored seventeen years to make it so. Never had he suspected that the dreamy boy who had believed in fairy castles and dragons and star-crossed lovers still thrived somewhere in the earl of Valcour's battered soul. Never had he suspected that this woman would take that grieving boy into her hands, gently, so gently, and breathe life back into his spirit, agonizing, unexpected life.

He loved her.

Sweet God, how could he have let this happen? How could he have stopped it?

Valcour groaned, flinging one arm across his eyes. Was this the Fates' final cruel jest? That he who had hated Alexander d'Autrecourt should fall desperately in love with the man's daughter? That he who had never forgiven his mother for falling prey to love's arrows had now bared his own breast to them, let them pierce him, deep, so deep.

What the devil did it mean? That tomorrow and the next day and the next he would feel this burning sensation in his soul, this agony? That he would spend the rest of his life completely vulnerable to this woman who had captured his heart? That he would be helpless, waiting?

Waiting for what?

For her to betray him? Betray him as his mother had betrayed him? As Alexander d'Autrecourt had betrayed him? As his father had betrayed him?

Valcour closed his eyes, remembering with nightmarish clarity what passion had driven his father to do.

Who fathered the bastard? Lionel St. Cyr had asked, so reasonably, his voice so soft, almost pleading. *Dominic, tell me the name of your mother's lover.*

Why hadn't he told? There had no longer been any reason to hide it. Death had already put the man far beyond Lionel St. Cyr's reach. Why hadn't Dominic spilled out the truth?

Because Dominic had felt it was his fault. Because then his father would know that Dominic should have stopped it, should have known. But he had been a foolish boy caught up in his own dreams, oblivious to the disaster waiting to engulf them all.

He hadn't seen the pistol until he was almost to the

door. He had screamed, flung himself at his father, but it was too late.

Valcour would never forget the stench of powder and sulphur, of sickly sweet blood and burned flesh. And he would never forget the hideous carnage that had been love's final legacy.

He had stood over his father's grave, a wound in the green earth, and he had turned away from life. Forever, he had thought. Until Lucinda had flung him back into the world of the living, until she had decided to love him.

An incessant rattle made Valcour swear, the racket deepening the throbbing in his head. What was it? Some housemaid run mad? A tradesman attempting to fix something? Valcour scowled, noting the direction of the sound. His bedchamber window? That was absurd—it was on the topmost floor.

Valcour levered himself out of bed and dragged on a banyan, fastening the flowing garment about his lean waist, then he stalked toward the sound, looking forward to lambasting whoever had dared rouse him at this infernal hour. Not that he had been sleeping, Valcour thought with irrational anger. Still, God knew he should have been!

At the window, the earl ripped open the damask curtains and froze, staring into the eyes of a dirty little waif wearing one of Valcour's own shirts. Tears streaked the boy's face—a face so battered, Valcour's gut burned with fury. The child's small fists pounded on the window, begging for entry.

"What the devil!" the earl swore. Shouts rose up from the ground beneath, and Valcour could see a cluster of his own servants, their fists waving, shouting threats as one of the footmen attempted to put up a ladder to fetch the miniature fugitive. For God's sake, it was a wonder the boy hadn't broken his neck already. From the looks on the faces of Valcour's servants, they wouldn't mind if the child had.

The earl carefully opened the window, then reached out and closed his strong hands about the child's arms and lifted him inside.

The boy had a distressingly moist nose and was hiccoughing in a manful attempt to keep his sobs at bay, but he seemed terrified that Valcour would evict him at once. Scrawny arms twined about the earl like living vines.

"What the blazes is this about?" Valcour demanded.

"Th-they wouldn't let me in! I told them and begged, but they wouldn't—wouldn't let me—"

"Exactly what business would you be having at Hawkvale, boy? Aside from stealing my shirt?"

"I didn't steal it! *She* gave it to me 'cause my other was so bloody after Pappy beat me! She said she would be careful, and then she didn't come back!"

Valcour stared down at that anguished little face, as if the boy were some strange exotic creature brought to display in a country fair. His experience with children seldom extended further than flipping one a guinea for holding his horse. But there was a quality about this staunch little fellow that touched something in Valcour.

"Easy now, boy. You're babbling. Who the blazes is this mysterious *she?* Your mother? Is your mother a maid here, or—"

"No, you great gudgeon! Never had no mother in all my born days! She said she had a pistol and a sword and that it would be a grand adventure! But I should'a known it would end disastrous. The ring was there on the moon."

A sick suspicion stirred in Valcour's gut. "Damn it, boy, who the devil are you talking about?"

"Your lady! Lucy. I gave her a note from Mad Alex an' she went riding off to find him."

Valcour's heart fell like a stone. In a breath, he was at the door between their rooms. He shoved on the panel. The damned thing stuck. "Lucinda? Damn it, girl—"

Raw panic pulsing inside him, Valcour slammed his shoulder against the door with a strength born of his terror. The door flew open, spilling the earl into the chamber where he had left Lucinda, pale and moaning the night before.

She was gone.

Valcour reeled back as if a fist had driven into his jaw. The entire scenario played out in his mind. Lucy, a master of deception, pretending to be ill, then riding off alone to face the madman who had tormented her these many months.

"No! Goddamn her hide to hell, she has to be all right! My God. I'll kill her myself!"

Valcour wheeled to where the boy still stood, shaking, his eyes wide, terrified.

"Please, milord, you have to save her! He took her, Mad Alex! I followed her, even though she didn't want me to. I saw him take her out, all limplike and laying there so pale."

"Where, boy? Where did he take her?"

"I don't know!" Tears shimmered on stubby lashes, then fell free. The boy scrubbed them away with one fist. "The streets were so crowded, and dark, and then Pappy Blood saw me and tried to take me back. And when I got away, I couldn't find her, so I took her horse and came here. But those bastards down there wouldn't let me in the door!"

"This man who took Lucinda, he must have said something, boy. Anything that could give me a place to start!"

"He was blooming crazy, talking to her real strange, even though she couldn't hear him. He said . . . said he was going to take her to meet Ann Cestors. Never heard of any one by that name."

Ann Cestors? Valcour grappled desperately with the cryptic name. Who the devil . . . "Please, boy. There must be something else. Anything—"

"He said something about a knight who fought in the crusades. And a ring . . . there was a magic ring—"

Wasn't there some story about that, attached to the infernal ring Dominic had given Lucy? Ann . . . That was it! He was taking the girl to her ancestors. And where else would he be able to find a knight who had been dead for centuries?

Valcour stilled, horrified, his memory filling with images of Lucy at the Avonstea graveyard, her skirts a splash of color on the grass, her chin jutting up, defiant, her golden hair ablaze with sunlight against a backdrop of wild-roving rose vines and a crude angel carved into a gray tombstone.

"Why would he take her to a graveyard," Valcour muttered aloud. "Unless she was . . ."

Dead. The word ran through Valcour's vitals like a knife, all but driving him to his knees.

No! She couldn't be dead! His belligerent countess with her sparkling eyes and devilish smile, her laughter and her raging temper, her courage and her wild, sweet loving.

"Damn it, boy, was she? Was Lucinda . . ." His voice broke. He couldn't form the word.

"I don't know for sure. I don't know. But I thought— thought I heard her make a little sound, like . . . like she was crying inside."

A tiny sound a frightened boy *thought* he heard above the din of the London streets. It was the most fragile thread of hope. Valcour clutched at it like a talisman.

He barely heard footsteps running toward him, Lady Catherine racing into the room, her hair in sleepy disarray, her eyes cloudy and disoriented as she clutched her bedgown about her. "Dominic, there was a disturbance, I heard—"

Valcour wheeled to face his mother, saw her raise her hand to her heart.

"Merciful heavens! Dominic, what—what has happened?" Wide, frightened eyes flashed from Lucinda's empty bed to the ragged urchin, then to Dominic's face.

"Lucinda. He's taken her."

"Who, Dominic?"

"Someone claiming to be Alexander d'Autrecourt."

A low, keening cry tore from Lady Catherine's breast and she staggered back, her face white as parchment. "Alexander? Alive?"

"God damn it, if he's hurt her I'll kill him! The minute I find him I'll . . ."

But what if he *didn't* find this lunatic? Oh, God, what if Valcour couldn't? Even now, this madman might be dragging Lucinda somewhere that Valcour could never find her. It might already be too late.

He wouldn't think it. If he did, he'd go mad himself.

"Boy, tell the groom to ready my stallion as if the stable were afire. I'm going after her."

The boy barreled out of the room. Valcour wheeled and raced into his bedchamber, grabbing up breeches and shirt, yanking on his boots. He was scarce aware of Lady Catherine trembling like a pale ghost, haunted.

"Dominic, where are you going? What are you going to do?"

"I'm going to the Avonstea graveyard, madam. If I find Lucinda—when I find her—I'll take her to Harlestone."

"Let me go with you."

"Why?" Valcour demanded. "So you can see if your lover still lives? My God, he's kidnapped Lucinda! God knows what else he's done."

"Alexander would never harm anyone."

Dominic straightened, his face contorting in rage and disbelief. "You would defend him even now?" He snorted in disgust. "You sicken me, madam. My hand to God, if anything happens to Lucinda—"

He bit off the words, then bolted down the stairs, the image of his mother's stricken face one more facet in the nightmare that would never release Valcour from its merciless talons.

Pain seared Lucy's throat every time she sucked in a breath of air, throbbed in Lucy's hands at the lightest twitch of her fingers. Something cold and hard grated against her cheek, a damp chill seeping into the very marrow of her bones. Where was she? She battled to grasp some tiny snippet of memory, some vague wisp of reality in this world of pulsating pain and relentless darkness, but all she could do was mouth the same word, over and over again, in a moaned plea.

Valcour.

Where was he? Why didn't he come to her? Pull her from this swirling abyss? Why didn't he drive away this hideous, crushing panic with the warmth of his love?

Love? No, he didn't love her. Could never love her. She flinched against the inner anguish the thought caused her, and fiery ribbons unfurled in muscles that seemed fused into place.

"So you are awakening, my darling lamb."

The words were tender, soft. Why did they make Lucy feel as if rats had just scuttled across her bare skin?

She tried to turn toward the sound, but her neck felt frozen. For a heartbeat, she couldn't breathe.

Sweet God in heaven. Reality crashed over her like stones hurtling down the side of a sea-battered cliff. My God, her father had tried to strangle her!

Her gritty eyes opened, pierced by shafts of light from a candle pressed so close to her eyes she could smell the faint stench of her curls being singed.

She tried to struggle back, away from the light, away from that eerie voice. But there was nowhere to go. She was wedged tight against something cool, like marble.

She battled to focus her eyes, felt fingers trail over her face in a gentle caress.

Her vision cleared. She was in a stone room of some sort, a cold, nightmarish chamber. Crumbling bones, shoved from the daises on which they had once reposed, were now piled in its corners. Branches of candles were tucked hither and yon, a chair and table in the far corner, while a feather tick was crowded beneath a stone tablet that read "Adam d'Autrecourt, his noble head severed at Chartres . . ."

My God, it was a crypt!

At that moment, a figure blotted out her surroundings, the light illuminating the gaunt, cadaverous face of her captor.

The blue eyes that had been so vague before were now restless and moist and terrifying.

"Lie still and be a good girl, Jenny," he crooned. "Papa has prepared a poultice for that nasty mark upon your throat."

The tenderness in his tones made her skin crawl. She wanted to scream at him, curse him, wanted to beg him to let her go. She wanted to writhe away from his touch. Instead, she clenched her teeth, groping for a way to escape this insanity. She had to try to find some way to reason with this man, who still had such twisted, abiding love for her in his disturbing eyes.

Could she reach past the madness somehow? Touch that part of the gentle musician that still remained buried beneath years of horror? If she could, perhaps she had a chance.

"My throat hurts," she croaked. "Why did you hurt me, Papa?"

His brow puckered, and he *tsk*ed at her. "You have grown very unruly since you have been away from me. It is a father's duty to teach his little girl better manners."

"I could have died from what you did to me."

"Were you afraid, sweeting? Papa is very sorry. You needn't worry ever again. You see, I am quite accomplished with this rope. Just enough pressure, so, and you drift off to sleep. Of course, there have been times I have lost my temper and applied a trifle too much. Then all is lost. But I am very, very sorry when that happens."

Sorry. Lucy could picture with bone-chilling clarity this man weeping copious tears over her corpse.

"The first time I lost my temper was with my father, the day I discovered that you had been stolen away from me. Only my brother Edward mourned with me—always we had been close, so close. Granville, the eldest, would have flayed the skin off his own babe if the duke had asked him to. Jasper, the impotent fool, just laughed. And my mother, she was cold, so cold. But the duke . . ." His eyes glazed. "The duke said what he had done was no different than tying a rock to a mongrel pup's neck and flinging it in the river. How could I let him say such things? I had to make him see what he had done." A shudder worked through Alexander, his bone-thin frame rocked by the memory.

"I was so angry. But he said I was a weak fool. I would do what I was told and never speak a word of what he had done to you and Emily and to me. He started down the stairs, and I charged after him. I only wanted to grab him, stop him, make him listen. But he fell." Alexander's voice cracked just a little. "He fell down the grand staircase at Avonstea. And laid there, with everyone screaming, his blood flowing across the white marble. I tried to push the blood back in, told him not to die. But he wouldn't listen to me. He would never listen to me."

"I—I'm sorry. It must have hurt you very much."

"Hurt me? No. Edward is the one the duke hurt, all the time. He would beat Edward until the weak fool did what he wanted. He would send Edward away and make him do things, things Edward didn't want to do. When you were sent away, Jenny, Edward was gone, in the West Indies. If I had only been able to reach him . . ."

Lucy stilled as she saw him pick up the silken cord and twine it about his long fingers. Was he so lost in his memories that he was going to use it again? Wrap it about her throat as if she were his hated father? Jasper? His mother?

Lucy swallowed hard. "Papa, the duke was a very bad man. Good fathers don't treat their children cruelly. A loving father would never hurt . . . hurt—"

For a frozen instant her gaze locked with his, and what she saw there made her hands tremble.

"Did *he* teach you that? What a loving father should be? Did my Jenny learn that from her mother's lover?"

The nape of Lucy's neck prickled in instinctive warning. She tried to steady herself. "I wasn't talking about me. I was speaking about you, your father—"

"You didn't answer my question." Alexander's voice grew a trifle more strident. "Did that bastard who is making your mother a whore ever hurt you?"

"Of course not! He was the most wonderful father imaginable! He taught me to ride and to shoot and to climb trees. And he . . ." The words spilled out, until Lucy saw that white, cadaverous face, saw his mouth twist, his eyes narrow. Oh, God, she had made a hideous mistake. How could she have been so foolish?

"He was the most wonderful father, was he, Jenny?" d'Autrecourt queried softly.

Lucy swallowed hard. "I didn't have you. I dreamed about you all the time. Every time I touched the pianoforte, I wondered what you had looked like, how your voice sounded. Every time I sung my "Night Song," I—"

"But that American rabble who is lying with my wife, filling her up with his bastards—that man never hurt you?"

"No! He would never—"

"But *I* hurt you, didn't I, Jenny? I can tell what you are thinking. I took this cord and I wrapped it about your neck, and you cried out before I crushed the air from your throat."

"Papa, you don't want to hurt me, I know that. Please, we need to talk . . ."

Instinctively, Lucy tried to squirm away from the figure closing in on her, the silken cord ready in his hands. But she was helpless, so agonizingly helpless.

"I don't want to hurt you, Jenny," he crooned. "You see, it is lovely, this cord. Silk, so it cannot tear your delicate skin. Silk for Papa's Jenny."

He wrapped the cord about her throat again and delicately tightened it.

He had killed his father, had been waiting to share with her the twisted pleasure of murdering his own mother. It was only a matter of time before he would "lose his temper" and murder her as well.

She was going to die, Lucy thought wildly. Die, here, in this hideous place with its leering skulls and moldering bones, with this lunatic claiming that he was her father.

The cord tightened enough to make her choke, and panic infused her limbs. She couldn't keep from kicking out with her bound feet, catching her tormentor in the midsection, but the blow only filled his features with roiling confusion and hurt. For an instant, she thought she saw tears shimmering in his eyes.

"You are a very naughty girl to make me lose my temper," he whispered as she sunk into darkness. "Go to sleep now, before I am very sorry."

How long unconsciousness had claimed her, Lucy didn't know, but when she awoke, it was to stillness. For a heartbeat, she wondered if this was her father's punishment for "naughty girls," if he had abandoned her here in this stone tomb, fastened the door, and left her here to stare at the crumbling bones. She wondered if, in his madness, he would even remember that he had left her here, or if he would stay away so long that she would starve to death.

Panic cut deep. Even if he had only left on some

331

errand, what if something happened to him? Some accident from which he never returned? Even if someone took him into their keeping, if Jasper found him or one of the other d'Autrecourts, would they believe any tale the man told of his prisoner? Would the d'Autrecourts care about her fate, or would they leave her here, gladly, their dark secret buried at last?

Jenny . . . dead at last.

No, Lucy berated herself, battling to stop the hysteria welling up inside her. She had to think! Had to keep her wits about her. She tried to lift her head from the slab of marble, her gaze catching on a small bone, perhaps a joint of someone's finger, still resting a few inches from where she lay. Horror clogged her throat, but she fought it, forcing herself to look about the room. A single candle, a whimsical rendition of the Three Graces dancing about its base, burned in a stone niche in the wall above the feather tick where Alexander lay sleeping.

If she could only get her hands free of the ropes and untie her feet, she could find some way to immobilize Alexander, then she could get away, she could escape. Harlestone was nearby. If she could reach the castle, no one could harm her.

If.

Her gaze fixed on the flame, a smear of orange hope against the dimness. If she could hold her wrists above the flame, the ropes would burn, wouldn't they?

But could she make it that far without collapsing? Her muscles still screamed with pain. She felt clumsy and numb and awkward, and the slightest mistake would mean disaster.

Lucy swallowed hard, the sensation of her neck being crushed playing out again and again in her mind.

She wouldn't fail. She wouldn't make a mistake. She was the Raider's daughter, for God's sake. The Hawk of Valcour's bride. She was going to live, damn it to hell. She was going to survive if it killed her!

Her parched lips twisted a little at the grim humor. Slowly, she managed to get herself upright, her eyes fixed with deadly intensity on Alexander's face, searching for any sign of wakefulness.

Lucy slid from the dais to the floor, jagged pain slicing through her as she attempted to half crawl, half drag herself across the narrow room.

She was agonizingly aware of Alexander d'Autrecourt snoring softly on the feather tick, but her breath seemed to rush with a sound like a gale between her teeth, tiny gasps of exertion escaping from her throat. Even her heartbeat seemed to sound like cannon fire. Inch by inch she tried to reach the stand where the candlestick stood. Heartbeat by heartbeat, she listened, prayed, swore.

The skin on her fingers tore, to bleed on the coarse stone, the delicate fabric of her shirt ripped at the elbows, which she used to lever herself across the floor. Three times she collapsed, her whole body quaking, the room spinning, her heart pounding. It seemed an eternity before she reached the stand. But when her fingers touched the claw-foot leg of the small table, her hopes began to soar.

Slowly, she struggled to her knees and poised her hands inches from the flames.

Lucy's stomach churned at the sight of her fingers, swollen and tinged a grotesque blue from the cruel tightness of the bindings. And she wondered if she could bear the pain of her skin burning with the rope.

Sweat beaded her face, and she bit her lower lip to keep from crying out as she lowered the silk cords that bound her into the searing tongue of fire. Her teeth cut into her lip until she tasted blood, the stench of burning silk filling her nostrils, sickening her. Fire seemed to leap from the candlestick into her veins, racing up her arms so fiercely she couldn't stifle a tiny whimper.

With what strength she had left, Lucy tried to pull her wrists apart. Silent tears ran down her cheeks, and she tried to picture something beautiful. Valcour, flinging back his head and laughing . . .

Suddenly the rope snapped. Sensation surged into her hands along with the flow of blood. She screamed inside, a terrible, silent scream. She feared she was going to be sick. But she held on to the image of Valcour and all the laughter she was going to draw from those beautiful, too-solemn lips.

After a moment the whirling in her head steadied. With great effort, she managed to loosen the loops of cord that fastened her ankles together. Then, abandoning the lengths of silk on the floor, Lucy returned her gaze to the candlestick. All she had to do was to take it and strike Alexander on the head. She wouldn't hurt him any more than was necessary, only enough to immobilize him until she could get away.

With fierce concentration, she forced her fingers to close about the candlestick. She was so tired, so damned weak, her fingers refused to obey her commands. But she had to finish this—no one, not even the all-knowing Valcour, would ever guess where to find her.

Slowly, she moved toward the grotesque phantom who claimed to be her father, the possibility that this man was Alexander d'Autrecourt still filling her with horror and disbelief. When she reached the edge of the feather tick, she froze, something rustling beneath her. She glanced down to see sheets of music, scribbled music.

For one frozen moment, she hesitated, the candlestick poised above Alexander d'Autrecourt's blond head, the compelling strains of her "Night Song" whispering in her mind. A hundred dreams of the father she had lost, the fantasies she had spun haunted her, hurt her.

No, Lucy thought fiercely. No matter what this man said or did, Alexander d'Autrecourt was dead. The gentle boy who had saved her mother from a cruel marriage could never take the actions this man had taken, never terrorize or hurt or conjure up sinister plots. If this was indeed Alexander in body, his spirit had been buried long before, buried by the family who had tormented them both.

Lucy caught her lip between her teeth, trying to force herself to strike, mustering the will to do so. There was no choice, nothing else to do. He was insane. God only knew what would happen if she did not escape. Once this was over, she would find some way to help him. Make certain he was safe, taken care of.

The thought shattered, horror tearing through her as the heavy brass piece slipped from her numb fingers.

She cried out as a sharp edge glanced off of Alexander's brow, slicing a nasty gash in his pale skin. He bolted upright with a yelp of pain.

Desperate, Lucy grappled for the candlestick in an effort to defend herself, knowing in her heart it was too late.

Just as her fingers closed on the object, a booted foot lashed out, cracking into her hands. Lucy screamed as she crumpled in agony.

Alexander towered above her, blood trickling in a macabre pattern down his face.

"You tried to kill me." He said the words softly, so softly. "That was a very naughty girl."

"I was only trying to get away. Please, if you are my father, I—"

"Jenny, you are a most ungrateful child. You leave me no other choice."

"Choice?" Lucy echoed, more terrified than she'd ever been in her life.

With chillingly methodical movements, he burrowed under the feather tick, withdrawing a gold-mounted pistol and a dirt-encrusted spade.

"You are not to be trusted alone. I shall have to put you where you will be safe." He hauled her to her feet, dragging her out into the twilight. Storm clouds roiled in the heavens, like Satan wrestling the angels, and thunder rumbled in the distance.

Sweet Jesus, where was he taking her? It didn't matter, Lucy thought, a faint hope sweeping through her. If she could scream, someone might hear her. Someone might come to her aid. Some vicar must tend the graveyard. Some villager or farmer might pass by. Someone, anyone, who might help her.

Alexander refastened Lucy's bindings, then settled her on the ground beside the tiny grave.

"I have lived here from time to time for almost a year now," Alexander said. "This is where I packed the box to send to you in Virginia. Virginia! Imagine Jasper's stupidity in letting such information slip into my hands. He would jeer at me, and tell me that you lived at Blackheath Hall. Sometimes it was as if he knew I wanted to find you. He knew I wanted to escape, make things right."

Lucy shuddered at the knowledge that the evil man she had first seen in the gaming hell could somehow have provided the catalyst that had brought her here—one more cruel jest that had spun out of control.

"Do you know, Jenny?" Alexander said. "In all the time I have lived here, never once have I seen a living soul. Perhaps that is because I am supposed to be dead!" He laughed, a hollow, frightening sound. Then he took the spade in his hands, fierce concentration furrowing his blood-stained brow. Despair rocked Lucy as the shovel tore a fresh wound in the earth.

"Wh-What are you doing?" Lucy choked out.

"Don't you see?" Those eyes met hers, soulless, empty. "Jenny is dead. I must bury her beneath the roses."

20

How deep did a madman dig a grave before he felt compelled to fill it with a corpse? Lucy stared at the top of Alexander d'Autrecourt's blond head with sick fascination, the man standing neck deep in the grave he was digging with such crazed precision. He had shaped the grave so carefully, uprooting the roses like a master gardener and setting them beside Lucy so he could replant them as "a blanket of blossoms for his darling."

Each chink of spade biting earth, each thud of the clods being flung into the growing pile of dirt beside the angel-carved tombstone signaled that she was one shovelful closer to whatever fate Alexander d'Autrecourt had planned for her in the twisted reaches of his mind.

Her hands writhed against the cords that bound her. And every time d'Autrecourt's face was angled away from her, she tore at the knots with her teeth, trying to loosen them. But they only snarled up tighter, cut even deeper into her burned skin.

There had to be some way to thwart him, something she could do. Suddenly the spade came flying up to land on the turf on the far side of the grave. Time had run out.

Lucy gave one last desperate twist of her wrists as Alexander d'Autrecourt pulled himself from the hole. Dirt clung to his clothing, his face so pale and deep with hollows that he seemed some ghoul come alive to stalk her from the grave.

She had to do something, think of something. If she could fool him, reason with him, play whatever insane game was running through the tangled labyrinth that had once been his mind . . .

Lucy shoved herself backward, the thorns of the roses Emily had planted so long before cutting into her skin as she collided with them. "No, Papa, you can't do this! Please, you have to listen—"

"I am going to put you in the grave now, Jenny," he said. "It is a very nice grave Papa has made for you."

"I don't want to be in the grave," she reasoned desperately. "I have only just found you again."

"Sometimes parents must do things their little ones do not like because the papa knows it is best for them," he said, drawing a pistol from his boot top. He caressed the barrel of the weapon, looking genuinely grieved. "It will hurt for just a moment, then you will be happy forever. You will be tucked safe beneath the roses where you belong. I will come and care for them, and I will talk to you, Jenny, when you are beneath the earth."

Lucy's gaze flicked to the edge of the grave, so near. An idea sparked in the midst of her terror. If she could startle him, make him fall backward, she might have some small chance to escape. "I won't talk to you if you put me beneath the roses," she insisted. "I'll hate you."

He flinched at the words, those vague eyes more befuddled than ever. "Jenny, you don't mean that," he cajoled, pacing toward her. "You could never hate your papa!"

Lucy grasped one of the thick branches at the base of a rose plant between her numb fingers. She sat, frozen, until he leaned over to caress her cheek. Then she lashed out with the thorny plant, lunging toward him in an effort to drive him back over the edge of the grave.

Alexander shrieked as the thorns slashed his face, the vined plant snarling around him. But he leapt to the side, avoiding the hole in the earth with the agility of a cat.

"You hurt me again!" he choked out, incredulous. "Jenny, why did you hurt me?"

In that instant, Lucy saw her death reflected in his eyes. She tried to shove herself away, but her numb legs refused to obey.

She thought of Dominic, wondered if he had discovered she was gone. If she died here, he would never know what had happened to her. The idea of Valcour tortured, waiting for her, when she would never come back to him wrenched at Lucy's heart.

Blast it, the Raider's daughter didn't give up! There had to be some way. Suddenly, as if summoned up by her thoughts alone, she heard something in the distance. Hoofbeats? Someone coming? Please, God!

Lucy pressed her bound hands against her pain-filled throat and screamed.

The sound was a raspy croak, one only Alexander d'Autrecourt could hope to catch. But whoever was approaching thundered toward them, as if drawn by her cry.

Alexander froze, staring in disbelief as a horse and rider crested the hill. Lucy let out a sob of joy as she saw Valcour burst over the horizon like one of the horsemen of the apocalypse racing toward them, his dark mane flowing, his face savage.

"Dominic! Oh, Dom—" Her choked cry was cut off as d'Autrecourt's hand knotted in her hair. He dragged her to her feet, twisting her until she was in front of him. The lethal kiss of the pistol barrel pressed hard against her temple.

God, no, please no, she prayed desperately, trying to

keep her knees from buckling. *Don't let Dominic see me die.*

Blood pounded in her ears and she struggled to keep her eyes fixed on Valcour's beloved face. His features were twisted with disbelief, his face ash-gray. If Lucy still had any doubts as to the identity of her captor, the incredulity raging in Valcour's eyes would have quelled it. The earl's mouth contorted in a feral shout as he reined in the stallion a cart's length from where they stood, the beast plunging and rearing as if it sensed its master's torment.

"Stop!" Valcour bellowed, flinging himself from the horse in a whirl of black cloak and desperation. "D'Autrecourt, no!"

For a heartbeat the barrel bit deeper, and Lucy waited agonizing seconds for the explosion that would end her life. But Valcour froze, his hands open to show he was unarmed. "D'Autrecourt, for the love of God, let her go!"

It was as if the mask of Valcour had been ripped away for the first time, and Lucy could see the man beneath. He who'd watched as his beloved father died the same hideous death that now awaited Lucy.

"Go away!" D'Autrecourt's cry shook Lucy from the horrifying thought. "I am not to be disturbed. I am taking care of my Jenny."

"Taking care of her?" Valcour raged. "You've got a pistol to her head!" Lucy could feel the pain throbbing in every sinew of his body, could feel him grappling to find some way, any way, to save her. During the duel in the gaming hell Valcour had been cool as ice. There was nothing cool and detached in his face now.

"I have to make things right at last," d'Autrecourt said. "Jenny belongs under the roses. St. Cyr, you above anyone should understand the need to end a misery too great to bear! Your father put a pistol to his head!"

"Because you drove him to do it!"

"You lie!" d'Autrecourt shrilled.

"I speak the truth!" The earl's eyes clashed with Lucy's. There was a plea for understanding in those midnight depths, a regret so savage she could feel it wounding him in places no one could ever reach. With his next words Lucy understood why.

"D'Autrecourt, you were the reason my father pulled that trigger," Valcour said, driving his hand back through the tangled waves of his hair. "You seduced my mother."

Lucy gasped.

"I'm sorry, hoyden, but it's true. Even on the night your *father*"—he fair spat the word—"caught the fever that supposedly killed him, he was leaving my mother's bedside after she bore him a bastard son."

"Aubrey!" Lucy felt the pieces in a macabre puzzle slide into place in her mind.

"No!" d'Autrecourt cried. "Jenny, don't listen to his lies!"

"They aren't lies!" Lucy could see the effort it cost Valcour to continue. This man who had always tried to protect those in his care was now making an effort to bring the madman's wrath down upon himself.

As Lucy watched those beloved features, she knew that the weapon Valcour was using against d'Autrecourt was savaging Dominic himself—that Valcour was revealing the most agonizing secrets of his life in order to save her, secrets he had not even been able to tell his own father.

"Lucinda wears the ring, the legendary love token you gave my mother."

Valcour paced, edging imperceptibly nearer, every muscle in his body vibrating with tension as he watched for any opening, any chance to reach her. Lucy tensed as well, waiting for the slightest signal in those dark eyes, trusting Valcour to the depth of her soul.

"You tried to get my mother to give up Aubrey." Valcour hammered at d'Autrecourt's nerves, relentless. "Told her that she couldn't keep the child. My father

341

would discover her infidelity. And so would your wife. It would destroy both of you."

"A bastard cannot be tolerated!"

"It wasn't Aubrey's fault that he was born, damn you! The boy had no choice in the man who was his father! Do you know how my mother cried the night you left her? How terrified she was to face my father? Lionel St. Cyr was a man with a temper to fear. He tried to beat the truth from her, but she wouldn't betray you, nor would she abandon her baby."

"Stop this!" D'Autrecourt's voice shattered on a sob. "Oh, God, Alexander would never—never . . ." The hand holding the pistol shook violently, and Lucy half expected him to pull the trigger in his distress. Either that or swing the gun toward his tormentor. That, Lucy realized, was Valcour's intent. To take the bullet for her, if need be, to give her a chance to escape. He was trusting in her ability to save herself.

Neither of them were going to die!

"You want to drive me mad!" D'Autrecourt raged. "You are one of them—one with my family. Next you will be telling me I am not Alexander! That I am Edward! That weak fool who stood by and did nothing when they sent Alexander away! Edward, who was helpless against the duke's fury!"

Valcour faltered for an instant, his brow creasing in confusion. "What manner of madness is this? Edward? The invalid? My God—of course! Edward was—" Valcour stopped.

Stillness fell, Lucy twisting her face to search that of her captor. The man was trembling as if stricken with palsy; what little color had been in his face seemed to have been sucked into eyes hot with insanity.

Valcour's own face turned waxen, and Lucy could see he realized too late that his words had shattered something in the man who held her captive, the man now wild with fury and denial.

"See what you have done! She doesn't believe in me now! My Jenny! I'll kill you, St. Cyr! Kill you for that!" The pistol tore away from Lucy's temple, shifting toward Valcour, but at that instant Lucy knocked d'Autrecourt's arms away, wheeling around to drive her knee with all her might into his groin.

The man shrieked and staggered backward, the pistol flying from his hand. Valcour was already lunging at d'Autrecourt. D'Autrecourt drove his fist hard into Valcour's chest, kicked and thrashed and battled, as the earl landed blow after blow to the smaller man's midsection. Finally Valcour slammed his knotted fist into d'Autrecourt's jaw. The man's head snapped back, and he cried out. He slumped to the earth, limp as a rag-stuffed doll.

For an instant, murderous rage contorted Valcour's face—a primitive thirst for the death of the bastard who had tried to take Lucy's life.

Her throat constricted by the unleashed emotion in those features, Lucy's voice was soft, gentle. "No, Dominic. He can't hurt us now."

Valcour looked up, his fists clenched as if aching to feel d'Autrecourt's neck crushed beneath his fingers. "When I think what he tried to do—"

"But he didn't. Because of you, he can never hurt me again." She swallowed hard. "Valcour, this isn't his fault any more than it is yours or mine. Please."

For a moment there was outright rebellion in those stormy dark eyes, as if he were battling for reason. Then his gaze softened, flooded with an emotion that brought tears to Lucy's eyes.

"My brave little hoyden. Oh, God, what he almost did to you!" Lucy trembled with relief as Valcour turned to her, his fingers carefully unfastening the bindings about her wrists. His heart-stoppingly handsome face was awash with tenderness, this man who had never flinched from danger, from ugliness, from his own faults; he winced every time he thought he caused her pain. Her hands were pathetic, battered little things, the burn marks from the candle flame reddened and blistered. The gouges the tight bindings had cut were fiery red, and her fingers were swollen and dirty. Valcour lifted them for a moment and pressed his lips on her fingertips. His voice trembled. "Oh, God, little one . . ."

"It doesn't hurt at all now that you're here."

Valcour's own eyes were over bright. "I was almost too late. Another few moments, and God only knows—"

"I would have been most put out if you had botched the rescue this time, my lord. I would have haunted you forever and ever."

"And I would have welcomed it. I would have waited for you in the darkness, Countess. Listened . . ."

A tiny groan from the inert d'Autrecourt made Valcour turn away. Dominic gathered up the coils of silk that had bound Lucy and used them to tie the man's wrists in front of him.

It was as if the fierce strength in Dominic's dark eyes had kept Lucy on her feet. Her gaze flicked to the pathetic man huddled against the grass: Alexander d'Autrecourt, or the mysterious Edward?

Would she ever know for certain? She crumpled onto the ground, sudden tears stinging her eyes. She should be grateful to be alive. And she was, God knew she was. But now, even after all that had happened, the mystery persisted. The questions, the sickening suspicions and fears that roiled inside her. Did it matter if the man Valcour was tying up was Edward d'Autrecourt or Alexander now that Lucy knew the harsh truth about what had happened so many years before? When Emily had been frightened and cold and desperate, her father had been sleeping with another woman, loving another woman.

Lady Catherine's words, soft, sad, echoed in Lucy's mind. *We never meant to hurt anyone.* But they had. And they were still hurting her husband with his bitterness, his despair, hurting Aubrey with rejections he could never understand. And hurting Lucy more than she would have believed possible, shattering her dream of the phantom angel coaxing music from the keys of a pianoforte.

Lucy wanted nothing more than to run to Emily, to bury her face in her mother's skirts and tell her everything, pour out her disillusionment, her heartache. But Lucy could never tell her mother the truth. Emily could never know.

"Lucinda." Valcour's voice, soft yet urgent, jarred her from her thoughts.

She turned to where he was bent over her captor's hands. Valcour's dark eyes were wide and amazed. "Countess, this man—he's not your father."

Lucy lifted up her chin. "I know that. Ian Blackheath is my father. He's the one who loved me, cared for me. This—this shouldn't matter at all. But it does, Dominic. No matter how much I try to pretend it does not."

"No, my love, you don't understand." Valcour caught her by the hand. "I mean, this man is not your father. He's not Alexander d'Autrecourt. I'd stake my life on the fact."

Lucy stared. "I don't understand. How can you be certain?"

"I spent hours watching your father's hands playing the keys of the pianoforte. There was a crook in his smallest finger, *here.*" Valcour cradled her hand in his, then kissed the bent joint of her little finger.

Lucy raised her eyes from Valcour's kiss to look at the madman's fingers—fingers that were perfectly straight. "Whoever he is, he lived at Avonstea. They kept him imprisoned there."

"Why?"

"He said that he accidentally shoved the duke down the stairs, killed him."

"The death of a father, a brother, the horror of such a betrayal could drive any man to madness," Valcour said softly. "No one knows that better than I do. But this man won't be imprisoned anywhere any longer. I promise I'll see he is taken care of. God knows, he is just one more victim in this horror. But it's over now. I promise you, it's over."

"I beg to contradict you." The malevolent voice made them wheel. Lucy froze, the light picking out the hate-filled features of Jasper d'Autrecourt. Valcour reached for his pistol, but Sir Jasper's gleamed, aimed straight for Lucy's heart.

"Move so much as an eyelash and I'll kill her," Jasper warned, a sword clutched in his other hand, a shimmering river of blue.

"What the devil are you doing here, Jasper?"

"I can hardly believe the fortuitous timing of my arrival myself. Imagine my amusement, watching this Cheltenham tragedy spin itself out, listening to you, Valcour, spilling out your soul, trampling upon your precious honor to save the life of your woman. Of course, I depended upon you being the same ruthless bastard you had always been. A quick sword thrust or pistol blast dispatching your enemy to hell. Who would have believed that Valcour could be tamed by a woman?"

"That still doesn't answer my question, Jasper."

The man sneered. "I've come to find my pathetic mad brother. And, I might add, I have gone to a great deal of trouble and exhausted a great deal of patience arranging this little meeting. He was desperate, you know, to recover Alexander's precious daughter. Year after year, I would come into the room, tell him snippets about Jenny that I had discovered. Anything to stir him into a frenzy. Then one day, I left him the keys to his cell."

"I don't understand," Lucy said.

Jasper chortled. "And here I thought you were a clever

346

child. It was a brilliantly simple plan. He was to leave the safety of Avonstea, and I would be waiting to make certain an appropriately tragic accident befell him. Who would have guessed that a madman could manage to elude me for almost a year? Who would have guessed that he would be canny enough to contact you all the way in America? And who would have guessed that you would be fool enough to come back to England to find him?"

Jasper shook his head in bemusement. "Had I not tracked him to the gin shop and beaten the truth from the hag who owns it, I might never have found him."

"Why would you want your own brother dead?" Lucy asked.

"A dukedom can be a compelling enticement to murder, can't it, Jasper?" Valcour snarled.

"Edward went mad when he discovered what had been done to Alexander and his infamous wife and child. My eldest brother was dead, as was Alexander. Upon my father's death, Edward was next in line for the dukedom. He was mad. I had a measure of the power inherent in the title. But it didn't matter. He was still the duke, damn his soul to hell! As long as he lived, I was nothing but a paltry knight, scorned and laughed at. Mocked because of my impotence. But when Edward died . . . all the wealth of Avonstea would be mine to command. I could revenge myself on anyone who had jeered at me."

"So you decided to murder Edward?" Lucy demanded. "Why not just creep into his cell? Do it quickly, cleanly?"

"Because my mother suspected my plans. Insane as Edward was, she did not want him dead. If she suspected I had killed him, the consequences would have been most unpleasant. She had him guarded night and day. I had to get him away from Avonstea."

"You sick bastard!" Dominic spat.

"What, Valcour? You try to play the saint? You are as ruthless as I am and as black of soul. I can only thank you for giving me the means to send you to the devil before me."

"It takes no courage to kill an unarmed man."

"Oh, but you're mistaken. You were armed, you see, with this so lovely sword." He twisted the weapon in his hand. "You came to fight my brother. Ran him through with your blade in fury at what he had done to your countess here. Burying her alive—quite a hideous death, but one that could easily spring into the mind of a madman. Unfortunately, you arrived too late to save her, and Edward managed to kill you as well. Three tidy corpses in a graveyard. It is an end poetic beyond imagining."

"Damn you, Jasper, this is between us," Valcour snarled as Jasper pushed his sword point against Edward's chest. "Settle it like a man!"

"Don't you remember what you announced to everyone at the gaming hell the night of our duel, Valcour? I am a coward. But no one will ever know. I will be quite heartsick when I come upon the hellish carnage in the graveyard. I will weep copious tears over my brother's grave, and then I will be duke of Avonstea."

Lucinda searched desperately for any way out. It was a miracle that they had escaped Edward moments before. There would be no miracle this time.

"Now, my lady countess, you will move to the edge of the grave. I think it wisest to kill your bridegroom first, before he tries once again to play the hero."

Lucinda cried, hanging onto Dominic. "I won't let you!"

"Then you may be the first to die!"

"No!" They all started at the groan from Edward. "Don't hurt Jenny! . . . Won't . . . let you!"

But Jasper's mouth twisted in a grimace of hate, his eyes never leaving Valcour's face. Lucy screamed as he rammed the sword deep into Edward d'Autrecourt's chest.

"Say farewell, Valcour," Jasper chortled, his finger tightening on the trigger.

Lucy flung herself in front of Valcour just as the weapon exploded. Fire blossomed in Lucy's shoulder, as the world became a fuzzy montage of scenes.

Edward d'Autrecourt's pain-ravaged face, the pistol he had held to Lucy's head clutched in his bound hands. The orange stab of the gun blazing. Sir Jasper shrieking in disbelief as the bullet slammed into his chest, tumbling him backward into the open grave. Valcour, wild with anguish, diving for his own weapon.

But it was over. Only the sound of Edward d'Autrecourt's strangled pleas shattered the deathly stillness.

"J-Jenny," he choked out. "I—I'm sorry. Didn't know Jasper . . . would come. I only wanted to take . . . care of you. But never . . . got anything right. Fool . . . weak fool, just like . . . always said . . ."

Her head spinning, Lucy edged toward the pathetic, broken man and took up his quaking hand. "It's all right, Papa," Lucy whispered, wanting only to give him some slight peace. "It's all right."

"You are . . . a good girl, Jenny. Like your . . . mama." He breathed once more, then his eyes rolled back in death. Lucy dropped his hand, waves of dizziness sweeping through her.

"Lucinda!" She heard Valcour as if from a distance, his hands—gentle, so gentle—scooping her up against his chest. "You fool! You damned little fool!"

Fire still raged in her shoulder as Valcour ripped open the torn fabric of her bodice, his breath hissing between his teeth in horror. Lucy could feel the sticky dampness of her own blood as he ripped off his shirt, wadding the fabric against the wound.

"Dominic." Lucy squeezed his name through numb lips as he tied the makeshift bandage about her. "You must . . . listen to . . . me. If I . . . die . . . not your fault. Blame self for . . . everything. Love you . . . Not your fault . . ."

"You're not going to die!" He gathered her fiercely into his arms and carried her toward the stallion. "I'm taking you to Harlestone. You'll get well there."

"Take me to . . . tower . . . room," Lucy whispered. "So beautiful. Music like magic. Want to hear . . . the rest . . ."

Her words twisted like knife blades in Valcour's chest. "Damn you, Countess! I order you not to die!"

"Always the . . . tyrant," Lucy whispered, aching at the pain in his voice. "But even tyrants don't always get their way."

Her head sagged against Valcour's chest, limp and lifeless. A wild, animal sound of grief split the night, seventeen years of pain bursting forth in the wake of the greatest anguish Dominic St. Cyr had ever known.

21

*F*or five days Valcour made certain the tower room blazed with candles, as if, somewhere in his tormented soul, he hoped their constant brightness could keep encroaching death at bay. But the physician who had left an hour before had told Valcour that the crisis was near. The countess would either awaken or slip away forever.

Lucinda lay like the sleeping princess in a fairy tale, silent, still, heartbreakingly lovely on the bed Valcour had ordered the servants to bring to the chamber that nightmarish night he'd carried her up the winding stairway to the setting of his childhood anguish.

Not once had the earl left her side. His face was haggard, his eyes burning with exhaustion. His voice rasped, hoarse in his throat. Hour after hour he ordered his countess to open her eyes. He raged at her, pleaded with her, challenged her in ways he knew would have brought his defiant hoyden to fury in days before.

But she only lay there, growing paler and more still, as if the dream she was having was so beautiful she couldn't bear to be dragged back into the ugly reality that had all but engulfed her beside the stone-carved angel.

Valcour sat beside her, his fingers clasping a brush of silver, gently smoothing the bristles through her hair. The silky strands curled about his fingers, so vibrant, so alive, the way they had the last night they had made love.

The thought of that magic night was almost too poignant to bear. The memory of Lucinda, her eyes wide with wonder as he loved her, cut Valcour more deeply than any lash ever could. He could have told her what he felt that night, confessed the raging emotions she had loosed in him. He could have opened his heart just a little and let her in. But no, he'd been too afraid, too raw to do so. And now it might be too late.

A strangled sound rose in Valcour's throat. How many times had he told her he loved her during this dark, desperate time? Now that her eyes were closed, her soft lips unable to receive his kiss? Now, when he couldn't reach her?

The brush trembled in his hand, hopelessness tearing through him. A soft sound made him turn to where Lady Catherine stood framed in the doorway.

She had arrived at Harlestone the same day Dominic had. And from the moment she had seen Lucinda, so helpless, it was as if Dominic could see her heart breaking as well. But in spite of all the anger, the fury, the resentment and ugliness that had been between Valcour and the woman he had blamed for his pain all these years, she had remained here, a gentle presence, always seeming to know when Valcour needed her. She had made broth to slip between Lucinda's lips and pressed Dominic to eat himself, saying he must be strong when Lucinda awoke. She had brought a blanket to wrap about his shoulders in the chill of the night and had held the basin of warm, rose-scented water while Valcour gently bathed his sleeping countess.

But never before had Lady Catherine intruded on the chamber without some reason, never before had she hovered there, unguarded love in her eyes.

"Her hair is beautiful, Dominic. So soft and silky beneath your hand. She looks like an angel lying there."

"An angel . . . should look beautiful, don't you think?" Valcour said, his throat thick.

Lady Catherine's voice was gentle, as if she understood his deepest fears, as she had when he was a boy. "She will not leave you. God couldn't be so cruel as to take her away."

"You, above anyone, should know how cruel God can be, madam. He gave you a husband you didn't love. He made you love a weak man who didn't deserve you. And he gave you a son so bitter he could never forgive you."

"Sh. You had reason to be hurt, to be angry. I made choices. It was only right that I paid for them."

"Forever?" Dominic curved his hand over Lucinda's cheek, a cheek pale and translucent as marble. "Is that how long I will pay for my mistakes?"

"Dominic, you did nothing wrong."

"I didn't love her until it was too late. I didn't guard her closely enough. This is my doing. All of it. If I had known what might happen, I would never have let her out of my sight for an instant."

"I know that, Dominic."

"She didn't trust me. How could she trust me after the way I behaved? An arrogant fool, a damned tyrant, never listening, never stopping to think. Do you know that is the last thing she called me, before she slipped away? I ordered her not to die, and she looked at me, those eyes, those damned eyes of hers so tender, so loving."

"She loved you from the first, I think, though she didn't know it. And you loved her."

"I never told her so. I was too caught up in my own stubborn pain. Too damned determined not to feel, not to let myself be vulnerable ever again."

"To the kind of pain your father and I caused you?"

Valcour turned away, stricken by the gentle anguish in

his mother's voice. "I didn't mean to . . . hurt you, madam."

"And yet, no matter how much we have loved each other all these years, we have done little else. Why is it always so easy to see what we should have done after disaster has overtaken us? When it is too late to change anything? It seems so unfair."

"I never understood what it meant to love," Valcour admitted, each word torn from his soul. "I never knew what you must have felt, how you must have suffered. I thought that if you had just put honor first, if you had only . . . only been strong, everything would have been all right."

"But that is true. I couldn't stop loving Alexander. I wanted to. Tried to bury the feelings I had. But——"

"All my life I have battled to save my honor. But I would cast it all to the winds just to see my hoyden smile at me one more time." Dominic's voice broke, his fingertips brushing over Lucinda's pale lips. "Do you know how many times I've dreamed of Lucinda carrying my child? Of a son with her fierce courage, and a daughter with her eyes?"

"You will hold those babies yet, my son. I am sure of it."

"I love her so much. Want so much for some part of us to be joined together forever, so nothing, not even death could ever part us. That is what you felt when you held Aubrey in your arms, isn't it? I think I knew that, even as a child. And I feared that—that you must love Aubrey, the son of the man you loved, far more than you could ever love me."

"I have always loved you, Dominic. Loved you both. You were the single good thing in my life for so many years. Aubrey was a tangible piece of the love Alexander and I shared. You were both treasures. I only wished that you might love one another."

"I didn't want to love him. It hurt too much. When I did, it made me so angry . . . angry at myself and you, and . . . I didn't want to love anyone. But Lucy wouldn't let me deny the truth any longer. She forced me to see that I was a coward, that I was lying to everyone, especially to myself."

Dominic gently lay the brush on the satin coverlets and turned toward Lady Catherine, his soul bared, his anguish there for her to see.

"Mama." He whispered the word for the first time since he'd watched his father die. "Help me. I can't reach her, no matter what I say. I don't think I can live without her."

Dominic felt his mother's arms encircle him, and for once the earl of Valcour let someone else share his burden of pain. He buried his face against her breast, racking sobs tearing from his throat.

"There was a time when mere words were never enough for you. Do you remember, Dominic?" Lady Catherine murmured, stroking his hair. "A time when everything you felt deep in your heart poured out each time you touched the pianoforte?"

"I can't. Not anymore," he said in a pain-ravaged voice. "It's gone, Mama. I know it is gone."

"I don't believe that. I—No!" Her sudden cry of alarm made Valcour raise his face, half fearing Lucinda had slipped away.

But his mother stared not at the bed where Lucinda slept, but at the tower door.

Aubrey.

The boy stood, windblown and travel weary, the expression on his face leaving no doubt he had heard every tortured confession, every painful truth about his birth.

"No!" Valcour swiped his hand furiously across his eyes, feeling as if a giant fist had crushed his chest. The earl jammed himself to his feet and wheeled. He paced away, leaning against the pianoforte in an effort to steady himself. "My God, boy. What are you doing here?"

"I came as soon as I heard Lucy was hurt." There was pain in the boy's face, confusion, and yet a kind of understanding that made him seem older. Older because of the pain he had suffered at Dominic's hands. Older because of the burden Dominic had just inadvertently laid on the boy's narrow shoulders.

"Aubrey," Valcour rasped, "I didn't mean for you to hear any of this. I wanted to save you the pain."

"You told me that you love me," the boy said softly.

"I do. God help me, I do. Yet I hurt you again. Just like I always have, since you were so damned small."

"I'm not a child anymore. And now . . . now I understand so much better why . . ." Aubrey shrugged. "Why my father . . . Why you . . . it must have been a blow to your honor—knowing that I am a . . . bastard." The boy tripped over the word.

"The circumstances of your birth don't matter a damn to me. You're my brother. I love you no matter what my stubborn pride made me do to convince you otherwise."

"It's all right then." Aubrey smiled a little. "We can begin again. Once Lucy is well and you are settled, I'll come and—and dandle your babes on my knee. I'll be their dashing soldier uncle, who comes riding in with presents. I'll spoil them terribly, you know. I never have had any notion of self-restraint."

Valcour's eyes burned, his voice quavered. "I don't deserve another chance with you, boy. I was wrong, so damned wrong all these years. There is no way to make it up to you."

"There is: Make certain we don't waste another minute on regrets."

Forgiveness. It shone in those eyes that had tormented Valcour so long with whisperings of the past.

"You are a better man than I am, Aubrey. A stronger one. A more forgiving one." Valcour reached out his hand to his brother across a chasm of pain and misunderstanding, regret and faint hope. Aubrey clasped Valcour's fingers with his own. Then the boy did something he hadn't ever done before. He embraced Dominic with no fear he would be turned away.

The candles guttered in the sconces, but Valcour hadn't the will to change them. The silence in the room seemed so damned loud after the hours he had spent with the quiet solace of his mother and brother, the almost unbelievable gift of their forgiveness after his stubbornness, his coldness all these years.

It was such a vast treasure that he wondered if the Fates would be willing to give him any more, after all the time he had railed against them, hated them, scorned them.

He wondered if the final price he paid for his folly would be the loss of this woman, this damned defiant little rebel who had breathed life and hope into his icy heart.

Valcour held Lucinda's hand in his, pressing it to his lips again and again. If he was to lose her, maybe, just maybe he could bear it if she knew how much she had meant to him. If she had any idea what he felt in his heart. That he loved her so much, even death couldn't separate them, that she would live in his soul, a part of him forever. That he would be faithful to her the rest of his life and accept his own death with joy when it came, if it meant that he would be reunited with his hoyden countess again.

But how could he tell her? How could mere words ever express it? *I remember a time when words were never enough.* Lady Catherine's voice echoed inside him. *When every emotion you felt poured forth in your music.*

The music, Dominic thought, more terrified than he'd ever been in his life. That was why Lucinda had wanted him to bring her here.

What was it she had said? That the music had been magic. But he had abandoned the magic that had brought him so much pain. He had betrayed his gift, because it had brought him nothing but betrayal.

He closed his eyes, remembering her, an angel of music garbed in moonlight, a wraith bringing melodies to life, trying to discover the last strains of the unfinished music somewhere in the mists of her imagination, as if those strains were a delicious secret the tower room was keeping from her.

Was it possible that the music could bring her back? Reach her as mere words never could?

He had burned it. The last step in erasing it from his soul. He couldn't remember. He couldn't possibly after all these years. And yet if there were the smallest chance . . .

Sweat beaded Valcour's brow, his dark gaze trailing with restless wariness from Lucinda's face to the pianoforte.

He went to her, knelt down and pressed a kiss to her brow, then slowly went to the stool and sat down at the instrument.

His fingers trembled, as if he expected them to catch fire the instant he touched the keys. Instead, a ripple of sensation pierced through to his soul as he forced himself to coax out a sound from the instrument.

His chest ached, and he closed his eyes, his hands motionless over the keys as he listened, strained to find the first webbings of melody.

It shivered to life inside him, flowing into every fiber of his being. Softly, so softly, he began to catch the wisps of music, turn them into beauty upon the keyboard.

It was as if he had opened an invisible gate inside himself, releasing emotions that hadn't been deadened as he had believed but dammed up inside him, waiting to break free.

How long he played he never knew, only felt the pulse building inside him, felt the waves carrying him away, away to the heartsick boy so afraid of being alone. A boy who had known even before he discovered the affair between his mother and the music master he loved that his world was beginning to crumble, that the parents he loved so much did not love each other.

The inexpressible yearning drifted into a sound magical, as if every hope, every fear in that boy's heart were distilled into music, as if every anguish the man Dominic had ever known were pouring forth from his fingers, covering the tower room with magic. It tore away the last veiling on Valcour's wary heart. Poured forth everything, until he was empty, aching. When the final notes drifted to silence, Valcour braced his arms against the instrument he had loved so dearly and cried over the woman whose loss was breaking his heart.

He barely heard the awed whisper, so soft and frail and filled with wonder.

"It was you."

He turned to stare in disbelief into wide blue eyes, tears coursing down pale cheeks. Lucinda—not carried to the angels by his song but brought back to him.

He couldn't speak, terrified that it was some heavenly dream.

"It was you," she said again. "You wrote my 'Night Song.'"

Valcour's throat felt as if it were closed, and his hands trembled. "I gave it to your father as a gift the day you were born. I did that often—gave away little compositions . . . as if they could be of any value to any one."

"It was magic, Dominic. All those years, when I was frightened and lonely, when I was hurting, I felt someone comforting me through the music—like a hand stroking my curls, cherishing me. I thought it was my father who was reaching out with my 'Night Song.' But it was you. You who wrote it for me. You who made the magic."

"It wasn't enough. I wanted so badly to protect you. You were such a winsome little thing. That was why I couldn't tell him. Couldn't tell my father that d'Autrecourt had fathered Aubrey."

"You knew me when I was a child?"

"Not really. I only saw you once. I didn't know it, but my mother had come to London to tell d'Autrecourt she was with child. She and I were at St. James Park when I saw you, this little girl, barely two years old, splashing into the pond. You had escaped your mother and were trying to catch a swan."

"I knew I remembered that place," Lucy said, her eyes glowing. "I remember laughter and sunshine. Joy."

"What you should recall is getting soaked to the bone," Dominic said softly. "You plunged in after the swans, and I . . . pulled you from the water. Your mother was so grateful, she insisted on telling my mother what a fine son she had, insisted on thanking her."

Valcour's voice dropped low. "I didn't know who she was until she introduced herself to my mother, told her she was Emily d'Autrecourt, Lord Alexander's wife, and that your name was Jenny. You were already racing off again, chasing fairies or sunbeams, your golden curls bouncing. Your mother turned to chase after you. I don't think she saw my mother start to cry."

Lucinda reached out, and Valcour came to her, catching up her hand.

"I knew my father would kill the man who had besmirched his honor. And every time my father asked me who had done so, all I could think of was you . . . a little moppet with golden curls, and a beautiful lady, laughing as we splashed toward her. How could I tell my father, Countess? No matter how much I loved him?"

"Dominic . . . I'm so sorry . . ." she whispered.

"My noble sacrifice was all for nothing in the end,

wasn't it? You were alone, stolen away from your mother."

"The 'Night Song' was with me always. Making me hope, making me dream. That is why I really came back to England. To find the person who wrote it . . . to find the magic. And I did. Dominic, I did."

Valcour looked down into her shining eyes. "I love you, hoyden," he whispered. "I tried to tell you so many times when you lay here, sleeping. I kissed you, I begged you—"

"More likely you were ordering me around again."

He smiled a little. "Sweet Jesus, girl, when Natty climbed through my window, told me where you'd gone, I was crazed with worry."

"Natty? That was how you found me?"

"The resourceful little rogue followed you. Then, when d'Autrecourt abducted you, the boy came to tell me. He'll never want for anything again, I promise you!" Valcour looked away, his voice husky. "Why didn't you trust me, Countess? Let me help you?"

"I was coming to tell you, but Aubrey was there. You looked so sad, I couldn't bear to distress you."

"Distress me? You drove me to madness, chasing after you, not knowing if you were alive or dead, lost to me forever." Valcour stopped, his voice wondering, awed. "But the music . . . the music brought you back to me, didn't it, Countess?"

She nodded.

"Aubrey and Mama are below stairs, waiting. They've been here from the first. They love you, you know."

He hadn't known any more joy could be squeezed into Lucinda's eyes, but they glistened, tears starting afresh.

"Aubrey knows everything. And the boy . . . the infernal boy always did know how to discomfit me. It seems he has decided to forgive me for being a—how did you put it, angel, a pompous ass? They're giving me a second chance. And now I have a second chance with you as well. I promise you, I'll prove worthy of it. I won't rage at you anymore or order you about or play the tyrant—"

"And I won't ever defy you again." She promised so solemnly, but her eyes were laughing, filled with so much tenderness, it broke his heart. "I am plotting a lifetime of rebellion against your tyranny, my lord. I count on you to be an adversary worthy of the Raider's daughter."

"I'll never be worthy of you, Lucinda St. Cyr," Valcour whispered. "But I promise you, Countess, I'll love you more than any man has ever loved a woman before. I'll try to be all the things you wrote in that letter to your parents. Try to be everything you ever dreamed."

"I only want you, Dominic. A stubborn, arrogant English aristocrat who kisses me until my bones melt and rages at me and loves me. I only want everything you promised me all those years ago in the 'Night Song.' A love so perfect no dream can ever compare."

Valcour lowered his mouth to his countess's, sealing his promise in a way no mere words could ever convey, his kiss as hauntingly beautiful, as filled with magic as the song he had written for a little girl so many years before.

Epilogue

*I*an Blackheath's eyes seethed with sullen hurt as John Wilkes's coach jolted on its way from the ship's landing, the bubbling excitement of the Blackheath children and the delighted chatter of Emily and Claree doing little to ease the sting of disappointment Ian felt at Lucy's defection.

He had been pacing the ship's deck from the moment England's shore was in sight, as if hoping to see bouncing golden curls and the saucy face of the daughter he hadn't seen for two years. But the ship had docked, the gangplank had been lowered, and the trunks cast off, and still there had been no sign of Lucy.

Instead, he was all but barreled over by a red-haired boy of about nine who looked distinctly uncomfortable in full dress regalia.

"You must be that Raider fellow come to see the countess," the lad had said, tugging at his neckcloth. "I ain't supposed to yank at it," he confided, "but the dashed thing's choking the life out of me."

"Who are you?" Ian demanded, nonplussed. "A messenger from my daughter? Some sort of page?"

"Hell no! I mean, *heck* no. I'm John Wilkes's new boy. Nathaniel."

Ian stared. "You belong to John Wilkes?"

"Just adopted me a month ago. It was a hard decision for me to make. I was right happy living in the countess's garden, you see. 'Specially since his lordship darkened ol' Pappy Blood's daylights when the bastard tried to fetch me back to a life of crime. But the Wilkeses wanted a boy real bad. An' they've got a stable almost as prime as the earl does." For an instant those button-bright eyes flicked longingly to Ian's gold watch chain. "Course, the lady keeps hugging me whenever I pass by her, and I still have the devil of a time not filching a body's purse when there's a delicious fat one just dangling there waiting to be pinched. But my new pa don't tolerate stealing."

"Ian! Emily!" The cry of greeting made Blackheath turn, to see John and Claree striding through the crowd, their faces alight with pride in the cheeky rogue standing at Ian's side.

"I found that Raider fellow for you," Nathaniel announced. "An' I didn't even take his watch, though the chain is dangling there just begging to be snatched."

"You've shown admirable restraint, boy," Wilkes said, ruffling carroty curls. "And I trust you also showed restraint in . . . other ways as well?"

"Not a word, sir. I was just about to tell 'em all that the earl and her ladyship misplaced the time of the ship's arrival."

"Misplaced the time?" Ian blustered. "What the devil is that supposed to mean? How could the girl forget what time her family was arriving after two years' separation?"

Natty smirked. "Her ladyship always has been a little shatter-brained. And anyway, countesses are much too exalted to come to the dockyards. She probably had a soiree at some duchess's house that was much more important."

"The devil you say!" Ian blazed.

"Ian, enough. Let's just get in the coach and go see her!" Emily passed the sleepy bundle that was little Jesse into her husband's arms. Ian took his first son and scowled into the toddler's face. "If that sister of yours has gone arrogant on me, I vow, I'll be back aboard that ship before she sails out again!"

"You're being absurd," Emily said in soothing accents, climbing in beside Claree. "I'm certain there is a perfectly good reason Lucy didn't come to meet us."

"Such as?" Ian demanded. "She's been climbing out windows? Playing ghost?"

"Oh, dear! I thought the earl had put a stop to such things," Claree interrupted, a worried pucker to her brow.

Emily smiled. "From what Lucy says in her letters, his lordship dotes on her to the point of madness, and is so protective of her—"

"I doted on her and *I* could never control her!" Ian groused. "There's not a reason in the world that girl shouldn't have been here to greet me . . . I mean, her mama. I know how disappointed you were when she wasn't there, Emily Rose!" He huffed, then lapsed into a fit of sulks that lasted until the coach rumbled to a stop. Ian looked up at an elegant townhouse, suddenly sure that if his Lucy came bouncing out the door he would forgive her anything.

But the door was closed, a hush blanketing the place, as if no one but the Wilkeses had any idea her ladyship's parents had just arrived from across the sea.

John's eyes were dancing as he opened the coach door. "We'll leave you to your reunion. You might mention to Lucy that she invited us to tea tomorrow."

"What? Has the girl become too dull-witted to bother remembering such trivial matters?" Ian thrust Jesse back into his mother's arms.

"See for yourself, my friend," Wilkes said with a grin.

Pendragon was in no mood for cryptic amusement, especially at his expense.

He bolted out of the coach, stalking up to the house, elated at the prospect of seeing his daughter again, sick with apprehension that the Lucy he knew would be gone.

A footman swept open the door, bowing low. "If I may be of service, sir?"

"You can tell me where the blazes my daughter is!" Ian snapped.

"You mean, 'her ladyship'? I believe she is upstairs, napping."

Napping? Zounds! It was worse than Ian had thought. Had the girl become one of these lazy English chits barely able to lift their cup of chocolate before noon?

"Lucy?" Ian bellowed, heading for the stairs. "Blast it, girl, where are you?" Ian called.

"Please, sir! Quiet!" The footman stammered. "The earl will not tolerate such noise right now!"

"I've not seen my daughter for two years! The earl can go to the devil!"

From the moment he'd received word of her marriage, Ian had instinctively disliked the man who had stolen his daughter away. This English earl, doubtless cold and aloof, bitingly arrogant, groomed by valets to sickening perfection.

None of Pendragon's preconceptions had prepared him for the man who charged down the stairway at that moment.

Dark hair tangled in a wild mane about a harried face, black eyes looking befuddled as the devil. A fine linen shirt clung in damp patches to his chest, the sleeves rolled up over well-muscled forearms.

"Be quiet, damn your eyes!" the man bit out. "Who the blazes are you and what are you doing in my house?"

"I'm Ian Blackheath."

Pendragon's glare had made whole squadrons of English soldiers turn and flee. But never had he seen such a singular reaction as the one on this man's face.

He slammed to a halt, blinking in abject confusion. "Yes! No! That's impossible! You aren't supposed to be here for days and days. Surely I would have remembered . . ." The man raked his fingers through his hair, then looked at Ian again. "What day is it, anyway? Thursday? Friday?"

Ian took a step back. God knew, he'd often suspected Lucy would drive her husband insane. But this was beyond even his considerable imagination.

"It's Saturday," he snapped. "What the devil have you done with my daughter?"

"A good deal too much, if the results are any indication," Valcour said cryptically. "Damn the girl, do you have any idea what she's done now? Of course not. She wouldn't do the sensible thing and prepare you! What fun would that be? You'll have to come see for yourself!"

Ian caught a glimpse of Emily's puzzled face, the children clustered about her. But Valcour was already charging up the stairs. Ian rushed after him, heard the others following in his wake.

At the far end of the corridor, the earl flung open the door to the most elegant chamber Ian had ever seen—a chamber obviously converted to a nursery.

Pendragon slammed to a halt, as if the earth had suddenly split before him.

Lucy stood in a gown of river-blue satin, her back to the door. She was totally unaware of her father's arrival, but her laughter rippled out. "It's too late, Dominic! I'm afraid you *will* have to 'hang the infernal fool' who made that disturbance."

"No, Countess!" Valcour interjected. "There's been a terrible mixup."

"But your daughter is wide awake again and demanding her papa!" Lucy called. "You swore you'd hang the next person who disturbed her."

The piteous wail that erupted made Ian stagger into the room, stunned. "A baby?"

Lucinda whirled, her face like sunshine—bright, filled with joy. "Papa! Oh, Papa!" She raced toward him, baby and all. "You're here at last! Where are Mama and the little ones and—"

She cried out, catching her mother and sisters in a delighted embrace as they entered the room. "I can't believe you're all here at last! I've missed you so much! And this is Jesse! Good morrow, little brother! He looks just like you, Papa! I swear he does!"

She turned to Valcour, relief in her eyes. "Dominic, I had forgotten what day it was! Thank God you remembered."

"That's what I've been trying to tell you!" Valcour insisted. "I didn't remember. Near as I can figure, the—the coachman did."

"John and Claree fetched us from the dock," Ian said, amidst the infant whimpers. "But they didn't say a word about a baby, by God's wounds! Girl, why didn't you write and tell us you were with child?"

"Lucy, are you all right?" Emily asked.

"You see why I didn't tell them, Dominic?" Lucy said, triumphant, then turned back to her parents. "I knew the moment you heard you would both be in a blather. I didn't want to worry you. And I wanted so much for it to be a surprise! But in the end, it turned out more astonishing than even I could have imagined, because—"

"Wait," Ian said, pointing almost accusingly at the little mouth contentedly sucking at the tip of Lucy's little finger. "That baby isn't crying."

"No, it's the other one's turn," Valcour said, as if that explained everything. "It's some sort of pact concocted in the womb. One awakens, the other sleeps; one is hungry, the other won't eat if God Himself commands it.

The instant there is a lull in the storm, they both wake up, bellowing to bring the house down."

"Both? You don't mean . . . twins?" Emily gasped, the color leaving her cheeks. "Child, did all go well?" The woman who had brought forth five children without a wisp of concern obviously found the fact that her daughter had been in travail daunting beyond belief.

"Did it go well?" Valcour moaned, going to scoop up his tiny daughter. "It was terrible! The worst night of my life! But Lucinda delighted in it. She adores nothing more than driving me wild!"

Lucy laughed at her husband. "You would think that since I produced a son, as our bargain required, the man would be elated!"

"I am, hoyden, I am, it's just . . ." Valcour looked at his wife, the anxiety he had suffered still shadowing his face. "I didn't know there would be so much . . . so much pain." His voice dropped, barely audible. "I didn't know I'd be so damned scared!"

"And here I thought Lucy was the one who had the babies," Ian observed wryly.

"You are a fine one to talk, Papa!" Lucy teased. "You and Dominic are exactly alike. He didn't leave my side for a moment. Not even when the midwife threatened to chase him from the room with a fire iron if he didn't calm himself."

Blackheath looked from his radiant daughter to the son-in-law he had been so determined to dislike. He grimaced. It was damned hard to dislike a man who looked so battle-dazed. "It was a bedwarmer when Norah was born. I can still see old Mahitabel waving that thing at me, cursing."

"But two babes!" Valcour echoed. "Why is it Lucinda has to outdo the rest of the world at every turn? For six weeks now, the whole house has been in an uproar. Of course, Lucy kept it in an uproar anyway, but this has gone beyond even that madness. My wife will not allow the so skillful nurse I hired to give any but the most cursory aid. No. She insists Mama and Papa be neck-deep in lullabies and cradle rocking."

"As if anyone can keep you from the nursery, my lord!" Lucy teased. "I vow, I wake three times a night to an empty bed and find Dominic bending over the cradles."

"I just want to be certain they're both breathing! They were so infernally tiny."

Ian nodded with abject sympathy. "I know. They seem so impossibly helpless. But next thing you know, they'll be climbing out windows in the middle of the night, raiding the pantry and terrorizing the servants."

The warnings fell on deaf ears, the new papa already enraptured again. "My God, did you ever see anything so beautiful? Beautiful just like their mama."

Emily touched Valcour's arm. "Perhaps you would care to introduce us?"

"This is Dante." Lucy indicated the tiny angel in her arms. "The one who is complaining at the moment is Aria. Dominic had just gotten her to sleep before you arrived. A feat that was not accomplished without considerable effort, I might add. The girl is incredibly hardheaded and opinionated for such a small person."

"I wonder where she would get such a trait," Valcour snorted.

"They're beautiful," Emily said, touching one tiny cheek. "Look, Jesse," she said, setting the boy on unsteady feet. "See the baby?"

"If you ask me, they look bald and squally," Norah piped up. "But I s'pose, in time, I can teach them to be quite naughty, don't you think?"

Valcour rolled his eyes heavenward. "Without a doubt, considering the chase their mother led me."

Valcour felt a small hand tug at his breeches and looked down into the face of little Hannah. "That horsie is too big for them. They'll fall right off," the child observed, pointing to a rocking horse of gargantuan proportions, a wooden sword and an doll house intricate enough for a crowned princess standing against the wall. "I could take 'tare of it for the babies."

"I would be most grateful if you would do so. My brother sends a new trinket every week for the two of them! He's a captain in the cavalry. A fine one. But he seems to consider it his mission in life to see that his niece and nephew are hopelessly spoiled."

"As if you aren't the worst offender in that regard," Lucy said, delighted. "The day after they were born, he ordered up matching ponies for the two of them, the most beautiful ponies with cream manes and tails and coats like aged gold."

"They adore their ponies. I've taken them out to see them a dozen times. I vow last time Dante smiled, and as for Aria—look at the hands on this girl! She already has the makings of a fine horsewoman!" Valcour flushed and took his son from Lucy.

The earl dipped down on bended knee, a baby balanced in the crook of each arm. "Look, children. A little man, and a little lady, both at once. Is your sister not the most amazing woman ever born?"

"No," Lucy whispered. "Only the happiest."

Ian chuckled. "You'd best brace yourself, my lad," he said to Valcour. "With this hoyden daughter of mine and two new babes to turn things upside down, your life will never be the same."

"Thank God for that," the earl of Valcour said, kissing the petal-soft brow of first his son, then his daughter, his eyes shining with reverence and gratitude as he looked into the smiling face of his wife.

It was well past three in the morning when Lucy finally left the bedchamber assigned to her parents. The three of them had talked until they were hoarse, laughing and teasing, catching up on two years of gossip. Valcour had excused himself two hours before, citing some business affairs to be put in order. He hadn't fooled Lucy for a moment. The man who had been so tyrannical, so cold, was the most thoughtful of lovers, and he had instinctively given her the gift of some time alone with the parents she adored.

It had been heavenly, for just a little while, to sink into the role of Raider's daughter again—cosseted, petted, teased and loved. And it had been wonderful to ease all her parents' niggling fears about the sudden marriage that had stolen her away two years before.

Valcour loved her—desperately, completely, with not the tiniest corner of his heart withheld from her. Even Pendragon remarked on it. And no one knew more than Lucy how much it had cost her father to grudgingly admit that her husband was a damned fine man, even if he was born English.

But when Lucy finally slipped up to the room she shared with Valcour, the bed was empty again.

She didn't even bother checking the study. She went straight to the open door of the nursery.

Valcour sat in a chair beside the window, moonlight streaming over features so serene, Lucy knew she would never tire of looking at them. Those strong arms she had clung to during the hours she had labored to bring forth his dark-eyed babies now cradled the twins as if they were the rarest of treasures. He was murmuring something to them, secrets that they alone could hear.

But the girl-child snuffled with impatience, her tiny fists waving in regal displeasure. Her father only smiled, a smile so peaceful it broke Lucinda's heart. Valcour knew what his little one wanted, and he gave her a gift still magical, still wondrously new, though the babies had heard it a thousand times.

Valcour's rich baritone drifted into the night as he sung the lullaby his children never tired of hearing. Dante

372

yawned, his lashes drifting shut in contentment. But little Aria's eyes were opened wide in the moonlight. She stared up at Valcour, her winsome face enraptured, her restless little spirit soothed in the haven of her father's embrace.

The Raider's daughter crossed the room and knelt at her husband's feet to watch in wonder as the strains of the "Night Song" enchanted another little girl, carrying her away to a magic place where tower rooms awaited and princesses awoke.

But the "Night Song" no longer whispered to Lucy of yearning but, rather, of hope fulfilled, dreams realized, and a love that would last forever.

She had tamed the Hawk of Valcour to her hand.

The reward was a sweeter one than she had ever known.

THE ENTRANCING NEW NOVEL FROM THE
NEW YORK TIMES BESTSELLING
AUTHOR OF *PERFECT*

Until You

by

Judith McNaught

AVAILABLE IN HARDCOVER FROM
POCKET BOOKS

POCKET
BOOKS

987-01

Judith McNaught
Jude Deveraux

Jill Barnett
Arnette Lamb

❦❦❦❦❦

A Holiday Of Love

❦❦❦❦❦

A collection of new
romances coming
Winter 1994 from

POCKET
BOOKS   1007

Pocket Books
Proudly Announces

STEALING HEAVEN

KIMBERLY CATES

Coming in Paperback
from Pocket Books
mid-April 1995

**The following is a preview of
Stealing Heaven . . .**

Sir Aidan Kane strode up to Castle Rathcannon as a footman scrambled to open the heavy door. Aidan barely returned the youth's greeting as he hastened through the corridors of the glistening haven he had built for his daughter, then took the stairs two at a time, unable to quell the strange tightness in his throat as he hurried up the spiraling risers that led to his daughter's room. When he reached the landing, the door was ajar, and he flattened his palm on it and gently pushed it wide.

Cassandra, half angel, half imp—a treasure that fate had foolishly thrust into a rogue's awkward hands—drowsed among coverlets sprinkled with gold-flecked stars.

With stealth acquired in years of practice, he slipped across the thick carpets imported from lands of spice and mystery, and saw his gilt chair drawn close to the bed. A blanket had been draped across its seat, and a small satin pillow placed atop it, small luxuries he knew Cassandra had set out the night before in an effort to make him more comfortable as he took up his customary vigil.

He could remember the first time she had devised the chair, heard her child-plea echo in his memory. She had been barely six years old, still reeling from her mother's death in the accident that had nearly cost Cassandra her own life as well.

She had grasped his hand tight in her own and stared up at him with wide gray eyes and that adorably determined tilt to her chin. *Papa, when it's time for you to visit, I wake up and think you are here, and run to your room again and again. If you slept in the chair, when I woke up I could reach out and touch you and make certain you are real.*

Aidan would have walked through fire for his daughter. It had seemed a small sacrifice, to please her by taking up a vigil in the chair on the nights he arrived at the castle. What he hadn't expected was that those night watches would become some of the most precious moments of his life.

Times when he could watch Cassandra's little face, soft, rosy, content, her lashes feathering across her cheeks. He could know that she was safe, that she was happy, and that, for a brief, precious space in time, nothing could hurt her—not even Aidan himself.

Slowly he reached out to draw back one of the bed's embroidered curtains. His gaze took in the tumble of silver-blond curls tossed across her pillows and, for an instant, he pictured her cuddling the doll he'd bought her in London years ago. He imagined his daughter's rosy little mouth sucking on two fingers, the way she had when she was small.

He had spent countless hours worrying that she would ruin the shape of her mouth, but as he looked down at his daughter now, he would have been grateful for such a minor concern. There were far more painful dangers drawing inexorably nearer to Cassandra with every day that slipped past.

She was growing up. Aidan's heart lurched as the morning light revealed the face of a girl on the verge of blossoming into a woman. Even in slumber, there was an expectancy in those features that were so familiar and yet suddenly so changed.

Since she was five, he had kept her safe, happy in her castle beside the Irish Sea—a princess running about her private kingdom in a gilded pony cart, begging for presents, hurling herself into his arms, laughing, laughing. He had marveled at her—a miracle of goodness in a lifetime ill-spent.

The only peril he had never reckoned with was the one overtaking them now—his bright-eyed moppet changing into a restless spirit, anxious to fly, a young woman with no understanding of the word *impossible,* and no inkling that a scandal from a decade past still had the power to harm her. The sins of her father and mother, emblazoned like some hideous brand upon her breast.

Aidan would have given the last drop of blood in his veins to spare her pain, but he'd been too selfish, too arrogant, too unthinking during that brief span of time or he might truly have fixed things for her. And now it was too late. There were some wrongs that couldn't be righted, some wounds that couldn't be healed. No one knew that better than Aidan Kane.

He reached out a fingertip to trace the scar usually hidden by the curls that tumbled across her brow, the faint white arc a poignant reminder of how close he had come to losing her forever.

At his touch, Cassandra's lashes fluttered open, revealing wide gray eyes so like her mother's, but instead of the vanity, the deceit that had characterized Delia Kane, delight shone unabashedly in his daughter's face as she scrambled out of bed in a flurry of nightgown and flung her arms about Aidan's neck. "Papa! You've come! You've come! If you hadn't, I would've been quite desperate!"

Aidan gave a strained chuckle. He gathered her close, his heart wrenching at the realization that she nearly reached his chin. He buried his face in her curls and breathed in the scent of milk and cinnamon and innocence. "Desperate? That sounds rather alarming, princess. Is there something amiss?"

"No!" she said rather too hastily. "It's just that . . . it's been forever since I saw you last!"

"Three months only," Aidan corrected. *But when I left, you were still a child . . .*

She drew away, and looked up at him with eyes suddenly vulnerable. "You used to think that three months was forever, too. Remember, Papa?"

Wistful. Wide. Her questioning gaze slayed Aidan, left him bleeding. *But that was before, when I didn't have to face how I've hurt you, simply by being your father. When I didn't have to feel this grinding guilt.*

"Perhaps I stayed away to save myself the embarrassment of making a disaster out of your presents, girl. Last time I came, I brought a length of muslin for a gown, and when I saw how tall you'd grown, I was forced to face the fact that there was scarce enough fabric to fashion a petticoat for you!"

"It's my very *favorite* petticoat!" she protested, a heartbreakingly beautiful smile tugging at her lips. "And besides, it is *my* turn to surprise *you* with a present! After all, it's not every day that a gentleman turns . . . how old is it? Eighty? Eighty-one? A great doddering age."

"Thirty-six, minx," Aidan said, pinching her cheek. "And seeing you is the best present I could receive. Except . . . perhaps one. Pray, tell me you have *not* baked me a cake again. The last one nearly poisoned me, if I remember rightly."

"I have a much better gift this year," she said loftily. "I worried over it until my head ached. But it was worth the agonies. It is absolutely perfect."

"I am positively agog with curiosity." Aidan made a great show of searching the room. "You know, it *is* officially my birthday," he observed, lifting the edge of the coverlet to peek beneath the bed, then turning to the dressing table and opening a trinket box to peer inside. "When do I receive this paragon present?"

Cassandra swirled about to grab up her dressing gown. "I don't know *exactly.*" There was an overbright quality to Cassandra's voice that set alarm bells rattling in Aidan's head. "Sh— I mean, *it* is arriving by coach."

"Ah hah! You nearly said *she!* Let me make a guess!

When last I was here, I told you that Squire Phipps was going to breed that delectable pointer bitch of his! I'd wager a hundred pounds you've sent for one of the pups!"

"I don't know what you mean."

"If you'd just written, I could have scooped her up and— No, you needn't put on such a sour face. I'll have her trained to my hand before the week is out! Make her the most devoted female ever."

Cassandra went quite pale. "It's not a dog! It's something ever so much more . . . more . . . exciting."

Aidan raised one dark brow. "Why does that particular adjective suddenly make me nervous?"

"Because you are far too stodgy and set in your ways, and you need someone to shake you up royally, sir," Cassandra said with a most disquieting gleam in her eyes.

"I see. And you are just the imp to reform me, eh?" Aidan lay one finger alongside his beard-stubbled jaw. "Come to think of it, I passed a coach on the road aways back, but between the darkness and the crazed pace I was setting, I didn't even realize that it could have been my own! Perhaps I should roust out Hazard and go make a search of it." He started toward the door, but Cassandra lunged for him, grabbing his arm.

"No!" She glanced at the window as if expecting the king himself to come racketing up to the door. "You should carry yourself off to make yourself quite handsome."

"I should, eh? Since when did you become so particular about my appearance?" Aidan peered into the gilt-framed mirror that graced one wall. His mouth tipped up in a rueful grin. Cassandra was right—he was looking even more disreputable than usual. Stubble shadowed his square jaw, his ebony hair wind-tossed and wild about his sun-bronzed cheeks. His eyes were reddened from a shortage of sleep and an overabundance of gin, and there was a most spectacular purple bruise across his left cheekbone. His cravat had been mangled by impatient fingers, while his breeches and boots were layered with a fine coat of travel dust.

"Your coat is deplorable, and your whiskers nearly burned my cheek raw when you kissed me!" Cassandra protested.

He rubbed at the offending stubble with one long-fingered hand. "I should hope these will be a minor irritation, since I doubt I'll be tempted to kiss my present!"

Cassandra choked, sputtering, "Y-you could make yourself presentable for me. A gentleman . . . well, I . . . Papa!" Her garbled scoldings vanished in a vexed cry. "What on earth have you done now!" Worry was edged with accusation.

Aidan frowned, confused. "I don't have the slightest idea."

"You have a black eye! Don't even attempt to tell me you ran into a stable door again for I shan't believe it! Tell me you haven't been indulging in fisticuffs at that awful boxing salon again!"

"I haven't even been to London!" He raised his fingers sheepishly to the bruised eye and groped for a plausible lie. "When I was riding out of the city, I was set upon by . . . by a pair of brigands who tried to relieve me of my purse."

"Brigands? Oh, Papa!"

"Yes, there must have been four big, burly fellows." Aidan paced to the window overlooking the castle drive, warming to his story.

"I thought you said 'a pair'?"

"Well, I was much confused. It was dark and, after all, I'd taken a devil of a blow to my head. I—" Aiden paused, nearly sighing aloud in relief as a reprieve came in an unexpected form—that of a coach rumbling toward the castle.

"It seems I will have to regale you with my adventure some other time," he said, tugging at Cassandra's curls. "My gift seems to be coming up the drive."

"Wh-what?"

"The coach!" Aidan said with diabolical glee. "I'll beat you to the door!"

Cass squawked, and started to dart out ahead of him. Aidan caught a handful of her dressing gown, reining her in. "Cassandra Victorine Kane, you are still in your nightshift, and a young lady shouldn't parade in front of the servants en dishabille."

"I won't if you'll wait! Papa! Papa, no!"

Aidan had never been able to resist teasing her. He raced down the stairs, making a deafening racket, while he heard Cassandra scrambling to get dressed. He had no intention of spoiling her surprise, of course, fully planning to wait for her in the grand entry to Rathcannon. But the man who had spent a good portion of time waiting for her royal highness to rig herself out was stunned when his daughter completely forgot her jealously guarded dignity and came racing out in record time, tugging the hem of a sweet muslin frock down about her legs as she ran, her bare feet pounding on the stone stairs. Her hair tumbled adorably about her face as she rushed past him.

The door flew open, revealing the face of Sean O'Day, Rathcannon's coachman, the burly Irishman looking as distraught as if he had just set fire to the stables. Ashen-faced, he railed at his young mistress.

"Miss Cassandra, what have you done? Oh, Jesus, Mary and Joseph, the master is going to flay the hide off every one of us, and I vow I'll hand him the knife to do it with!"

Aidan stepped into the coachman's line of vision, and Sean looked as though he were about to be judged at the seat of Lucifer himself. "Come now, man, don't be so hard on the girl!" Aidan soothed. "I promise not to resort to violence unless I'm severely provoked."

O'Day's wild eyes slashed to Aidan, his big hands clutching at the front of his travel-dusty livery. "Sir . . . oh, sir," he mourned, "I was hopin' you weren't here yet . . . that there'd be time to fix things somehow. . . . But we wouldn't be able to right this in a hundred years! You have to believe me, sir, I had no idea what Miss Cass was about or she couldn't't'a dragged me off to Dublin bound with chains! But if I hadn't gone, what would have become of her? Didn't know what the divil to do once I had her . . . didn't dare to tell her . . ."

"Tell who *what?*"

"The lady, sir! There she was, standin' at the dock plain as the wart on Cadagon's nose, with a letter in her hand and her thinking you wrote it. But I knew the truth the minute I saw it."

It was as if O'Day's rattling was stirring up the dregs of gin in Aidan's head, starting a painful throb in the base of his skull. "You're blithering like a half-wit!" Aidan bit out. "Just tell me what mischief the child has kicked up, and we'll sort it out somehow. You're acting as if she committed murder, for God's sake!"

"It's *you* who might be tempted to that, Sir Aidan, when you see what lurks out there!" O'Day waved one hand toward the open door.

Fists on hips, Aidan stalked to the threshold, glaring out at the scene before him. Slivers of light drove beneath his eyelids, and he swore, rubbing his fingers impatiently across his suddenly blurry gaze.

He didn't have the slightest idea what he expected to see as the mist cleared from his vision—the hounds of hell tied to the coach wheels, a tribe of gypsies setting up camp on the front lawn, or the horsemen of the Apocalypse, their steeds kicking up their hooves in an effort to separate old Cadagon's teeth from his gums.

The only thing Aidan *did* know was that he didn't expect to see a footman unloading a spanking-new trunk with the trepidation of a man who expected the thing to explode at any moment while a lone woman stood looking on beside the coach.

Aidan took in the wide brown eyes and dusky curls peeking out around a heart-shaped face that looked rather pale under the shelter of a bonnet brim. A rich blue pelisse that should have seemed the height of fashion and elegance flowed about her slender figure, but instead of setting her charms off to advantage, the garment made the woman look, for all the world, like a child caught dressing up in her mother's finery.

Even the object caught in her arms seemed designed to accentuate that impression, for she was holding on to a child's doll with white-knuckled fingers.

Yet when she looked up at him there was something about her . . . that stiff-necked English propriety, that sense of control that had always set his teeth on edge. His face twisted into a black scowl as he stalked down the stairs.

"What the blazes is going on here! The coachman's raving like a cursed Bedlamite!"

The woman raised those melting-dark eyes to his. "He's been acting quite strange since the moment I met him," the woman confided. "As if there is some sort of . . . confusion. If you could just take me to your master, I'm certain it can all be untangled."

"My master?" Aidan echoed.

"Yes. I'm looking for Sir Aidan Kane. If you could . . . find him for me?"

He eyed her warily. "What the devil do you want him for?"

Color flooded her cheeks. "It's rather difficult to explain. But I can assure you that he's expecting me."

"The devil he is! I mean, the devil I am. I'm Kane."

The revelation seemed to cast her into dismay, and Aidan was excruciatingly aware that he looked like absolute hell. The sensation irritated him beyond belief.

"Who the blazes are you?" He cursed himself, unable to keep his hand from creeping up in an instinctive effort to straighten his tousled hair.

"I'm Norah Linton." She looked at him as if the name should explain everything. But Aidan just watched her, tension coiling at the back of his neck.

"I—I answered your advertisement," she stammered out. "The one you placed in the *London Times.*"

Aidan folded his arms over chest in challenge. "I never entered any advertisement."

Disbelief streaked across her delicate features. "But of course you did. I have your letter right here, and you . . . you arranged my passage from England—"

"I didn't arrange a damn thing!"

"Miss Linton!" Cassandra cried, rushing up to the woman, beaming. "It's so wonderful to meet you at last!"

"You know this woman?" Aidan glanced at his daughter. What he saw made his stomach knot. "Cassandra, what is this? Some sort of crazed joke?"

"Joke?" What little color had stained the woman's cheeks drained away. "You can't mean you had no . . . no idea—"

"It's not a joke, Papa," Cassandra said breezily. "Miss Linton is the present I told you about."

"My present?" Aidan choked out, casting a wild glance from his daughter to the woman standing in his carriage circle. "What the devil is she supposed to be? A maidservant? A governess?"

"Don't be ridiculous. You don't need a governess."

"You drag some strange woman from God knows where and tell me she's my goddamn present, and then say *I'm* being ridiculous?" He sucked in a deep breath, battling for inner balance. He knew damn well he shouldn't ask the question Cassandra was so obviously anticipating, but he couldn't help himself.

"If I don't need a governess, what in blazes *do* I need?"

The girl raised her chin with a pure Kane recklessness that always presaged disaster.

"What you need is a *wife*."

Look for

Stealing Heaven

Wherever Paperback Books
Are Sold
mid-April 1995